Critical Acclaim f

"In a single, radiant package, by turns astonishingly funny and ———ing, this perfectly pitched and gorgeously written novel captures the passionate intensity of familial bonds."
—Andrea Barrett, author of the
National Book Award–winning *Ship Fever*

"Nelson's writing is refreshingly earthy . . . her excursions from the predictable are frequently inspired."
—Ken Foster, *San Francisco Chronicle*

"Home is where the heart is, as Antonya Nelson beguilingly demonstrates. . . . Impressive."
—Lee Milazzo, *The Dallas Morning News*

"*Living to Tell* is full of razor-sharp character portraits and a constant, dizzying, forward momentum."
—Hillary Rosner, *The Village Voice*

"The story's hard-won . . . ending is a satisfying benediction upon this ensemble cast, about which the reader has truly come to care."
—Emily Barton, *The New York Times Book Review*

"The complex loves, betrayals, and loyalties of family life are carefully delineated in this novel. . . . When Winston, the killer driver, is allowed again behind the wheel, entrusted with the life of the child whose great-grandmother he killed, it is a moving triumph."
—Barbara Fisher, *The Boston Globe*

"Readers familiar with Nelson's previous two novels and three collections of short fiction will be pleased to find her abundant gifts on display in this ambitious new novel: her wild wit, piercing insight, and fearless candor. . . . One question may remain after the final page: how does Nelson manage to be so funny, so tenderly scathing, and so wise?"
—*Publishers Weekly* (starred review)

"With each new book, Nelson's award-winning fiction reveals ever more resonant truths about the human condition. . . . Nelson avoids melodrama with her wisdom, dry humor, and gift for quirkiness and offhanded moments."
—Donna Seaman, *Booklist* (starred review)

ALSO BY ANTONYA NELSON

Nobody's Girl

Talking in Bed

Family Terrorists

In the Land of Men

The Expendables

LIVING TO TELL

A Novel by

ANTONYA NELSON

SCRIBNER PAPERBACK FICTION

Published by Simon & Schuster

New York   London   Toronto   Sydney   Singapore

SCRIBNER PAPERBACK FICTION
Simon & Schuster, Inc.
Rockefeller Center
1230 Avenue of the Americas
New York, NY 10020

First Scribner Paperback Fiction edition 2001
SCRIBNER PAPERBACK FICTION and design are trademarks of
Macmillan Library Reference USA, Inc., used under license by
Simon & Schuster, the publisher of this work.

Designed by Brooke Koven
Manufactured in the United States of America

1 3 5 7 9 10 8 6 4 2

The Library of Congress has cataloged the Scribner edition as follows:
Nelson, Antonya.
Living to tell : a novel / by Antonya Nelson.
p. cm.
1. Family—United States—Fiction. I. Title.
PS3564.E428 L58 2000
813'.54—dc21   99-088529

ISBN 0-684-83933-4
0-7432-0060-8 (Pbk)

Chapter 8 of this novel was previously published in a
slightly different form in *The New Yorker*.

*Dedicated to Juliet Ruth Nelson
and F. William Nelson*

For wise advice, my thanks to Z, Kath, David "W,"
Andrea, Laura, Bonnie, Jane, and Robert;
my indebtedness to invaluable helpmeets Jill and Marta;
and love to my favorite girl and boy, Jade and Noah.

Finally, who shall blame the leader of the doomed expedition, if having adventured to the uttermost, and used his strength wholly to the last ounce and fallen asleep not much caring if he wakes or not, he now perceives by some pricking in his toes that he lives, and does not on the whole object to live, but requires sympathy, and whiskey, and someone to tell the story of his suffering to at once?

VIRGINIA WOOLF, *To the Lighthouse*

Hoping to die, but surely living to tell . . .
When it comes to
matters of the heart
there is nothing a fool won't get used to.

MICHAEL McDONALD, "Matters of the Heart"

PART ONE

PART ONE

I

O N THE RUNWAY, passenger Winston Mabie began to narrate his flight home in the manner of his own obituary.

Or, since he would note the milestones of survival, maybe it would be more proper to call what he was constructing an antiobituary. "Winston Mabie did not perish on takeoff, nor shortly after," he observed to himself once airborne, the plane struggling under him like a goose, urging itself upward, on a wing and a prayer. "Winston Mabie has survived the first minute of his trip." A former girlfriend once told him that most airplane accidents occurred in the initial forty-five seconds after the wheels left the ground; her habit had been to count slowly to forty-five and then relax, reassured by statistics. Winston gave himself a full three hundred measure, good and easy—"two hundred fourteen, two hundred fifteen"—before even pretending to slacken. He tallied as he breathed, glancing over his seatmate out the window where the gray riveted wing protruded like a ledge. He hated that wing, because now he was going to watch it from here to Wichita, waiting for it to fall off, to wobble and creak, to leak greasy fuel or burst into flame. And didn't those rivets need paint?

"Remember that *Twilight Zone* gremlin?" he said, sort of to himself, right after whispering "three hundred."

"Beg pardon?"

"I hate to fly," he murmured. His companion nodded distractedly. She'd already unpacked a load of work, her hands flashing over a computer keyboard, their ten gleaming fingernails the color of freshly minted pennies, thumb firm on the space bar. *Copper,* the nail polish would be named. Her toenails, he thought, would match.

The plane climbed and banked, shimmering as if relieved if not amazed at its own ability to lunge, once again, into the wild blue yonder. *I thought I could, I thought I could,* it seemed to be saying. Apparently it wasn't going to be caught unawares by a wind shear over the greater Kansas City metro area.

He would have preferred being driven to his parents' house, and ideally by his little sister Mona, but the ticket had arrived from his mother, her last missive addressed to him at Larned, and, since he was the son of depression era Democrats, both of them frugal and practical, he knew it had cost her more than its dollar price, and accepted his boarding pass without protest. Accepted it, and then handed it over as if in exchange for his life. Flying he hated; yet what awaited him, at the other end, he would no doubt also hate.

Winston surveyed, as best he could, the aerial view of his homeland. How would it be to die today, above the wheat fields and the grain elevators? From overhead, the elevators didn't resemble toilet paper rolls, as you might expect, but simple gray disks in the otherwise green landscape. It was *awfully* green, as rain had been falling ceaselessly in the Midwest this week, flooding and letting spin with the tornadoes, typical spring behavior. The Missouri River was swollen, as was the Kaw, the various declines around the countryside filled with water, reflecting the hazy sun back at the sky. The plane's shadow passed over the land like a premonition. Green and gray, puddles, patches, a great black looming storm approaching from the west, which was the direction Winston was aimed. It irked him that he might endure all the trauma at this end of the flight only to perish at that end. If it had to happen, he wished it would be now, save him the trouble of agonizing and brooding for the next hour. . . .

Wouldn't it be queer, down there, to find the body parts of an airline accident? Scattered digits like buckshot, pieces pelting the tin farmhouse roofs and QuikTrips and the heads of farmers, the parking lots and their cars, the vast empty stretches of the north or south forty? But maybe the Midwestern farmer was prepared for the impact of parts, having been through cyclone season, all the wind-tossed objects driven by supernatural force into their phone poles and front doors.

"Winston Mabie did not succumb to turbulence over Olathe." Below him, just north, sat his alma mater, the University of Kansas, his former dorm rooms and housemates—he latched on to one in order to claim his attention, direct his anxiety to the category of memory, what was she called, that strange roommate, *Jennifer,* who'd changed her name to Cassandra, who thought she was a witch, who couldn't drive her car so instead painted it with psychedelic house paint, crosses and bats and other funky discordant iconography. . . .

He hadn't flown in more than five years, but it was all coming back to him, surging over him with familiar fears and hopes. Your comrades, sitting in alarming proximity, might be sensitive to your fear, or nursing their own, or they might be bemused, ignoring your presence despite your knee knocking against theirs, your cough in their ear, their collar and dander in your face, elbows sparring on the armrest, parry, thrust, retreat. Other passengers seemed to think of flight as either an opportunity to reflect with closed eyes, or to read a book, or to open a computer screen or magazine or catalog or safety guide from the elasticized pouch before them. They might casually consider the 747 diagram provided them and learn osmotically how to exit in case of emergency. The calmness of most passengers only served to exaggerate his fright; someone had to keep the thing aloft, praying and parlaying and striking unkeepable bargains.

"I hate to fly," he might comment moodily to his neighbor, as he had to this one, who on other flights might have agreed, she or he did, too, or who might smile indulgently, noncommittally, and return to an open, popular, poorly written novel. This person might strike up a conversation, might indulge some horror story of flight, might ask what he did for a living. How Winston relished the anonymity of this forced intimacy—there beside him sat someone who could believe nearly anything he had the balls to create. He could be anyone: author, playboy, student, surgeon. Loyal son, zealous uncle, caring brother. Into most of this invention entered an aspect of truth, or at least of desired truth. In the abstract, climbing to 30,000 feet, Winston certainly *wished* he were honest and wise and humble and kind, modest and temperate and pious and sweet. His seatmate surely wanted it. Perhaps all the passengers of Flight 500 felt the same, hopeful for his success. Or utterly indifferent, either response one he could embrace. It was the response waiting for him on the ground that troubled him.

Down there there would be guardedness and suspicion and pity and solicitous kindness.

He imposed an exercise in distraction. First, didn't he want a cigarette? Wasn't he a pack-and-a-half-a-day man? Oughtn't that to be absorbing him at present? Wasn't his system hungry for his friend nicotine? And what about those flight attendants, two hefty middle-aged women, twin grinning Vikings, red-faced, ample-bodied frumps, zealously detached during the safety procedures, their cavalier treatment of the oxygen mask and the seat-belt buckle enough to make anyone see how perfectly safe he was in their hands, how needlessly worried . . .

Still, even though the flight wasn't full, Winston took a moment to stew about the stewardesses' heft. What if the plane were too heavy to hurl itself smoothly from here to there? What had happened to the regulations that had kept previous stewardesses trim and shapely, role models of anorexic teenage girls, subject matter of male pornographic fantasy? How the hell had these Wide Loads squeaked through flight attendant training. . . .

It stunned him how quickly his thinking had shifted from its recent course to its older habit, how swiftly he'd moved out of prison. Never would he have guessed that flying would still frighten him. He'd thought he'd found subsuming fears to occupy him. But with each subtle bump, every minor instance of turbulence, his heart pattered.

He touched the smiling scar at the base of his skull, the little zipper of wrinkled flesh two inches long. To touch it brought a sweet nausea, a wave of willed discomfort, punching the built-in punish button. This was *his* pain, his and no one else's. It was a queasy combination, guilt and horror and simple sadness—to touch it brought back a particular flashing moment, the interior of the car just after impact. And inasmuch as it tormented him, it also reminded him of who he was. This was his scar, his memory, pitiless and private, possession and stigma.

He *used* to be a driver, behind the wheel, in charge of his craft and master of his fortune. Of course, he had not driven a vehicle since the accident that had landed him in prison. This was a change he would have to accept in his character. He had now no desire to drive. In prison he had worked hard to adopt a philosophy that would permit him not to need a car. Something along the lines of a reach never exceeding its grasp, a destination never being other than one within walking distance.

Or on a bus line, he supposed now, observing the sheer space of his home state. Perhaps in a large city one could live without a car, but in the rural Midwest? In the boxy horizontal scatter of strip malls and suburbs and the long empty stretches between? Where property was habitually described in terms of acres and counties? He should have taken the bus home from Kansas City.

"Keep your nose clean," advised Sonny Noisome, Winston's favorite of the guards. Sonny had only one eye. Winston had come to trust the advice of the injured, the damaged, those who had lived to tell.

Over the PA system rustled the voice of the captain. His name was James Taylor. Winston sort of liked James Taylor the singer, even though he whined. In music, Winston's taste tended toward the sentimental, the ballad, the whiners. His little sister Mona liked to listen to people who were in some deeply developed stage of outrage or irony, nihilism ad nauseam. He loathed her music.

But James Taylor the pilot sounded more like John Wayne the cowpoke. He said he was taking the plane "upstairs"—and on the way they might experience what he called "chop." Winston marveled. See how the world went on inventing new ways to say the same things? Even in his absence, this had happened: planes went upstairs, under the threat of chop—and people like James Taylor were doing their best to "keep it smooth."

Down below, Winston believed he could pick out Emporia, which reminded him of the six years he'd spent making pit stops there, en route home from Lawrence, cotton-mouthed, red-eyed, aimed toward the weekend of doing laundry, eating his mother's cooking, sleeping in his giant bed, cranking up to return to school. College had suited him, better than anything else. Education, before college, had been to a large degree about avoiding conflict—the conflict of the playground, of boys, of team sports. Winston hated competition. But once he'd hit the university, his difficulties passed. His natural inclinations—sympathetic teachers had always labeled him "sensitive"—had worked in his favor. He grew out his hair and started wearing sandals. The loveliest girls wanted to sleep with him. In a class on feminist literature, he had actually been mistaken for a girl; the professor opened her anthology, scanned the length of the long seminar table, and declared how glad she was to see a roomful of women. And this hadn't appalled Winston, not in the least. At East High he would have balked, he would have never lived it down, but at the University of Kansas he felt thrilled, included, camouflaged to advantage. He'd slept with four of those women over the course of the semester, including Dr. Ringley.

He would never experience that same ease in the world again. He felt suddenly sorry for himself, a wave of despair upon him. He had looked toward release from prison, had marked that time as his goal, his one concrete objective, a focal point in an otherwise monotonous landscape. You could be free, he thought, flying mysteriously through the air, and still trapped. Trapped by former happiness, by a knowledge of diminishing returns, by a cowardly nature. He ran his finger over his scar again, just to locate himself, just to feel his unique queasy pain.

The service cart was coming down the aisle, the seat-belt lights had gone off, the nose of the plane seemed satisfied with its altitude and allowed the tail to catch up, make itself level. Cruising altitude, his captain claimed cockily. Statistically, this was the part of the flight least likely to kill a person, but Winston could not reconcile the reasonability of statistics with the irrational and ludicrous fact that he was 33,000 feet above land. What sort of fool put himself in a vessel such as this, an aged flying bus whose interior shimmied as if to shed its exoskeleton, and allowed himself to be catapulted into the atmosphere? Preposterous. Of course millions of similar fools endured air travel every day. Of course it was more likely he'd smash off the interstate driving to the airport than explode in his plane—the same ex-girlfriend of the forty-five seconds had also told him it was more likely he'd be hit by a meteorite than die in an airplane. Surely his odds of getting knifed in the exercise yard over five years' time were better. Yes, plenty of people survived many years of air service, there was probably an entire squadron of retired stewardesses, they probably had reunions, maybe they chartered a goddamned airplane for their reunions, what about old Chuck Yeager and Charles Lindbergh and all those military personnel, prevailing despite bombs and bad weather and tricky sworn enemies whose whole raison d'être was to blast them from the skies, all sorts of ill-fated adventures during all sorts of wars. Think of his own father, veteran of World War II, lying in the bomb bay of a tiny little plane, coming home over the Atlantic . . .

The 747 lurched suddenly, seeming to fall in the way of the roller coaster, a plunge that registered first in the groin, then throat, then head. No matter your thinking—the body would always betray: Winston was still terrified of flying. The drink cart clanked. Instantly the seat-belt light dinged on. James Taylor–John Wayne came over the public address system, all mellow cowhand reassurance: "Well folks, we're experiencing some unexpected turbulence, just a little bumpy air, so I'm gonna—" He cut off abruptly. What was he gonna? Winston clutched his seat arms, touching the pale cream sleeve of his seatmate with his elbow. She removed her arm without missing a beat in her typing. *Unflappable,* Winston thought. "Winston Mabie and his unflappable neighbor made it through a bit of bumpy upstairs air."

"I *hate* to fly," he repeated aloud, sincere and contrite. The plane shuddered once more. "Winston Mabie made it through the bumpy air?" he narrated weakly, a kind of plea. It surprised him to find that he did not want to die; he'd thought he did, a time or two lately.

Meanwhile, the service cart proceeded toward him. He tried to take solace in the serene expression on the stewardess's face. Surely she was destined to reach retirement from American Airlines, see her fiftieth or sixtieth birthday, fly in much worse circumstances and come through those trips, too, make it home to greet her husband week after week. Maybe he was a pilot: doctors married nurses, professors married coeds, pilots married stewardesses.

His grandmother Bunny had enjoyed flying, he remembered. That ought to cheer him, that someone as wise and ancient as Bunny had liked to fly. Simultaneous with this relaxing memory was Winston's recollection that the anniversary of her death was disturbingly impending. Or was it past? This week, certainly, odd he couldn't remember which day. Five years. Just the sight of a certain kind of old woman's hair made him remember his grandmother, a wavy yellowish gray, bobbed, her hands cupped under her ears, bouncing the skirt of her coiffure, still a little vain even in her seventies, eighties. She had a way of tipping her head like a bird listening to the noise underground, cocking her glance in your direction, a half-smile, big blue eyes like his, the narrow nose his sisters always claimed to envy, her thick hair he also had inherited, not hay-colored like hers but black, wasted on a boy, according to his sisters . . .

A baby began crying, its shriek blood-chilling. Winston's heart leapt. Infants, like animals, might sense danger before the average dulled adult instinct would. It was a premonition, an omen. When flying, everything became an omen. For instance, the lipstick smeared on the stewardess's lower lip—could such slovenliness be tolerated from the mannequin sensibility of flight attendance?—or the "human organ" cooler box he'd noted in first class, blaze-orange tape lashed round its contents as if they'd just been pulled, warm, from a dying body, or even the trash left in his pouch from a bag of candy orange slices deposited by the last occupant of seat 13D. Thirteen D?!? *Thirteen?* Why, if high-rises were erected without a thirteenth floor, if elevators went without mentioning the number, surely the airline industry ought to know better. Good god, how could he be sitting in . . .

The plane bumped again, boat on rough water, toy falling down the steps, forcing Winston to remember the way the ground crew had been scuttling around just before takeoff. What had they been doing out there? Had that been panic on their faces? Were they trying to communicate something to the pilot, who was probably guzzling at his hip flask and adjusting his Stetson instead of concentrating on the business of piloting? Should Winston have intervened, buzzed his buzzer, notified authorities? Had something flammable leaked from a fuselage?

What was a fuselage, anyway?

Some asshole was always proclaiming nothing to fear but fear itself. This did not take into account death, dismemberment, heartbreak, or financial ruin. It neglected pain of all sorts. It passed over rejection, betrayal, public speaking, pink slips, and Dear John letters. Anonymous phone calls, rabid dogs, toxic toadstools, loneliness, crowds, boredom, or hyperactivity. The loss of memory, paralysis, eviction, the big bad wolf, temptation, consummation, Mack trucks, motor scooters, wild geese, alligators, the dark, the basement, the attic, the creepy antique dealer. The killer on your left eating pork and beans, the child molester on your right eating the same, the arsonist, the rapist, the man who fed his wife rat poison. Flying. *Fear itself,* separate from its subject, was just another bodily function, a revved bloodstream, an anatomical jump-start, a swift kick in the adrenal gland.

Winston's flight seemed cursed, as all his flights had. Perhaps this one seemed particularly treacherous because he hadn't flown in such a long time and he'd lost the knack. He'd survived a relentless and humiliating and terrifying incarceration, and now, free, had to suffer more of the same. The time he'd worked toward appeared to him, in his heightened fear, a hopeless fantasy. Life was not going to be necessarily easy, this flight home was teaching him. This was step one.

All around him seemed people destined to die. The women behind him, for example, across the aisle in seats 14A, B, and C, all three clutching dolls as if they were real babies, rag dolls wrapped in scarves, swaddled near their armpits. The women had their eyes closed. Were they in a cult? Grief therapy? What the hell were they doing on his flight? Why in the world should the three of them anticipate seeing the light of another day on this planet?

Directly across the aisle, 13C, sat an older woman who kept placing her paperback on her little tray table only to have it slide to her lap. Over and over it slid. Perseverating behavior, he recalled from some psych class, indicating a certain kind of brain trauma. Despite trusting the message of the damaged, Winston did not like to be cargo with misfits. He wanted to be counted among the able, the worthy, those who fit and were necessary. Everyone on this flight seemed utterly expendable, even the partial person in first class, the "human organ" in the cooler box, on its way to some poor one strapped in a hospital bed. A tragedy in the wings. Winston looked around, seeking out military types, CEOs. Those people just kept surviving; where were they when you needed them to secure your own survival? He wanted to snatch the sliding book away from the woman and fling it down the aisle, right into the backside of the stewardess as she trundled nearer with her ominous cart of fluids. Beside him, the businesswoman typed complacently, aggressive thumb banging on the space bar. Winston attempted to read her screen, but it was not text. It was a pie graph. She was consulting numbers and then blipping to another place, so quickly Winston couldn't track the data. Almost imperceptibly he registered her knowledge of his peeking, the way she shifted slightly, sighed, requested ginger ale when asked.

Ginger ale: the beverage of the fully actualized adult.

"And you?"

"Scotch," Winston blurted. His heart pounded in his throat. He hadn't had a drink in five years. But what better time than now, at 33,000 feet, seated in the chariot conveying him to his death?

"ID?" asked his looming stewardess.

"ID?" Winston repeated, not understanding.

"Identification. Are you of age."

Beside him, the computer woman finally looked up. Winston

reached automatically for his wallet—despite not having reached for it in years—elbowing his seatmate in the upper arm as he did so. "Sorry," he murmured, his face burning. He did not have a driver's license, revoked at the accident scene, and his K.U. ID had expired in 1988, when he'd last matriculated. His other cards he did not wish to extract, the feeble effects of a marginal citizen, the freebies: social security, local library, obsolescent video rental. "I'm thirty-three," he said, turning his face upward to the stewardess. And her expression registered his age, he thought. It registered a face he'd learned to make during his stay at Larned, new to the world outside that place, one that insisted you shalt not fuck with me. All his life, he'd been mistaken as younger than his years because he smiled a lot, because he was handsome. It wasn't intentional, it was just the way his face went. A laid-back face, a girl-friend had told him once. A beautiful laid-back face. She liked to study it after sex. Her own, she'd claimed, was not as nice.

But now he'd scared the stewardess with his other face.

"Coffee," Winston said. "Forget the scotch." In the unserved seats behind him, Winston could sense restlessness; he'd taken up enough of the stewardess's time with his foolishness, people needed their pretzels and soda, they were entitled. He was handed a cup and a tiny packet called Whitener. "Whitener?" he said to his seatmate, who had gone back to her pie graph. Winston laughed hollowly.

Suddenly the plane dipped again. Winston clutched his seat as if holding it might help right the thing, as if he could steer them through turbulence from back here, the extraordinary power of sheer nervous energy. But they kept dipping, the nose aimed downward, his whitened coffee trembling at a definite declined angle, the surface quivering like Winston's hands. If he were a farmer in a field, would he look up now and watch the little 747 fall out of the sky, over there behind the wheat fields, silently, a tiny problem of someone else's, a mess of shrapnel and gruesome human body parts in a fellow farmer's barnyard, a fire in the haystack, a trail of black smoke pluming not unaesthetically heaven-ward? *About suffering they were never wrong,* Winston remembered, those helpless scissoring feet in the distant pond while the grim farmer went on fulsomely tilling in the foreground.

Again he remembered college, the adrenaline of insight, the inten-sity of the sun on the front porch of the last house he'd lived in, with the witch and the computer nerd and the alcoholic premed student and the working girl, Jeannette, with her romance novels and peculiar sleeping hours. Jeannette worked at the plastic factory, checking those margarine tubs night after night, reading her romances during the day. Jeannette, Jennifer née Cassandra (or was it Cassandra née Jennifer?), Oliver, McFarland, Winston himself, the string hammock on the porch, the diamond-shaped impressions it left on your thigh skin like butcher-netted meat, the fall-winter-spring sunshine, the pile of books and the deadlines of essays and take-home exams and the brilliant campus on the hill like the Emerald City, like El Dorado, the trilling campanile, the pond and the big tail-waving dogs with Frisbees and their useless purple or red bandanna collars, and garage bands, and pickup volleyball, and keggers, and long strung-out nights on coffee and saxophone broadcast live from Kansas City, meanwhile ideas rocketing through the body like the new substance of all vital fluids, blood, saliva, sweat, tears, and semen, holding forth with good-hearted girls who felt the same, who fell into bed weary but willing, perfect, more perfect, most perfect. He could cry to think all of that was over, forever, for him.

More descending. How much descending could a plane do before it found itself nose-dived in a bog? But his captain returned to inform them this ear-popping plunge was intentional, nothing more than the initial descent into Wichita, the old air capital city herself, that explained the dipping, the activity in Winston's ears, the return of the wide-bottomed stewardess with a plastic bag to collect debris. His seat-mate clicked off her screen and snapped shut her computer, which resembled a small bathroom scale. "I've never seen a computer that tiny," Winston said.

"Yes," she answered, unsurprised, as if she'd been aware since having had the bad luck of landing next to him in the seating lottery of his lack of savvy in the world of computers, fashion, grace, and flight. She couldn't have been much older than he but seemed quite firmly established in another camp, on the other side of an important line drawn somewhere in the sand, the side that made money and decisions, the side that ran industry and commerce. On the one hand, she depressed Winston. His good looks weren't charming her. He seemed to have lost his touch. But on the other hand, she was quite definitely a survivor, which meant he would ride her coattails to terra firma. His older sister Emily was like this woman, competent and able, the sort Winston had liked to undo, in the old days.

Beneath him Winston felt the wheels erupt from their cargo space. Out the window, a section of the ledge-like wing rose, another opened out, flaps and props. The improbable whirring gadgetry of approach. Irrationally, this was Winston's favorite part of flying because it meant he was closer to the ground. Statistically, he seemed to recall that it was the most dangerous, the forty-five seconds at the end of the journey, but he was happy to recognize landlocked objects, highways and cars and barns and cows. Good old cows, chewing through their days. Surely his odds were better than any one of the cows' down there? They weren't standing in a pasture because they'd been spared the rendering plant— they were just waiting. "Winston Mabie's flight did not culminate in a lightning strike or tornado as he entered the Wichita region, home of Pizza Hut and Boeing."

The paperback woman now slid her plastic drink glass down her tray table, over and over, until the stewardess made a last pass. Then the woman hid her cup, folded away her tray until the stewardess had gone, then let it down again to continue her game.

"Hey!" Winston said, clinging to rules and propriety as a way of ensuring salvation. "You're supposed to close that thing."

Her face, when she turned his way, terrified him. On it he saw a fear much larger than his own, shimmering on the scrim of her features. Her pale blue eyes were filled with tears, her small mouth trembled, her loose cheeks were the crepey pink of fair skin grown old. "I'm sorry," she mouthed soundlessly. She handed Winston her cup, righted her table, then pushed herself against her seat back so hard her gnarled knuckles turned white on the armrest, blue veins so prominent they ought to have burst. Though she was nothing like his grandmother, the woman made Winston remember his Bunny, and this made him sigh. He had been responsible for her death, five years ago, and although he could long for Lawrence and his college days, his actual destination was Wichita and his family. Not his past, but his future. His parents, his two sisters, the house where he'd grown up and become who he was.

He found himself praying that "Winston Mabie wasn't going to belly flop on the landing strip." Reverse backthrust would now explode into its appropriate parachute-like anchoring use, and Winston Mabie would survive.

Oh, maybe all of this was useful, this preparation for death. If he dreaded seeing his family so, perhaps it would be just as well if the plane fell earthward, met its demise, sucked in a hapless pigeon or duck to tangle its engine. So long cruel expectation, so long to his own cruel disregard of the same. They would forgive him, he thought, if he died today. They would stand at his grave and regret his death. And wasn't that all anyone could expect or hope for? Their grief made him swear to himself to be good to his family, should he make it through this loud and terrifying landing.

Winston recalled other bargains made with God for his survival through a flight. Hadn't he sworn to stop lying? Stop belittling fools? Stop drinking? Now he'd be punished, harassing an old frightened woman, attempting to purchase a scotch, lying and bleating to God as he approached yet another arrival, a hurtle onto the ground from the air on indelicate wings. Now God would get him for reneging, put him through the whole of this tortuous flight only to obliterate him in the last act, just like any meaty tragedy, save the spectacle for the end. Forget that old deus ex machina today, bub. Ha, ha. For Winston Mabie's promises meant nothing, absolutely nothing, less even than nothing, and God knew it very well.

2

"YOU ARE A BIG fat ugly baby," Emily's brother said to Emily's baby. "How in the world did I end up with a nephew as ugly as you?"

"Niece."

"Gads. Worser and worser." Her passengers all three sat in the backseat while Emily drove, like a cabby or a chauffeur. She was working not to take it personally. It occurred to her that her brother had some trepidation about sitting in the front seat; he'd had a bad accident involving an automobile, and perhaps this was the result. He sprawled between her children in the back of the Volvo like an unstrung marionette, head flopped on the seat rim, legs hinged open, palms splayed on his thighs like starfish. This was a pose typically associated with comfort—or coma—but she could not believe her brother felt comfortable.

"*What's* your name?" little four-year-old Roy inquired of Winston for the third time.

"Lance," said Winston without raising his head; he could banter effortlessly, all the livelong day. "Lance Boyle."

"No sir," said Roy. "Your name is Winston."

"You've been sorely misinformed, my man. It's Harry. You say 'Harry what.' "

"Harry what?"

"Harry Butt."

"Harry *Butt!*" Roy crowed. Winston would have won him over simply by sitting beside him in the backseat, unheard-of adult behavior.

"And you're called Spanky, am I right?"

"Roy."

"Maybe Macon Bacon?"

"ROY!"

"Carl Buncle?"

The child banged his head on his new uncle's shoulder, Emily was both pleased and alarmed to note; it reminded her of her own childhood with Winston. She trusted him and adored him, and then he broke her heart.

Her brother had not seen her in five years, and before that, they hadn't been close, as siblings, since the time when they were very small, since they'd shared bunk beds and a fear of the dark. Then, their stories in the night had exhausted and therefore saved them. They talked until one of them stopped, or until both of them breathed evenly, air instead of words. Winston would have been roughly Roy's age then, Emily two years older.

But their little sister Mona had come along during those years, splitting the vote, dividing the constellation of four that had seemed to Emily organic, the logic of dollhouse families, the mother, the father, the girl, the boy. She and Winston had grown apart—"grown apart," Emily contemplated, a strange phrase, like the lost object "found missing"—moved to separate bedrooms and bedtimes. Never to share nighttime fraternity again. Three children was a mistaken arrangement in family planning; odd numbers might always be. Because they tended to pair up and therefore exclude, inevitably two to one, girls against boy, older versus youngest, youngest versus oldest. Now Emily had to glance surreptitiously, when traffic allowed, to the rearview mirror in order to catch glances of this large, limp-bodied man who was her only brother. She and he had not been allies for years; they'd grown apart, their intimacy had been found missing.

This, she realized, was the way the entire family would be looking at him, slyly, in mirrors and from discreet angles, checking not only his physical presence but watching for signs of changes in his character, the matter of his long-gone soul. He'd brought into her car an unfamiliar odor, mildew possibly, something she associated with old swimming pools, with places closed for the winter, and cigarette smoke. This habit he'd either taken up in the last five years or simply permitted to be now public. In the walk from terminal to parking lot, he'd lit up in the manner of the addict, desperately sucking, relief spreading on his face.

She hated herself for fearing that he might do something to her baby in the backseat, but fear for her children was Emily's defining feature. Because she'd given birth two times since Winston's departure, he wouldn't know this about her. He wouldn't know that she, too, smoked—just one a day, secretly, on the roof of her attic quarters. But what he didn't know about her was utterly eclipsed by what she could not possibly know about him.

"You guys okay?" she asked. Nobody answered; after all, the question was about Emily, not them. "See the lightning?" In the west was the green sky of tornado weather, the beginnings of an approaching storm.

Roy wouldn't shut up, chattering at his new freaky relative, but Emily's daughter was ignoring Winston—she'd been doing so since sizing him up at the airport gate. Eight months old, she did not recognize his comeliness. Everyone else did: leaving the terminal, Emily had remembered what association with her brother had always brought her, looks of interest from others, who scanned him first, head to toe, thinking he was undoubtedly a celebrity, someone traveling incognito, then glanced quickly to check his companion second, more swiftly, and wondered about the connection between the two of them. Winston was just that handsome, just that alluring, a particular blazing kind of pretty— like Tony Curtis, their grandmother had claimed, sparkling ivories, deep baby blues, a dimple—tempered by a modest spirit. Her brother was not smug, did not pull punches, did not love himself. His was a humble radiance, if that were possible. All it afforded him—which was actually a considerable advantage—was a slackening of other civil energies; he always started a relationship with his foot in the door.

But Emily's baby wouldn't comprehend any of that. What use did a baby have for handsomeness? He was a big stranger, someone her mother was ready to hug long and tight, a hug full of forgiveness, one that spoke of clean slates, new beginnings, squeezing the baby between them like a stuffed animal, just that neglected. The baby had wailed at her supplanting, Winston had recoiled at her noise, and now he sat between her and her loquacious brother in the backseat, trying to enlist her in his fan club. The child's cheeks were so fat and heavy she could not smile unless thoroughly amused, beside herself with mirth. Her head was bald and her fontanel throbbed. She was a tough audience, and most people considered her sullen, not worth buttering up. They grew afraid of making her cry, tired of grinning into her impassive, judgmental face.

Winston wasn't much easier than the baby, as far as conversation went. What did you say to a man who'd just gotten out of jail? Small talk landed you squarely at his cell. He'd not seen any recent movies, eaten at any restaurants, traveled or shopped or barhopped or hiked. At the airport gate, Emily had resorted to: "Your plane was late."

"Yeah," he'd responded, "I told that damn pilot you were waiting." And then they'd walked swiftly out of the building, Winston with no real baggage, lunging ahead in his distinctive gait, hands jammed into his pockets, tilted forward as if too tall, as if late, as if racing his companion and prepared to present his nose first at the photo finish. It was no use to speed up; he merely did the same. He did not want you abreast; he wanted you behind him, like a shadow.

"See?" Emily offered now as she pulled her solid Volvo onto the highway, "the construction still isn't finished on Kellogg." He'd missed so much in five years she ought to have had a thousand conversational entries, but each she entertained seemed tainted by innuendo. For instance, why had she mentioned Kellogg, where Winston had had his fateful car accident, an accident that in some ways, as a matter of fact, had been due to the construction, diversion, unfamiliar stoplight? What sort of unkind unconscious did she possess?

But Winston was talking to the baby; he'd always been good with children, and he wasn't going to let this one ruin his reputation. "What do you think of this, you big protoplasm? Does this tempt you?" He had the baby scowling cross-eyed at his stuck-out tongue the next time Emily checked the mirror, fat fingers reaching to touch something Winston had placed on the end of it.

"*Protoplasm!*" howled Roy.

"Bwake," Winston said around the impediment on his tongue—an item black and plastic, from the filthy backseat floorboard, a Hot Wheel connector. Emily screeched to a halt just before the bumper of the Coors truck ahead of her.

"Sorry."

"'Sokay."

Emily felt tactless traveling on Kellogg; soon they would reach the site of Winston's accident, the stoplight he'd failed to anticipate, the intersection he'd sailed through at a speed calculated to be, roughly, seventy miles an hour. But Winston himself seemed unperturbed, his knees spread like clamshells, seat belt unheeded until Roy—rule-tender—made a stink about it. That was another of Winston's gifts—serenity. Placidity. Like a Zen monk, he seemed. The world did not often ruffle his pretty feathers. Emily remembered—in her body, it seemed, a flare of revulsion, frustration—the resentment his composure often inspired in her.

"What will you do first?" she asked over Roy's chirping narrative—there was McDonald's, there Shepler's where the cowboys shopped, Kmart, Towne West—aware that her brother never answered a question directly. It was against some mysterious principle of his to behave like anyone else, like a polite human. Or maybe he wanted to point out that Emily was asking the wrong questions.

"I'm afraid to see Dad," Winston said, apropos of absolutely nothing, and as if trying to prove his vulnerability, as if having read Emily's skeptical mind, as if set on disarming her. "Dad scares me."

"Dad scares me, too."

"Does he scare them?" he asked, nodding toward his companions in the backseat. He meant the whole of the next generation, one of its representatives frowning as she tried to steal his black gadget while he twirled it lazily before her in his long fingers.

"I don't think he scares them."

"*Who* doesn't scare me?" Roy demanded.

"They have their own dad for that, I guess," Winston said.

"Dad," Roy said wistfully, a faraway look in his eyes.

"Maybe," Emily said noncommittally. Her children's dad was now her ex-husband and he lived in the Florida Keys—facts her brother either had forgotten or wished to allude to, it was hard to know. For Emily, it was difficult to give Winston the benefit of the doubt, although she had pledged to try. When he smiled, he not only had a dimple but fangs—yet he couldn't help the inherited incisors, could he? "Sometimes *I* frighten them," she offered, about the children. "Just the other day I had a terrible fit in this very car. They were driving me crazy, screaming back there, and I hadn't had much sleep, and I had this doctor's appointment . . ." Single parenthood wore Emily out. There seemed to her nothing more pathetic than raising children solo. She could hand the children themselves over to her parents, to her sister, but she had no one to whom she could hand her fear. Like pregnancy, you just wanted to get some relief, detach the bulk of your womb and dance lithely about for a few hours. In the same way, no one shared her fear, and that, truly, was the gnawing, wearying thing, her inability to leave it behind once in a while. "Anyway," she continued, "we pulled into the Safeway parking lot and I just lost it. Sat there screaming about my feelings, don't *I* have feelings?, I yelled. If you cut me, don't I bleed? What about *me*? Enough about you guys for a while, WHAT ABOUT ME?! That shut 'em up in a hurry. Sat there sniveling, terrified." In the rearview, Winston looked unimpressed. "It was kind of funny," Emily finished lamely.

"I wasn't sniffling," Roy said. As usual, a story about himself had silenced him, made him thoughtful and dissatisfied. His mother always got some detail wrong.

Someone else might have sympathized with Emily's overwhelmed motherhood, might have at least chuckled, but not Winston. He was just like her baby daughter, hard to please, unwilling to fall into the conventional decorous responses to conversation and anecdotes. Emily decided that was okay with her. She could profit by some undercutting of her self-pity, some reminders that, despite her setbacks, she still had her children, her family, her job, a hefty bank account. What did her brother have? She checked her mirror once more and caught him in profile as he watched the fatal street pass, Hydraulic Avenue, the vaporous early summer light turning his eyes aquamarine. Its exit was cleaner now, five years later, the mighty highway flowing over it, the wide off-ramp splintering smoothly to the side, light pole below long ago repaired, nothing to distinguish it from all the other minor cross streets these days. He had a bad guilty memory, that's what he had.

"Lightning, Mama!" Roy announced.

"I see, sugar."

Her brother looked sad, and therefore more tragic. The chromosomes had blessed her brother, blessed him with all the cosmetic loveliness of a saint, blue-eyed, black haired, too beautiful. Emily and her sister Mona often complained of the injustice: they with their dull brown hair and big noses. For his part, Winston suffered his beauty, as a saint ought. Until he was in college, he had kept his hair clipped short to hide its sheen and wave, and he rarely washed it. He would go weeks without shaving so that a scraggly bunch of whiskers would wind unappealingly down his chin. In high school, his admirers had been of two sorts: the vaguely dweeby—brainy girls, choir girls, SAT champions—and the druggy—girls with nicotine habits, poor posture, raccoon eyes, bad reputations. His policy had seemed to be never to intentionally hurt any of those girls. He returned their calls and talked for hours, lying in the upstairs hall with his feet on the wall going "uh-huh, uh-huh, I hear ya, exactly." There were heel marks on these walls, still. He ate at the houses of his devotees, played with their siblings, sat in the park in their nasty cars and smoked their pot, attended their debate competitions, tutored them in their weak subjects, met them for winter walks and wandered for hours around the neighborhood, listening. He was of both sorts without fully committing to either. At home, his favorite activities had been getting high, reading books, playing guitar, building elaborate model cities, and learning bridge from his grandmother. This reminded Emily of another set of girls who found Winston charming: her grandmother's club members, the old women who played duplicate at the Ladies' Center. It was his talent to actually enjoy them, to tease them, to make them laugh flirtatiously, to spend his summer afternoons in their cool dens while the rotating fans dispersed their mentholated cigarette smoke. He had only a couple of male friends, two markedly unattractive boys named Philip Mills and Marty Song, boys who still could be found in Wichita, one bartending, the other driving a delivery van for the chocolate factory. Marty Song made a point of phoning up for Winston every few months, asking how he was doing, his name cycling in his mind like a dim planet, in sight every now and then.

"Marty's been calling about you," Emily told him.

"Your mom thinks he's a hairball," he said to Roy.

"I don't," Emily cried. Roy laughed.

"Hairball!" he said. His uncle had the most amazing vocabulary, and Roy loved words. For months, he'd been fixated on *panty hose,* cackling it like a punch line again and again and again. Before that, *bumbershoot.*

"I don't think Marty's a hairball," Emily insisted, although she did consider him a loser. She shook off an angry regret, a foolish high school evening spent in this loser's bed. Marty Song: he was a stoner, a slacker, with the requisite irksome lazy laugh.

But Winston didn't care what she thought. He was busy folding a road map into a hat or mask, something that would slide over his face and through which his pink tongue poked. Emily's daughter startled everyone, herself included, by suddenly laughing. Unlike all else about her, she had a pretty laugh, rare as it was, and it made Emily smile to hear it. Her brother had succeeded. In the mirror, he looked pleased, too. Maybe this was his first success in his new free life. Emily wondered why he felt such urgency to charm the child, but apparently none to charm her, his sister. Why all the teenagers and old ladies and babies, and not his older sister, the one who used to pour her heart out to him from her top bunk, to attend to the same, coming from below?

Through the window, she watched their hometown go by, curious about how it seemed to Winston. They had left the west side, with its outlet stores and Mexican restaurants, passed downtown, the river, Hydraulic Avenue, their old high school, the graveyard, exited, and now took the smaller streets, arteries, they were called, toward home.

Winston said, "What else, Emily?" Finally he was meeting her gaze in the mirror. His eyes seemed newly spooked to her, and also a little challenging. Emily could not imagine how difficult this was, coming home. She wasn't going to ask him about prison. She wasn't going to mention it, but she knew it was going to lurk around beneath everything he did for the rest of his life, circulate like some illness he would always test positive for yet never actually exhibit. She could identify only in the most superficial ways; she'd had nightmares, for example, in which she'd performed some irrevocably bad deed—murder, negligence, buried evidence—and her guilt and fear and horror would trail her around not only during the night but for the whole day following. Those things, and the gorgeous relief at having wakened unencumbered: free. What must Winston feel like, living this nightmare, sans the relief?

So when he asked "What else?" she assumed he meant: what had he missed? There were Emily's two children, neither of whom he'd met until today, and her ex-husband, whom he'd known only as a despised brother-in-law. Emily wasn't ready to tell him the whole family now referred to Barry as The Excrescence, a fitting label Winston had coined long ago.

A lot of things had passed in five years, but, when they pulled into the driveway of the old family home, Winston noted aloud how conspicuously unchanged the place seemed. "Mona already told me about the cat," he added. If she'd told him about that, Emily thought, there wasn't much she would have neglected to tell him. Mona had been the family's go-between, ambassador, arbiter, traveling to Larned State every few months to visit.

"Mona's home," Emily noted, surprised; the Toyota was parked only halfway in the garage, which was as far as Mona would take it into that small space. Their father always eased the car fully inside, and Emily, when she drove it, always left it right beside the back steps because she had packages. Their mother did not drive.

Emily parked her Volvo and they all four looked up at the pigeons in the eaves, those oddly menacing creatures who looked right back at them. Both parties, human and bird, had long been engaged in a turf battle. Poor Roy feared the birds and frowned mightily in their direction, but the baby, made of sterner stuff, never failed to give them a piece of her mind.

"Ahh, ahh!" she cried.

There was the Virginia creeper covering Mona's bedroom window, and the trail of rusty water that leaked along the drain, staining the white plaster like old blood. A piece of red tile, from the roof, sat precariously near the gutter where it had sat forever, theatrically not falling. Their house was eighty years old, containing over eight thousand square feet of rooms, nestled in a jungle of flora and fauna that, despite its urban location, included poison ivy and opossums. The Mabies had lived here for thirty years. The place had consumed and enclosed so much of their lives that there were a hundred ways to feel about it, a hundred roles it had played: warmth, foreboding, entrapment, shelter.

Winston reached around Roy to try to open the car door.

"Hey," he said angrily.

"It's a *child* lock," Roy said, pained at having to explain the obvious.

Emily quickly unfastened her seat belt and stepped around to yank at the handle. "It wasn't on purpose," she said as her passengers huffed out.

"You didn't have to lock me in back there," Winston said. "I'm not going anywhere." As if to prove this, he dropped to his knees and touched the old cement driveway with his lips. "Thank god I'm on the ground," he murmured.

"He kissed the sidewalk!" Roy crowed. It was clear he could not let this new uncle out of his sight; no telling what he'd miss if he did.

Oh yeah, Emily thought, remembering an aspect of her brother's character she'd forgotten, which was restored to her as a gift of sudden sympathy, and which made her want to hug him all over again. He was afraid of flying.

3

MONA MABIE was supposed to be at her therapist's office. She was supposed to be talking to Lydia about her depression. It needed sedating, her depression, it needed, occasionally, tricking. Mona carried it about like a vaguely feral pet, the unpredictable monkey, the sleeping weasel. For weeks, it would pretend to have run away, leaving her at last a happy average girl, and then she'd wake to find it back once more, rabid beneath her skin. Its return never failed to surprise her. Mona was like a child, in that way, having yet to abandon hope.

But she'd not only left her job early to go to therapy, she'd come home early from therapy to stand looking down at the driveway from her bedroom window. Her period had started in Dr. Lydia's office waiting room. "Of course," she had said there, out loud to the empty space.

"You'd think," her sister told her once, "that after nearly twenty years, you'd remember these things happen. With some sort of regularity. Pre*dic*tability, even." On *her* period, Emily put P's on the calendar, the one hanging in the family kitchen.

"They just keep throwing me a curveball," Mona replied. It was true; she was never ready. Emily, who took no chances, began inserting tampons prophylactically, days before necessary. Not so, Mona. Mona had, this time, left a tiny ragged valentine on her therapist's floral love seat, a single drop of blood. It startled her out of her thoughts, made her blush, look around for witnesses, although there were none. Just her in the anteroom, waiting for the client ahead of her to be done. Her doctor had a back door, like a circle drive, like the chamber lock of a spaceship, so that coming and going were done through different doors. You never knew who was in there ahead of you; perhaps a faint scent hanging in the air, aftershave or perfume or the musky residue of somebody else's elusive beast. And of course the velveteen rocker was still warm.

When you went to the dentist, you brushed your teeth; before the gynecologist, maybe you douched. But how to prepare for the shrink? Mona had been reviewing a few subjects for discussion with Dr. Lydia, hating to come unarmed for her sessions, feeling an obligation to entertain. Entertain, or at least impress with her week of thoughtful self-analysis. This habit was one they had discussed, she and Dr. Lydia, Mona's status as youngest child, the one who felt extraneous, the one who felt the need to justify her presence, prove her worth, earn her keep. Occupational hazard, Dr. Lydia named it. Her therapist, in fact, was the only person Mona knew who actually wanted her *not* to think about pleasing others but about herself twenty-four hours a day, seven days a week. Everyone else frowned on that kind of selfish navel picking.

Today she was angry with her sister for being the one who drove to the airport to retrieve Winston. Her two siblings did not particularly get along with each other, and hadn't it been Mona who'd gone to see him in prison? Why was it automatically assumed that Emily would pick him up instead of Mona? Why were the adult responsibilities habitually handed over to her older sister? Mona was twenty-nine years old, old enough for everything, but her family still treated her like the youngest, the one who would get it wrong.

Never mind that she had this expensive appointment and couldn't have gone to the airport, anyway.

In the office bathroom, Mona fashioned a toilet paper pad for herself, winding the roll around her hand. At least she was not wearing white pants to add to her embarrassment. "The good news," her sister always chimed in, "is that you're not pregnant."

"Just humiliated," Mona said now to her image in the mirror. "The usual bad news."

Back in the waiting room, she sat on another chair, giving the love seat a scowl, as if some other forgetful soul had had the bad manners to leave a bloodstain there. Once again, she reviewed topics, juggling them like tennis balls, air-filled and funny-colored and fuzzy today. Her beast seemed subdued, shrunken. She was happy, Mona thought; she had nothing really to say. Her therapist saw dozens of clients, all of whom had multitudes of problems, yet still Mona had some desire to stand out, to show up on time, well dressed, polite, and with at least one or two lively anecdotes up her sleeve. She had learned this from her family, who appreciated nothing better than a good story, who didn't mind yawning in your face if you bored them. And Dr. Lydia's magazines were ones that let you know she had higher expectations in this world than other doctors. None of those insipid housewife rags. No *People* or *Modern Maturity* or *Sports Illustrated* or *Highlights* or *Newsweek* or even tony *National Geographic*. In Lydia's office, it was all *Architectural Digest* and *The New Yorker. W* and *Rolling Stone.*

Dr. Lydia had not been the first therapist. Oh, no. There'd been a few before, ones who wanted Mona to ride horses for therapy, or attend matinees, or just plain get over herself. They'd reminded her of her parents, or well-meaning teachers, but what she needed was an animal tamer. They'd not possessed the ability to zoo keep. There'd been some bad prescriptions and vertigo, some copious weeping and pounding of the face with her own fists, some afternoons of having to be literally pulled into the backseat of the car, then out of that same backseat and through the doors of a scary building. Inside, she might have to discuss religious conversion or support groups, yoga or herbal antidepressants, dream journals or self-affirming Post-It notes on the bathroom mirror. Dr. Lydia was the one who had saved Mona. Dr. Lydia with her short short nutmeg-colored hair and her pierced nostril and her blue fingernails and her sarcasm. Dr. Lydia whose first words to Mona had been, "Great shoes."

Great shoes. And they weren't even shoes Mona had borrowed from Emily. They'd been *Mona's* shoes, platform mules of faux zebra fur.

Three years earlier, Mona had tried to kill herself. The attempt, she was convinced, had not been very serious, although her family thought otherwise. All the therapists before Dr. Lydia looked askance when Mona downplayed the go at suicide. They didn't believe her. She'd stood before her parents' medicine cabinet in the wee hours of a February morning, lonely and failed, her face in the mirror the most hideous thing she had ever beheld, rubbery and splotched, unlovable. Her lover had just notified her, an hour before, that he would have to end their affair. He had sneaked out of his house to phone her, Mona waiting impatiently to hear from him. She did nothing but wait for him, every-thing else filler. His voice, his presence, him. For the hour following his call, Mona had been spinning, her sadness so profound she could not envision carrying on. That wild animal inside of her had begun eviscer-ation, liver, spleen, heart. Her lover's guilt at deceiving his wife, his dis-traction concerning his infant son, it was all getting to be too much. He was sorry—Mona could hear it in his voice how sincerely sorry he was—but deception didn't suit him. He kept saying that he would call her every day for a while, that they could talk, step down from the pas-sionate relationship they'd been carrying on for the last three months. In the background she'd heard cars passing, his call coming from a phone booth not far from his home, which was not far from her house, either. It was cold outside, and she could hear his eagerness to hang up, to return to his wife and son and radiant heat.

But Mona felt as if she could not breathe, that as soon as he hung up, she would be without air entirely, as if torn from life support, his essential embrace, his sustaining body abruptly denied her. Nothing would suffice. Sure enough, once the receiver had returned to its cradle, she found herself reeling like a spun top. Directionless, abandoned. Even her face, reflected in the mirror before her, she could no longer rec-ognize. Who the fuck was that, inside that skull, under that wiggy hair, behind those green marbles?

She started with a few muscle relaxants, just to relax her muscles, the pounding one caged in her ribs most of all. Her parents' medicine cabinet could make you cry, so full of pills was it, row upon row of small brown vials, each with a childproof cap, each bearing a variety of neon stickers to demonstrate its potent danger. Mona moved through the shelves taking four or five of each—a fistful of pretty colors— wanting, in her own strange logic, to kill herself without inconvenienc-ing her parents, without consuming all of their available drugs.

It was this restraint that accounted for her failure. Vodka to wash down the mess of painkillers and sleeping aids—she *wanted* to kill pain, she was *dying* to sleep, but instead she merely swooned. She meant to poison the presence that tortured her, that thing that was and was not *her*, that slippery fiendish force. She'd intended to fall into her bed, oh but the floor would do, in a pinch, and if she were going to have to vomit, well, better here on the threshold than in the sheets and blankets, all that dry cleaning. . . . Her poor pets worried, the dog nudging her hand with his dry nose, the cat who watched uneasily, pacing, sniffing, mewing restlessly. Was that what woke her mother, the cat? The cat could mimic a child, when she wanted. Her mother's startled cry had nearly pulled Mona back to consciousness. So animal-like, so squawking a sound from her mother. The cat like an infant, the human mother like a creature—maybe they could find each other to comfort? Mona had the urge to reassure them both but could not quite muster the necessary words. Noise came out, she thought, burbled ululation as in a frustrating dream.

"Self-inflicted," the ambulance attendants said. How simple would it be, Mona wondered during her stay in the ER, for someone else to drug you to death, to jam handfuls of pills down your throat? Already the event had begun to leave its narrative residue, the small bits she extracted for use in a joke. The polite suicide who doesn't want to ingest *all* the pills in the house, doesn't want to be greedy. Or the inept murderer who attempts to stage a drug overdose, coaxing pills into the maw like you would have to an animal, stroking the throat, petting the head . . .

Strangely, and something she could not quite convince her family or those first therapists of, Mona had not really intended to die. She had intended the *gesture,* had felt it absolutely necessary to kill *something.* Her lover had broken her heart, although she'd known that, as a rule, affairs with married men were doomed relationships. She had a kind of prescience about her life that did not aid her in making wise decisions; she seemed to believe also that she would be the exception to the rule. Or—this was Dr. Lydia's angle—Mona looked to be punished, sought out the futile affair.

When she'd begun sleeping with her sister's husband she told herself that she would have to be content with a small portion of his life and love. That he would not choose her, push coming to shove. And she understood that. Her sister would win, as she always did, presiding. Mona told herself that sleeping with Barry was about competition, nothing more. She'd proved she could seduce him, he her, they'd both taken whatever revenge they'd felt necessary on Emily, and now it was over. Emily won, though the victory had a vague tarnish on it, didn't it?

The problem was that, after the competition part had been satisfied, Mona managed to fall in love with Barry.

She'd fallen in love even though she knew she could not have him, had never even hoped it. Taking her parents' pills was a similar decision; she understood somehow that she would not go the distance, that her death would not be now, just as her affair had not been destined to thrive. Her pets, who attended her in all times of crisis, had seemed the wisest beings she could envision. Their kind troubled eyes and devoted solicitude had reassured her as she flowed in and out of consciousness. They had some contact with the untamed animal inside her, sensed its writhing and her wrestling, cheered for Mona to prevail. They did not want her to die, they loved her just as she was, warts and all, and she kept sending out to them reassuring messages on that topic, that this early morning disaster would end, soon enough, and she could rise to follow them to the kitchen, set down a few saucers of milk.

Still, everyone else seemed to feel that the suicide attempt was a symptom of something grander. Oddly enough, it had the effect of washing away some portion of Mona's obsession with Barry. She managed to conflate her love for him with her desire to die, two unhealthy urges tangled together in a nasty knot, purged from her heart as parts of her past. Summoning his image, she brought with it the accompanying sensation of her own lapse in consciousness, the bitter gritty taste of pill vomit in her mouth. This fusion was good, she believed. Her grief over her affair had been derailed, and that was a relief. Meanwhile, her family fretted. Mona did not mind the attention, although she often felt fraudulent as they stepped gently around her. There were lasting repercussions: the medicine cabinet now held only the mildest of drugs. Where were the rest? Hidden, she supposed, in the thousand secret places her parents alone could know. Also, whenever there was mention of suicide—in movies, in the newspaper, in conversation—there was an awkward beat, a moment when all thoughts in the room converged on Mona's attempt, on the relief that she had failed, on the possibility of her trying it again.

And, maybe oddest of all vestiges: she still had a strange sensation in her throat when she swallowed, as if the pumping apparatus had injured her there, scar tissue in the larynx, a checkpoint to monitor just briefly whatever passed its way for acceptability. Occasionally she felt her body's reluctance to take down what she wanted it to swallow, wary of her intentions.

Two beneficial side effects were, one, the assumption that Mona would continue to live at home, cared for, and, two, sessions with a psychologist. Mona enjoyed going to Dr. Lydia's office every week. Dr. Lydia was the only person to whom she could talk about absolutely everything, her affair, her anxiety about her family, her fear of stepping into the world alone. Dr. Lydia's worldview was at least as bleak as Mona's, tempered with a shy generosity that Mona thought of as the pearl: clamped down tightly inside her therapist's tough shell. Dr. Lydia never had to pretend to be in a good mood, never appeared to smile without meaning it, and, when she spoke, did not lie. She met you with a direct gaze and said precisely what was on her mind. There wasn't subterfuge or pussyfooting. No patronizing or second-guessing. Just candor. She reminded Mona of a kind of religious ascetic, someone thoroughly convinced of the salutary effects of her profession. She liked Mona. She thought Mona worthy and her family curious. Dr. Lydia adjusted Mona's stories slightly by her brief comments. These small insights helped. "Your mother's eye problem sounds like a self-fulfilling prophecy," she had said once. Yes, Mona thought, of course: her mother didn't want to see what she was being forced to see. No wonder she was going blind. Knowing this, she had revised her relationship accordingly. Dr. Lydia's success was in explaining the characters who surrounded Mona, clarifying them, pinning them and their motives to human forms instead of allowing them to orbit like idols or blurry planets. She put the world into scale, week after week, cracking the whip over the rearing head of Mona's personal weaselly beast, scoffing at the daunting superiority of Mona's constellation of intimates. This was Dr. Lydia's great gift, calibration. Steadiness in a tipsy universe.

"How's tricks?" she asked flatly today as Mona stepped in.

"Good," Mona replied; Dr. Lydia had broken her of the habit of saying "Eh," which had been the old answer, a kind of Catskills Jewish comedian's expression—"Ach, who can complain?" Once she'd held up her bare leg, which looked battered, as if somebody had taken a pool cue to her, knocking bruises up and down her shins and thighs. "I bruise easily," she'd told her therapist, knowing how well Dr. Lydia loved making symbols, spinning metaphorical, analogical castles in the air, only to knock them down later, detonate them.

And sure enough, Dr. Lydia had smiled discerningly, agreeing entirely, Mona bruised easily, a big sensitive piece of juicy fruit. The trick was not in changing her nature, but in keeping from getting squashed.

"Bruises are sexy," Winston had told Mona when they were in college. "My brother thinks bruises are sexy," Mona repeated for Lydia.

"Imperfection is interesting," Lydia remarked. "How's he feel about varicose veins?"

"My brother is coming home," Mona said today, glancing at her watch. "As we speak." And so they could discuss Winston, which Mona preferred. The other topic option was her new boyfriend, Nicholas Dempsey, who was another married man. She hated having to do it, but she was going to have to lie to Dr. Lydia about Nicholas Dempsey. It was obvious Dr. Lydia didn't want Mona to date another married man; the other one had taken such a toll. And since Mona was happy in her affair, there seemed no point to discuss it. Happiness sent the hungry rodent inside her into hibernation. Didn't obliterate it, merely stunned it.

Mona loved Nicholas Dempsey in the dangerously obsessive way that was her method. She fell in love like Alice into the Wonderland rabbit hole, heedless head over heels descent, reckless and with no sense of the bottom, no hope of a parachute or net. On occasion, she felt that Nicholas Dempsey had made a similar plunge, down a similar hole, but of course he had a wife and two children, consummate net and parachute. Even if she'd wanted to, was there any way to adequately share this sensation with someone on the outside? Wouldn't it all sound like faint murmuring?

"He's been safely tucked away," Dr. Lydia said, of Winston.

"Yeah. You know, for a while I've been able to feel just exactly the same about him, every day. Sorry for him, worried, but I always knew where he was, and that he and my father wouldn't be having any fights. Now . . ." It was good, ultimately, that Winston had been gone, that, for a while, he could call Larned his home. Now, Mona had images of terrible things happening; it made her nervous to be here, at her appointed hour, talking to Lydia when she ought to be at home, waiting to protect one of her family members from the other. She didn't trust happiness, she thought. When she was a little girl, she had, but not anymore. She didn't trust Winston's homecoming, nor Nicholas Dempsey's love.

Mona's eyes teared unexpectedly; she looked to her therapist, trusting, it seemed, only her. "I feel like I can't trust feeling good."

"*You* can't," Dr. Lydia said, taking up her pen and making a note.

This tendency of hers, suddenly writing, was the one part of therapy that still threw Mona. Something was worthy of committing to paper, but what? Or maybe Dr. Lydia was doodling, trying to stay awake, constructing a To Do list? But to think like this was to lose track of what Mona had actually been saying, feeling.

"You are encumbered by thought," Dr. Lydia had diagnosed her, long ago. It still pertained, the habit of anticipating trouble, fretting over it, creating a hundred versions of the way the family would split itself, the dozens of wrong responses she might make in any given situation. At night she woke alarmed, the dark a forest of ill-advised paths, snakes of the future hanging overhead, rats of the past nipping at her heels; it was Dr. Lydia who recommended turning on the light, listening to the radio, taking a bath.

"Right."

Her therapist had made her sign a contract stating that Mona would give Dr. Lydia one call, one chance, before doing the deed. They'd shaken hands, very solemn, Dr. Lydia squinting mightily, two lasers piercing Mona, defying her to betray such a pact. Mona was torn as to whether this agreement could be called binding. Who, after all, would object if she didn't fulfill her end of the deal? Only Dr. Lydia would know, and only after one of the Mabies notified her, Emily no doubt, and what kind of person would feel right about complaining to the bereaved family? Mona enjoyed a fantasy in which her therapist and sister discussed her suicide, the two of them who knew each other only through Mona. They wouldn't like each other, she thought. They were too much alike, and they would want to stake similar claims to Mona's life, that of confidante, mentor, the person who knew her best.

Or maybe they'd become bosom buddies, agree about every aspect of Mona's fucked-up cowardly behavior, meet for lunch, admire their mutual good taste in matters of fashion and diet and foresight. Now that Mona was out of the way, they'd probably develop a friendship the likes of which Mona could never fathom.

"Mona?" Dr. Lydia said. "You don't trust feeling good . . . ?"

"Well . . ."

"You're drifting."

"My sister," Mona began, but it wasn't her sister exclusively, it was the whole clan. "I have to go," Mona said, rising so quickly from her chair that she grew dizzy; her blood was slow, torpid; some of it spilled warmly between her legs. Today it seemed imperative that she set aside her so-called personal problems in the name of some greater task. Inside she could feel her parents' reluctance to show enthusiasm for the day, her brother's trepidation—these were the source of her headache, which was growing now like a gathering pressure system in the western regions of her skull. She had to attend to her family, explain them to one another.

"I understand," Dr. Lydia said. This was one of her famous sayings, her blessing. It was convincing. She smiled knowingly, reassuringly as Mona thanked her and left the inner office, passing through the decompression chamber where sat the receptionist boy who made your next appointment. He seemed capable of nothing more than precisely that, booking your future appearance, period. Today he looked at his watch, eyebrows raised in dramatic vexation.

"I'll be back next week," Mona promised, as if the guy cared.

"Rock on," he said blandly, turning to his calendar.

Speeding home, Mona was tempted to head toward the airport, intercept her siblings with flashing lights and blaring horn before they came to blows. Still, she found herself in the driveway of the house ahead of them. No one else was downstairs, the place quiet except for ticking clocks, as it always was this time of day, the hour of her mother's nap. The only movement was the dog's tail as he stood waiting in the kitchen: one old dog lonely for his friend who'd disappeared, the one old cat. Kojak and Inkspot.

Upstairs, at the door that for nearly thirty years had been her bedroom door, Mona bent to use a key. This was a recent installation, in preparation for what, Mona wasn't sure. All she knew was that she wanted a deadbolt on her door. It had gone unmentioned in the house, her parents either not noticing or, as had become routine since her suicide attempt, not wanting to make an undue fuss. These days they would choose their battles, Mona guessed. The only person who'd said anything at all was her sister's son Roy, who liked to visit Mona's toys, and now had to knock.

Behind the locked door of her room resided her collection of animals, a veritable zoo of stuffed creatures, their button eyes and synthetic whiskers facing her as she lay in bed. A room of watchful toys, benevolent and beloved. She'd been collecting them since she was a baby, first the lion and tiger, huge in her childhood, the size of beagles, a tiger lying curled as if suckling young, a terrific place to tuck your head, her golden eyes calm as a mother's. And the lion, standing on his haunches, watchful, front feet splayed, black thread sewn to indicate the different toes. For years, Mona had considered them married, the lion and the tiger, even as she understood the intricacies of breeds and species and geography. The standing father lion, the prone mother tiger: parents to the rest of the menagerie, pelican, porpoise, panda. They were all she ever got for Christmas. The objective now was the exotic, animals no one had ever dreamed of replicating in her childhood, crabs and spiders and hummingbirds, as well as the stubbornly uncute, the beluga, the ant, the pea-brained dinosaurs. Mona owned and treasured them all, arranged on shelves and bureaus and chairs and windowsills around her bedroom, some unceremoniously jumbled together in a hammock-like net strung in one corner. The room was soft, Mona thought. Children enjoyed visiting it. You could lie on a fuzzy white rug in one corner and listen to music, surrounded by the kind open eyes of a virtual forest of friends. They worked well as pillows, many of them, and she still nestled her skull into the open tummy of the mama tiger. The way to escape her family was to wear her headphones, turn her music up very loud, and nuzzle with her animals.

Her music, unlike her decor, was harsh and jagged, intensely unsentimental and full of shrieking profanity, unmelodic anger, unadulterated despair, sharp as glass shards. Her music disturbed even Winston, who was not easy to disturb. It was the one thing he could not understand about Mona. That was okay with her. She required it. It bespoke a darkness she could open herself up to, and in the proper setting, like this soft pretty room, playing the music here as opposed to hearing it in a club, the bleak void was bearable. This was music that the wild weasel understood. Raw, abandoned, raging, hopeless: it made Mona feel connected with a whole anonymous culture of like-minded souls, their scrabbling secrets.

But it was not a group she wished to meet in person. At bars or in the face of live music, Mona sometimes was known to go hide in the bathroom or outside, fingers in her ears—everything was bleak and unbearably lawless, desperate, addicted, self-hating and full of doubt, the noise, the crowd, the liquor itself. Other times you might find her suddenly in tears. Why? No balance, she thought. She knew that the music spoke of the true shape of the world, truly doomed, godless and unkind, unethical, immoral, and needing escape at just about any cost. You could fall off a world like that, tip right over the edge and descend like a stone off a roof, senseless, careless. Yet her childhood still tugged at her heart, a sweet toehold, and no matter what horrors her musical taste dredged up and sent through the stereo speakers, these beautiful creatures, these stuffed emblems of perfection with their stitched whiskers and clear marble eyes, wouldn't let her betray that little girl who was also her.

Her family thought she was wild, and her friends thought she was tame, a hayseed, and the truth was, she was both, wild *and* tame, sweet *and* unsentimental, soft *and* hard.

The telephone, like the deadbolt, was another recent installation in her room. Her own line, on which she hoped to receive calls from the man who currently held her heart in his hands. It gave her a certain pleasure to study the new equipment on the shelf above her stereo, the cute toy-like cordless phone on its stand with both a green and red light lit on its face, the efficient answering machine beside it, a bright painful o illuminated in its messages received window. A red zero. Before Mona was a large window, on the other side of which was the damp summer world, trees undulant in the Kansas wind, pigeons muttering among themselves on the roof eaves. She could look out of this window and watch the weather arrive, watch the downtown skyline for nighttime glow, watch for visitors to the house—today, her brother Winston. Then there was the tiny window in the black box, and it was the window responsible for forecasting the real weather, barometer of the soul. All evening she would be running upstairs to check her messages, and if she received one, she'd be happy. If she didn't, she'd be hopeful. And then, ultimately, heartbroken. Mona sighed. She did not like this aspect of herself.

Below, Emily's Volvo arrived, and Mona leaned forward, watching as Emily let Winston out. "Child lock," she murmured, smiling.

On the driveway, her brother was on his hands and knees, kissing the concrete. This was not a typical Winston-like gesture; it had too much of the mawkish in it. But maybe mawkishness would be what prison had taught him. That wouldn't be absolutely fatal, would it? His coming home a sentimental, grateful fool? Of the family, only she and their cousin Sheila had gone to visit him in Larned. She had driven her mother there—her mother who could not see well enough to sit behind the wheel of a car, her mother who had arrived at the prison parking lot and remained there, unable to enter through those gates—and then left her for an hour in the car, reading a road map three inches from her face, studying the narrow route that would deliver her home. Still, it had been six months since Mona's last trip to Larned State; he had changed since then. Or maybe it was seeing him finally erect, in the outdoors under natural light, wearing something besides blaze-orange coveralls, his fine hands out in the open instead of stuffed inside pockets. It had an aspect of the surreal, him there on the driveway after five years, as if he were an actor from a much-watched movie stepping from the screen into the audience. From the top of his pretty head shone a bald spot the size of a quarter, something he might not yet know about himself. It was sad to see his looks failing him. A tear fell on Mona's cheek, followed by another. She was so happy he was free, and so scared. She was so delighted her brother had returned, and so anxious.

And there was that nerve-racking o on her answering machine.

Her nephew Roy was running circles around Winston; of course he would love his uncle. Mona felt a jealous pang: this was how Emily would take precedence in Winston's life, through her children. This was how she'd become close to their parents again, too, by producing infants. Not by acting like an infant herself, Mona thought wryly, not the way Mona had behaved . . .

Winston looked up, then, right at Mona, and waved. He knew she was there, waiting. She smiled broadly, forgetting that she and Emily were competing for something. Her brother was the prettiest of all the Mabies, the distillation, the essence. Their grandmother had loved him best, and some of it, Mona thought, had to do with his undeniable attractiveness. You wanted to look at him. You wanted to be with him. At Larned, Winston had confided to Mona that many of the other inmates felt that same urge.

"What do they do?" she'd asked, imagining the worst, the hideous grubby sodomizing, tools made of scraps and nails at his throat. She'd been reading literature about prison, her heart beating wildly as she placed her brother among the savages in their cages.

"Stare at me," he'd answered. "Make what we call suggestive remarks."

"Gross."

He laughed. "Mona, you know I'm a hugger, not a slugger."

"Whatever."

"One of the guards watches out for me. I do Monty Python for him. He likes that."

"Big fat liar," she said. She knew her brother's life inside prison was unmentionably awful, nothing that a rendition of the cheese shop or the dead parrot or Mary Queen of Scots could salvage. In the eyes of the men around her when she'd visited, she saw nothing resembling humanity, and her greatest fear was that Winston would emerge having traded himself for this same look. "Bad boys," his lawyer, her current boyfriend, had called them with a knowing grimace. Her brother had gone to live among the bad boys.

Mona was careful to lock her bedroom door from the outside as she left it, stooping slightly to fit the key hanging from a chain worn round her neck. She liked to think of herself as a kind of tenant in her parents' house, somebody entitled to a bit of privacy, someone like Emily Dickinson, who might be composing literature in there. In fact, her living at home was a product of inertia, a compilation of circumstance. The house was large, far too big for merely two people; her mother was going slowly blind and needed a driver; furthermore, Mona had suicidal tendencies. But mostly, she liked her bedroom. She liked her family. She didn't want to be alone.

For a second she waited at the door, listening for the phone. Then carefully she walked downstairs, avoiding by habit the treads that squeaked, the third, the eighth, the thirteenth, not wanting to interrupt her mother's afternoon nap.

Down in the kitchen her sister Emily stood trapped by her children, the baby in one arm, Roy wrapping himself around her other side, her purse strap choking her. Motherhood, Mona thought, ball and chain, straitjacket. She stepped to the mudroom. "Where is he?"

"Taking a tour of the grounds. He didn't believe a tornado got the tire-swing tree. Roy, unhand me, you're tearing my panty hose. Will you hold her?" She passed the fat baby to Mona, who, as always, felt guilty distaste concerning the girl. She was such an ugly child, not one redeeming characteristic to save her, dour, gloomy, coarse featured, charmless. She comported herself like a Buddha, a toad-like entitled somebody others ought to be grateful to hold and serve. Now Roy climbed into his mother's arms like a monkey, so that when Winston came through the door Mona could not hand off the baby to give her brother a hug.

"Where're the Aged P's?" he asked, stooping ever so slightly at the threshold between mudroom and kitchen, although the doorway was high enough to accommodate him. Once more, there was his slight bald spot, tipped toward Mona, a small circle of susceptibility like the fontanel of an infant. He glanced around the kitchen rather than look at Mona's tearful face.

"Mom's sleeping. Dad's off with Billy."

"Billy," said Winston thoughtfully, as if he'd forgotten the existence of his curious uncle.

"Mom made chocolate raisin pie," Mona said. "Your favorite," she reminded him, in case he'd forgotten. Her heart swelled to picture her parents, their separate retreats now that their only son had come home. Neither wanted to be found awaiting him. Both wanted to walk in as if it had been they who were gone, they who were returning, expecting welcome. "I'm so glad to see you, Winnie!" She embraced him one-armed while her niece leaned awkwardly away, threatening to topple the threesome backward. She was a heavy counterbalance, that baby. Mona's brother had just smoked a cigarette, she could smell it on his breath.

"Hey scum," Winston said fondly, releasing Mona and opening the cupboard behind Emily to take down a glass. He held it up to the light, as had always been his habit, to check for dishwasher sand collected on the bottom. Dissatisfied, he picked up another.

"You'd think they would have bought a new dishwasher by now," Winston said, shaking his head over the dirty glasses.

"They did," the sisters said together. And the three of them shared a smile.

"Could it be the cocktail hour?" Mona asked happily, glancing at the clock to see if it would give her permission. Her sister shot her a look that reminded Mona that their brother was not to drink, these days. Or was he? The clock said 5:15, which was a quarter of an hour advanced into happy hour.

"I'm having a beer," Mona declared. It was a refutation of Alcohol as Problem. "Anyone else?" Her brother, to her relief, declined. But also to her disappointment. Alcohol had made the family kinder to one another; without it, they would not have laughed as hard, touched as often, told soppy stories of their affection, their shared adventures and humiliations. Happy hour preceded dinner, the preparations of which pleased everyone, especially when executed under the gentle fuzziness of a glass of wine or gin and tonic. Even now, Emily began moving between kitchen and pantry, between pantry and dining room, doing her part, assigning her son the task of locating silverware, setting the baby in her high chair with a pile of crackers and grated cheese, stopping every now and then to sip at a glass of wine.

In the face of their older sister's busyness, Mona noticed that she and Winston were falling into their shared lazy habit, watchers, peanut gallery to Emily's competent performance in things domestic. He sat at his old kitchen chair, she at hers, beside him.

"So, Inkspot ran away," she mentioned.

"Died," Emily said. "Turn the oven to three fifty, please."

"She didn't die," Mona said. "She'll be back."

"Doubtful," said Emily. "Three fifty," she reminded Mona, whose chair rested directly in front of the stove.

"What are we having?" Winston asked. He'd been looking at the kitchen from his spot, studying a wall and then shifting his gaze to the next wall, as if creating a panoramic image in his head. Like her sister before her, Mona found herself attempting to get her brother's angle on the room, working to think what he thought. And like her sister, she was struck by how alien his point of view had become. She could only make guesses based on his body, which seemed to be breathing a bit heavily, a series of sighs, like defeat, or perhaps merely acclimatizing.

"We're having halibut," Mona told him jauntily as she poured every last drop of her beer into her glass.

"Just for the halibut," Emily and Winston said together.

4

"I WISH SHE'D learn to park the Toyota *in* the garage," Professor Mabie said, pulling into the driveway in a two-tone Lincoln Continental Mark IV with a white-soaped asking price ($1,999.99!!!) defacing its windshield. Professor Mabie sat behind the wheel; his younger brother Billy sat beside him, staring through the numerals while his nose dripped. His posture was bad and his nose leaked; when he opened his mouth you saw his teeth, which looked like the remains of a broken cup of coffee, jagged yellow porcelain all jumbled in a bunch.

Professor Mabie handed his brother a napkin, which Billy swiped hopelessly beneath his nostrils. They were test-driving the car for Billy's daughter, who was sixteen, a spoiled girl who got everything she even dreamed of asking for. *Sheila*—even her name suggested the seedy, and seemed destined to direct her into a line of work involving G-strings and raunchy music. "What's the point of parking halfway in the garage?" Professor Mabie asked. His family seemed to hold many halfway members, his daughter Mona among them.

"What'll Sheila think of this auto?" Billy asked contemplatively. His daughter baffled him the way teenage girls had always baffled him. Billy would not grow up, and that meant that his older brother would have to watch out for him.

"Hmm." Professor Mabie didn't think Sheila would like the car, and that made him temporarily favorably inclined. He was an unlikely patriarch. His nature was shy, self-effacing—yet he had been so often put in the position of authority, he'd adopted a look and tenor of assurance even when he didn't feel it. Now he grunted, unhappy not only with the Continental's appearance—it looked like a certain kind of men's wing tip, dotted swiss and shyster-ish—but also with the rumble of its engine. There was something of the faulty lawnmower in it, something just barely noticeable but fatal, something that would sputter and expire in a puff of blue smoke in the not-so-distant future. He pictured sullen Sheila, hiking her short skirt over her thick thigh on the highway, thumbing a ride after this hideous two-tone shoe of a car broke down. . . .

"There's Emily's Volvo back," Billy noted quietly.

Professor Mabie nodded. Both men knew that Winston had now returned. Neither planned to say any more on the subject. Professor Mabie's brothers, all four of them younger than he, would never prod him to respond to difficult news like this. They would give him invitations to converse, and then let him choose to pick up the ball. Three of them lived in California, but Billy, the youngest, lived across town in their mother's old house. The house had been willed to Billy when their mother died; she'd known who the needy in her family were, the ones who could care for themselves, and the ones who'd require her help.

Her money she'd willed to Winston. Bunny had bequeathed a quarter of a million dollars to the boy who'd driven her into a stoplight and killed her. Professor Mabie thought his reluctance to greet his son might have had something to do with the fact of that dreadful irony. As executor of the estate, Professor Mabie had had to put himself through the awful dilemma of considering a lawsuit against his incarcerated son—"wrongful death," it was called, and nothing had ever seemed so correctly named to Professor Mabie, *wrongful death*—but word came that Winston refused his inheritance. He did not give it back, but refused to take it. As was typical, he created more work with this gesture. Winston had an obstinacy, a prideful loafing grudge that precluded his making something simple for his father. One might think that Professor Mabie would have given up his antagonism when the money had been settled, but that wasn't what happened. To Professor Mabie it seemed as if Winston were ungrateful to his grandmother, as if he didn't need money. He was arrogant, confident in the way of youth.

His lack of humility, his disdain of the money, *something* bothered his father.

Professor Mabie sincerely wished there'd been litigation. For the first eighteen months of his son's imprisonment and his own mourning of his mother, he had imagined arguing his case. The boy's need to learn the value of human life, let alone monetary windfall, played an enormous role. And then Winston had upstaged him, declaring as soon as he discovered the contents of his grandmother's estate that he wanted nothing to do with the money. Momentarily, Professor Mabie had flown into another rage, a contradictory fury: how dare his son spurn this treasure, the hoarded bounty of his mother's difficult life? How dare he so cavalierly refuse her gift?

His wife merely wept, but his best friend Betty set him straight. "You won," Betty declared, having had enough of him.

"I didn't win."

"Just because he wouldn't fight doesn't mean you didn't win," she went on, in what he thought of as a patronizing manner. He hated teacherliness in others, recognizing his own habit, the knowing tone and superior weariness. He wasn't petulant, he wanted to convince Betty, he was entitled to a full-fledged dispute. Maybe his son deserved the money; how would they know, now? Had there been a court of law, one that would have come down on his side or his son's, there would be no outstanding debt, no leftover prickly, nagging rancor.

When Billy phoned earlier, the ostensible reason had been to ask for advice, but in truth he was gauging his older brother's mood and unrest. Professor Mabie knew this. He knew this foolish test drive had little to do with Sheila's need for a car. All four of his brothers still turned to him for leadership, but they now also looked out for him, attempted to protect him from his second family. The brothers understood his feelings about Winston in a way that none of the women in Professor Mabie's contemporary family could. After all, it had been their mother who had died.

"This is a lemon," Professor Mabie declared of the Mark IV, which grumbled beneath him, then occasionally hiccuped, a big drunk shoe.

"I think so too," Billy said. He sighed, looking around. "It's roomy, though, comfy."

"I wouldn't think that would necessarily be a virtue."

"A pimpmobile."

They glanced at their watches and came to the same relieved conclusion Mona had, inside: cocktail hour.

"A drink?" they said together as Professor Mabie turned off the rumble and jostle of the weighty machine, which took a moment to recognize that its trip was over.

They stepped out of the car but hesitated while the doors creaked heavily on their hinges.

"Let me show you something downstairs," Professor Mabie said, guiding his brother to the house's second back entrance, the one that did not lead to the mudroom and kitchen but to the basement, the back stairs. Inside, you could turn one way, climb a long winding set of steps, and end up in the old servants' quarters on the third floor, the apartment where his daughter Emily now lived with her two children. Turn the other, and you found yourself going down into the basement: coal room, furnace room, wine cellar, workshop. Ancient appliances, dark corners, moldy walls. This was the enclave of the masculine, the place where furniture was fixed, where fish got gutted, where pilot lights were lit, where paint was splattered and noxious glue uncapped, where the mighty shop vac took care of the mess.

They stepped stealthily downstairs and into a dank room with a drain in its center, the ceiling of which was crisscrossed with ominous-looking pipes, stained white tails dangling everywhere. Billy said, "Lotta wicks." Wicks were the Mabie solution to leaks; a torn scrap of bedsheet was lashed around the corroded plumbing, soaking up the water, permitting it then to evaporate. They hung all through the basement of this house as well as Billy's, like rusty neckties or bloody bandages, like forgotten macabre party decorations swinging from the leaden pipes.

When they looked up into the latticework, they understood they were directly beneath the kitchen, where everyone always gathered. "He there?" Billy whispered, as if he wished only to suggest the idea of Winston, as if hoping his brother would intuit his question rather than actually hear it, in case he didn't want to be reminded, in case he didn't want to answer. Professor Mabie appreciated this deference, this care. His wife and daughters did not indulge it, perhaps did not understand his love of subtlety, his great respect for the under- or unstated. They seemed to think he was avoiding them when he didn't directly answer their questions. They didn't see that some questions should simply not be asked.

"I can't hear him," Professor Mabie said. He heard his grandson Roy hopping in his boots, clodding from kitchen to dining room. He could hear the baby babbling. His daughters laughed their similar open-throated laugh; you could not tell them apart, laughing. Cupboards squeaked and the floorboards trembled; water pulsed through the leaky pipes in short bursts—rinsing vegetables, filling cups. Then he smelled cigarettes.

His brother smelled smoke, too, Professor Mabie could see the scent register on Billy's face, a tremor of fear. It was a nostalgic smell; their mother had smoked. Mentholated cigarettes, long and slender, her head tipped back and her lips pursed, a woman exhaling a kiss of scented wind.

"I better get that piece of shit car back to Chuck Self's," Billy said, to remind his brother that a drink had been promised. He knew there'd been nothing to be shown in the basement and he wasn't going to mention the maneuver of entering the house that way. "I don't guess Sheila'll be driving a Lincoln Continental to school anytime soon." He and his wife had only one child, which was plenty. She ran their household, insolent and spoiled and loud and slutty. Of course, he couldn't see this about her, blind the way some parents were. She amused him, stunned him. He seemed to feel that his obligation in the world was to make her happy, to impress her the way one would a queen or future date, as if he were her minion, her dweeby admirer, and now she wanted a car. Since Billy wouldn't think of purchasing anything as big as a car without his brother's advice, they'd gone to check out the Continental together. Together they consulted *Consumer Reports* and *Motor Trend,* window-shopped, test-drove, sat at the kitchen table and debated ad infinitum. This dead earnest concern with the spending of money eluded Professor Mabie's women. His wife merely refrained; she didn't need anything. His daughters had the irritating inclination of the impulse buyer. Even Emily, the cautious one, the driver of the prudent Volvo, the one who seemed most like him, even Emily had an impetuous streak that landed her in trouble. Look at her marriage to the cocaine dealer, for instance . . .

In the basement, Billy was mulling his plans for the next day, thinking aloud about Sheila's school schedule, his lunch hour, his wife's return from her training session in Dallas. The Mabie brothers settled on noon, back at the Chuck Self pre-owned lot on the west side.

"You could stay for dinner," Professor Mabie suggested.

"Oh, nah . . . Sheila's cooking up something." He frowned, his memory of the evening's plans collecting behind his eyes like cherries in a slot machine. "But I think she's bringing it over here?"

"You're eating with us," Professor Mabie recalled.

"Oh yeah." Billy smiled, jackpot! He and Sheila ate with the Mabies when Billy's wife was out of town, a not-uncommon scenario. The brothers smelled smoke again, as if Winston's exhalations were being piped down specially, right through the little hole in the ceiling where the children used to deposit their unwanted vegetables, Brussels sprouts, asparagus.

"Let's get a drink in my study," Professor Mabie suggested.

By instinct, Billy checked his watch again to make sure they were clear for alcohol.

THROUGH THE warren of musty basement rooms they stole like burglars, up the other, public, stairs, which were dark because the men had entered the basement backward, against the light switches. Professor Mabie was relieved, at the top of the steps, to find the entry hall and living room unoccupied and quickly crossed them to the safety of his study, where he closed the door. The house was large enough to negotiate a passage without running into others, without being detected, and the study, like home base, seemed the end of a tense game of hide-and-seek.

Both men relaxed immediately upon entering.

Like the basement, this was a male space. It had been everyone's study before Professor Mabie's retirement, but he'd evicted the accessories of his family when he made his move home from the university. Out went the trashy yet much-handled paperbacks, the ancient Underwood, and all the dusty esoteric musical instruments someone thought he or she should learn, autoharp, recorder, bongos, castanets, saxophone. Out went the half-filled photo albums, fish aquarium, plastic fixer trays and all the other antiquated darkroom equipment, and the collection of ceramic frogs and the bygone schoolwork and the piles and piles and piles of old *New Yorker* and *National Geographic* magazines. Good god, how those things collected, all the unread information, accumulating as testament to the vastness of the world, to the proliferation of writers and photographers, not to mention their endless, exponentially mutating subjects, and, mostly, to the shabby guilty indifference of subscribers. The study, previously, had been the place you wandered into when bored, when looking for something you'd lost track of as an interest. All the casual detritus of his family's halfhearted hobbies disappeared when Professor Mabie took it over. The room acquired square footage. He installed a telephone, leather chair, computer, heavy drapes, stereo system, liquor cabinet and stemware—as if he were opening some swank business where his cronies might come and discuss high finance or Mob hits. He alphabetized his serious thick-spined hardbound biographies, unstuck the stuck door so that it would fully close, and then instructed his family to knock on it rather than burst in, as had been their habit.

He prohibited his grandson Roy from spinning in the chair or playing with the mouse of his computer. He did not exactly encourage the subsequent gifts he was given—cigar humidor, indoor weather station, sheepskin scuffs—but neither did he return them to the arcane shops from which they'd been acquired. His family embraced his notion of *study*; they wanted to equip it with all the proper masculine amenities. Once a week, Professor Mabie actually cracked the window and puffed on a cigar from his pricey climate-controlled box.

Billy took the chair facing the desk, dropping the Continental's keys on Professor Mabie's spotless blotter. Professor Mabie poured them each a bourbon.

"No rocks," he explained, although he had an ice bucket and in general remembered to fill it. Today he'd forgotten. He pinched the tongs abstractly.

"No problem," said Billy, taking a delicate wincing sip. He wasn't much of a drinker. That is, he drank, but he wasn't good at it, he couldn't do what the other brothers could: hold his liquor; drink and drink and drink and never show drunkenness. He just became very sleepy, face soft as a hankie clutched round his broken teeth. Professor Mabie's daughter Mona was exactly like him, first silliness and sentimentality, then slumber. Perhaps that was a trait of youngest children, susceptibility. Trust that someone would lift you from the floor, tuck you in, cover your tracks.

They talked about the car. How grand to have a subject that wasn't their intimate feelings, that wasn't their personal problems. The quest for Sheila's car would give them weeks of each other's uncomplicated, unstrained company. These projects—always in the form of house maintenance or proposed purchases—had become their way of being together. Why couldn't his other family understand the appeal of Billy's company? "You like him more than us," Mona had once cried to him. "You'd rather be with your brothers than your own children." *Your own children.* That had the ring of someone else's phrasing to it. Well, he loved them all, both families that he'd had to raise, but with his brothers he felt an ease he just didn't with *his own children.* With Billy, for example, he was never without a conversation topic. Between them, they were never without a thing to do. So today they were not hiding in Professor Mabie's study, fortifying themselves with a stiff drink. Nossir. They were discussing the disaster of an automobile that sat leaking grease on the driveway outside the study window; already, Professor Mabie was envisioning pouring kitty litter over the pool of oil it would leave. And after they finished with the Continental, Professor Mabie was going to show Billy how computer solitaire was easier on arthritis than the traditional variety. He supposed he should find things his daughters enjoyed doing so that they'd have subjects, too, but their tastes ran toward the confessional, the conversation, the intensely depressing nerve-racking focus on feelings.

"Don't guess any of the others are at home, out on the West Coast," Billy said.

Professor Mabie checked his watch. It was only 3:45 in California, and the three brothers would still be at their offices. When he and Billy ran out of steam, they phoned up one of the others. Long Beach, Sausalito, Fresno. Somebody was always in the market for something, mulling a trade on a car or home or hunting dog, contemplating the installation of a swimming pool, bemoaning a college flunkee offspring, rectifying a household disaster or visiting a physician. Medical problems were not openly discussed until after diagnosis, and sometimes not even then. When their mother had been alive, she had often been their topic. Phoning the brothers today seemed a bit obvious, even to Billy Mabie. After he finished his bourbon, he stood a little woozily. "I'm gonna go drop that bomb back at Chuck Self's. I'll see you for supper."

Professor Mabie handed him the Continental's keys. His brother left the house through the side door, avoiding the kitchen and mudroom, skulking around the driveway and closing the two-tone car door quietly. There wasn't, Professor Mabie noted, an oil stain after all.

Now he poured another bourbon and sat alone in his study while the sun, burning behind the thick yellow clouds, refused to sink. Summer. From his window he could observe his animal habitats: wren house, martin house, little beehive, bat box, finch feeder. He loved most wildlife and birds, all but pigeons, and of course they plagued him. Before him on the desk sat his computer, on which he was supposed to be writing his book, at last, and therefore needing his solitude. When he had retired, he'd had in mind a text on teaching, his lectures and strategies for engaging the uninterested student in American history via art and literature, image and narrative, gossip and sidebars. His target audience was the teenager; by the time students got to him, in college, it was too late. By then, their indifference had taken hold. History = death. "It's all about war," they complained. "Battle of this, battle of that." Professor Mabie came to understand that they could not care about the winners. History was about winners, and his students did not, typically, identify.

His progress on this textbook had been thwarted by his own indifference. Now that he didn't see these students, he couldn't much get inspired to help them out. They'd become ghost figures, difficult to imagine or remember; his own children had grown up, passed out of teenage scorn and into adult shame of their deficiencies. They certainly couldn't remind him of why his book was necessary—and his grandchildren were far too young, just yet. And how could he ever envision his niece Sheila interested in anyone's drama but her own? His own fervor had been inspired by his ignorant students, like bad weather from which to take immediate shelter—and now the disaster was a thing of the past, he himself unruffled by wind. He could forget what they didn't know. His hearing was fading, whatever roar had once summoned him now a modest hum inside his own head. Most often, he sat in his comfortable leather chair, admiring his privacy, playing on his computer, preparing to work. Getting ready. Tracking his feathered friends. He had all his props, plenty of time, the patience of age, the wisdom of experience. Perhaps he had too much of each. So he sat sipping a preparatory drink or playing computerized solitaire or hearts, some times slipping into a gentle nap, listening to the radio or watching the birds for whom he'd made life easier, waiting for the phone to ring so he could chat with his friend Betty or counsel his obedient brothers, for the mail to arrive, or his family to show up from their forays into the world. He liked to hear what was going on out there without having to investigate for himself. His daughters brought news in the form he liked best: stories. They each had an ability to turn a simple trip to the grocery into a lively anecdote. His old friend Betty Spitz he counted on for gossip, news of his former colleagues, their enduring friends, lore of the city at large. Their friends were succumbing: fleeing to the golf course states, Florida and Arizona, or contracting diseases, or plain dying, in all instances disappearing from Professor Mabie's life without replacement. If it hadn't been for Betty and his daughters, for his brothers, for his solid quiet wife, Professor Mabie might have wound up like his old neighbor, Hans Vaughn, who had died last year alone in his basement next door, undiscovered for four days, unmissed. It was the four days that frightened Professor Mabie; his own downfall would be noted much sooner, he knew. Still. Hans's children—those strange creatures whose development over the years had served as reassuring contrast to his own children's normal growth, the Vaughns' odd height, protruding eyes, thick glasses, bizarre apricot-colored springy hair and nearly albino skin—now departed for other cities, their lives unknown to Professor Mabie. His wife would know; her nature was to contain things. Nearly every day of the year represented somebody's birthday, to Mrs. Mabie. That was her sense of history: the milestones of personal passed time, anniversaries, birthdays, seasonal holidays and their attendant decorations, flags or pumpkins or elves.

And of course Professor Mabie had his brother Billy and Billy's worthless daughter Sheila and his ambitious absent wife. Billy was still his project, lo these many years. Billy helped Professor Mabie feel connected to a less demanding world. On most days, Professor Mabie could enjoy his retirement, could overcome the knowledge that it was step one on the road to death, the public death, retirement from the professional world. Personal death would be later, private, abundantly solitary.

Most days he could bypass all of that, be pleased not to have to greet the same dull colleagues he'd been greeting forever and with forced joviality in the hallowed halls of the history department, but today, anticipating the reunion with his delinquent son, he could almost wish he had somewhere to go, some group of uninterested students to bore. He opened a document file he'd created recently titled "Obit," which contained the eulogy he was authoring for his best friend, who was still dying, but his mood was not sufficiently focused on Betty and he could not summon his true melancholy to add to his notes today. Even his ongoing game of hearts failed to occupy him, though the screen obligingly offered up its hands, the funny utterly gratuitous shuffling noise that usually amused him, the quick flap of its swift dealings, the opponents whose names he was allowed to invent and change, Pecker, Swifty, Fathead, and the endless forgiving option the screen offered him of taking back a play when he'd made a mistake and was about to lose. He swirled one hand on the mouse, rested one over his fly. Funny how his genitals attracted his palm, the soft pouch, the friendly bundle. Having a closed door between him and his family of women permitted him the luxury of laying his hand there.

His problem with his son was irritating because it involved a paradox. As an academic, Professor Mabie was supposed to be charmed by paradoxes, but this particular one just went round and round in his head, dividing itself like a cell, dodging him, enraging him, laughing at him as it sprang nimbly about in his mind. He believed, on the one hand, that no child should have to endure the life he himself had. Depression era gloom, coughing and kicking dead center in the dust bowl, poorly fed with colorless food, made to grow up quickly, skipping from knickers to navy issue, four small brothers looking up with hungry eyes of awe. Their hero. Professor Mabie, as eldest, became their inadvertent father figure when only a teenager himself, as yet ignorant and unlaid. So much of his life seemed dictated by default. His own father had died young—younger by twenty years than Professor Mabie today—leaving his wife stunned, skill-less. She'd gone to work—what choice was there?—and Professor Mabie had overseen the boys, James, Edward, Theodore, William, rising up in the thoroughly unglamorous blasted soil of hinterland Oklahoma. He read John Steinbeck and tried to feel plucky, heroic, unsung but stalwart. Eventually, Professor Mabie was proud for having pulled through, for seeing these boys into their own adulthoods, for simply surviving. Bad as it was, it had also held the real risk of sucking them down into something worse. Theirs had been difficult, unhappy lives, and Professor Mabie hadn't wanted anything more desperately than to prevent his own children from living ones just like them.

So they hadn't, and he'd made sure of that. His vision of their lives led him through his twenties and thirties, guidance as demanding as a set of commandments. Before he acquired a wife he'd gotten himself educated and tenured. He drove a used car and bought a giant fixer-upper of a home that he then fixed up. His children—of which there were not too many—had not had to work their way through college; his son had never had to quit school or move home or join the military just to help make mortgage payments. There'd been saving accounts for all three children, private lessons at instruments and art, semesters abroad in countries other than their own, tours of the world's wonders—his children, he'd sworn, would never stand gawking, eyes teary with astonishment at the ripe old age of twenty-five, at the simple extraordinary sight of a skyscraper. Professor Mabie looked back on his younger self, his four country bumpkin brothers, Jimmy, Eddie, Teddy, Billy, with a kind of proud pity that still had the effect of twisting his heart. Their naïveté, and its cost, still stirred him—poor Billy, hoping he could find a used car for a decent price. Yet Professor Mabie could not have wished the circumstances of his own youth on his next set of charges.

And what was the price of this better life? Predictable enough, he supposed. Having spared the rod, what had he expected? His two daughters lived at home—both unmarried, both in varying ways dependent—and his son, at age thirty-three, the identical age at which Jesus Christ had already died, for God's sake, his son had not just done nothing, had not just not succeeded, but had completely failed. Done damage. Was in arrears. Was an ex-con. Was a murderer. Only in his head did Professor Mabie call his son a murderer, only under the soothing blanket of bourbon. He did it with something like irony, with something like hard-heartedness, which was to prevent him from something like total despair.

What could he have done, over the course of his son's life, to prepare him to be a man? This was his dilemma. He'd not wanted his son's life to resemble his own, and so it did not. But neither did it resemble what it ought, something productive and moral and improved. Why couldn't a man expect an evolution of ethics? But he suspected his son had the ethics of a person raised in the circumstances of destitution. It was embarrassing, confounding, humiliating, frustrating. And so this paradox taunted Professor Mabie, had been taunting him for years. How was a parent to behave?

It was the coldest of comfort to think that Winston had now suffered imprisonment. Was that what it would take, to cure a spoiled child of his ways? Would a slap in his niece Sheila's face actually remove the snotty smile from her lips? Might she be scared straight in the pen? Had that happened to Winston? Unfortunately, Professor Mabie remained a liberal in his thinking on incarceration. Prison, like the military, he believed overrated for its rehabilitating effects.

The paradox he had to entertain concerning his son did not trouble him when he considered his daughters' lives. True, they showed similar inabilities to grow up and move on, but Professor Mabie didn't mind having them at home with him. In fact, he thought he'd be lonely in this house without them. If they moved out, took their clatter and children and colorful clothing and exotic friends, then he and his wife might have to move out as well, into something smaller, something scaled to their needs, which were few, really. No more cavernous insulation, isolated privilege, no more luxury of useless space. Or perhaps they'd simply close entire floors of this house, the third, possibly even the second, seal doors and heat only the tunnel of rooms they actually used as a couple, kitchen, living room, bedroom, bath, study. The connecting hallways and stair, all others shut off and cold, lightless. Professor Mabie, though he complained about it, sort of enjoyed hearing his granddaughter cry in the night, or his grandson run up and down the back steps, pounding in his cowboy boots to the third-floor apartment he shared with his mother and sister. Professor Mabie did not mind seeing his youngest, Mona, in her pajamas before the television, just where she'd been twenty years ago, happily watching while eating popcorn or ice cream, many of the same tinny, silly sound tracks ringing out, *Here's the sto-ry, of a man named Bra-dy* . . . Mona: who always jumped up to see if he wanted something to drink, ready to change channels or do a crossword puzzle with him or fix him a sandwich. He thought of their living arrangement as a kind of experiment in the extended family. They liked one another, they got along, they helped one another out, preparing meals and baby-sitting, taking messages and making appointments, driving to day care and pharmacy. Weren't sociologists and anthropologists always complaining of the family's disintegration? Wasn't the Mabie household bucking tradition, rectifying a wrong, going against the grain in the most humane and logical way?

If you owned a house that had a half-dozen entrances, seven bedrooms, five bathrooms, four fireplaces, two kitchens, separate flights of stairs, rooms as big as ballrooms, and even an empty elevator shaft, what better use for it than to install your children there, forever? It was a mansion, a castle, a barn, a compound.

And why did his son's arrival suddenly make all of this look like a problem? How come his son couldn't come live with them, too? Why was it different for this particular boy? Why did Professor Mabie both want his son to suffer the same life he himself had suffered, as well as to be spared that suffering? Why did Professor Mabie not care if his brothers failed, proved themselves weak and unreliable? Why did his daughters' weakness not bother him so? Why did Winston bear the burden of this expectation of better behavior? Because Winston was his son. Winston was supposed to carry on the tradition of taking care. Not being cared for, but the reverse. He was supposed to be strong, not weak. All of the rest of them were Professor Mabie's charges, but Winston was his heir. And his heir had failed him. There was no imaginable forgiveness; for some reason, the rift ran just that deep. His son was weak. Weakness in all the rest of the world did not so deeply offend Professor Mabie as it did in Winston. In Winston, he saw too clearly his own tendencies, his own forsaken paths. Winston was precisely what Professor Mabie had chosen not to become.

It was during his third bourbon that Professor Mabie fell asleep in his chair. He dozed as if rocking in a boat on a sun-drenched river, warm, buoyant, destinationless. It was joy without context, this kind of sleep. At ten after seven, his youngest child rapped lightly on the study door, cracking the obscure and fragile shell of his nap. She'd known where he was, and what he was doing, and now called gently that his dinner was on the table. "Papa?" she added—he loved his name on her lips—"We're eating in the dining room." Professor Mabie was on his feet—fuzzy yet hungry, appetite engaged—before he remembered what awaited him.

5

B<small>UT</small> M<small>ONA</small> <small>HAD</small> been premature in summoning her father. Dinner was not quite ready to be served. Mrs. Mabie was not her usual efficient self. Her son, who had been so long gone, prevented efficiency.

"Hey, Mom," he had said, casually, when she came through the kitchen door. She had slept her ritual afternoon sleep: dreamy trance into which she entered as if hypnotized and from which she woke with her heart stuttering as if she'd missed a crucial appointment. She often woke in a faint panic; her parents, long ago, had died while she slept. Nowadays her fear was that she would find no one home, that all at once they would leave and she would be orphaned, again. She hurried clumsily down the stairs today, gripping the banister and feeling blindly with her toes for the next tread. For years she had been losing her sight, yet sometimes the tight focus in the center of her vision made her mission clear, her aim true. She came looking for her boy as if sniffing him out. When she found him, he hugged her hard. Breathtaking, dwarf-making, earthquaking: he took her breath, he made her small, his was a seismic presence. She had not visited him in prison; he had insisted not, although she'd once made it all the way to the gate before surrendering to his wishes. He'd forever had a stubborn resistance to embarrassment. As a boy, he'd hide his failures, bury the bad report card, run to his room to shed tears unseen. And so he'd retreated to prison, don't look at me, leave me alone. Because Mrs. Mabie no longer drove, she had ridden with Mona that one time. From the moment they left the driveway she had known she would renege, return to the safety of her house, its smells, its textures, its objects that bore the imprint of her belonging.

"Honey," she said into his tattered flannel shirt collar. She had not seen him for five years, but she and Winston had exchanged letters, Mrs. Mabie hurrying with hers to her bathroom, where the light was bright and where the doors had locks, read them two or three times, then burned them, as if from a lover, let them swirl away into the plumbing. Like a lover, she did not want to share him. Like a lover, she believed she knew him best, loved him more. Whatever was between them had nothing to do with her daughters, his sisters, or her husband, his father. He had been with her, these five years, through the mail, via penmanship, a correspondence that had its own distinct existence, a friendship, a courtship, a fluent conversation. Despite the crude editing by the capricious hand of the Larned State censor, Winston's letters had provided his mother reassurance. She liked letters; in them, people made the polite efforts that had been forsaken in other modes of communication. *Dear,* they began; *Love,* they ended. There was no exasperated sighing, in a letter, no sloppy slang, no hammering overuse of *like.* There was no boredom or savagery, no cold shoulder or jeering.

In her most frankly honest moments with herself, she admitted her relief that he was accounted for, his sentence a kind of purgatory, preparation for what came next, shelter and protection—protection from himself as much as anything else. His car accident was not the first time he'd been cited for driving drunk. His next one might have taken him, too. Her husband did not share her belief that there was luck involved, but Mrs. Mabie would happily have sacrificed her mother-in-law for her boy. She was grateful he had been spared. As the world grew dark around her, as her degenerating eyesight made it close down, she wanted the people she cared for contained, like money in the bank, like food in the cupboards, like hands in pockets.

She squeezed him again when she felt him ready to step away, realizing as she did so that they had left behind their former intimacy. She had always been better on paper than in person, her prose style more convincing than her corporeal presence. *Orphan,* she thought, recalling her husband's words from long ago. *You act like an orphan;* he'd been complaining about her passivity, that gratitude for small favors, her over-whelming aspect of *un*-entitlement. Officially, she *was* an orphan, justi-fied to play the part. But her husband had also meant something less literal. He meant that she seemed stray, abject, nobody's girl. Now her son was here, home, and he wouldn't talk to her. Not the way he had in his letters. She would lose him, she thought, she would become wall-flower to the more vibrant forces in the house, four-year-old Roy and adoring Mona, his skeptical big sister Emily and his bitter father, the professor. His blind orphan mouse mother would recede, Mrs. Mabie believed, fade once again into the backdrop of more insistent relations.

Yet, for that time he was gone she had sustained him, she thought, and he her. There wasn't any point in begrudging his noisier affections, these people she moved among daily and harmoniously. She loved them, too, and when they called upon her, she was there, obliging, ready. Winston had needed her differently, these five years. The news he sent back had been intended to reassure her, never to frighten her, and in this way he had taken care of her. He had protected her, from that great distance of 250 miles, despite the layers that separated them, walls of stone and walls of simple alienation, a boy's absence and guilt, a mother's disinclination to look; he had done her the favor of shielding her from the gruesome world he had unluckily stepped into. Her daughters, she knew, would not extend to her the same generosity. Her daughters, she thought as she let go her son's embrace, believed her both gullible and goody-goody, in need of a rude awakening. Her son, like his father, had a gentleman's refusal to sully such a trait.

"You oughta hit the bottle," Winston said to her as he patted her head. He meant hair dye. He hadn't had to tease her, through the mail, but he had to do so in person. Mrs. Mabie knew these things. There was hardly anything she didn't know about her children, the mother's peren-nial curse, and they despised her knowing, which she also knew.

"Do you think there's been an accident?" Mona's mother asked.

"You always think there's been an accident," Emily said, frowning at her mother's fearfulness.

"Billy runs late," Mona reassured. "Especially when Wenda's away." Her sister and mother took turns checking the driveway, Emily annoyed by the tardiness of her uncle and cousin, Mrs. Mabie frightened.

Neither Mona nor Emily enjoyed having Billy to dinner without his wife. Wenda wouldn't let him tell his vile jokes, and in her presence, Sheila became sullen instead of flamboyant, murderously silent instead of obnoxiously ebullient. Without Wenda, anything could happen.

"Billy's just a great big child," Emily said. "Incapable of the grown-up niceties like arriving on time." He treated Emily like some sort of hothouse flower, more civilized or snotty than him, casting himself as crude to play against her prude. Mona thought that, had this act been sincere, Emily might have been flattered. In the past, Winston had been known to take up this tone with Billy around. Winston was never one to pass up an opportunity to have fun at someone else's expense. Billy would say something vulgar—he had a passion for puns with sexual innuendo—then slap his palms over his mouth when he realized Emily had heard.

Mona didn't like Billy because he didn't afford her the same consideration he did Emily. He thought Mona was a black sheep, like him, and was as raunchy with her as he was with his daughter. He claimed that Sheila shared his sense of humor, which was of the bathroom genre. Sheila had known farmer's daughter jokes since she was seven years old.

But Mona had some sympathy for her uncle because he had once suffered a severe breakdown. Many years ago, as the result of an obscure episode at an overnight camp, Billy had ended up for several long months in the basement of his brother's home, rolled in an army blanket, staring at a black-and-white television that received only one channel, and that one poorly. This was before Professor Mabie had earned his doctorate or met his future wife; this was before the widespread availability of socially acceptable pharmaceuticals, before *depression* had been shifted from a national economic situation to an individual mental one. When his brothers were forced to retreat from the world, they turned to Professor Mabie. His was the phone number they dialed when romances went sour, when bank accounts came up empty, when job prospects fell flat, when cars rolled off roads. Their relationship with her father was not unlike hers with her sister Emily: oldest siblings kept their feet on the ground, a fact which left the younger free to drift, if necessary or unavoidable.

"Finally," Emily said, as her uncle's black pickup came barreling into the driveway, bright headlights on, voluble radio. Mrs. Mabie smiled in relief, taking this arrival as her cue to open the oven, from which a great cloud of steam emerged. Through it she pulled a stack of pork chops sizzling in a bath of molasses. Mrs. Mabie had a talent for making up recipes whole-cloth; the book she claimed she one day might author was of her culinary inventions. She made beautiful things—food, gardens, needlework—but she was not beautiful any longer herself. She was plain now, fading, her daughters sometimes said as they pondered their own future appearances. Their mother's lips had no color. She stood closer to things as if seeking the steadying benefit of solid objects, moving in a graceless fashion through her own home. Her eye disease was called retinitis pigmentosa, and it meant that she saw less and less of what was not right in front of her face. It meant she counted on her family to shelter her, shout warnings, see what she could not.

"Did I get a call?" asked their cousin upon entering. Sixteen-year-old Sheila paraded in the kitchen stitched in black, instep to clavicle, the general trussing interrupted here and there by patches of leather. *Faux* leather, she told them, because she didn't believe in killing innocent animals.

Mona and Emily simply exchanged looks. "*Guilty* animals," they said, together. Wenda, they felt certain, did not know of the existence of this outfit. Their uncle Billy followed Sheila, holding a half-threaded leather belt in one hand and a Tupperware tub full of diced fruit in the other.

"Fruit compost," he said. He grinned his snag-nasty grin, yanking the belt through its loops after depositing the rocking container of food on the counter.

"Com*pote*," his daughter corrected. "Like my scent?" Sheila waved her wrists as she wiggled through to the pantry phone. Her young body was chubby and pale, the result, Emily had always suspected, of being the girlfriend of black boys. Sheila had had black boyfriends several years now, challenging her parents' professed tolerance, stretching to the point of bursting the open-minded policies of her older aunt and uncle. Emily thought these boyfriends had kept Sheila from falling into late-twentieth-century girlhood troubles; she certainly didn't starve herself or bake her skin brown, the way Emily and Mona always had. Sheila's boyfriends seemed to want to squeeze her like a soft loaf of bread, as well as display the profound contrast of their flesh tones. Sheila's problems, it occurred to Emily, had a nostalgic, retro ring to them, *Guess Who's Coming to Dinner?*

Billy pulled a beer out of the refrigerator, asking if he could freshen anyone's drink, as if he were the host and they his guests. Their father appreciated Billy's making himself so thoroughly at home that he confused whose home it was, but the Mabie girls gave each other a tucked look.

"What stinks?" little Roy asked.

"Is this what you smell?" asked his grandmother as she piloted the pork chops through the cluttered kitchen and into the dining room.

"Poison," Sheila told him. "It costs thirty dollars *per ounce.*" She sniffed her own wrist appreciatively, then, since it was near her face, glanced at her thick-cuffed watch. Her gestures fell in the sometimes-charming, mostly awkward gap between childhood and adulthood. She didn't usually get it right or graceful. "Eddie's coming, too, after a scrimmage at the college. Did he call?" Eddie Shakes was Sheila's current beau, a starting tackle who'd just graduated from high school and was already the darling of the local college coaches. Sweet enough, Eddie seemed to have suffered some sort of head injury along the way. Sheila bossed him around mercilessly. She liked to sit in his mammoth lap and kiss him, waiting, it seemed, for someone in the family to object. Now she looked up through a thick clot of mascara, remembering tonight's novelty anew. "Where's Winston?"

"Winston," Roy repeated, reverently.

Mona asked if Sheila's serpent tattoo was permanent.

"Nah," said Billy, smiling, then frowning. He'd dropped himself into a kitchen chair after popping his can of beer. "Is it?" he asked Sheila, who told him *he'd* never know. Her fruit compote had a hair in it.

"Sheila said poison," Roy told Emily, tugging on her shirt as if tattling.

"She meant perfume," his grandmother said, returning for potatoes. "Would everyone like to sit down? Take your drinks, everyone, please sit. Sit."

"It it," yelled the baby, imitating her grandmother.

"Winston?" Sheila's voice called enticingly as she meandered through the lower floor of the house. "Winston?"

WINSTON was outside having a smoke. Emily had seen him exit through the side door just before Billy arrived. Emily had a talent for tracking the motions of her family. No one else paid the kind of attention she did. It was what made her a good mother, she thought, this diligent awareness. It was what had led her to uncovering her husband's affair with her sister, years earlier. She'd watched them at the very dinner table she was now lading with food. In the large areas—rendezvous, phone calls, love notes—they'd been scrupulously discreet, but at the micro level they'd failed. One evening Emily had watched Mona simply lift Barry's cup and sip at his coffee. Just that small moment, that piece of thoughtless intimacy and Emily knew they were sleeping together. To this day, they did not know she knew. She'd given Barry a blow job that night and told him he had to end his affair, pronto, naming no names, citing no evidence. He was in the habit of being wowed by her; he complied with her wish as if afraid of her enchantress abilities, as if he might otherwise end up a toad. But hers was a personality incapable of letting anybody go unnoticed for long. Was it sensitivity or nosiness, she wondered. Her brother had disappeared into the foliage of the side yard, sitting with the rabbits and snakes and who-knew-what-else that lived out there. Cigarette smoke might keep him safe.

"Where *is* Winston?" Mrs. Mabie asked her, fingers on Emily's arm, no doubt imagining another awful thing had happened to him as soon as he stepped out the door. The table had been readied, Professor Mabie summoned from his study, Roy and the baby seated and occupied with bread sticks, lights dimmed and candles lit. How dare Winston not materialize in this kind illumination.

"Let's start without him," Sheila suggested as she returned from her search. "I'm starving."

Emily said, "You're not starving. You're anything but starving."

"I am so, I haven't eaten since—"

"He'll come," Emily interrupted Sheila, putting a hand on her mother's shoulder.

Mrs. Mabie looked over the beautiful bounty she'd laid out on the linen cloth; Emily read her mother's admiration of its flawlessness, the easy steam beneath the chandelier, the plump unpunctured flesh of the chops and red potatoes. Her mother was rarely afforded the opportunity to behold the pretty product of her busy hands. The house would not stay clean, the garden would not go unraided, the food would soon be reduced to carcass and cold remains, the dishes dirty, the napkins unfanned and soiled, dropped to the floor. Emily was struck, for a moment, by her mother's willingness to put forward this effort, to have continued energy for and optimism about the goodness of such gestures.

Billy had dropped into his customary chair and hoisted the first thing he could lay hands on, the basket of bread he nudged leftward, passing it to get everyone in the mood.

"Where's Winston?" asked Professor Mabie, his eyeglasses reflecting twin images of the wavering candles. Another pair of women might have seen sternness but both Emily and Mrs. Mabie saw trepidation in the burning flames.

PROFESSOR Mabie felt safely cushioned. Drinking encouraged that buffer. Conversation occurred outside his hearing, although the large oval table seemed to radiate from his heading it, Emily and her children on one side, Winston and Mona on the other, Billy at his right elbow, Sheila at one o'clock, his wife anchored at her far end, facing him. They talked, probably assuming that Professor Mabie was listening. He wasn't. He was considering his son, his abiding paradox, once more.

Winston had seemed to crawl in for dinner, absent when Professor Mabie had looked upon his plate of pleasant colors, then present when he lifted his head. Sneaky, Professor Mabie thought. Ashamed, ungrateful, wily as a ferret slipping into his seat. Was he? Bourbon had set Professor Mabie's thoughts into a swirl like a shaken paperweight of snow, lucid crystals floating randomly behind his eyes.

"Chuck Self says check out a Caddie coming in tomorrow," said Billy suddenly, on his right. Professor Mabie blinked at his brother. What was this utterance, this garbled gibberish? Billy's knifed eeked on his plate as he sawed vigorously at his meat. "Can you see Sheila in a Caddie?"

From Billy's other side, Sheila squealed, claiming she'd have to let Eddie drive her around if she owned a Cadillac.

Billy waved his knife at her. "You are not to let anybody else drive your car, you hear?"

"Dad-dy," she said. For shock value, she opened her mouth full of chewed food and metal orthodontia. This never failed to close a subject.

"Mama owned a Caddie," Billy recalled, then snapped his mouth shut, no doubt recalling that their mother had also died in that Caddie, and that its driver was back among them for the first time since then.

The table was silent just long enough to make little Roy look up, curious as to why the grown-ups had stopped talking.

Then the others hustled on to discuss the neighborhood, the resurfaced church parking lot, the pastor's house, the new family next door where the Vaughns had always lived. His grandchildren went back to making their usual racket, spilling milk, refusing any but the blandest food, dominating Emily's and Mrs. Mabie's attention. Mona and Winston carried on some conference that ran underneath the others in the room; Professor Mabie remembered this about them from childhood, the way their secret dialogue went on as if they were spies or critics. It reminded him of his own younger brothers, who'd looked to him as their leader, whose conversations of this sort were not cocky but frightened, not acerbic condemnation but whispered intimidation.

"We should toast!" Sheila suddenly shouted out. She'd only been eleven when her cousin was sent to jail; who knew what she knew? "To Winston," she said, lifting her can of Coke. "Welcome back to Wichita!"

"Whoo-ee," said Billy, who never refused a reason to drink. Others followed, the table too wide for them to make clinking contact with anyone other than the people on either side. Roy beamed, knocking his plastic cup against Emily's wineglass again and again. Winston held his water up, hardly three inches above his plate, while staring down at its contents.

The phone rang. The rule was to let it ring, during meals; Billy actually laid his hand on Sheila's to keep her in her seat. But this caller seemed to know the family and to disregard their rule. On and on the phone bell sounded.

Finally Sheila could bear it no longer, and dashed away, leaving her fork clattering in her plate, napkin on the floor, chair rocking on its sturdy legs. She believed her boyfriend was on the line, but soon returned, dropping churlishly in her seat, reporting to her uncle that it was for him.

"Make her call you back," she told him. "I'm expecting Eddie."

Her could only be Betty Spitz. Professor Mabie stood, surreptitiously checking his zipper as he did so. It occurred to him that his son would never bother to check his zipper, and that was the difference between them. He could not reconcile his own awkwardness with his son's composure. With that beauty. There Winston sat, grinning as he ate the food these three women—four, if you counted Sheila and her bowl of worn brown fruit—had made for him, in honor of him. Their adoration irked Professor Mabie. It was such unearned love.

On the phone was his old best friend Betty Spitz, medievalist. Betty was dying of lung cancer, so had every right to interrupt a meal with fifteen jangles of the bell.

"How're you holding up?" she croaked.

"Fine," Professor Mabie replied.

"He there?"

"He is."

"Just keep drinking," she advised, coughing suddenly and desperately into the line. Behind her, Professor Mabie could hear her parrot, who'd picked up Betty's smoker's hack over their twenty-year companionship. Now the ugly bird would outlive her. As would Professor Mabie.

"Shut up, Guido," Betty said routinely to the parrot.

"Be quiet, Betty," Guido would reply.

"Chin up, Mabie," she now told her old cohort in the same manner she addressed her worthless pet.

"Be quiet, Betty." Her illness had only exaggerated a prerogative she'd entertained with Professor Mabie during their long years together in the history department. They'd been hired the same year, 1953, assigned offices next door to each other, and allied themselves as the upstarts, the bleeding hearts, the perennial junior members of the department, neither of them ambitious in the way of their colleagues, neither aimed in an upwardly mobile direction. They marched for hopeless causes, they signed petitions, they passed failing students, they shunned committees. Once their nameplates had borne the same dated typeface; now they both had *Emeritus* placed, in new face, beneath. Hers had been doctored, as she'd donated her office for a coffee-and-gossip chamber for the graduate students who didn't hold teaching assistantships. They needed fellowship, Betty had insisted. She wouldn't be using her space anymore. Her students called her Betty without her requesting it, undergraduates, graduates, devotees and whiners, one and all—this cluttered room was now the Betty Room; soon it might be the Dead Betty Room—while in his case it had always been Doctor or Professor Mabie. Why was that? Never in a hundred years would he have thought to bequeath his office to graduate students.

She collected jokes, and now told him one to perk him up. It involved a duck and a pet shop. "Got any duck chow?" Betty quacked merrily. Three times the duck returned to the pet shop, three times and with increasing annoyance was told by the owner that there was no chow for it. When warned that his webbed feet would be nailed to the floor, should he ask again for duck chow, the duck only returned to ask, "Got any nails?"

As Betty laughed, Guido joined in. Perhaps, thought Professor Mabie, Guido had not been mimicking her hack all these years, but her laugh. That would be a comforting thought.

"I knew you'd laugh at one of my jokes, now that I'm so sick," she said.

"I always laugh at your jokes."

"A good friend laughs at bad jokes."

"A good friend finds them funny," he replied.

"Well, I'll be up late," Betty told him as they signed off. "I sleep even less than usual. You can call."

"Who was that?" Mrs. Mabie asked when her husband returned to the dining room.

"Betty," he said, watching for the tart pucker his wife's mouth used to take when his colleague came up. She seemed to have left behind that long-standing jealousy, or maybe just temporarily forgotten, given the evening's knottiness. "Can I get anybody anything?" Professor Mabie interrupted the general din. "As long as I'm up?"

They turned their eyes his way. He remembered to smile. His smile made him look foolish, but he put it on regardless.

"A refill," said Winston, hoisting an empty glass.

"Coke?" his father said. Later he would recall that his first words to his son in five years were these, the list of sanctioned beverages. "Orange juice, apple juice, Diet Sprite?" His wife had filled the refrigerator with nonalcoholic fluid just so Winston would have options. "Perrier? Chocolate milk?" There were twenty kinds of things Winston could want, yet he insisted on city tap water, flat and tepid and full of chlorine. His son wanted his mother to feel bad, Professor Mabie thought. Then shook the thought away from himself. He did not want to be ungenerous.

Dapper, Professor Mabie imagined others might say of him, as he stood at the kitchen sink. If a compliment was required, *dapper* was as good as he could expect. Winston's problem was that he was too pretty. His beauty had come from two women, his mother and his paternal grandmother. Professor Mabie had admired those female beauties, taken pride in them. In the first Mrs. Mabie it had been the tender prickly pride of a son, confused and often shamed; he could not bear to have been born of her, to figure so prominently in her bodily life. In his wife, pride took on the dimensions of ownership and possession, a confidence he had earned by having persuaded her to love him, to choose him and thereby marry her particular fortune to his absence of the same.

But in his son that wealth of beauty mocked him: it surpassed his own plainness. It opted against his less dramatic, pedestrian features. He did not trust his son's aristocratic looks. He could not decide if he trusted his son who resided inside them. They were only skin deep, but who was in that pretty packaging? Funny how it was beside the point in the case of his wife, had been so in the case of his mother, too.

Before he returned to the table with Winston's water, Professor Mabie checked his zipper once more. His son would not have troubled. Winston would be aware that no one attended to his zipper, they were transported by the surprising pleasure of his return, his lovely presence. His presence that absorbed all available light, like a black hole. But Professor Mabie's hand dropped automatically to his pants, forefinger on the tiny metal tab, secure, always secure. Embarrassment he could not afford, even—perhaps especially—here, before his family. His brother, wife, niece, grandchildren, daughters; his stunning boy who drew the other faces at the table the way the sun did the faces of flowers. In that analogy, where did Professor Mabie fit? Planet Pluto, he supposed, far away, barely visible, these days arguably a mere moon rather than planet. Professor Mabie reined his anger in familiar fashion, turned it inside out, amused himself. It was imperative in life to amuse oneself; others could do so only infrequently.

He set Winston's glass of water before him, as well as a pitcher full of the chalky stuff, then sat down himself.

From nowhere came his Mona. "Have some wine," she implored her father. She touched his arm and held the bottle questioningly over his empty glass.

He could not resist little Mona, his best girl. It was touching how she attended to him. And she had such faith in all of them, in the redemptive power of their being together. How could he do anything but behave himself? He'd not wanted her to come into this world, had argued against the pregnancy that produced her, but was now supremely grateful. "Thanks, honey," Professor Mabie said, and smiled, letting her pour him a swollen red glassful.

THERE WAS nothing Mona liked better than her family's large dining room meals, Christmas, birthday, anniversary, or simple reconvening. Kitchen meals were not the same, nor were the drinks. There it was beer, milk, water in jelly glass tumblers. But to her mind, once the elegant stemware and expensive alcohol were involved, the evening spoke far too fervently of occasion—of celebration, of ceremony and ritual—ever to fall into a tone of soddenness or pathetic abuse. Over countless meals they had sat laughing with the wine bottles standing in the midst of the evening's collapsed debris, initial detritus cleared, plate of desserts, crumbs and spills, odor of roasted meat, sheen of rich balms, butter, gravy, glaze, the pretty bottles and the pretty glasses to hold the pretty liquid, their pretty names, Champagne, Chardonnay, Claret, Merlot, Cabernet, Burgundy, Beaujolais, Pinot Noir. Was there ever a sexier name than *Pinot Noir*? And after the tall grand green bottles were emptied of their thin liquid, and the tall thin glass stemware drained and smudged and rimmed with waxy lipstick, then came the decorative and more substantial squat decanters, colors amber, gold, maple, with their accompanying tiny sweet tulip bud glasses, cut-glass tumblers, glistening pristine from the leaded glass cabinet, fragile as flowers, furnished with aromas intoxicating and unique as an array of perfumes, Amaretto, Cointreau, Cognac, Benedictine. The transparent bowled beauty of the brandy snifter, sheets of its syrup swirling gently down, blurring as if melting its very vessel, a heady vapor rising to the nostril, wavering seductively to the brain.

What could be sinful about this scene, the Spanish chandelier with its muted peach fixtures, dimmed, hanging over the large dark stained wood table, its heavy clawed feet and white lace linen nearly reaching the solid animal's toes, which dug into a thick red carpet, the milky candlelight shimmering, diminishing in holders, white wax slowly oozing into soft molten shape, reflecting in the eyes of a set of sated diners, who either leaned forward or back, spines weak, elbows on table, or feet stretched beneath, nearly yet not quite touching the legs and feet of others, the relaxation of indulgence, a platter of sweets indolently following the crystal glasses, going round and round from hand to hand losing its contents adagio, invisibly, lips following a brandy with a dark truffle, a swirl of cream on the base of a blood red plate, the fingertip that stirred a brief lazy pattern and then was placed languidly between lips, the pattern on the plate slowly dissolving away, closing its interrupted scrim of thick rich ivory, the surface of which was too tempting not to disturb, once more and once more until empty. Until done.

And each time tonight, Winston gently refused, smiling briefly. His need to consume water told Mona that he was working not to be tempted.

Once, as Sheila went on and on about her boyfriend Eddie Shakes and his tardiness, Winston brought everyone up short by banging sharply with his water glass. "Two times means pass the water," he told four-year-old Roy, his new nephew and neophyte. "If I only banged once, you'd be expected to hand me the salt and pepper." That was all the mention he made of his time away, but it broke Mona's heart. Dinner was over, so she beat a hasty retreat to her bedroom, knelt to unlock the door, whose keyhole was blurred by her tears, locked it again from the inside, and lay on her bed among her stuffed cheetahs to sob.

On the answering machine, as yet unnoticed, a red number flashed. Three messages.

"She never does the dishes," Emily complained.

"She's a romantic," said Winston. "She's weeping."

"How do you know?" But he wasn't going to answer this. He'd said it, and she knew it was true: Mona wept. "You never used to do the dishes, either," Emily went on, putting her sister out of her mind.

He shrugged. "Fuck romanticism." In fact, he seemed sort of delighted to be carrying the china in from the dining room, handling it delicately, looking it over with interest, rinsing it in the sink and letting the warm water cover his hands. It had not occurred to Emily that he was much of a sensualist, but this ordinary chore gave him a peculiarly intriguing pleasure. He had also enlisted little Roy to assist, assigning him first forks, then knives, then spoons. The child trudged back and forth, bringing only these things, then butter dish and bread basket, then balled cloth napkins, which Winston coached him in tossing into the mouth of the open washing machine in the mudroom.

Sheila languished on the telephone, tormenting Eddie Shakes as he explained his college curfew. The Mabie brothers had descended to the basement; Mrs. Mabie bathed her granddaughter; Mona cried in her room. Emily and Roy and Winston finished the dishes.

Then Winston ducked outside once more to light a cigarette, and Emily watched him from the window. The family—even Roy, who'd been indoctrinated at day care about the evils of cigarettes—seemed to have reached some silent agreement not to mention his new habit; better, she supposed they were all supposing, this one than another habit he might have chosen. Why the human need to put things to the mouth? Emily realized her own use of a brandy glass as prop, that she would not be drinking brandy in any other kind of glass because it wouldn't be as much fun to hold, that the brandy inside had grown body temperature warm, that she rolled its stem between her thumb and forefinger mostly for the effect of the action, that she cupped the glass to feel something warm and curved in her palm, something like a breast. Didn't men hold breasts that way, like snifters? Mightn't that be the appeal of a container of warmed brandy?

Roy sucked his thumb; Winston popped in his cigarette, pulled it from his mouth, held it pinched in his upper knuckles, fingers flexing with the ash trembling on the end. Their grandmother Bunny had smoked like this, her other fingers held by the thumb, like someone making quotation marks or taking a pledge. And those two fingers, with their cigarette, would curl as if she were beckoning. They curled more quickly when she was annoyed, Emily remembered. Her crossed leg would jump, her fingers would curl, her eyelids would twitch, her mouth would purse. Ordinarily calm, outwardly polite, she had some gestures that betrayed her irritation.

And then a hearty, hooting laugh. How her grandmother had liked to be amused. Bunny had been on Emily's mind today.

"I'm cruising," Winston announced when he came back inside, meaning he planned to take a walk.

"I'm going with him," Roy told his mother. "Please can I go with him?"

Emily had some nervousness about permitting this. It was her test, she realized. Outside, the day had finally lost its light, but that wasn't the source of her anxiety. Other people's children she would not have hesitated in sending along with her brother, but her own she could not afford to lose. When she agreed it was only because she planned to follow them, surreptitiously, a block or so behind.

Winston and Roy started out the front door, Emily moved through the back, leaving the baby with her mother. As an excuse, Emily took the family's accidental dog, their grandmother's animal who had come to them after her death simply because he had nowhere else to go. Family: the gang that not only has to let you in when you come knocking at their door, but who also has to take in your miserable pets.

"Kojak," Bunny had named him after her favorite detective. "Jack-off," the Mabies had modified. There was a well-known urban legend about this sort of dog, the story that explained how an American tourist had picked up a pet in Mexico, a hairless Chihuahua, the snaky tailed creature. That would be Kojak. He had the pointed face and big ears of a bat, the tiny tense body of a rodent, the hair-trigger yelp of an alarm clock. No one liked him based on his own personality, but he'd been their grandmother's beloved companion. They loved her love for him, and that had saved his miserable ratty life for the last five years. Because he was small and of no particular breed, his life expectancy was astronomical, only nine years of which he'd used up. Kojak was not grateful, nor was he charming, nor well behaved or good at guarding the grounds or even performing the most basic of domestic dog duties: floor cleaning. He disliked men, hats, masks, cats, other dogs, the automobile, fireworks, tile floors, leashes, and dry kibble. He was selectively deaf. In his left ear he had a bite mark because, along with all his dislikes and fears, he had an alarming habit of attacking dogs much larger than himself. This notched ear was the result of such a confrontation with a German shepherd.

His leash was the size of a phone cord, springy that way, too. He trotted along from side to side ahead of Emily, lifting his tufted rear leg—alternating left and right—and dribbling his ludicrous markings on every protrusion in the urban landscape, shrub, lawn ornament, sprinkler head, fast-food trash. Ahead, Emily watched her brother and son. Roy had one hand on the back of his jeans, holding them up, and the other in Winston's hand. He was too thin for his clothes, but he'd adapted without much complaint. Maybe he thought the rest of his life would include walking one-handed. Belts didn't work because he could never unfasten them quickly enough to make the potty. Making the potty was often a matter of a mad dash to the bathroom, a slap of the lid, a hurried burst, just in time.

Emily's brother Winston was careless, and let Roy walk balancing on the curb, inches from the street. His carelessness had had some appeal when he was younger, but now it simply made Emily annoyed. It had been combined with good humor, goodwill, a charm of silliness, as if it were nearly conscious, flirtatious. But now that he was thirty-three, it had lost its comic tone and taken a more serious one, something potentially pathetic, not to mention lethal. It seemed something he might never outgrow, now, an aspect of character that would take him down. Emily's central concern, this evening, was that it not take down her four-year-old son, too.

Ahead of her they ambled, Roy dropping his uncle's hand to dart ahead, then rush back. The wind blew, as was common in Kansas, splashes of wetness either from the tree branches or from the sky that dappled Emily's face and arms. The sky seemed unable to come to a conclusion about rain: should it, or shouldn't it? At the first corner, Winston failed to take up Roy's hand. Emily jerked Kojak so hard that he skidded his hind legs on the pavement and squealed out.

Roy turned to look behind him, but not Winston, who had made it to the other side of the street and was still ambling along. Roy stopped in the middle of the street indecisively, looking back, then ahead, but Emily had ducked alongside a stone wall so that he could not see her. There was no moon, the street was poorly lit, there were no cars or headlights to pick her out and blow her cover.

"Uncle Winston!" her son cried out plaintively. "Wait for me."

He ran, hand holding his pants, feet slapping in the duck-like way they did. Emily's ex-husband would have been disappointed at how unathletic their son was. Roy was afraid of balls. This would perhaps be the thing that united him with Winston, Emily realized, their mutual dislike of athletic competition. Competition in any way. Roy refused to let his mother know his dominant hand, for example, refused to settle for left or right. He seemed not ambidextrous, but the opposite, ambi-incompetent: neither one functional. He was only four, Emily reminded herself, sighing. Tonight he was trading off, holding his jeans with one hand and then the other, trotting to keep up with Winston.

At the next corner, her subjects hung a right. This was Devonshire

Avenue, the street where the friend Winston had named a hairball earlier today lived. Marty Song, the chocolate delivery boy, also aged thirty-three. Emily herself was thirty-five years old, former Vista volunteer, part owner of a boutique that her husband's nefarious business dealings had helped finance, mother of two children, sponsor of two other children in Guatemala. Good daughter. She'd seen various members of her immediate family through their difficult times—her mother's degenerating vision, her father's retirement, her sister's near suicide—not to mention her own pregnancies and divorce. Her brother she'd put on the back burner. She thought his time in prison might rescue him from what surely seemed waiting. That view was not one her sister shared, but one her parents had had to take themselves. Sometimes Emily felt like an extra parent to her younger siblings. They weren't much younger, not really, but those brief distances seemed to have made all the difference.

Winston turned into the driveway of Marty Song's house. Roy followed, stopping to check out Mrs. Song's birdbaths and statues. She collected modern art; much of it was incomprehensibly huge and frightening. Roy wandered the inside of a rusty tripod and dipped his fingers in several bowls before joining Winston on the porch. The house was utterly dark, but Winston rang the bell nonetheless.

And, oddly enough, the door opened—black cave. The two of them stepped inside, leaving Emily half a block away holding the coiled leash of Jackoff, who had already marked everything he could find and was tugging to move along.

"Shit," Emily whispered. "Now what?" she asked the dog. They continued along the broken concrete of the block. The neighborhood she'd grown up in was a vintage one, full of grand old houses accustomed to money and huge families, beef-eaters and bankers and Catholics, the confidence instilled by the aircraft manufacturing days of Wichita, cattle and wheat and fighter planes, staples of a bygone time. The trees lining the parkway and canopying the street were so ancient and rooted that they'd toppled the sidewalks, disrupted the brick cobble, dispensed with the confines of underground to erupt onto the surface. Overhead their massive arms swayed majestically in the wind. Kojak peed and peed, every gnarl and uplift worthy of his attention, and Emily tripped, keeping her eyes on the Songs' dark house.

A light went on deep inside the house. Of course Marty Song also still lived at home, that went without saying. Hadn't these structures invited it, after all, so large and comfortable that a child need never leave? The Song girls had married and moved away, Mr. Song had finally died, leaving his wife alone now with her boy. He parked his chocolate truck out front every evening and probably brought her seconds, the white rabbits without ears, the almond clusters with too few almonds or a misplaced pistachio. What was Winston doing with little Roy in the home of Mrs. Song?

Kojak now mutinied. Emily had forgotten that his little legs went only so far, three blocks max. Her mother had a route marked out, around the block of their home, cutting through the Blessed Sacrament church parking lot as a kind of shortcut, Jackoff urinating on the signs meant to preserve parking for the priest and his assistants, cooks and Sunday school leaders. Now Jackoff simply sat, then lay on an upended chunk of concrete two doors down from the Songs' and would move no farther, despite Emily's vicious tugging on his leash.

"Asshole," she said, lifting him. His fur was not soft but coarse, his rear end damp, his ratty tail cold as a snake on her forearm. His fur was the color of dryer lint. She sat across the street from the Songs' on an uneven concrete half wall, out of sight but watching. In the house beside the Songs' lights blazed, a television clear in the window, figures moving about and cupboards opening. Nothing like it at the Songs'. Pure darkness except for that one light, far away in the house's bowels, most likely the rear den. It occurred to Emily that she could sneak around the yard and look through those windows. She'd been in that den often enough, when Mr. Song was alive and he and his wife were away at the social events befitting a surgeon—charity balls, symphonies, auctions—when Marty had held his famous parties, beer and pot and poker and fucking, plenty of bedrooms for high school fucking. Emily had had sex a few times at the Songs' house, once with Marty himself. Their house, like all the houses of the teenagers in this neighborhood, was so big that the children could move about it without detection, leave it and enter it without disturbing the trusting—ignorant, oblivious, unimaginative— sleep of their parents. Marty Song had been the worst of the party boys. He had two front teeth knocked out while trying to sneak into a concert—why sneak in? Emily had always wondered. His parents had money, he could have bought a ticket, a raft of tickets, and entered legitimately, why pretend he had to go the difficult route. At the back gate he'd been caught, chased by zealous roadies, knocked flat on the parking lot, and left without his front two teeth. The substitutes seemed of inferior quality despite his father's connections to orthodontists and dentists; those white replacement tiles always retained the color of whatever he drank on whatever evening, red grenadine, green crème de menthe. Tinted teeth, Marty's pride as he smiled at his guests.

Marty Song. Emily had spent a long evening kissing him once, stoned, happy, ready to glom on to the first pair of lips that desired hers. He hadn't been bad at kissing—nobody kissed as well after high school—but later she'd never felt happy about having let him sleep with her. It gave him some sort of vague power over her she'd rather he didn't still own. Did her brother know about that?

The wind blew, more water fell. She lifted her grandmother's hideous dog and made her way across the street, up the driveway and past the delivery truck, which smelled of stale chocolate, into the backyard, also full of odd sculpture, and around to the party room, where the television was playing. Ah, nostalgia. How many nights had they all sat there, she and Winston and even underage Mona, watching TV and smoking joints, laughing with their accumulated neighborhood gang. She'd liked to get high with her siblings. They were among the few people in the world who didn't make her a paranoid basket case when under the influence.

Marty Song lay in a recliner staring cross-eyed at a bong the size of a tenor saxophone. To his credit, Winston seemed to be abstaining. He was showing Roy Foosball, in which Roy was thoroughly engrossed. Maybe a four-year-old would not understand even the remotest thing about a bong, would not recall his father's similarly smelly pipe. Bong water, Emily thought. Was there anything more dreadful? She could summon its distinct repulsiveness in a flash.

Kojak suddenly began squirming in her arms. She dropped him, letting loose his leash accidentally. Away he ran, the little shit, heading toward the busier street at the other end of Marty Song's block. He'd pretended exhaustion just so he could make her crazy. Emily had no choice but to pursue him. He was fast, given some motive, which no doubt was the motive of annoying the person entrusted as his caretaker. Emily hated this dog, even though she'd loved her grandmother, who'd loved him. Her grandmother had a talent for loving the unlovable. Maybe it was that talent that made her lovable herself, saintly in her way.

Could Emily trust Winston to bring Roy home? Was her job to stay spying at the window, or to chase her grandmother's rotten dog before he threw himself under the wheels of a sports car on Douglas Avenue? Of course she had to go after the dog. She took one more peek in the Songs' window, long enough to see pudgy Marty Song weighing an eight ball in his hand, head now lifted with the held reverence of someone filled with marijuana, before she went in pursuit of the ratty varmint, the last vestige of her beloved grandmother.

So HER SISTER wasn't home when the Lee twins visited. Mona came down to the kitchen to find their identical skeptical faces. The dishwasher was in its last cycle and the room was nicely warm and damp. The Lees had been Emily's best friends for so long they didn't have to call in advance, nor knock when they arrived. They simply took up residence, helped themselves to a cookie, and tonight were here to look at her brother.

"Moni baloney," said one of them, the typical greeting.

"Where's everybody?" asked the other.

"And what are you all dressed up for?"

Mona blushed, looking down at her skirt as if she'd forgotten. It wasn't just that she was dressed up for her late date with Nicholas Dempsey, the married man she couldn't brag about as a boyfriend, but also the fact that the twins would be evaluating the fashion statement itself. They owned a clothing boutique, partners with Emily, and they had extremely critical remarks to make about dress and accessories. Mona did most of her shopping in vintage and used stores; tonight's ensemble was a '50s tulle tutu-like skirt over a black bodysuit, topped by a monogrammed bowling shirt. *Calvin,* said Mona's shirt. It was not the sort of combo the Lee twins complimented. Mona sighed; the thing about having an affair was that you didn't get to relax very much in areas of appearance. She had to bathe and dress up whenever she saw Nicholas Dempsey—his wife could be relaxed and frumpy, she told herself. It took an inordinate amount of time to always be prepared, smelling good, wearing birth control. She had only had three real relationships, and two of them had been with married men. Her first boyfriend, Michael, she had lived with for two and a half months. That had been nice. Near the end, she'd gotten to relax a little, but then he'd gotten cold feet and they'd had to break their lease. She scared men, although she wasn't sure why. Apparently it was her intensity that alarmed them. "You are so intense," they were always saying, never in a pleased tone of voice. She wasn't really a model mistress because she had the aspect of the marrying sort. Maybe she misled them, these men she slept with. How had she acquired only three in her nine years of so-called sexual activity? What was it about her? Her boyfriends were married, her job was that of teacher's aide. Of adulthood she seemed to have acquired a taste for the twice-removed title: not wife but mistress, not teacher but aide. Even her clothing had been owned before.

The Lee twins were Roberta and Tonya, friends of Emily's from high school. Frog and Toady, they were called, practically members of the family. They'd come to gawk at Winston, the bad boy, the idol. They loved to be tormented by his familiar fraternizing, as if he had four sisters instead of two. Mona had named her sister's friends the Just Wait twins because they were forever lording their experience over her. They and Emily would sit around discussing men or gynecology or middle age, always turning their tired refrain on Mona.

"Just wait," they said ominously. Mona hated being told to just wait. It seemed she'd been hearing that for far too many years. Always someone had arrived ahead of her. Always they wanted to fill her in. They liked to alarm her, scare her with a vision of her own future behavior, her body's mutinous betrayal. Frog was married, but you'd never guess, since she rarely spent any time with her husband, who was named Fred. A lot of her "just wait" advice had to do with her marriage, despite the lack of contact hours. "You'll be counting minutes until he gets off," she would say, of sex.

"Watching the digital clock . . ."

"Going 'forty-seven, forty-eight, forty-nine . . .' "

"Just wait." Or, on another topic: "The worst thing is gray hair. Then you know you're old, plucking gray hairs. Just wait."

"I have gray hairs," said Mona flatly, wondering why she should be bragging about gray hairs.

"*Pubic* hairs?" Toady said.

"Gross."

"She hasn't found any yet," Toady told the others. "You'll see," she said to Mona. "I went into back spasm once, plucking gray pubic hairs. Just you wait."

In their eyes, she was still the tagalong runt she'd always been, trailing after them desperately, so eager to join them, to accept whatever shred of attention they might offer.

"How's Winston?" Frog asked, taking a chair at the kitchen table. She always chose Professor Mabie's captain's chair, never seeming to understand that it was forbidden.

"Winston's fine," Mona said.

"Look any different?"

"Act any different?"

"Got any sick stories?"

"I don't know," Mona said, wondering if she'd remembered lipstick. "I have to go."

"Where's the fire?"

"Who's the guy?"

"You can see through that skirt," one of them called as she dashed out the door. "Just FYI."

Mona wasn't scheduled to meet Nicholas for another half an hour, but she didn't want to stick around with Frog and Toady. From the row of hooks by the back door she took the Toyota keys. The agreement was that Mona would be available for errands for her mother. She sincerely hoped there was nothing to fetch tonight.

6

I T WAS NOT her vision alone that seemed to be failing Mrs. Mabie. Her self, she sometimes thought, was turning inward, collapsing in the way of other life-forms, container no longer robust, insides going hollow. Her face, at roughly the age of forty, had quit wanting to smile. For a while, she reminded herself to make the effort, to cheer her children, to encourage her husband, but soon she'd tired of forcing that falseness and instead settled on what seemed the reflexive dwindling of her facial enthusiasms, positive as well as negative. What remained was not precisely a pleasant expression, nor unpleasant, more along the lines of . . . inert. She could feel this inertness in her flesh. When she peered into mirrors, she saw it without true recognition; her corporeal self seemed to have little to do with who she was, anymore.

Now Mrs. Mabie lay on her back in bed noting how her face felt as it contorted itself, emphatic as a tragic mask because she was trying to cry. She had the urge; she could recall crying in bed with clarity, the way your ears filled with tears. Still, this crying would not come. She might squeeze out a tear, but it would not have made her truly unhappy, any more than smiling would have made her glad. Perhaps it was hormonal; perhaps her passions had simply been used up.

Her husband flopped on his side of the bed beside her like a fish,

turning his back on her. He was pretending not to notice her wakefulness, which was fine with Mrs. Mabie. Soon enough he would be asleep,
heaving his heavy breaths. He'd used to worry over her weepiness, but
time had worn thin his concern. Moreover, he knew as well as she did
that there was nothing he could provide for her; his specialty was the
more dramatic episode, the verifiable disaster. Cryptic nighttime nerves
merely confused him. Better that he sleep, if he could, and leave her to
her own more subtle devices.

After all, neither was a stranger to insomnia. In some ways, Mrs.
Mabie looked forward to the tension, as it seemed to signal that she had
not given up. Given up what, she might have asked herself, but that too
was mysterious. Just: she felt troubled, amphetamized, a lively intent
swam in her veins. She'd lain awake many nights worrying for her children, and this night could in no way be called the worst. There had been
terrifying early mornings when they hadn't even been safely in their
beds, when their literal absences tormented her. Tonight she worried
over less concrete concerns—they were here, safe, present, but *who*
were they, these presences? She was accustomed to bringing up the
parental account, and weighing her role in the balance, but her children
were now thirty-five, thirty-three, and twenty-nine years old; oughtn't
there to be a statute of limitations? Oughtn't she be off the hook by
now?

Winston's bedroom was two doors down from his parents' room, and
although she had cleaned it in his absence, Mrs. Mabie had not altered
it. His drawers of clothing awaited him, as well as his books and models
and papers and the scruffy easy chair he had favored—a furry plaid,
named by the children "the raccoon"—placed under a lamp so that he
could read. Her son enjoyed sitting like an old man, reading in a comfy
chair, drinking hot tea. Like all of the Mabies, he suffered nighttime
wakefulness—Four in the Morning, they called it, this contagion—and
rather than creak down the stairs in the night, he stored the makings of
tea on his desk, electric kettle and tea service of his own, one his grandmother Bunny had given him for his eighth birthday, a rotund little
group, patterned in Blue Willow, cup, sugar bowl, lively pot with its lid
missing and replaced by the white top of another. A jolly-looking set like
something from a children's cartoon, nearly animate. Winston's bedroom could never be anyone's but his, with its navy blue walls and window shades, its gamy rugs and its odd decorative hangings—pages from

a wallpaper book, nine-by-nine squares featuring stripes or ʃ
other modish 1970s designs, applied with lumpy paste to the
notices—and his king-sized bed, a sagging voluminous hand-mc-い.
from his tallest uncle Tommy, the headboard elevated with building
blocks to prevent nasal congestion.

As a baby, he'd stayed in the nursery just off the parents' bedroom,
longer than either of the girls. Boy babies, his mother had heard,
required longer indulgence. Mrs. Mabie had spent many nights of Winston's childhood sleeping with him in her arms in there, upright in a
rocker so that his sinuses would clear, so that his breathing would be
easy. He'd had a tendency toward croup, his whole rib cage prominent
as a poultry carcass beneath his fair skin as he burbled and percolated.
Oh, those footed pajamas he'd worn, thin as Emily's Roy when he was
young, coughing and snuffling in his mother's arms as if he'd die there,
exhausted and ill, damp with fever and exertion, unless she held vigil. In
those nights there'd seemed nothing in the whole universe but the two of
them, primal and necessary, her watchfulness and his distress, the black
closed world just outside the foggy window, the sleeping forms of all the
other family members in their peaceful rooms. In the nursery the
steamer whistled and wetted the air and she rocked him and rocked him,
humming, occasionally dropping to sleep herself, face against his
sweaty scalp, elbows relaxed on the chair's damp wood arms. She
missed the scalps of her children, their soft children's hair, their smooth
foreheads, their long weary lashes closed over clear kind eyes. Her children's childhood selves were a source of grief for Mrs. Mabie, so far
gone, so intangible and irreconcilable. She'd once held them in her
lap—she'd been able to, first off, and they'd desired it, secondly. Pregnant with one, clutching another, full of baby. People were always telling
you what a joy grandchildren were: restored children—without the
worry. But Mrs. Mabie missed the worry. She couldn't love her grandchildren the same way, that intensely fearful way that kept her up at
night and sent her visiting their beds as they slept, that made her cry
with complicity and fullness. It was fullness, wasn't it? She simply
couldn't claim fullness in the case of her grandchildren. Their time away
from her did not plague her as her own children's had; she forgot about
them for hours in a row. And she couldn't entertain the same anxious
knowledge that she would somehow be punished, that something terrible would happen to them in order to exact revenge upon her. Nothing

would befall her grandchildren, she thought, not because of her. It quite frankly was not the same.

Not to mention that Petra and Roy did not love her best. All her life, Mrs. Mabie had been happiest occupying the exclusive places in people's hearts: daughter, wife, mother.

Winston had been the most gorgeous, sweet child, his shining dark curls, his magnificent blue eyes and the dimple in his cheek, the sensitive disposition, the impishness and kindness, his desire to make his parents and sisters laugh, his weakness in the face of all passing infection, his phlegmy bronchi fragile as jellyfish. Why was it that such a boy could seem so damned? Why couldn't the world accommodate him? What made him now seem so ill suited to carry on? Once more Mrs. Mabie felt the central conflict of being her son's parent: how best to help him. Protect him? Shelter and indulge? Or thrust him into the world to fend for himself, shutting the door behind him? She and her husband traded positions on this, neither of them certain how to proceed. For the last five years, they'd let the world have Winston. Now he was back, and what was it that the world had taught him?

"Sweetie?" she whispered, suddenly needing company in the dreadful darkening night. She felt as if she were falling down a deep well.

"Hmm," her husband said, asleep.

"Sweetie, I'm worried."

"What?" He was going deaf, she was going blind—soon their married dependence upon each other would be urgently literal, they'd share only one set of intact senses between them.

"I'm worried," she repeated.

"Don't worry," he answered wearily, rolling over and laying a limp weighty arm over her. Now she was not falling; she was pinned to a humid bed by a human arm. Her husband had been nervous over dinner but now he was solely tired, full of drink and sleep. This might be the rare night when he could clear the decks of his conscience and push like a cruising ship through the night sea.

"I'm afraid we did the wrong thing," Mrs. Mabie went on. "We should never have let Winston go to jail."

"Oh," her husband sighed. He really wasn't up to this conversation tonight; having it would require sitting up and putting on his glasses.

He shut down after a day's engagement with the world. It was taking more and more out of him to get engaged, so it seemed particularly unfair to make him snap to action in the middle of the night. "Our hands were tied," he said blandly.

"They weren't. Don't be ridiculous. You know perfectly well they weren't. Go on back to sleep, we'll talk tomorrow."

"No, I can talk. Just let me wake up."

"Go back to your dreams, I'm fine."

"Is that the wind?" Outside the big mulberry trees groaned, small wind chimes at the neighbors' house tinkled desperately, and the rain splattered the sidewalks and street as if tossed from buckets. Mrs. Mabie wanted to be alone with the storm, so she patted her husband's shoulder and apologized again for waking him.

Mrs. Mabie rose then and pulled on her bathrobe. She slipped down the hall to Winston's room, the door of which was closed. Across the hall, Mona's door was also closed, the keyhole to the deadbolt Mona had had installed a few months ago once more a source of pain. No less painful was Mrs. Mabie's secret concerning this lock: nobody knew that she'd called in a locksmith to help her pick it. Mrs. Mabie had waited until Mona was visiting Winston in Larned, then broke into her daughter's bedroom to investigate. The locksmith did not appear even moderately surprised to be unlocking a deadbolt inside somebody's house. His lackluster response made Mrs. Mabie curious about the stories he could tell, the transgressions he had helped perpetrate.

Mona's room smelled like no other in the house, of thrift store and sunshine, dusty toys and clothes all exuding their odor of the past. Her daughter did not shrink from this, Mrs. Mabie thought, though she herself felt her lungs constrict. The place appeared unchanged, stuffed animals everywhere, pillows, secondhand shoes and dresses and purses hanging and flung, on the dresser top an array of powder-covered boxes containing costume jewelry and political buttons and old hard candy and dried makeup tubes, incomprehensible stereo equipment and music collection stacked beneath the window, not one familiar name in the lot, a tidy pile of technology, topped by a telephone. She picked up the receiver and listened to the burring dial tone.

"Hmm," she said. Mrs. Mabie had let the locksmith stand while she surveyed the room, as if there might be a live alligator awaiting her among the stuffed toys. Did he expect an explanation? Mrs. Mabie took an employer's prerogative, and did not supply one. "Can you make me a key?" she finally asked.

"Sure," he said dramatically, pronouncing the word to rhyme with *sewer*. Now, if she wanted to, she could enter her daughter's room. If the time ever arrived when Mona felt the need to down dozens of pills again, Mrs. Mabie would be ready to reach her.

At Winston's door, Mrs. Mabie laid her head against the wood, listening. His light was off, she could tell by the darkness at the cracks, but she smelled smoke, felt the cool breeze on her feet from his open window. Was he sitting by that window having a cigarette? Or was he sleeping, the smoke stale?

Upstairs, in the third-floor apartment, Emily and her two children slept. Some nights Mrs. Mabie heard her eldest daughter rise, walk across the floorboards of her own maternal insomnia as if to measure its length. Her mother could have told her just how endless such calculation was, but of course it was not possible. Emily would not have welcomed her mother's company, although they were often the only two awake at those terrifying early hours. Mrs. Mabie would have liked nothing better than to join Emily then, sit with her in the little kitchen upstairs and drink tea, discuss the nightmare or anxiety that had woken each of them. But Emily's face would have registered annoyance, had Mrs. Mabie intruded up there. She would tolerate her mother, yet not welcome her. She wanted her privacy, as a mother. And, to be honest, Mrs. Mabie found it hard to imagine just what form their conversation would take. She did not have enough conviction to barge in and demand intimacy; she had lost that confidence with her children when they'd learned to do for themselves: feed, dress, bathe, think. Tonight she and Emily would endure their wakefulness separately, one right on top of the other, two forms in bathrobes, moving uncomforted across the lighted windows in an otherwise blackened house.

Downstairs Mrs. Mabie could hear clocks ticking, Kojak wheezing on the couch where he'd been told again and again he could not sleep, the muffled noise of a passing car on the street through the thick layers of hedges and trees. A branch scraped the window outside Emily's old bedroom, which had become the guest room. Some nights Mrs. Mabie wound up there, pretending she was in a hotel, pretending she had no family to clutter her thoughts and trouble her sleep. She would compose a letter to Winston to post the next day, a mission that often satisfied her. Like the key she held to Mona's room, her letters required the immediate focus of her love, the manageable task of expressing it. Loving grown-ups proved challenging to Mrs. Mabie. They were big, they had their own ideas. Some nights she simply hoped that the coolness of other, clean, sheets would be enough to send her back to slumber.

Winston's bed gave a sudden creak behind the door. This noise soothed his mother. Her son was home, having a dream, turning in his old bed under his old blanket as if he were his old self. Did she want his old self? Could she trust his new one?

She tiptoed to the guest room and, briefly, missed her letter-writing days. She pulled back the sheets, lying in the welcome of solitary rest on Emily's childhood canopy bed. Everyone alone in his or her bed, she thought, all of the solitude that sleeping alone represented. Once they'd been a family that moved fluidly from room to room, Emily sleeping on the bunk above Winston, Mona between her parents as an infant, Mr. and Mrs. Mabie naked, the doors open, the shared baths, the pleasant necessity of an utter lack of privacy or self-consciousness, the house of need. Mrs. Mabie missed that. Now she sensed the separate sleep all around her, the beds each occupied by only one. All of the masturbating that had gone on in these beds. All of the wild dreams. The crying. She did not want to pursue thoughts about her family's adult lonely lives; she could not bear the fact of their secrets. She knew secrets she didn't want to know. Most people enjoyed secrecy but not Mrs. Mabie. Secrets did not make her feel ownership or superiority or kinship or intimacy. Secrets made her uneasy.

So tonight she thought instead about food, the table where they would gather, the menu she would contemplate tomorrow, the trip she would make with Mona down the enormous aisles of the grocery store, her own basket tethering her there in the infallible abundance of that place she loved named Safeway.

MONA MET Nicholas Dempsey at the White Glove Motel, which was located on the other side of the airport, a motel where the western farmers might stay when they had flights out of Wichita. The parking lot held pickup trucks; Nicholas had been here since late afternoon, the hour he'd told his wife that his flight to Cincinnati left. She'd dropped him at the airport and within minutes he had routed himself right around, taken a cab less than a mile west on Kellogg. This was the second time he and Mona had stayed together at a motel, so his heart was not beating so percussively when she arrived that evening. It surprised both of them how simple it was to carry on this way, to make up names, to pay cash in advance, to be for an evening lost to anyone in the world who might seek them, anyone but each other.

Nicholas Dempsey let Mona choose the motels, the White Glove this time, the Top Hat last time. He acquiesced to the '50s decor, the retro aura she preferred. Left to his own devices he would have gone for the major chains, Comfort Inn, Best Western, mattresses that hadn't been fucked on for forty years in a row.

"Winston's home," she said, pressing her forehead to Nicholas's shoulder. One of Nicholas Dempsey's great virtues was his sympathy with her brother's case. They'd fallen in love slowly, meeting only now and then over the intricacies of Winston's accident, incarceration, and inheritance. Nicholas had defended him in the first trial, the state's vehicular homicide case, and then recommended another lawyer for the case that the family had considered bringing on, the one called wrongful death. He'd suggested that although he could continue to represent Winston, the better plan would be to find a lawyer more experienced in civil court. He'd seemed reluctant to lose his contact with the Mabies, and so he'd kept track of them. The moment Mona's feelings had shifted toward him had been at the brief meeting in March, in the downtown courthouse, discussing Winston's imminent release. He blushed when he met Mona's eyes over that table. He had a habit of clearing his throat, and in the instant just after, speaking some important bit of information, a necessary aside that seemed ventriloquistic, as if Nicholas Dempsey himself would not like to claim it, but thought it essential to broach, nonetheless. Like a conscience, a faint murmuring echo.

In his car, the first time he'd kissed her, he'd cleared his throat this way and said, "Yes" when Mona asked if he still loved his wife. That did not displease her. He was not a liar, he was not shallow. He loved his wife, and kissing Mona made him feel guilty. At the White Glove, this wind-racked stormy night, he had a bottle of Jack on the dresser beside the plastic pail of ice. The television played music videos at a low level. Because Mona liked music, Nicholas Dempsey was trying to reacquaint himself with it. He'd bowed out a few years back, too busy with his career and his family to keep up. So he had bought *Spin* at the airport before grabbing his cab. Mona was touched by his study of her. It was as if he were substantially older, although the difference in their ages was only a few months. He'd been sent to prep school, catapulted out of the misspent youth of their Midwest high school culture at an early age, aimed for an aristocratic, Eastern Seaboard sort of life.

"So this *Beck* person," he said now. "What's his deal?" He grinned at Mona, removing his glasses. "Must they yell?" he'd asked worriedly, of countless bands, like an old person. "They must," Mona had assured him.

"You kinda look like Beck," she told him tonight, "if you want to know the truth. He has rosy cheeks, too." He was as angelic looking as a little boy, she did not add. He made her heart a faucet of love. Nicholas Dempsey had very few opinions about things other than his job. His wife, it seemed, whom he'd met in college, back East, made decisions about what he wore and ate and watched and read. They were predictable choices, Mona thought, and they had given Nicholas confidence because they seemed so popular, so overwhelmingly endorsed, so evident on politicians and financial giants and the whole big business corps. Mona liked to confuse him by questioning these choices. And to his credit, he seemed to enjoy having them shaken; he was enjoying the White Glove, for example, the light fixtures shaped like bowling pins, the orange-and-green checkerboard carpet. The two of them would not have noticed each other in high school; he would have been always in a group of boys, smart and clean-cut yet condescending, boys destined to belong in groups, football team, college fraternity, country club. And Mona would have been the girl wearing black whose ears were plugged with Walkman headphones as often as possible, skulking through classes with one eye always on the clock, ticking off minutes like someone being tortured, forever labeled an underachiever.

But despite being a follower, Nicholas Dempsey possessed an appealing curiosity. He only rarely let it supervise his life, yet it explained his brief lapse in college when he'd taken nothing but art classes for a semester. It accounted for his uncharacteristic insistence in naming his white white children after black jazz players—Miles and Ella. It permitted his love affair with Mona.

"All the interesting things you do are the ones everyone else advises against," she noted.

"Hmmm," said Nicholas Dempsey the lawyer; he needed further evidence. "No doubt I'd be advised against a number of other things."

"Such as?"

"You know, crimes of all sorts. Just because a few wild hairs worked out doesn't mean I ought to go shoot up heroin and rob banks."

Mona laughed, raising herself above him in bed. Never had she met a less likely drug addict or criminal. Perhaps that was part of his appeal: he was as unlike her last lover as possible. Nicholas Dempsey was a wage earner, levelheaded, capable of following through. He gave Mona gifts and called her every day. He was always able to come up with an erection. And whatever vacuum the disappearance of her last lover had left in her heart, Nicholas Dempsey had arrived to mostly fill it.

Sometimes, however, his clean living saddened her, made her miss Barry with an insistence that sent her reeling. His had been a more kindred spirit, she thought. Once, for instance, in a motel bed not unlike this one, with Barry, Mona had woken to find herself soaking wet. They'd been drinking and then fell into drinkers' sleep, the four-hour catatonic sort, only to wake simultaneously, four eyelids popped open like the slap of cheap window shades, when Barry peed the bed. She had loved him so much she didn't care. She loved him so much she laughed. How could he have betrayed a love like that?

Nicholas Dempsey would never wet the bed. Nicholas Dempsey was not excessive, and every now and then Mona missed excess. She approved of excess. Moderation seemed dull, cloying, like milk. So she encouraged Nicholas Dempsey's nascent vices, his drinking, his adultery. He would take to them, she thought.

"Pretty girl," he murmured now, squeezing Mona's breast. His wife, Mona knew, was small and blond, wore one of those brimmy hat things and power-walked with a double stroller in front of her. Her shoes were white, her hair confined to its ponytail, her weight always in the double digits. These facts floated in the casing of Mona's brain, to be interpreted differently depending on the occasion. Tonight, she felt delighted to be slothful and heavy and dark; tonight, those things seemed exotically European instead of merely ugly.

"It's so easy to be in love with you," Nicholas Dempsey said dreamily after they'd fucked. Mona fell asleep on his chest, breasts beneath his chin, as happy as she had been in years. Her brother was home, and her lover was beside her.

THE TORNADO siren went off after midnight, the climax toward which the day had been building all along. Its howl did not surprise so much as satisfy Professor Mabie; this was what he had been awaiting. Despite his grogginess when his wife had tried to rouse him earlier, he now rolled calmly—completely sentient—from bed and pulled on his bathrobe. It was true that he did not rise for the fevers or nightmares of his children, but in the case of acts of God, he was prepared.

He went to rap on the other doors of his children, while his wife, emerging blind and wrinkled and frowzy from the guest room, gathered bedding and pillows to carry to the basement. Flashlights and radios were already there, fresh batteries loaded in their chambers, all the accoutrements of what some might name paranoia, and others preparation. Once his immediate family had been stirred, Professor Mabie took a moment to phone his brother Billy's house, in case Billy had had too much to drink and didn't hear the siren, or in case Sheila was playing her music so loudly that nothing could be heard. Why he thought the jingle of his telephone call would reach them if the mighty blast of the air horn couldn't was a very good example of his heightened sense of importance in the lives of his brothers. Such was his fraternal power, fiercer than the emergency civil defense system.

"Billy, where are you?" Professor Mabie asked when his dazed brother finally answered.

"Talking to you, I guess obviously. In my bed."

"Well, get out of bed and head for the cellar. Didn't you hear the warning?"

They both paused to listen to the rotating howl. Then Professor Mabie swiftly hung up his receiver; rumor had it that you could get electrocuted speaking on the telephone during a storm.

Poor little Roy had grown too heavy to be carried down three flights of stairs by his mother, whose arms were full of her sleeping daughter and her daughter's sleeping apparatus, anyway, stuffed toys and milk bottle and pacifier on a string and clip. "Will you carry this?" Emily asked as she passed her father, offering the sticky bottle, using her newly freed hand to grab Roy's arm. "Single parenthood sucks," she muttered as she tugged him down the basement steps.

Baby bottle in hand, Professor Mabie circled the main floor opening windows and switching off the lights. The open windows were to decrease pressure and prevent implosion; the extinguished lights were to discourage a fire, should a lamp blow over in the wind. And the wind blew magnificently through the freshly ventilated room, the curtains flew up like ghosts, sheet music sailed from the piano to the carpet, the doorbell chimes clanged tunelessly. Professor Mabie's chest thrilled; there was something undeniably intoxicating about an emergency, about herding his family from danger, about being the last down the steps, door sealed against the upper floor and the stormy elements.

Except that he wasn't the last down the steps. Where was Mona? Where was Winston?

"Where is Mona?" he demanded of the two women and the two children. "Where is Winston?"

"Where's Jackoff?" asked Roy.

"Kojak's hiding, honey," Emily told her son. "Dogs know when to hide from storms. Dogs have good sense about storms, don't you fret." Emily felt hypocritical but entitled; she knew better about animals and storms. She'd passed through twelve years of Kansas public schools where she'd been annually shown apocalyptic footage of the family pets, lifted from their homes and deposited twenty miles distant, stranded on grain silos, embedded in billboards, steamrolled by Mother Nature.

"Wah," said Roy melodramatically.

"That helps," his mother said.

The siren went on and on, screaming its stern message. Lightning sizzled and the lamps flickered. Mrs. Mabie, woozy from lack of sleep, tuned the radio so they could listen as the surrounding counties were polled, floods in Cochise and McPherson, flooding rain in Sedgwick, 120-mile-an-hour winds outside both Emporia and Hutchinson, air traffic of the whole vicinity diverted to Oklahoma City. Upstairs something fell—the piano bench, thought Professor Mabie, spilling the remainder of the sheet music, all the old tunes his mother had loved—then the basement door opened and Winston thumped down. In his arms he cradled Jackoff, who was shivering. The dog, who apparently assumed Winston was to blame for the fracas, snapped witlessly at his wrist.

"Here's Kojak," Emily told Roy.

"Little shit," said Winston, dumping the dog on the tile. Instantly the animal fled beneath the pool table, making his distinctive noise. "Growling," the family pessimists would claim; "Groaning," argued the optimists.

"There's enough pillows for everybody," their mother told them from her place near the hearth. Since she was slumped in the rocker, it wasn't necessary for her to say she was taking it, though she did. Her face seemed deflated, bearing its sleep wrinkles like the collapsing skin of an old apple.

"Mona's fine," Emily assured her father, who looked concerned. "She's fine, Dad." Emily assured him although she had no idea where her sister was. Mona was not forthcoming with her love life, even though the sisters were close. Since her affair with Emily's husband, Mona didn't like to broach the subject, as if it might lead, like a single string, to the knotted source.

Professor Mabie sighed, but this was nothing new. It was his fate, someone's perpetual absence. Someone, somewhere, was not safe under his watchful eye. He thought of Betty Spitz, her home without a basement. Hers was the personality that sought out tornadoes, brought a camera and thrilled in the sighted funnels. Danger excited rather than frightened her; or maybe her fright expressed itself in the form of delight rather than rage, able as she was to submit to it, like people who rode roller coasters or sky-jumped, giddy with their lack of control.

The all-clear was not due for another two hours so the family made their pallets on the couches and floors and chairs. Because of its bumpers, the pool table received the baby. Roy's grandmother set him up on the love seat in the corner, explaining as she did so why he was perfectly safe, that there were no windows nearby, that the tornadoes would pass, that he would wake up tomorrow to a sunny day. It was always very sunny and clear after nights like this, she told him, yawning her dusty breath on him, the sun tomorrow was something to look forward to, and she would bake him a peach dumpling. Roy liked the word *dumpling*, it reminded him of a big soggy pillow, so he let her kiss him, then sat up to see where his mother lay in case he had to find her, later, and then flopped back on the scratchy surface of the love seat, pulling his sheet around him. His view was of a painting he'd never noticed before, hanging on the wall at the end of his new bed, there where he could not help staring at it.

He lay unavoidably studying this piece of art for a long while, the wail of the siren and the urgent voices on the radio somehow blending with the images on the canvas. The picture and the noise would stay with him for the rest of his life, a memory of uproarious abandonment, of being wholly alone even though the people he loved best lay all around him. The painting was of a burning house, flames leaping from all the broken windows, black birds like fighter jets hovering anxiously around it while a man and woman hid from each other behind a corner and a shrub, the man with a garden hose, the woman clutching a broom whose straw had also caught fire. They were both hiding from, and looking for, each other. Roy thought they were parents, something like his own, and he wondered where their children had gone, if the children were still inside the house, in the flames. Outside the house's picket fence stood a funny-looking dog, white with a head like an anteater, watching its owners and the birds. Where was the mother's boy? Roy could almost see himself inside that burning house, crying. He was not surprised this picture had been tucked away down here in a neglected corner. Because he had not lain on the basement love seat before, he had not known what view awaited him during his night of terror. He sincerely wished he'd been left upstairs on the third floor with his own pictures to stare at, Buzz Lightyear, Yosemite Sam, even Eeyore, the gloomy donkey, he would have preferred. He thought he'd rather take his chances with a tornado than spend the night contemplating the flaming house and the evil couple with their menacing tools.

He also wished his mother were positioned somewhat closer to him, or that his sister were older so he could say something to her that she'd understand. When she was born, his mother had promised him he would have a friend, a little adoring chum to follow him about and do what he said. Not so, so far. Now he would have liked to hand off some of his terror, spread it around so that it involved him less. The person closest was his new uncle, who lay a few feet away in a brown sleeping bag. Roy wouldn't have minded lying in that bag with Winston; its soft red lining was emblazoned with images of friendly black dogs and the quail they pointed their noses toward. . . .

His new uncle suddenly turned to face him from the floor. He squinted at Roy as if sizing him up. Roy wondered if he'd cried aloud, if Uncle Winston planned to give him a spanking. Then, as Roy quietly inhaled, Winston crawled out of his bag and to the love seat, his face level with Roy's. He flinched, certain Winston was going to bite him. Instead, his uncle asked him to scoot over and then sat practically on top of his head.

"Sorry," he said, shifting his haunch from Roy's ear. He was wearing shorts and crossed his hairy legs, smelling of smoke, as if he had emerged out of a fire himself. Roy sniffled a few times, wishing his mother would know to come over here, wishing she weren't sleeping on the other side of the pool table. He was going to have his dream about the invisible man, the one who constantly went around opening windows and inviting in large monsters through them, and he hated that dream so much. This painting he'd just noticed reminded him very strongly of that dream; maybe he *had* seen it before, maybe it was where the dream came from when it found him. The invisible man bore some vague resemblance to some aspect of Roy's father, whom he remembered in blurts, like a quick flip through all forty of the TV channels. Maybe this Winston person was his father? There was something familiar about him. . . .

His new uncle said, "Is that picture keeping you awake? Is it bothering you?" Without waiting for Roy to admit as much, he hopped off the couch and not only spread his arms and hefted the painting from the wall but banished it to another room. Faintly, Roy heard a door close in the workroom. Before he knew it, the smoke smell was back, and his uncle's voice was near his ear, saying, "Now you can sleep." And sure enough, now he could.

PART Two

I

WHEN WINSTON had taken a brief break in his career as student and flounderer, he and his grandmother adopted each other as companions. School, he realized in a lucid moment, would wait for him. That was its classic beauty, its incorruptible presence— venerable grounds, benevolent faculty, lofty library full of books; pen, page, mind. Waking without the threat of failure hanging over him had a certain appeal. So he moved home in 1988 after almost finishing his BA, and took up with his grandmother. They thought of themselves as gadabouts, at loose ends, lazybones. Winston's life had yet to assume direction; his grandmother's was nearing closure.

In the mornings, she phoned him to chart the day's course. Alone in the big family house, Winston sat among the residue of leave-taking: newspaper, cereal bowls, skunky scorched coffee odor, porky maple haze. The place had the feel of phony sick day, of illicit malingering. In his position, either one of his sisters would have snooped but Winston had no such inclination. He sat fuzzy-headed and hungover before the morning newspaper, waiting for his grandmother to call him and make plans.

Antique stores interested her, as did Chinese restaurants and of course the bridge societies she belonged to. They spent some time at the art museum to which she had bequeathed a few paintings, and the university campus where Professor Mabie taught, peering at statues, eating pastries, drinking wine. Wine! In the middle of the day, in the sunny atrium of the downtown Hilton, the two of them comfortable with long silences. His grandmother enjoyed people-watching as much as anything else, the lunchtime hurly-burly on the downtown streets, the bartering and bickering in stores, the funny habits of her bridge cohorts. Alternately, she would tell him about herself, the anecdotes that stacked up like building blocks or attached themselves one to another like body parts to have made the person that was *her*, and no one else. Slowly he was gathering her life, accounting for her whereabouts during the bulk of the century. In her company, Wichita had taken on new dimensions for Winston; he felt a growing entitlement to its streets and corners, as if it had been he who'd lived there for the last forty years.

They shared a love for napping. Midafternoon found them on separate Mabie sofas in the long dark living room slumbering companionably, clocks ticking, excluded from the rest of the world, the gainfully employed and occupied. When they woke they wanted fun, and had in common a delight in pranks. Once Winston found his old trove of saved molars; Bunny immediately hatched a plan, baking the biggest of them in an angel food cake. Together she and Winston watched as the bridge club took refreshment, the brilliant dawning moment when enormous obnoxious Nell Crandell pulled the tooth from her mouthful of gooey sweets, horrified and discreet, convinced she'd lost one of her own.

The day his grandmother's long life had ended, Winston had been squiring her home from a casual round of duplicate in which they'd made a killing. He and Bunny sailed through their city in high spirits; their victory had inspired a fit of bad manners from several of her long-time friends, a grumbling bitterness born of an antagonism that was not supposed to exist in the friendly circle in which they played. His grandmother loved the times her fellow humans revealed their weak jealousies and petty concerns. It made her happy to see rancor over the meager winnings of a Saturday bridge club, that part far better than the booty, which rode in the backseat, an irrelevant basket of bath oils, cookie cutters, Christmas ornaments, toilet water.

"Good job, Winnie," she told her grandson. He smiled sanguinely, drunkenly. With the proper combination of alcohol and concentration, he could play quite well. He hit stride, able to, at the same moment, retain the rules, track the whereabouts of the face cards, carry on his flirtatious teasing, and execute a thorough rout. Bunny's mood all afternoon had been high—pleased with her own trim figure, flat tummy and silk skirt covering it, proud to have produced the charming handsome young man who did not behave like the other grandsons, who were polite and patronizing, checking their watches. No, this grandson sat among them, looked them in the eye, made faces at racist remarks, told bawdy jokes with them, had the great good manners to discern among them, to remember the names of the ones who interested him, to dislike a few.

His grandmother preferred that he pilot them home since he was the better drunk driver. His high energy was only slightly modified by alcohol. He became quicker-witted, relaxed into a breathtaking spontaneity, managed without much difficulty to keep the left front fender aligned with the flashing white lines of the road. Bunny's tendency was to sleep, recline into her stupor, and laugh at his antics. She *could* drive and she often *did;* she owned a very fine Cadillac whose interior and exterior both pleased her, comfortable as well as beautiful, although occasionally difficult to fit in small parking spaces. Like the king of beasts, it insinuated itself among the lesser beings as it eased through traffic, others moving deferentially out of its way. When she and Winston took it cruising at high speeds their excuse was always that it needed its carbon blown out, whatever that meant.

Bunny had never believed she would be powerful in the world. But her grandson made her feel impervious, special, lucky. How rewarding to have finally been given someone to make her laugh.

Winston's eyes were his grandmother's, and people who looked long into them, especially properly intoxicated or sentimental or both, might fancy they were seeing Ruth Bangor Mabie once again—some gleaming wit in Winston's blue gaze. She had been a delicate beauty, turned to a birdish frailty in her later years, eyes in her head dauntingly forthright, blazing, formidable. You often found yourself feeling peeled, discovered, undone.

She'd been ordinary—never distinguished herself particularly from others in little Lawton, Oklahoma—until a strange incident in 1921, when she was fourteen years old and visiting Oklahoma City with her parents. At the Hotel Rio they sat for lunch in the formal dining room, even though they weren't paying for a room at the hotel. This was a compromise worked out between Ruth's extravagant father and penny-pinching mother: they stayed overnight in a cousin's extra bedroom, Ruth sleeping on a pile of woolen blankets smelling like barn animal. But noon meals, those were taken in restaurants, Coca-Cola in a glass. Ruth insisted on using the Rio bathroom three separate times. She liked the negress who handed her towels as she stepped from her mint green tile cubicle. She tinkled only briefly, thin warm trickle, then yanked the chain with relish. The woman accepted her nickel the first two times, then seemed to have taken a break when Ruth appeared yet again. Why did she love the bathroom so? Its wallpaper, its small soaps, its large clean privacy, and its keeper with her stool and towels. But the third time she stepped into her cubicle—a new cubicle, the third of three, the one against the far wall—and released her sparse offering to the clear water below, a hand reached from the stall beside her and grabbed her ankle.

It was a man's hand, a white man, she noted, with dark tufts of hair on his knuckles like a monkey. His grip was on her flesh, just above the anklets she'd bought yesterday at Kresge's along with her other school clothes. She'd come to the city in order to purchase those clothes, an act of pride she now would pay for, just as some Baptist ninny was always proclaiming. In the instant he snatched her leg, she renounced vanity. Look where it had gotten her, these wages of her sin. Now he shook her ankle as if trying to rattle nuts from a tree. "No!" she cried, and from his cubicle came his chuckle. Or perhaps something else, she thought later, after she was grown up and married, savvy about the noises a man might make in the throes of sexual gratification. That man's gurgle might have been his climax, the vocal analogue of his dirty happiness. As for herself, she sprang from the bathroom noiselessly and raced toward her parents' table, underclothing damp, skirts askew. Once there, she took a moment to turn her slight ankle, study the imprint of his fingers still visible at the fold of her white cotton anklet. He'd not resisted her departure, there in his adjoining stall. She did not consider telling her parents, or anyone, a thing about it.

In later years it came to her differently. At first she considered it her great wisdom, the thing she knew about the masculine species that her friends and other girls did not. Later, she appreciated how little it had taken on his part to defile her, and she harbored a victim's anger. Later still, she understood her luck. His satisfaction could have extracted more from her; his lesson for her was one a girl required in this world, and she had learned it so thoroughly, so early, so easily. He'd left no scar, broken no heart, and yet she came away equipped for life. Nothing would ever take her by surprise in the same way. When her own affections turned sometimes sinister, this did not catch her off guard. Who could say how the heart would flutter loose from acceptable loves? For example, during her marriage she'd fallen in love with another man—out of conceit, she thought, out of weak will. Instead of allowing this affection to flower and fade, like others, she forced its dramatic declaration. She had an affair. She'd made a mess of her marriage for a few years—critical years when her sons were young—although her husband never guessed the source of disharmony. He thought it psychological. Mortal, perhaps. Her husband had an appealing habit of thinking better of Ruth than she did of herself. Hadn't that habit saved most marriages, most love? Wasn't that how children prospered, being seen as the pure innocents of their adoring mothers' eyes? Wasn't it up to total strangers to let you know your common brutal heritage, your dark desires? A man had taken her by the bone and shaken possibilities into life.

"Winnie," she said to her grandson, seventy years later. "Winnie, did I ever tell you about that fellow that grabbed me in the ladies' room?"

"Left or right?" her grandson asked, steering them home after bridge club, concentrating on the white lines dividing him from the lane beside him. "I always forget on Hydraulic."

"Old Water Ave.," his grandmother responded dreamily. "Left," she added, then began her story about the hand that reached into her cubicle while her underwear was down. Perhaps that man had been able to see her panties; perhaps he was reaching for them. But, no, the touch had brought him some pure pleasure, she was sure of that. She wondered aloud if Winston had ever experienced a moment like the one she described, when the most unthinkable thing pops out of nowhere and changes everything, the rush of fear, adrenaline churning even when the source of trouble has disappeared. What more unlikely object than a man's hairy hand would a fourteen-year-old girl have anticipated while in a public women's rest room with her bloomers down? And you know what, she said excitedly to her grandson, of course it was symbolic for all the rest of that fuss and nonsense, the puberty and the lust—why, some man was always going to be reaching into your private place and wobbling your leg, startling you out of serenity, making you afraid. And *good* afraid, afraid in the *best* way, the way that will prepare you for everything to come. Isn't that what your sisters would say? Oh shoot, she told him, not left, but right, I'm sorry, hon.

And those were her last words. She was sorry, hon. Overcompensating, swinging a hard right, sort of vaguely envisioning his grandmother's long-ago pantaloons, Winston lost sight of the fact that he was traveling seventy miles an hour on an access road, and plowed them into the thick unforgiving metal base of a brand-new stoplight. He'd been involved in the story of his grandmother's not-quite molestation seven decades earlier in the Oklahoma City Hotel Rio bathroom. The thing about his grandmother he liked best was that she could remember being young, recall it physically, viscerally, and she did not romanticize the experience. She had never once expressed a desire to return to some halcyon past, she'd never waxed nostalgic about lost manners or the dreaded youth of today. She'd had a hard, unfair life, and she found ways of telling Winston that the history of humans would resemble her experience forever. Why this lesson of unending hardship and injustice should comfort him, he did not know. Just that it did. And then he managed to kill the messenger, which perhaps would have surprised her not one whit. In fact, Winston believed that very peculiar truth about her death. She had her profoundest faith in coincidence and irony and poetic justice. That the boy she loved best in the world would drive her into a pole and kill her would have seemed fitting to her, especially since she had just given him bum directions.

And so he did not suffer the guilt his family might have expected. To do so would have been a sentimental betrayal of his grandmother. With him he carried an image of her as a fourteen-year-old girl, sitting on a mint green toilet with a chain in one hand, a billowy skirt in the other, blond hair thick and bobbed at her neck. He costumed her in a sailor sort of suit, white dress, blue tie in a square knot at her chest. Bloomers at her knees, possibly whistling through her teeth. Alone in the sparkling bathroom she sat happy, new clothes, novel chain pull. And then the dark hand reached for her, and shook her, and nothing afterward was quite the same.

Yet his grandmother had decided to see the event in different lights as the years went by, revising its symbolism in her life. It continued to mean something to her, but a different thing each time she considered it, like pieces of music or profound novels, revisited in later, wiser times. In the end, she'd decided that a much worse fate could have befallen her, one instructive yet too much so, or of a lesson one oughtn't learn. Her own lesson had the advantage of relative harmlessness. Powerful, yet ultimately benign. She'd thought of the bathroom today because the dish of meltaway mints at bridge club contained three colors of candy: Pepto-Bismol pink, margarine yellow, and the shade of seafoam green that had been the precise pigment of the Rio bathroom stall tile. The woman serving them was a large black woman, and it was this combination, the black woman and the green mints, that brought back her strange experience.

She liked telling Winston about it. Funny how talk defused the explosive while also substantiating it. He was her confidant, although she recalled that confidants were in general female. And then a great blank wall threw itself before her, stunning as a hand emerging from another realm, and everything was over.

2

BETTY SPITZ would die before Christmas, Professor Mabie thought. At Saint Francis Hospital, on the first day of November, his friend held court in her semiprivate room. In attendance were Professor Mabie, his brother Billy, Billy's daughter Sheila, and Sheila's boyfriend, football powerhouse Eddie Shakes. Sheila and Eddie were trying on the disposable rubber gloves that hung in dispensers on the wall, Sheila's pink, Eddie's blue, predictably enough. Billy wanted to know if any of the tanks in the room were laughing gas. But Professor Mabie couldn't find much fun in a hospital. He hated hospitals; this room and its apparatus frightened him. Of course, without this machinery and intervention, Betty would have already died. Her bad habits would have already killed her.

He did not so much regret the fact that Betty Spitz had maintained her bad habits as appreciate her passion for the side effects of the same. Smoking and drinking were responsible for her illness and decline and imminent death, and there could be no real question of what toll had been taken and how costly, and yet . . . she'd been the top of any list of party invitees, in her day, as well as throwing wonderful parties herself, parties guaranteed to be discussed come Monday morning, parties famous for their unpredictability, their lives unto themselves that whirled with utter volition once set in motion. She loved occasions; she would celebrate the national holiday of any nation, would don masks, cook regional or seasonal treats, hire bands, purchase Champagne by the case. She might phone you up on Boxing Day to go into the slummy side of Broadway for a belt in the barrio; she might make mint juleps on Kentucky Derby day and run a betting pool. She liked gathering with people, never mind the event, and she liked almost everyone she met, for she could forgive their weaknesses, and cherish their jokes and their jollity and their lapses. Professor Mabie forced himself to remember her pleased expression when a stranger, a new acquaintance, had made her laugh. She was both ready to meet new friends, yet also poised to be disappointed, at once. She had little patience for boors, snobs, pretentiousness, or simple dullness. She cultivated the eccentric, the hilarious; she imitated mercilessly. Her house had more than once been the site of extravagant and wayward parties, a hodgepodge of guests garnered from the far corners of her lively circles of friends, every debauchery imaginable tolerated, if not outright encouraged. People jumped naked into her swimming pool, or brandished knives, threatening to scalp her pets or each other, and, as a result of her boundless goodwill, always a few grateful graduate students stayed around after, shoveling up the bottles and caps and tabs and wrappers and cigarette butts, which were insistently and forever everywhere.

Alcohol and tobacco. It could not be denied that she would not have been the same without them. Certainly Professor Mabie knew others whose pleasures in this life had been reduced to the indulgence of one or more bad habits; his own mother had been a heavy drinker. The thing about Betty was that she'd managed to uphold all the business that went with her bad habits, even as they did her in.

For example, in her hospital room, despite the absence of customary props, she was delighted to see Professor Mabie and his collection of companions when they showed up for a visit. Professor Mabie had been afraid to come alone, and so he'd brought along some alibis.

"Sheila, who's that with you?" Betty cackled from the bed, although she knew full well who Eddie Shakes was; his photograph had already appeared numerous times in the *Eagle-Beacon* sports section.

Sheila had merely mentioned Eddie's Western civ instructor, and Professor Mabie had seen his opportunity. "Come along and talk to Betty," he'd told his niece. "Bring Eddie." His friend still had influence with the graduate student who was threatening to flunk Eddie. Flunking

Western civ would mean Eddie was ineligible to play ball, which would endanger his scholarship, and that, probably, would endanger his relationship with Sheila. His niece, for all her daftness, struck Professor Mabie as a more pragmatic scheming type than he'd given her credit for previously. And this made him optimistic that she might excel in the world after all. He didn't think Billy was prepared to have his daughter live with him indefinitely, the way Professor Mabie was. Wenda wouldn't permit it. So it was all for the best that she make her bald appeal to Betty Spitz, who, frankly, was thrilled to have a problem laid at her feet, pleased as punch to be thought the one who could solve it. Betty liked to remain powerful, influential in the world of academe, even as she dwindled under the tireless reign of cancer.

Most important, having Sheila and Eddie and Billy in the room meant that Professor Mabie was not there alone with Betty. Their goodbyes were coming; he wanted to put them off.

Sheila was bleating away nonsensically. "I helped him write his research paper on plutonic love between Greek gods. It was great." Professor Mabie cringed but Betty laughed raucously; her parrot barked his laugh from his cage. How had she managed this? Birds in the hospital: unthinkable. Didn't they communicate some horrifying diseases? Scabies, or something related to winged vermin? Weren't their very droppings, come to think of it, carcinogenic? Professor Mabie had tried without any success for many years to rid his home of pigeons. He'd tried plastic owls, rubber snakes, Chinese noisemakers, high-frequency sound waves, and shotgun pellets, all to no avail. The birds flapped grudgingly away during the application, then returned, either clever (they knew they'd win) or stupid; hardy (destined to outsurvive the human race, like cockroaches) or merely unimaginative. As a historian, Professor Mabie was interested in what survived. But his interest in the large birds murmuring and sighing outside his bedroom windows did not compel him. Their laconic looks and plump forms, their assured blustery entrance to the eaves of his home, did not give him faith in the endurance of life. They were neither beautiful nor noble—they were merely prolific, competent at breeding. He wanted to shoot them, each and every one of them. He wanted to frighten them, if he could not kill them. He wanted them to go away. They made him angry, he thought, because they made him ridiculous. Nothing upset him more than ridiculousness.

En route to Betty Spitz's hospital room, he'd had to give chase to Kojak, who'd squirted out the back door as he was leaving. Some neighborhood mutt was in heat, no doubt, and Jackoff, often without wherewithal or motive, had picked up the scent. So off down the driveway and street the two of them had run, Kojak sprinting with his tongue out, Professor Mabie cursing in his loafers. He hated frenzy, the ruckus of mishap, clumsiness. Back when he'd received student evaluations someone had written *He doesn't really go with the flow.* His brother Billy, however, was quite adroit at happenstance, accident. He rolled with punches in an admirable way. He did not mind looking like an idiot; he'd figured out that people appreciated a buffoon. They were in favor of his clowning, in favor of somebody's willingness to play the fool. This was not in any way Professor Mabie's nature, fool-playing. Somehow his brother had latched on to it, however, and Professor Mabie wondered if he ought to admire him.

Sheila and Guido the parrot were doing all the talking today. Sheila, still wearing her pink latex gloves, went on and on about Eddie's TA, gesticulating while Eddie cast his glance about the small room. Everything he saw seemed to cause him embarrassment, the bedpan, the intravenous drip, the sundry pill bottles and sterile pads, the curtain separating Betty from her mysterious silent neighbor. He twitched in his letter jacket as if bitten by bugs. Guido's cage was covered by a hospital gown, the ineffectual tie strings dangling. Guido kept noting the time of day, "Good morning," he insisted over and over, hinting broadly that someone might want to take away his wrapper. "Good *mor*ning!" he squawked.

Betty stared unblinkingly at Professor Mabie as she asked Sheila for more details about Eddie's bad class. Did she know that he was not ready to be alone with her for the last time? The class was being supervised by one of her favorite students, the crazy boy with his wacky allergies. His physician had sent him to Kansas because there were fewer of his particular irritants in the air than elsewhere; also, the university had accepted him into their program. Every week a delivery company showed up at the history department main office with a shoe box–sized parcel packed in dry ice. This was the boy's rabbit, the only protein his system could allegedly tolerate. A secretary signed for it, then set the box delicately on the mail shelf. He wore a mask to teach in. For eight years he had been working on his doctorate, taking semesters off now and then to break down, then reappearing at the first department meeting of the year, hunched sullenly in his synthetic clothing and sterile mask. Before the building had gone NO SMOKING, Betty had liked to torment him by lighting up when he came to see her. It pleased her enormously to hear how he hated Eddie Shakes.

"Of course he wants you to fail," she rasped at the football player. "You're everything he's not. You're big and successful and you can probably eat anything in the world you want, and you don't carry around an inhaler, and you don't wear a veritable *charm* bracelet of allergy warnings, and you haven't any"—she abruptly hacked, throwing her head against her pillows, her nose growing red, Guido joining her in his own coughing fit from behind his pale blue dotted covering—"you haven't acne," she finished weakly. "Poor Louis Kramer also has acne."

"Doctor Kramer made me come to his office," Eddie said, the first words he'd spoken. He had a deep, belligerent voice. Belligerent, yet appealingly innocent, a small boy unjustly accused, complaining in an offended baritone.

"Doctor?!" Betty howled, laughing so hard her thin, thin legs curled up under the hospital blankets, her lungs racked with activity. Professor Mabie saw the curtain twitch between her bed and the neighbor's, as if the person lying there had blown against it. Or maybe that was just the heat coming on. "You tell that moron he can be fired for passing himself off as a"—cough cough—"Ph.D.," she whispered. Eddie's smile, which only involved half of his mouth, a small tuck turned upward beneath his round brown cheek, was particularly gratifying. You couldn't help smiling with him.

"Good *mor*ning!" shrieked Guido. "Good *mor*ning!"

"Shut up, Guido," Betty sighed. She took a few shallow breaths, recovering from her paroxysm. Professor Mabie was frightened by her expression, she who'd been sharp and discerning, she who'd always attended to others shrewdly, always knew what you were thinking, what your true nature was by simply giving you the once-over. Why she had adopted him as her friend had never been clear to Professor Mabie, but he certainly wouldn't turn away from her affection. She had rescued him, professionally, made his job bearable, his relations with other department members civil. It was Betty Spitz who'd explained him to their colleagues, who'd explained their colleagues to him. Like a wife, she bridged the awkward chasms between men; like a hostess, she prevailed with her own version of manners when manners failed others. She had an admirable ability to see to the heart of things, to neutralize polarities, to defuse institutional bombs. For some reason, her faith in people's general good will and nature had made the history department a respectable and decent place without turning it sanctimonious. Now Professor Mabie found himself breathing very deeply, as if to coach her in the procedure, as if to do it for her, since she was having such trouble. He would have liked nothing more than to help her. It seemed the least he could do.

"Shit," she gasped at last. "I can't take any more of this hilarity, boys. I'm tuckered. Will you let Guido see some light?" She waved a clawed hand toward her pet.

Professor Mabie moved to the cage, which hung on an IV holder. It was on wheels, so he brought the animal around to Betty's side. "I'm precious," the bird said to Betty.

"Hey bub," she responded. All their years together, this was how she greeted Professor Mabie, too. He'd heard that parrots lived for a hundred years or more. Betty had owned Guido for thirty-five of his life span, which meant he might be around for two more generations. It suddenly struck Professor Mabie: some animals lived longer than humans. Trees, he'd grown accustomed to, planting them as often as he did. He liked to imagine them reaching into the sky after he'd left the earth, shading his unknown great-grandchildren. But parrots? Tortoises, elephants? What else—dolphins? Whales? How was it possible that *Guido* would be laughing and hacking and speaking Betty's odd phrases in her smoky voice long after she'd gone? How in the world could such a thing be? It made him want to knock the cage over and trample the little snotty parasite.

Pigeons and parrots.

The bird pecked at his water pan, then grabbed hold with his beak and claws, and slid expertly down the black bars, maneuvering his iridescent green body as close to Betty's fingers as possible. "Howsa hangover?" he asked her wryly.

"Shut up, Guido," she responded.

"Does he know what he's saying?" Sheila asked. "Do you know what you're saying?" she asked the bird.

"I'm precious," the bird squawked. "Can't be trusted."

"Coo'," said Eddie Shakes.

Professor Mabie would have liked to sit down, but the only chair in the area was shrouded with ominous white sheets that he did not wish to touch. Betty would not leave this room. She would not see her home again, would not take another walk around the neighborhood, would not have another meal in a restaurant. None of those simple things. That was why her bird was here with her. Professor Mabie reviewed the annoying process by which he had arrived at her hospital room today: the onus of having to go in the first place, having to capture the dog, who'd traveled the circumference of the block and then crawled beneath the car wheels like a rodent, refusing to come. Kneeling beside his car, whistling for Kojak, snapping his fingers, swearing all sorts of revenge. He'd finally had to retrieve a broom, swing the thing menacingly at the animal, then chase its short-legged dash into the garage where he grabbed the dog fiercely, not unhappy with its breathless yelp. Into the house he tossed it, slamming the back door and stomping to the car. At Billy's, he'd had to wait for Sheila to get dressed. Eddie Shakes was in her bedroom with her, a state of affairs that troubled Professor Mabie. Wenda was at work; surely Sheila's mother would not have permitted the boyfriend in the bedroom. But Billy, as usual, seemed vaguely oblivious, or perhaps simply too trusting, to worry. Eddie was his daughter's friend, and he was in her room with her as she got ready to go visit Betty Spitz at the hospital.

When the waiting was over, Eddie decided to drive himself in his Camaro, Sheila installed at his side. Professor Mabie had watched from his rearview as the two of them nuzzled and necked, then stopped for a hitchhiker on the interstate. "Your daughter is picking that guy up."

Billy turned around to look. "Vietnam vet," he diagnosed. Eddie's car disappeared from view as the Mabie brothers plunged on.

"Quite possibly *not* a vet," said his older brother. "You can buy camouflage clothing just about anywhere. After World War Two, you would always stop for a vet. It would have been unthinkable not to. But I wouldn't stop for anyone these days."

"No one?" Billy asked.

"A relative," Professor Mabie amended. "A student or neighbor or friend. Perhaps not a neighbor, hard to say." He pictured his new neighbor, the fellow who'd moved into the Vaughns' old house. He didn't think he would stop for him; his eyes were beady, his opinion always communicated in a glare.

"What if it was a tiny child crying?" Billy asked after a moment of silence.

"Yes, of course. Damned if we aren't out of gas," said Professor Mabie, noticing the needle trembling on the E. Long ago, his daughter Mona had innocently believed that E stood for Enough, and F for Fill 'er Up. But Mona knew better now, and she had been the last driver, her passenger Winston. It was Winston who bothered Professor Mabie, as usual, who acted as reservoir for the collected annoyances of the day, Winston whose character might stand on the side of the road pretending to be a Vietnam vet, cardboard sign insisting he wanted to work when anyone who knew anything knew that any money he received would go for liquor or cigarettes. . . .

Now Betty wished to know how he was doing. "How's Winnie?" she asked. As she'd done with Mona and her suicide attempt, she labored at engendering some sympathy from Professor Mabie. She thought Winston had cleared the slate when he returned his inheritance. She admired the gesture, brushing aside Professor Mabie's contention that the courts would have found against him, regardless.

"Then he saved you a lot of trouble and legal fees and time," Betty had told him. When she asked how Winston was now, Professor Mabie could not be terribly forthright, given the others in her room. And how could he hold a grudge, he asked himself, when Winston had served his term? Here was the justice system in action; hadn't justice been upheld?

"Looking for work," he said, but did not believe, picturing his son on the side of the highway, hitchhiking, freeloading. Since June, his son had been allegedly *looking for work*. Sometimes the phone rang; often Winston disappeared for lengthy walks; and most nights he could be found playing his guitar. These things did not seem to Professor Mabie an indication of job search. They looked more like summer vacation, now extended unnaturally into the fall. Having been an academic, Professor Mabie was still tuned to the school calendar. It was time for Winston to get up and go; summer was over, school was in session. . . .

Betty gave him her piercing glare. "Sit," she said, patting her blanket. "You're awfully tall when you're not sitting." Professor Mabie complied, covering her hand with his. On her dry face grew a series of pale velvety lavender patches—he felt he could brush them off, then apply an ointment to ease her constricted skin, and then somehow purify the cancerous bellows of her lungs. In the end, she'd smoked her slender cigarettes with a filtered holder, looking for all the world like an old film star. He liked her so well, cranky wizened Betty, and relied on her so thoroughly.

"You're never alone, when you're married," he'd told Betty once, "but you're lonely." He'd expected her to agree, be impressed by his intelligence.

"I'm not going to feel sorry for you, bub. You're lonely when you're not married, too," Betty Spitz had instead corrected him. "People are by nature lonely, that's the way it goes."

"Why won't you let me feel sorry for myself?" he asked, trying for the joke.

"Why should I? Pity is a terrible emotion, the worst. I'd rather hate someone than pity him. Pity hasn't got any teeth. Pity is a limp dick." So now Professor Mabie wasn't going to feel sorry for her, if he could help it. The others in the room, reading his intimate seat on the bed beside Betty, receded through the doorway, leaving Professor Mabie to say his good-byes.

"You forgive him," Betty said, meaning Winston. "You'll eat yourself up, otherwise, inside out."

He nodded, not really listening. His conversions, as inspired by Betty, had almost exclusively happened because he'd brought to her a problem, which she would then address. She couldn't force him to think of Winston as his problem. Winston would have to do the work, he told himself stubbornly. Winston was the one in the wrong.

"What can I bring you?" Professor Mabie asked his old friend.

"Bring Winston," she suggested. "I want to lay eyes on the boy."

"Hmm."

"I want to give him some advice."

"He won't take it, believe me."

"But I want to give it."

"Bossy cow." He didn't want his son in Betty's room. He didn't want to share her with Winston.

Betty tried to laugh, but couldn't summon the energy.

"Don't talk," Professor Mabie told her, taking her hand and squeezing. "You don't have to entertain me. I'll just sit here for a while. They can wander around out there. Billy'll find a newspaper, and Eddie can maul Sheila here as well as anywhere. Don't worry. I'm right here." Professor Mabie put himself in her position, alone with her terminality. All you could ask for was company, he thought, interested company in your lonely life and its inevitable end. And that, he could provide.

ACROSS town, Emily and Mona sat on the side porch. The sun, despite its lower position in the sky, shone more fully on the yard and house because the leaves from the dense growth of trees had fallen, or were in the process. Leaves the shapes of hands, and hearts, and spades, and skinny minnows fell spinning, slowly, as if through water to the ocean's floor. This floor was yielding, padded by vinca, Boston ivy, poison ivy, other leaves now strata of undistinguished mottled mulch, and a layer of hay Professor Mabie made an annual ritual of spreading over his favorite plots of plants, blanketing them in preparation for the hard freeze. Two intact bales sat waiting for unleashing—you snapped their plastic tines and watched them sag like uncorseted bodies. Over the months, their bulk would diminish—picked at by rodents for insulation, by birds for nests—and their gold color would tarnish, turn to dung brown.

To walk through the yard was to send up a flurry of small animals, the frantic beating of unseen wings, the rustling shimmer of an escaping snake, and to appreciate anew the evergreens, pine and juniper and spruce and cypress, suddenly the most florid objects in the urban forest. The white bark of the birch seemed freshly skeletal; the badly pruned old catalpa empty and gnarled and witchy, its hollow bean pods hanging like severed fingers.

"Scurvy, scurvy, scurvy," sang one bird.

"*Loser*," said another, scornfully.

And the crows all laughed, relentlessly, coldheartedly: "Ha ha ha ha," a creepy chorus.

Emily and Mona had come to the porch because it had been summer's favorite spot, now grown nippy. Despite the warmth of the day, the metal porch furniture held an icy chill, and numbed the backs of your legs and arms in a foreboding way. To be honest, the porch had rarely been perfectly comfortable; if not too hot or full of mosquitoes, then an irksome proximity to the neighbors' noisiness on their driveway was unsavory.

"Listen!" Mona said. They froze. In the distance the ice cream truck tinkled. *Playmate, come out and play with me . . .*

Emily stilled the gentle rock of the glider. Her sister reclined her head against her hammock pillow and they listened to the melancholy jingle. "He's got to be a dealer," Emily declared. "Nobody could make a living selling ice cream from the back of a step van."

"Maybe that could be Winston's new job," Mona said. "Popsicle man."

It was the Sunday after Halloween, and, despite the traditional bitter sleet of last night, today had struck as a sudden Indian summer one, seventy-five degrees. The air seemed thick, smelling of hay and the rot of leaves and mulch and pumpkin meat, which reminded Emily of body odor. Tangy, rank. Perhaps the reason the family had often sat on the side porch last summer was because Winston came out here to smoke— he'd reminded them of its pleasures. Parts of 133 N. Pearson went without hosting its inhabitants for years on end, then suddenly became popular. Perhaps it was the fighting clan next door that had contributed to the summer's setting of choice. Separated by the honeysuckle, a moat of ground cover, contained by a hedge of pine, the neighbors' driveway was still within easy listening distance, and if the side porch were the Mabies' favorite place during the hot months, the driveway next door was the neighbors'.

Also left over from the past summer was the drink Mona and Emily sat sipping, Champagne in which floated scoops of orange sherbet. Emily didn't think much of this drink—the sherbet created a funny scum on the delicate surface of the Champagne and seemed to be killing the carbonation—but Mona had invented it and, further-more, was willing to bring it out to her in a beautiful cut-crystal glass that rested solid and sharp in her palm, so she wasn't going to com-plain.

Mona said, "You know, it didn't seem weird that we lived here with Mom and Dad until Winston moved back."

"Tell me about it. Last night, when I couldn't sleep—"

"You had Four in the Morning."

"Right, I had Four in the Morning, so I came downstairs, and there was everybody." She'd suffered her typical wakefulness, strange fully conscious hours lodged smack dab in the middle of the night—but instead of staying upstairs with her children and books, with her anxi-eties and futile pledges of self-improvement, she'd descended to the main floors to check what was on television. She'd felt too confined up there with only herself to contemplate. She missed being in love, had dreamt of it and then woke longing for it, actually aching for it, sorry for herself, desirous of a man's touch. It seemed such a meager thing to want as badly as she did, ordinary yet impossible. In her dream, a shy man had taken her hand, a stammering customer who shopped at her store for his wife. Even in the dream, she'd looked at her gratitude for his touch with some measure of contempt. See what she'd been reduced to, the woman who thrills over a nebbish's casual grasp.

So, armed with the sputtering electronic baby monitor, she had arrived at the living room, hoping to locate an old movie on the cable station and lose herself in overwrought black-and-white melodrama. Instead, there sat her father before the silent television, reading the blaring captions of a news report as they appeared like teletype at the bottom of the screen. Emily liked neither her father's wakefulness nor the menacing invasion of news in the middle of the night—shouldn't the world take a break from itself for a little while? Her father did not hear her enter the room, his profile seeming like chiseled ice, cheekbone vivid blue as it reflected the screen, and she decided not to startle him. In the kitchen, she'd found not only her mother up and about—pink bathrobe, tan scuffs—but her brother as well. Her mother's Four in the Morning was well established in the family, industrious insomnia (housekeeping often took place overnight, everyone rising to discover the refrigerator scoured, clean laundry sorted and folded in the pantry), but Winston stood in front of the open refrigerator as if it were midafternoon, studying the appliance's contents disappointedly. It was true that the refrigerator almost never yielded exactly what you had in mind. He and his mother had been talking, Emily could tell. Their words hung in the air like smoke above their heads, waiting. She looked at the clock, just to check for the strangeness of it all.

"Why is everyone up?" she asked. It occurred to her that she was dreaming, that in fact nobody was awake, not even her, that she was walking through a vivid figment of her own imagination. In her hand, her children's breathing could be heard over the monitor, steady and static.

Winston didn't bother to turn from the Frigidaire, although her mother peered in her tunneled way, wiry hair pushed up on one side from sleeping on it earlier. "It must be hereditary," she said mildly. "We wake up." Winston wasn't wearing pajamas, Emily noted, his shirt and pants and flip-flops those he'd worn the day before. Perhaps he was just coming home from somewhere. Or maybe he slept in his clothing.

"You people," she grumbled, as if she weren't one of them, and returned to her garret.

"I was awake, too," Mona said when Emily finished telling her about it. "Like around two or so. We all were. A whole house of insomniacs."

"I don't like it," Emily said. "Not one bit. The best thing about being awake in the middle of the night is the fact that no one else is awake. I want to be alone."

"Same here," Mona said. "Well, maybe not. Maybe it's better if somebody else is up, too. Like, I'm always glad to hear your footsteps overhead, going around, or your toilet flushing. It's less lonely. It makes me feel like I could go talk to you, if I needed."

"Sure you could," Emily said. "You could even wake me up, if you want. You know that. I try not to flush, in the middle of the night," she added, just to point out her consideration.

"Thanks. I bet it's the men who flush, Dad or Winston."

"Men would. Leave the seats up all day, then flush at night."

They sat quietly, listening to the hubbub of the neighbor children, the clatter and racket. Emily's children were in the basement with her mother, so her attention to the noise was calm instead of alert.

"The weird part is," Mona said, returning to their initial topic, "the weird part is that you and me and Winston are all three here, just like we never left, the way we were way back when."

"The house is big," Emily pointed out.

"Humongous," Mona agreed. "And Mom can't drive anymore . . ."

"Dad likes us . . ."

"And your kids make things different . . ."

"Mom loves those kids . . ."

"The house is so big," Mona said, "it would be stupid to go rent another place. There's so much room here. Too much room."

"Totally wasteful not to take advantage of it."

"Totally extravagant. I couldn't afford it."

"I could. But why bother? And we do help with maintenance."

"I answered the door all Halloween and gave away the candy so Mom and Dad didn't have to."

"Fred replaced the sump pump," Emily recalled, her friend Frog's husband. Then she realized that Mona wouldn't have had to answer the door for Halloween if their mother hadn't had to watch after the baby while Emily took Roy around. Roy had been dressed as a robot in silver spray-painted boxes. He was a robot like Rosie the Jetsons' robot, a 1960s notion of the future. For his dangling arms they'd duct-taped dryer tubing to his box. It had been a project all three siblings could throw themselves into, Winston rigging a battery-operated light panel on Roy's chest. Roy himself would have been happy with a cheap store-bought costume, sagging fireproof suit and flimsy mask snapped to his head with a rubber band. "Remember when our trees used to get toilet papered?" Emily asked Mona.

"You don't see that so much anymore, do you?" Mona said. "Now there are plastic bags in trees. There were never plastic bags in the trees when we were little."

Emily considered them, flapping up there. Plastic bags in trees didn't bother her; at least up there her children couldn't get hold of them and suffocate themselves. She could be glad of that. The blue Safeway bag whipping on the branches of the mulberry was one Emily didn't have to imagine over Roy's or Petra's face. "Let's send Winston to get it down," she said.

"There you go," said Mona. "See? Mom and Dad wouldn't know what to do without us." But she didn't seem convinced, as if unable to confess the reverse: what if their parents knew exactly what to do without them? "Still," she sighed. "It is weird, all three of us. I thought I was the only one who thought so." She sounded disappointed to hear of Emily's hesitation. Just a few days earlier Emily had discovered a box of grown-up diapers in her parents' bathroom. She'd been looking for Epsom salts, and found Depends, instead. Long ago she'd uncovered their birth control methods through just such an accident; that had been part titillating, part nauseating (no, she didn't want to imagine a flimsy rubber cap full of goo inside her mother). And the same reaction applied here, substitute pity for titillation, dread for nausea. Which of them, she wondered, found a diaper necessary? Was she going to be checking for telltale padding beneath their clothing?

From next door a man's voice shouted out, "Stop trying to control me!" He emphasized *control* oddly, as if it had taken him a moment to find it as his word. "Jesus H. Christ, if I wanted that I would of stayed with my fucking mother."

The Mabie sisters, on the side porch, hidden by thick trellises heavy with crisping, decaying honeysuckle, gave each other a long glance. "I don't think you should say 'fucking' in front of 'mother,' " said Mona at last. "Do you?"

"Well, no."

"I mean, *mother fucker,* yes, but *fucking mother,* no."

"Exactly."

"Just picture Roy doing such a thing, saying 'my fucking mother' about you."

"Roy will never be tempted to utter such nonsense, never." Emily couldn't imagine Roy getting any bigger than he was, knowing any words he didn't now know, growing pubic hair or an Adam's apple or pimples, let alone developing antagonisms toward her. It was preposterous.

"And why Jesus *H.* Christ?" Mona asked. "Why not Jesus P. or W. or T. Christ?"

"Grow up," came the neighbors' conversation, this time the flat tiredness of the woman. "I wish you would grow the hell up." She meant she had *enough* children, all of them riding their riding toys up and down the driveway, plastic grating against concrete, the slap of bare feet. The couple probably sat on the steps, arguing as they just barely kept the kids from pitching into the street. The steps, Emily thought, would be cold like the metal furniture. She remembered having sat on those steps many years ago, with the daughters of the old family, the Vaughns. Funny, she'd been good friends with Hannah and Heather, but now had no idea what had become of them, none whatsoever. This family was new to the neighborhood, having lived there only eighteen months, replacing the Vaughns, who'd occupied the big brick house previously and forever. The last Vaughn, the unpleasant dad, had died in its basement, barricaded in his bomb shelter. Now a new nameless clan lived there, and if you pried apart the pungent honeysuckle you might see a youngish harried woman wearing athletic clothing and her three towheaded children engaged in some raucous activity on the driveway, and, occasionally but by no means always, an older man with a beard and ponytail who could have been the father. The Mabies called this group The Naked Family, because the urchins ran amok wearing no clothing most of the time. Also, all family business was conducted in this driveway or on the side steps, absolutely no sense of decorum.

"You know what Winston thinks of them?" Mona had told Emily. "He likes the fact that they have no shame. He's in favor of The Naked Family. He thinks it's healthier to go around in the buff and have fights in the driveway." Emily pictured her brother, eavesdropping in amusement, strumming his guitar, alternately poking a lit cigarette in a Folgers' can of sand, or in his mouth, or in the loose sharp end of a wire string on the instrument's neck. He avoided talking much to Emily, but through Mona, she learned of his thoughts. Another of his purported notions was that Roy should go play with The Nakeds. Emily was reluctant, afraid her son would come back without his shorts, spouting some wholesome soul-opening wisdom.

"It's so public," she said now, unhappy with her own discomfort.

"I know," Mona said, sighing.

Despite the cool imprint of the outdoor furniture, their drinks and the orange fall sunshine were making them sleepy, the fight next door hazy as the backdrop of a distant television. Again the ice cream truck tinkled, like memory, like the sound track of bittersweet nostalgia. "I love this drink," Mona said, defensively, as if she, too, had grown tired of the taste. The Champagne still churned weakly around the amber ball, as if trying to get rid of it.

Emily went on. "If they didn't want us to listen, they'd be inside. They *want* an audience."

"We want a show, so we're a good match, The Nakeds and us."

"It's pathetic that they feel they need an audience."

"Maybe we're more pathetic," Mona said, closing her eyes and dropping one foot to the tile from her position on the hammock. Mona wore boxer shorts, in honor of the last warm weather, and had never in her whole life shaved her legs, so the soft hairs lay sleek and smooth as an animal's. Emily watched her shove her toes against the cool floor to make a gentle swing, saw the furry calf muscle flex, relax, flex. On occasion, her sister's movements struck her as so essentially sensual she wanted to imitate them, use them in some future seduction. On these occasions, she understood her ex-husband's attraction to her sister. Mona lifted her drink carefully above her tummy to avoid spilling, then raised her head only as far as necessary to tilt a swill of fizzy orange across her lips. She weighed probably ten pounds more than Emily, and this extra layer made her succulent, fleshy where Emily seemed stringy to herself.

"I think it's weird that they don't know a thing about us," Mona said, of the neighbors.

"I should send Roy over to tell them."

"That's what Winston says."

"Goddamn that damn Winston," Emily said mildly. "How come he doesn't say it to me, anyway?"

Mona went on, "But Roy doesn't know anything about us either."

"True."

"We must look like a bunch of recluses over here, all these trees, and the cars in the driveway. The mysterious comings and goings. The lights on at all hours."

"All these grown-ups." Emily took a moment to contemplate the phrase "a bunch of recluses." Was that possible?

"Those Nakeds are going to grow up being scared of our house," Mona said.

"I wonder if they know Mr. Vaughn died in their basement?"

"Probably not. I don't recall that in the real estate literature. Remember how we were scared of the pastor's house? And there wasn't anything to be scared of there except the pastor. At least he mowed his lawn."

"He had a lawn to mow. This place would require a machete."

"I know." Mona sighed again, reclined with a foamy peach mustache on her lip. The tips of her long dark hair brushed the dusty tile floor, swept over it gently like a handful of paintbrushes as she swung. Emily considered the problem of their overgrown yard. It was easier to maintain a jungle than a golf course, let nature have its chaotic way, that was true, but perhaps the city would sometime raise a civic objection. Her father's alibi was simple: "We're chlorophylling the neighborhood." For every tree his neighbors felled, Mr. Mabie planted two or three new ones. The yard's canopy had reached the house's second story, so it took a trip to the third-floor roof—to Emily's apartment—to view the city skyline, to assess the weather, to admire the stars. Underneath, all was dense growth and shadows. The wind blew, and the plastic bags rustled, the leaves fell.

"Go ahead," the woman next door shouted as the sound of footsteps could be heard, the man moving to what? Then the car door opening, slamming, laughable insect engine revving, Naked children scrambling out of the driveway, scraping their toys with them, the sound of a Volkswagen puttering in reverse, whirring out the drive, hesitating, then first gear, then fainter second as it roared its feeble four-cylinder roar and faded away down Pearson to Douglas.

"He turned left," Mona said in the aftermath.

"Heading for the hills. What a crybaby. What a jerk."

"Is *she* crying?" Mona asked, looking worried. The sisters listened. The three children next door, stunned, had not made any noise for a few moments. The woman must be alarming them somehow, weeping silently into her hands, prostrate on the cold steps, destitute and alone. Then came the distinct music of electronic buttons, seven tones, and the woman began talking on her telephone. "Tiffany? It's me . . ." And one of the Naked kids yelled out, "Get the bikes, everybody!" and they were off again, racing up and down the driveway, their mother on the phone, spreading her story, her thoroughly divulged problems.

Emily was relieved. Nothing impelled her or her sister to make a visit next door. Everything was fine, clamor and craziness, cheerful children riding their toys back and forth, back and forth, bare and beautiful, Halloween loot stashed in the house for necessary rejuvenation, wrappers spilled on the old Vaughn carpet like confetti. Their father's leaving reminded Emily of her ex-husband, the man her family pretended had never existed in order to spare her embarrassment. "The Excrescence," Winston had named him, before his own hell had all broken loose, before Emily's ex had proved his worst nature.

The thing about Barry was that he was, basically, gentle and benign. But he was also a sucker for stimulants. It was hard to sustain a relationship with a partner as weak as Barry because you could never go slack yourself. You had to be fortified, ready to prop him up, call his boss or scrape him from the floorboard of his automobile. He humiliated her, mostly, although she occasionally could work up an elaborate anger, especially if she happened to drive past the house they'd owned on the other side of the park. Such dramatic waste, such ample illustration of failure. When she'd returned to her parents' home, during their separation, Barry had simply continued to use the place as he had with Emily, crash pad. Her absence from the house was clear—the fishpond went undrained all winter, the porch unpainted or shoveled, the flowers unwatered. The electricity had been cut off, eventually, and a thick yellow extension cord had then been run from the neighbors' house across the driveway and into the window. Weeds filled the yard, and then, as if to declare more emphatically his complete disdain for Emily's love of its charm, Barry banged his monster truck into the house and dislodged a full panel of plaster, which fell to the ground and lay in thick puzzle-like chunks, killing the grass beneath. The bricks left exposed still struck Emily as a kind of wound, a big gash in what had once been her home. She had not told Barry about her second pregnancy. While he was demolishing their marriage, she was busy enlarging the scale, adding another voice to the fray.

To this day, he did not know he had a daughter. If asked, Emily would have declared another man baby Petra's father.

"Mona," Emily said suddenly, anger turning from her ex-husband to her brother, who'd known Barry's nature from the beginning, but how? How dare Winston call him The Excrescence not three minutes after meeting him? "I've been wondering why Winston never cared what I thought about him. I mean, he was so understanding and nice to all those girls and old ladies, but why was he so mean to me? Why didn't he turn his charm on me?"

Mona swung, half asleep. In the past, she had told Emily that Winston resented her bossiness and what had seemed like the unfair ease with which she'd entered adulthood all those years ago, back when Barry was wealthy, and Emily had owned a home, partnered in a business, seemed properly weaned and ready. In those versions of Winston's rudeness, he was merely jealous of Emily's competence, her no-nonsense approach to the world, her survival instinct, her moderation.

"How come he tells you stuff, and talks to you, and seems to hate me? Why?"

Mona's face was sad. "I don't know," she told her sister, eyes going glassy. Emily understood then that Mona felt worse about it than she herself did, so she did not press.

"Damned child," said their neighbor to her friend Tiffany on the telephone. "Does he really think I need another child? I saw this inflatable man in a catalog, and I was thinking I would order one. He won't talk back. He won't leave his shit all over the house. He won't be an asshole."

"Inflatable men, unlike inflatable women, probably don't have orifices," Emily said wearily.

"Probably not," Mona murmured. "And probably not protrusions, either."

3

By evening, clouds had rolled in and rain had started. Unfortunately, Mona had a blind date tonight. In effect was a storm advisory, which meant that the Mabie household had the television turned on with the sound down, ears pessimistically primed. Mona was too old to be reprimanded about going out during bad weather, but she felt her parents' disappointment as she dressed and drove away. They couldn't say anything, but they could sigh, imply that, sure enough, she would never learn.

She was to meet her blind date at The Replay, a bar across from the university. Winston called it The Pre-lay. Its location was the only thing that sustained it, accessible to all the dorm students and athletes, those matriculating beer swillers without wheels. Mona thought it a safe bet for a blind date; atmosphere certainly wasn't going to dizzy her from the reality of her partner. She wouldn't get carried away by a chandelier or a sultry jazz combo wearing tuxedos. No, The Replay was never anything but itself, concrete floor littered with peanut shells, black-light posters on the walls, bathrooms labeled Studs and Fillies, bartenders whose only employment proviso was the ability to tap a keg.

Frog and Toady had arranged this date. They'd tried to set up Emily, but Emily tended toward more dangerous types, could not see herself with a math professor who measured five feet seven inches in height. Mona, listening in inadvertently, had volunteered. Why not? What she especially liked was the thought of telling Nicholas Dempsey she'd had a date, his jealousy. She would have liked meeting *him* at The Pre-lay, or, barring that, waiting for his call. If the evening had to happen without him, she would prefer that it had already passed, that the date was already behind her, now useful as a story to tell Nicholas Dempsey. From all of her daily adventures, Mona culled the parts Nicholas might be interested by, saved them to report later, in the instance of a phone conversation. He was her secret audience, her gauging instrument.

What hurt was having to wait. She reminded herself of her missing kitty, Inkspot, who adored it when you scratched her above her tail, loved it, loved it, loved it, and then, abruptly, bit your hand. As if she'd been tormented, teased by the pleasure, and couldn't take it any longer. Mona felt like that, like an overpetted cat with her tail in the air, eyes closed in pleasure, and then ready to sink her teeth into somebody's hand.

So she drove into the storm, suspecting her sister and her friends of perpetrating an elaborate practical joke, not unlike the pranks they'd played on her when she was young, spooning something faintly toxic into her mouth, coaching her to speak profanities, providing her with her first pharmaceutical highs—always the patsy, the guinea pig, the chump.

The sky was the color of ice; trees bent over both sides of First Street as if to make a tunnel. Up ahead Mona watched a man walk against the wind, hands deep in his jeans pockets, face bowed, wondering why on earth he wasn't inside, then recognizing him as her brother.

"Winston!" she shouted as she honked, pulling into a deep freezing puddle at the curb. He climbed in without seeming surprised.

"Isn't it amazing, Winston?" she asked as they took off. "Mom and Dad must be beside themselves, worrying about us out in the sleet."

"Turn here," Winston said. He smelled of coldness and cigarettes, of camping.

"They must think they haven't taught us anything, that their example was worthless." Overhead, a tree limb cracked. Mona had yet to meet another car on the streets. Aside from the obscure visibility, she enjoyed the wildness of the evening, enjoyed having rescued her brother. "Where are you going?" she asked him.

"To Marty's," he said. "Don't pull in the driveway, his mother doesn't like anybody to block her car."

"She drives that?"

"Not the van, the Riviera." Winston pushed open the car door, climbed out, then put his face back in to tell her to wait.

"I'll wait," she called, over the noise of the wind.

Soon he and his friend were back.

"Oh good," said Marty Song. "It's you. Winston said his sister . . ." He trailed off. Marty was afraid of Emily because Emily couldn't stand him, which was because she'd accidentally slept with him once. Mona was glad that hadn't happened to her. For some reason, Emily had a weakness in the area of sex; she'd fucked a lot of unlikely partners, stupid men, strangers, women, one-night stands. If their parents were asked which of their daughters was the promiscuous one, they would both, without hesitating one minute, name Mona, not Emily. She could hear their chorusing voices: Mona. Mona the slut. Occasionally Mona was tempted to set them straight. She herself had standards. She would never have let Marty Song touch her, for instance, drunk or not. To her sister's credit, it did seem that Marty had unusually good luck with women. He was not handsome, but he possessed a kind of slothful charm, an easy laugh, a way of keeping track of what you were saying and complimenting you a lot. His tongue seemed unusually large, and he had a habit of unrolling it when he laughed.

"Sleepy Hollow rec hall, over on Thirteenth," Winston said, directing her to his destination.

"What's there?"

"AA," Marty said. "Winston's dragging me to an alkie meeting. You think they'll think I'm a drunk?"

"You *are* a drunk," Mona said.

"You don't have to lie," Winston told him tiredly. "Say whatever you want. Say I made you come."

"You did."

"Say it's your first time."

"It *is* my first time, man."

"Who said it wasn't?"

"You just made it sound, I don't know, like I was lying."

"Is this a gun? Am I holding it to your head?"

"We should all be in a basement," Marty grumbled, lashing himself into a shoulder belt in the backseat.

"The rec center is underground," Winston added, after a few moments silence. "If that makes you happy."

"What would make me happy is my own twelve-step program. Step one: slake that thirst. Empty that bottle. Fill that scrip. Smoke that blunt. Et cetera."

"Where you going?" her brother asked Mona.

"The Replay."

"The Pre-lay?" said Marty. "What in the hellfer? That place is for footballs. Meatloaves and footballs. God I hate that bar. I get a hangover just thinking about that place, it is the soul of crapulence."

"I have a date," Mona told them.

"Ahh so," said her brother.

"Who with?" asked Marty, unbuckling himself and leaning over her shoulder to talk. Marty was like a pet dog, Mona thought, a big sloppy loyal mutt. That tongue. But she had a special fondness for Marty that had to do with his reaction to her suicide attempt. Her stomach and throat had still been raw from the hospital pumping when Marty came to visit. He'd given her a big hug and said not one word, happy as a hound to have her home. That was that; no residue, no patronizing, no tiptoeing. If she'd requested it, then or now, he'd hand her a pharmy, no problem.

Outside they drove without meeting any traffic, north across all the number streets, fording the deep dips, accompanied by the sound of the hopeless wipers slapping frantically at the windshield. It was exciting.

"Who's your blind date?" Marty repeated.

"A math prof," Mona said. "Somebody Frog and Toady know."

"Not Garth Blewski?"

Mona looked in the rearview. "Why?" she asked.

Marty fell against the seat, shaking his large jowly head.

"Why?" Mona asked. "What's wrong with him?" A specific kind of dread filled her: the horror of being duped, fooled into thinking she wasn't pathetic, lulled into hoping she wasn't headed for the doomedest blind date of the century, something even an anecdote afterward wouldn't salvage. For a second Mona envisioned Nicholas Dempsey somehow in on this setup, preparing her for his inevitable leave-taking, conspiring with Emily and her friends, all of them sitting around laughing even now. . . .

"Oh, he's okay," Marty said, unconvincingly. "In a gay sort of way."

"You guys are coming with me," Mona said, passing right by Central instead of turning toward the rec hall. "I'm not going to meet some weirdo professor without accessories."

"Yes!" said Marty, cheering immediately. "It's a shithole, but I'd still rather go to The Replay than to an AA meeting. No offense," he added, looking at Winston.

"None taken."

"Should you go to your meeting?" Mona asked her brother. It was just too hard to believe that it wouldn't be preferable to head out to a bar with him. How tired he must be, of being himself. How sad to lose all those crazy nights of maniacal laughter, all of them initiated in circumstances such as these, a mixture of happenstance and foul weather, unlikely cohorts, absurd destinations, hapless new acquaintances. Mona's favorite pastime was the acquisition and later disclosure of these nights—the twenty-four-hour stoned grocery store runs, the back roads and lost articles of clothing, cigars and circus peanuts and strange girls, evasion of the parents, the dullards, the police. Surely Winston wasn't going to have very much fun at an AA meeting? But surely going to a bar was not going to sit well with his probation requirements. . . .

"Fuck it," Mona said. "I'll just run in and tell him I have to drop you guys off. If he's decent looking, I'll invite him along. If he's a loser, I'll give him a rain check."

"It *is* raining," Marty Song pointed out studiously, then added, "and I took a class from him, so I know he's a loser."

"Really?" Mona asked, sighing. In the rearview, he made his thumb and forefinger into an L and flapped it to his forehead: the international sign for loser. In her secret hopeful heart of hearts, she'd been looking forward to her date. She was afraid of her obsession with Nicholas Dempsey; she wanted a backup, a diversified attention, some sort of Plan B.

"But what the hell do I know?" Marty asked rhetorically. "My relationships last, max, one month. Maybe I'm the loser."

Neither Mona nor Winston corrected him; their family tended not to understand the expected response to self-deprecation, the way they were supposed to contradict his self-hating, No, Marty wasn't a loser. Instead, they just agreed, politely silent about it: indeed, loser.

At The Replay parking lot, Mona left the car running, dashed inside and stood awkwardly gaping around her. The other patrons gaped back. Her date was supposed to be sitting as near to the pool table as possible, salt-and-pepper hair and beard, cowboy hat. The only cowboy hat in the bar sat snug on the head of a fat blond boy whose hand was being tightly held by the hand of a fat blond girl, two bloated objects washed up from the bland Midwestern sea. Mona scanned again, breathing in the beer and cigarettes and dampness. Beneath her feet, the concrete floor was slick with rainwater and spilled drinks. "Super Freak" played on the jukebox, pool balls cracked as somebody broke, and a small man waved from the bar.

To Mona he seemed dreadfully small, breakable, the petite type who has embraced his effeteness and turned it against others. She felt like an Amazon beside him, and instantly began taking notes for the story she would tell Nicholas Dempsey.

He shook her hand, grimacing as if injured by her grasp. "Garth Blewski," he said.

"Nice to meet you," Mona replied. "I left my car running."

Garth indicated the barstool next to him.

"No," Mona said. "My car is running. My brother is waiting."

Garth Blewski raised his eyebrows. He had very expressive eyebrows to go with his tiny frame. He probably swam, Mona guessed. Swam and drummed and chanted and did yoga under the influence of herbal tea and incense sticks. He didn't eat meat, she suspected. He looked *quite* lactose-intolerant. His drink, she noted, was clear, as in club soda or Perrier. On his feet were sandals, raw woolly socks; the word *hemp* went walking around Mona's brain. His cowboy hat was a crushed straw model, overly worn out, urbanely abused. He blinked at her blissfully; what was she going on about, brothers and running cars?

"Do you want to come with me to drop off my brother?" she asked finally. "I have to drop him off. It's raining. Him and his friend."

Garth Blewski carefully laid a crisp dollar bill on the bar and stood, stretching his fists over his head and then bending side to side in the manner of the well-lubricated yogi. None of this was good, Mona thought. Winston and Marty would eat him alive, not to mention Emily and Frog and Toady. And what about Nicholas Dempsey? Garth

Blewski was not someone Nicholas would find threatening, would in fact probably perceive as a puny adversary, one that did not speak well of Mona's taste, nor of *Nicholas's* in *her*. . . . She wished she were a little drunk. In fact, what was to prevent her from downing a shot of tequila before plunging back to the car? Winston's AA meeting couldn't start very soon, if he had planned to walk all the way from College Hill to Sleepy Hollow.

Garth Blewski disapproved of the tequila, but Mona could ignore his pursed lips as she licked the salt off her thumb and threw back her head. After all, she was bigger than him, and younger, and prettier. Ah, lime. She'd not eaten dinner so that her tummy would lie flat in her jeans, and the liquor went immediately to her head. Much better. "Okay," she told her blind date. "I'm set."

"Marty Song," Garth Blewski said as they climbed in the car. Winston and Marty both sat in the backseat now, leaving Mona at the wheel and her date in the passenger seat, where he swiveled to check out his riding companions. "I still have your semester project, you want it?"

"Oh I'll come get it some day," Marty said. "If I can find a parking spot over there."

"This is my brother," Mona told Garth. "Winston. And I guess you know Marty."

"Where are we taking you?" Garth asked as Mona pulled out.

"To a meeting," Mona said quickly, her foot on the gas pedal matching the speed of her words. They lurched through a deep noisy puddle, the car seeming to float briefly—like a wild unlikely thought.

"Twelve-step?" asked Garth Blewski.

"That's right," said Winston quietly. And that was that.

When they stopped at the rec center on Thirteenth, Garth asked if it was an open meeting and, when Winston nodded, climbed out, too. "We could all go," Garth suggested in a teacherly manner to Mona.

She frowned, the warmth of the tequila still in her limbs. "Maybe I should have a breath mint to kill the alcohol?"

Marty snorted. "Maybe," he said. But no one had a breath mint on him. Mona found a chalky moist towelette packet in the glove box and rubbed its lemony astringence around her lips, once over the surface of her tongue. Truthfully, it wasn't much different from doing a shot with lime.

Inside, she realized she needn't have bothered: everything smelled of wet animal. The rec hall hosted canine obedience school just before the AA meeting, and a few dogs remained in the foyer with their masters, damp and moody, no doubt plotting some act of exuberant transgression once they left the premises. Their owners most likely were thinking of the mud. Mona averted her eyes from dogs and people both, embarrassed to be entering an AA meeting, embarrassed to be embarrassed. The one consolation was the presence of Garth Blewski, a potential source of embarrassment now subsumed by larger categories of shame. At least she wasn't sitting alone with him at The Replay drinking club soda. But why wasn't she driving somewhere secret with Nicholas Dempsey, parking at Riverside or near a farm, paying for a room at the Top Hat Motel . . .

In the full fluorescent light of the rec hall, she discovered Garth Blewski's true appearance. Yes, petite, yes, knobby and pale, salt-and-pepper hair, beard stubble like iron filings, old man yellow teeth and long toes flexing in his socks and spatulate sandals, a wandering eye, hands dainty as a woman's. Still, taken together his features did not add up to ugliness. It was Mona's peculiar habit to see attractiveness where it didn't legitimately exist, to make a case for the unappealing. In the company of her beautiful brother, this was harder to do. His perfection tended to cast a shadow on the looks of others. Compared to her brother, the other three members of her party must have appeared scruffy, damp and wretched as the dogs they'd just passed, a set of mongrels escorting their purebred friend.

Winston's presence meant that Garth Blewski focused on him, instead of Mona. This was always the case, Winston acting as centerpiece, Mona left in the penumbra. Perhaps Emily's problem was that she did not like to be penumbral, where Mona sort of relied on it, found herself comfortable narrating from the sidelines.

"Let's sit near the exit," Marty suggested. Mona, covering her tainted mouth, agreed by moving that direction. Garth, by virtue of his age or perhaps habit of his profession, led them to seats and positioned himself between Winston and Marty. This was fine with her; she still held the moist towelette near her face, like a hankie soaked in smelling salts, something to keep her from passing out. How she longed for another shot of tequila. Gritty salt, burning liquor, absolving tangy lime.

The meeting felt to Mona like a class, a group of people gathered to discuss an esoteric topic the outdoor world cared not one shred for. Outside, the wind blew and the sky roiled in its huge purple dramatics, while inside a few people were taking turns confessing the very local turmoil they suffered. It was a humbling enterprise; when her turn came, Mona shook her head shyly, proclaiming that she'd rather just listen, if that was okay.

"You're among friends," the leader assured her. He was a furry blond sort, hair sprouting wildly from his polo shirt at his neck, balding but bearded, straddling his folding chair in the confident manner of the buff high school coach. His demeanor declared that he had been around the block, hoo boy, but he wouldn't hold that against anyone. His eyes were a startling clear blue, like Winston's, like a zealot's, and they penetrated in the same manner, which made Mona avert her own gaze.

Her brother cleared his throat. He told the ten assembled people his name and that he was an alcoholic. They chorused back a greeting; Mona lip-synched. "I'm here because it's part of my probation. Not that I wouldn't come, anyway, although I probably wouldn't . . ." he trailed off. "I haven't had a drink in over five years. I think about it all the time, however, which sort of seems like drinking. Lusting in my heart, if you follow." A couple of people nodded, smiling. Mona scrutinized his audience, which was smaller than usual, the leader had explained, given the weather. They looked merely ordinary, which made Mona wonder what she had expected. She didn't know any of them, not the tense skinny woman with her limbs all wrapped around themselves, not the older woman blinking like an owl behind her eyeglasses while she knitted. The others were men, the leader—Van, he'd said his name was, although these names, as they were spoken in the circle, sounded to Mona like aliases, like they had quotation marks around them, AKA. Next to "Van" sat "Paul," a rich-looking, well-dressed professional who refused to look up from his feet, as if he were busy stepping on ants down there, and in a cleared space on the other side of him, a nervous fellow in a wheelchair who rolled forward and back as if in a rocker—"Sergio"—and a guy wearing a phone company shirt, heavy boots most likely intended for climbing poles. His beeper sounded as Winston began speaking, and he switched it off without giving it a look. Mona liked that about "Tony."

But she didn't like hearing her brother speak before strangers, even if they didn't seem to be paying particular attention. They were waiting for their turns. They, like Winston, smoked with a kind of urgency that seemed desperately unhealthy. Her brother's speech disturbed her terribly, as if he were confessing to a crime he hadn't committed. She wanted to amend his guilty offering, provide counterpoint to his point.

"I always come back to wondering if the desire isn't truly worse than the act," Winston was saying. The guy in the wheelchair was frowning mightily: what was this bullshit? Hadn't he just gone on and on about avoiding temptation, forsaking that bottle, this invitation, his awful friends who refused to buy his serious intention of quitting the party life? Others had provided much more concrete examples of success. No one else, so far, had been sober for five years, although Mona suspected "Van" had a long history of not indulging. Forty-five days of sobriety to the guy in the wheelchair probably represented quite a feat, so no wonder he didn't want to hear about Winston's existential stance, five years in. He was probably hoping that in five years he'd have forgotten all about drinking. In five years, he'd have other fish to fry, yet here sat Winston declaring otherwise. For a second, Mona felt the full impact of Winston's words; that's how she'd felt when Barry left her, the whole stretch of life without him and the unbearable ache of it, obsession, obsession, obsession. And for a second, she anticipated Nicholas Dempsey's departure, the cliff she was about to be shoved off. . . .

"This place is a drag," Mona said during the break.

"What she said," said Marty. "And my turn's coming, too. I was thinking I'd talk about my mother, blame her for all my problems."

"She *is* kind of overbearing," Mona agreed.

"Says who?"

The four of them—her team, Mona thought—stood under the sheltered portico watching lightning, shivering with their Styrofoam cups of weak scorched coffee. Garth, she thought, was definitely a homosexual. Clearly he'd grown smitten with her brother, as everyone did, and hardly had a moment to cast a glance her way. Now that her appeal as a blind date was in question, Mona found herself resenting his lack of attention. He was the loser in this combination, not her. Didn't he realize that? He and Winston were discussing college classes; apparently Garth taught one that Winston would enjoy. Her brother was not only beautiful but tolerant, the sort of mild man that homosexuals propositioned, a factor in his favor. Perhaps her brother was purely bisexual, able to fall for the individual, regardless of gender or age, drawn to the self lurking inside, amorphous and without corporeal shortcomings. Was this the result of being so comely himself, his not caring much for beauty in others? But surely he wasn't going to fall in love with tedious Garth Blewski. Was he? Mona was developing a very strong dislike for her blind date.

Garth started the second round of stories. He'd done everything, it sounded like, and in combination. Mona particularly mistrusted the way he referred to drugs, ludes and beauties and poppers, names like forsaken dances, the mashed potato, the monkey. His drug habit sounded phony, to her. He seemed overly proud of it. The turning point, he was saying, was when he woke up in a hotel room in Tucson, Arizona, and realized he'd been sniffing STP engine fluid, the room totally trashed, curtains soaked in the stuff, television shattered.

"Horseshit," Marty whispered in Mona's ear. She nodded, vaguely bothered by Marty's mouth so near to her ear. Or maybe bothered by the fact that she'd gotten a little charge when he spoke. This was the product of her Nicholas Dempsey problem: readiness, like an open wound, susceptible to any passing touch. Others besides Mona resisted Garth Blewski's confessional. The older woman looked skeptical behind her specs, her knitting needles clicking maniacally, and the skinny woman wrinkled her mouth, twisting her pretzel-like arms and legs tighter. The professional man not only continued staring at those ants on the floor, but now began grinding his heel methodically. Garth Blewski was a complete denial of masculine virtues, soft where masculinity demanded firmness, slight where it urged bulk. His shoulders sagged where they ought to have stood out, his midsection round, his knees knocked. He resembled the bottle-like form of the Virgin Mary, the sloped containment of two parentheses. Mona did not like herself for finding him repulsive, but she now found him so, regardless. He held up his small hands, What? Me Worry? Style, and claimed he'd been sober ever since Tucson.

"Congratulations!" "Van" said finally.

Mona decided to be attracted to "Tony," and leaned forward to listen to his story with obvious undivided attention. He would be her blind date, when this evening became a story to tell Nicholas Dempsey. "Tony" worked for the phone company and had the hands of a mechanic. He had a habit of saying "uh" between every third or fourth word he spoke, "I was sorely uh tempted for most of uh the week uh to . . ." Mona frowned, wanting to commiserate, extending the most forgiving of first impressions, but this "uh" thing was tedious. Her family had always prized articulation. "Tony" had a bad beer habit, was still drinking, but cutting back one beer a day. He'd been doing this for a week and a half, and still managed to put away a case by bedtime.

"Wow," Mona said, not quite as far under her breath as she intended.

Marty whispered in Mona's ear, "Once I took this big white pill, it was supposed to be Vicodin, but I found out it was a suppository."

"Ick."

Marty shrugged, his mouth loose, tongue unrolled; his part in this life was to be the butt of jokes, the happy-go-lucky shaggy dog.

They sat through an inspirational chat given by "Van," who hoped they'd be back next week, or tomorrow, or whenever they felt the need of solidarity. He clenched his hands together in the air as if to rally the surly group; Garth Blewski raised his own fist in brotherhood.

At the car, Mona said, "I need a drink."

"Amen," chimed Marty.

"Look at the stars," Garth Blewski noted, like a parent using the distraction technique. Above, the clouds were scurrying off in wisps like torn cotton, leaving the piercing clear sparkle of the stars. It was much colder now, as if deep winter had dragged its scythe over the city, shaving warmth away like a layer of skin.

Garth's ten-speed had been stolen from The Replay. "Shit!" Even his cursing didn't sound authentic, somebody trying on the vernacular. Nothing he'd said this evening seemed exactly him, as if he were summoning personae as the occasion demanded. Now he wanted to be the indignant victim of a bicycle theft. "Shit," his character spoke.

Mona sighed. She'd had it with her blind date. Maybe he was an alcoholic and pillhead. Maybe he had trashed a hotel room like a rock band. And maybe he'd managed to become a math professor regardless. That didn't mean she had to like him, and she didn't. She probably didn't like Nicholas Dempsey either, when you got right down to it, but she loved Nicholas Dempsey, and that was going to get in the way, no matter who she had a bad date with. Thank god her brother and Marty were along. Imagine if she had to wait here alone with Garth and the sullen bartender as the police were called, reports were filed. After all was said and done, Mona still had to drive him to his apartment, which was on the other side of campus.

He leaned back into the car to say his good-byes, yellow teeth bared in a crooked perverted smile. He'd had an exciting evening, despite the outrage of losing his "wheels."

"Come see me, Marty. Thanks for the ride, Mona. And Winston, think about that statistics seminar." He lifted his eyebrows meaningfully at Winston, who said, "Check."

"I have the worst luck," Mona said as they drove away, bouncing over speed bumps a little carelessly on her father's axles. "What a fucking dork. And isn't this apartment complex for retired people? I am going to kill Frog and Toady, just throttle their sorry throats. Did you believe his story about STP?"

"No way in hell!" Marty said. "Can I ride up front?" He rolled over the seat as Mona turned onto Twenty-first, knocking her shoulder with his boot heel. "Sorry."

"'Sokay."

"Garth Blewski," Marty howled. "He has the worst BO."

"I'm sure he doesn't *believe* in deodorant."

"I remember him going into this whole lecture about beef *by*-products, how everything we touched was basically a beef *by*-product, paint, toothpaste, beer."

"Did you ever go to the slaughterhouse on the west side? My fourth grade took a field trip there."

"Uh-huh."

"They served us hot dogs for the grand finale, if you can believe that. I was like, give me some peanut butter. Winston? What did you think of Garth Blewski?"

"Spry fellow," he said. In the back, by himself, he'd been sitting silently, as if involved in loftier considerations. Although Mona could feel his knees pressing against the back of her seat, his presence had otherwise been unremarkable. Now he stared out the window when Mona looked in the rearview mirror. It seemed he didn't have the energy or urge to dissect poor Garth Blewski. "Find me a Seven-Eleven," he said wearily. "I need cigarettes."

"Another beef by-product," Marty said. "Tell me something, Mona, is it true that women love addicts?"

Mona thought about it, her past passion for Barry. "Many women love fuck-ups."

"Your sister loved a fuck-up." Marty said this with reverence, which made Mona see that he still held a torch for Emily, despite being terrified of her. It figured. Just when she'd been briefly thrilled with his breath in her ear, there he was pining for her sister.

In the QuikTrip parking lot, Mona asked, "You guys want to do anything else, or should we call it a night?" Wind shook the traffic lights ominously at the intersection of Thirteenth and Oliver; they swung like old-fashioned lanterns over the street. Puddles were freezing and turning opaque before their very eyes.

They were old, it seemed, and could not come up with any merry pranks.

"Remember when we used to do Whip-its at Safeway?" Marty asked nostalgically. "Those were the days."

"Why do you like Marty?" Mona asked Winston after they'd deposited him at his mother's house. She was annoyed with Marty for reminding her that not only had she loved Barry, an undisputed fuck-up, but that *he'd* dumped *her*. At least Emily had kicked him out.

"Why do we like anyone?" Winston responded. "He's been hanging around since third grade, plus he's messed up in a way that interests me."

"You probably helped get him the way he is."

"Probably."

"Tailor made."

Their house was lit only with night-lights, dim glowing peachiness through a few windows, lights to guide your sleepless feet as you prowled in the early hours. On the porch steps Mona laid her head back while Winston smoked a cigarette. Upstairs, her answering machine would report its number and determine absolutely Mona's mood for the next twenty-four hours, evil zero, acceptable one, reassuring two, thrilling three. The concrete slab beneath her had turned cold, and wouldn't warm up, Mona thought, until April. Winter had arrived.

4

EMILY WENT to visit her gynecologist, whose unlikely name was Dr. Love. He hesitated, frowning, between her spread legs.

"What?" Emily had no particular shame before Dr. Love. He'd delivered her babies, appreciated her sense of humor about labor and birth, been forthcoming with the painkillers, told her she and Barry made beautiful children, and had not asked where Dad was during round two. She'd made her appointment because of the ache in her left ovary. She recognized the feel from her former days of sex; occasionally, when Petra nursed, Emily's ovary responded, deep inside of her and up high, answering somehow the tug on her breasts. She caught her breath, readying herself as if for penetration. It was strange, and it reminded her of sex, although she tried not to let it do so. Feeding your baby was not a sexual experience, she scolded herself.

Still, the mouth pulled at her breast and inside, between abdomen and groin, something replied, the answering ring of a bell chain.

She tried explaining this to Dr. Love, babbling in the way that was her tendency in the face of professional blankness. "Maybe it's hormones?" He told her to lie on the table and scoot down.

Scoot, she thought. What an idiotic word.

Into the icy stirrups went her heels, the two parts of her flimsy paper gown rustling and bunching. A perfectly worthless garment, the disposable medical cover-up. The speculum squeaked as it was ratcheted open, then slid coolly between her legs like two metal shoehorns.

"Relax," said Dr. Love.

"You bet," she responded, and she could feel his breath on her inner thigh.

He probed at her in the method of the Thanksgiving cook, one hand inside, one out, tapping, pressing, pushing. Emily had heard that cancer did not hurt, so at first she tried to take solace in the excruciating pain he was able to produce. He'd found the little bell that Petra had rung, and he made it clang as if to deafen her.

"There's something here," he said over the jangle in her ears, the chorus in her bowels. Because she was crying, Emily heard his words as if through water, as if she had suddenly been dunked in his office, the room flooded and she swept away.

"Ultrasound," he said as he floated from her view, door swelling shut behind him. Emily lay with her hand over her tender abdomen. What had her baby unearthed, inside there?

The sonogram also alarmed Emily, as it was scheduled overnight, the usually impassable doors of medical procedure swinging wide open to address her trouble. When she entered the office full of waiting women, Emily had the distinct impression she was cutting in line, promoted to the front by virtue of the magnitude of her affliction. Here, she wanted no special favors. Here, as in no other place, she wanted ordinary treatment, routine investigation. She wanted to blend with the masses and wait for hour upon irritating hour. She wanted corroborating statistics that said all of this was to be expected, within the norm. Frog and Toady, in whom she'd confided, stepped forward instantly to say that was so; there wasn't a medical procedure involving stirrups that they hadn't suffered.

"Cyst," Frog assured Emily.

"Hysterectomy, at worst," Toady went on.

They sat with their identical hazel eyes full of empathy, Emily's best friends. Her gratitude for their presence was supreme. They'd brought tequila and limes, hauled out the shot glasses and salt shakers from the cupboards, settled in for a spell. For reasons that eluded Emily, she was not yet ready to include her mother or sister in this news. She'd wait until they had to be included.

Over the scooped bowl of her pelvis floated the lubricated device.

She'd had sonograms with both children, and now missed the reassuring hoofbeats of their infant hearts. Hers thumped stolidly along, lonely and slow. "What?" she asked the technician, whose face was a murky turquoise in the monitor's reflected light, as if she were studying aquatic life-forms. She took notes but made no reply to Emily, who, superstitious, did not want to annoy her with further demands, as if the woman could produce a bad result with the flourish of her pen, whimsically.

Not only did there appear to be a mass in her left ovary, but her Pap smear results came back bad. These things were separate, Dr. Love explained, Emily back in his office wearing her paper apron. Now it was her cervix in question, her colon, her rectum, all of the adjoining organs.

"I feel like bruised fruit," Emily said, though what she really felt was rotten, gone radically bad.

"Cauterization," Frog told her.

"Hysterectomy," Toady repeated. "You can live without your female parts."

At her colposcopy, Emily shook noticeably. The technician showed no sympathy, leading her to a room and providing the ubiquitous paper garment. Emily had brought a lofty book, *The Journals of Virginia Woolf,* and tried to read while she waited, avoiding the menacing array of obstetrical equipment lining the shelf beside her table. There was something mad-scientist-like in the appliances, anachronistic as Bela Lugosi, a resemblance that wasn't reassuring. The doctor was a stocky woman with a great deal of makeup covering her acne-scarred face. She entered after giving an alarming rap at the door, smiled broadly, extended her hand, and told Emily to relax. They were always so sure you ought to calm down. That you *could*.

"Lean way, way back, and put those feet in the stirrups," she commanded.

Looking up at the ceiling, Emily noticed the poster someone had applied directly above her head. One of those infuriating blurred images that, under some hypnotic gaze, stopped vibrating long enough to reveal a band of dinosaurs or flock of birds. You were supposed to suspend some aspect of vision in a way Emily could only rarely achieve, stare into the middle ground like a somnambulist and then the picture would unveil itself to you.

"This'll sting," said the doctor. Emily lifted her head, peered between her own knees to see the magnified fishy eyes of the doctor as she studied Emily's cervix with a big scope.

"What is it?" Emily asked.

"There's something," the doctor replied, vaguely, squinting her amplified eyes, "something I can't see the end of."

"What do you mean, you can't see the end of it?"

"I'm going to do a biopsy." She wheeled herself toward a tray of tools, lifting a scalpel. Tears ran down the sides of Emily's face, pooling in her ears, dripping noisily on the paper bedcovering. Paper everywhere, rustling and plaguing. She could feel the scraping, the blade of cells that the doctor took away in a tube. She could imagine the peppery trail of cells left behind, their endlessness burning inside her. Before leaving, the doctor told Emily to dress, to take a sanitary pad from the drawer if she needed it, that she'd hear back in a week or two. Such dispassion, such cold evasiveness, as if Emily weren't obviously crying, as if she didn't ache, on top of the terror, as if there were no difference between a week or two. As soon as the door closed, the stocky ugly doctor gone, Emily jumped up and ripped that impenetrable poster off the ceiling, flung the pushpins across the room where they pinged on the blasted medical equipment, and then shredded the thick coated paper, left on the table a pile of bright-colored trash.

MEANWHILE, her son stayed happily with Winston. "When I was your age," Winston said to Roy at the kitchen table over playing cards, "I used to be afraid in this house. A lot."

"Scary house," Roy said. For a second, Roy envisioned that painting his uncle had taken away during the tornado warning last summer, the flames and anger, the mom with her burning broom and the dad with his shooting garden hose, birds dive-bombing the place . . . Winston was teaching him Twenty-one. Roy was winning, which meant he got to shell the pistachios. Kojak sat waiting for crumbs to fall. In his amazing way, Uncle Winston could make the dog yawn. All he had to do was look Kojak in the face, yawn himself, and the dog would yawn right back at him. Roy loved that trick.

"Sometimes I used to put a knife beside me," Winston said, patting his palm on the table surface.

Roy gazed up at the knives on his grandmother's magnetized holder above the sink. There were several that interested him, but he saw them as companions to one another rather than weapons, the cleaver was of course Dad and the serrated bread carver Mom, their children the smaller knives. One of those is what Winston had at the ready. Or perhaps a pocketknife, tiny blade folded neatly away in its abode with its small relatives.

"Hit me," Roy said, and Winston laid a three on his pile, making yet another perfect twenty-one. Roy clapped. "Will you make Kojak yawn?" he asked. "Please?"

"Later. I'm telling you about knives right now. Listen up. Knives are dangerous," his uncle insisted, gathering the hand, pushing the pistachios Roy's direction. "But being scared is dangerous, too."

"Okay! Now the yawning?"

"Now the yawning."

"STD HOTLINE," Mona said, answering the phone.

"Don't do that," her father said, after a pause. What he meant was, don't make me think I've dialed a wrong number. Don't make me think I've failed at something so simple as calling my own home. He could be so easily undone. How had Mona missed that fact, all these years?

"Where are you?" she asked. That was the important question.

"At Saint Francis. Please tell your mother. I don't know for how long."

Visiting Betty Spitz; his voice was more tired than irked. "Okay, Dad. Tell Betty hi. And Guido."

Her mother was jamming the vacuum cleaner against the base of a couch, bam, bam, bam, a fierce expression on her face. She cleaned this way, with a vengeance, with a fury. Yet she never complained about her mission in this life, was not bitter about the eighty-five hundred square feet of home she alone oversaw. She was a housewife, and with her it was a profession, one she'd embraced in a time when she didn't have to. She could have gone the career route; she could have hired a cleaning service. She could have asked her professor husband and urchin children to divide the labor with her. But it was clear that she took some pleasure in maintaining order. Emily claimed it was because she wished to push thoughts out of her mind, that dusting and scrubbing and rearranging and sorting was a way not to think. If their mother was in constant motion, she didn't have time to mope or get melancholy. At nightfall she was legitimately exhausted, tired in a way that sent her to sleep wearily fulfilled.

Mona considered her own tendency to sit at her west bedroom window brooding, staring out for hours, listening to music, waiting. Waiting and waiting. Maybe she should take up housework.

"Mom!" she yelled into the roar of the old vacuum. She waved her hands, slashed her throat with her flat hand to ask for a moment. The antique Electrolux died wheezing. Her mother looked up expectantly, a bandanna tied round her wrist so that she could blow her nose, as she was, in the tradition of the martyr, allergic to dust. "Mom, Dad's at the hospital. He'll be home late."

Her mother thanked her. Mona could not read her expression as she wiped the bandanna beneath her nose. Because she was going blind, her mother looked often to be intently studying you, but Mona didn't believe this was the case. Was she jealous of her husband's affection for Betty? It was not her mother's nature to reveal insecurity. Another kind of woman might have railed, nagged, mistrusted, but to give in to small-minded insecurity would betray a pettiness that was, to Mrs. Mabie, unseemly. She was not a silly jealous weak wife.

She raised her eyebrows, asking if there were more Mona wished to say.

"That's all." Mona shrugged. "Just that he doesn't know when he'll be home."

Her mother nodded, switched on her noisy cleaner, and resumed her assault on the sofa.

Mona and Emily disagreed about their mother. Mona claimed that she embodied patience, maternal affection, unconditional love. She knew everything, dark as well as beautiful, and embraced it all, choosing to celebrate only the good, absorb the evil, digest it, filter it, turn it pure. "She's the family's liver," Mona said one inspired drunken night. "She's processing our yuckiness."

Emily had another opinion. She thought that their mother had checked out early in the game. She thought her eye disease was psycho-somatic, symbolic. "She didn't want to see what was going on around her, and now she can't."

"She was going blind!" Mona said.

"She was blind before she went blind," Emily countered.

"You're cold."

"I'm honest."

"Just because you're not happy," Mona argued, "it doesn't mean you can't be glad for *her* happiness."

"Her happiness is so *blindered*. She walks around ignoring things. I spent six years of my life throwing up food in a bathroom during the day and stumbling home drunk at night, every single night. Where was she? Reading her books. Watering her plants. Spraying Pledge."

The past had a way of sneaking up like this and scaring Mona. She'd been happily ignorant, too, it hadn't just been their mother with tunnel vision. For many of Emily's troubled years Mona had been in her bedroom with her stuffed animals, listening to music, spinning a fantasy life for herself that had, as its props, many of the elements of her older sister's life. It made for a strange friction, now, to hear how miserable Emily's real life had been. From the outside, it had looked better than fine, and Mona felt that she'd somehow contributed to its horror by admiring it so, by wanting it for herself.

"What would your therapist make of this?" Emily had asked, frowning suddenly, analytical.

Mona thought, working on being smart. "She'd wonder what you were angry about now. Your anger about the past is justified, but it's in the past, over and done, so what is it these days that you're angry about? What makes you need to rehash the past to justify feeling the way you feel?"

"Really, that's what she'd say?"

Mona sighed. "Dunno. Maybe."

They'd pondered that briefly, then gone roller-skating, depositing Emily's children with their mother, zooming without speaking around and around and around the Joyland Rink. "*Joy*land," Emily shouted when she passed Mona; the name never failed to amuse them.

THE LAST thing Betty Spitz said to Professor Mabie was: "Not quite." As in, she wasn't ready?

"What's gonna be your last words?" his daughter Mona had asked him, when she was in second grade. It was a famous question, in family lore. *What's gonna be your last words?* Now he could not remember the last thing his mother had said to him, before death, nor his father, nor any of the others he'd known and lost. Their absence in the world was what he registered, the stunning erasure. Gone, forever; the house, empty. You had nowhere to hold them but in your mind, and that was an unreliable vessel, a sieve, a piece of permeable cloth where only the obvious bits of flotsam got caught, the unsubtle chunky nuggets of memory. Who knew the immaterial dissipation of soul? Or the petty dregs so stubbornly clutched? You sometimes visited the places where the dead had been, saw their motions or heard their phrases—you committed those movements and words yourself, dredged from who-knew-what river of reminiscence—and the dead would be there once again, vivid, in your whole body, animating you with ghostly gestures not your own, vital remains, these missing characters whose only existence lived within you.

"Not quite," she'd said, perhaps meaning that death wasn't turning out to be what she'd expected, a slight variation on the theme she'd been considering for years. This was the day after Thanksgiving. True to her truest nature, she'd struggled to make him laugh, even as she could hardly part her lips. "Light in the tunnel," she murmured, the preface to her favorite joke: That light at the end of the tunnel? That was the oncoming train. She was sleepy, which was not her nature, and Professor Mabie had given up fighting his tears, which ran steady as drainpipe rain down his face. Had he asked her something? Had she been answering? "Not quite." And what would the question have been?

This was two days before she died. Everything was the way that had become normal. You could get impatient for an ending. No roommate but the bird, Guido clacked in his cage. Professor Mabie stood surveying the sight, the oddness now that it no longer seemed odd.

"This won't do," Betty said, "you upright, me lying down. How can anything go right with us like this?" It took some strength to hold one index finger up, and the other one flat, illustrating her point. Her hands trembled.

So he got into bed with her. It was crowded. They stared at the ceiling, their hands chaste on their chests. The smell was not good. Nausea passed over him like ether.

"Finally," Betty said, gaze held upward. And he knew what she meant. At last they had arrived in bed together. For years they'd circumnavigated physical touch, both aware of its loadedness. Later, he supposed, he'd look back on this scene as tragic. Later, in bed beside his wife, he would have nights recalling the visceral fact of lying next to Betty Spitz—a bodily memory of her dry papery presence, late and guilty intimacy, appealing unappeal—layers of tragic enigma. But for now it seemed daring, riveting. Every now and then arrived a moment that vibrated like this, one in which almost anything could happen and the course of the future hung in the balance. He wished a nurse would arrive and express something pleasing on her face. He wanted to see how this looked to someone else. His unaccustomed unconventionality.

"You're hoping somebody walks in, aren't you?" Betty said. Her voice, flat, gravelly, disappointed, made him understand that she loved him, had always loved him, had wanted to lie in bed with him long ago and for a long while. She didn't need witnesses. She'd had enough of novelty. She wanted nothing to do with wonder. She wanted him.

"I *hate* your wife," she said passionately. "I always have. She doesn't appreciate—"

"Please don't talk," he said. "It sounds like it hurts."

"It's not hurting *me*," she said. "You have to let me talk." He assented. And with a great deal of trouble she told him what she believed. That he had been a caretaker too long, for too many, including his wife, who was weak. "I hate weakness."

"She's not weak."

"You need some relief."

"I'm fine," he assured her.

Betty nodded. Her eyes seemed preternaturally open, slightly dry, their surface lusterless. Oxygen flowed through the clear pretzel tubing into her nostrils. She rested for a moment, and Professor Mabie did not object. The pillow they shared was unforgivably firm; he himself could sleep on nothing but a barely down-filled model that conformed to his neck. The ceiling above had little to offer, a series of flimsy pockmarked panels hiding the wires and pipes and insulation. Functionally efficient: pop one out and you could replace or repair whatever had gone wrong inside. Nothing like Professor Mabie's own house, its ceilings of lattice and plaster, mortar and mouse dens. A physician might wish the human body were designed like this hospital, accessible and delineated, a structure of plastic pieces, all of equal weight and volume, you could snap apart and inspect, discard the faulty part, pick up its substitute at the hardware or toy store.

"But *caretaking*," Betty began again, the word like a curse, "it can't be satisfactory for long, can it?" This made Professor Mabie recall his daughter Emily's ridiculous husband, Barry, and how Emily had ultimately failed in reforming him. He didn't like to think about Barry, a young man utterly unworthy of his daughter's ministrations. He could not even be said to have a particularly reassuring gene pool, so obviously chemically unbalanced. But Emily's attachment to the boy, the blatant way she required a project, a soul to salvage, seemed clearer than his own possible need for the same. After all, he'd never sought it out. It had always fallen into his lap, in the way of family obligation. A person did not abandon his family.

"*You* took care of me," he told Betty, which was the truth. She had been his shoulder to lean against, when need be, more so than his wife, which was probably why he didn't want to hear Betty bad-mouth the woman. Betty had been his wise colleague, the spirit he looked to for guidance, his best friend. "There's always someone who's restless, in a marriage," she'd told him years before. "That's one thing I've noticed. The restless one, and the one who's steadfast. She holds on, your wife, and you twitch. I bet you chase women in your dreams. Don't you? A woman at a cocktail party, who's always leaving the room? You're always following *that* one, seeing her back, her heel."

He had envisioned the woman as Betty spoke, a figure from many dreams, bare-shouldered, beautiful, elusive. True, it had never been his wife he pursued through those ephemeral doors, but it had never been Betty, either.

"What are you thinking?" he asked now, lying beside her two days before she would die, hands clutched over a heart pounding to hear that she loved him. Why did he need to hear what he already knew? What made him want to make a dying woman work so?

"None of your beeswax," she said raspily. "But I'll tell you this: You are going to have to forgive Winston. That's all there is to it. You are not the sort of person who makes war on his family. If you don't forgive him pretty soon, you're going to hate yourself. You can't even invite him to come see me, can you?"

"He's—"

"*He's* not the issue," she said. Often her advice concerning the children was for Professor Mabie's ultimate benefit, explaining what otherwise would purely have frightened him. It was she who had convinced Professor Mabie to send Mona to a psychologist. On the morning of her suicide attempt, when his wife and daughter had ridden off in the ambulance to St. Francis he had stood blinking before the telephone. His son was in prison, his daughter on her way in a screaming ambulance toward the hospital. Whatever domain he'd felt secure in overseeing had been exposed as severely corrupt. He did not know whom to call first, so he consulted his own desires. To whom did he *want* to talk?

Betty was not surprised to hear that Mona had overdosed. Saddened, but not surprised. "You've thought of killing yourself," she admonished him. "Admit it."

But he hadn't, really. Too much of his life had been about *not* killing himself. About saving himself and everyone else around him. He was the one who dipped into the pocket, who held down the fort, who offered the strong shoulder, who reminded one and all to be sure and buckle up, who inflated the lifeboat as the ship went down. He paid insurance bills, he consulted *Consumer Reports*. His role, in this universe, was preserving life, not playing recklessly with it. No, he had never considered suicide. Suicide, he thought, was for sissies. As he and Betty talked, he understood how angry his daughter had made him, how completely besieged by rage. How dare she ruin what he had worked so hard to protect?

"You're mad at her," Betty said calmly. "That's all right. Just admit it, and move on. You have every right to be furious."

"I am furious."

"Of course you are." Despite the early hour, Betty had been lucid and smart. Nothing in the whole wide weird world would ever shock her. How could he explain his gratitude? Every now and then, Professor Mabie had heard her inhale on her cigarette, clank her coffee cup against the receiver. He had been pacing in the upstairs hall, the site of his daughter's sickness just twenty feet away. He'd cleaned up her mess first, sponged and mopped and swept, vomit, blood, the icy mud tracked in by EMTs. It had seemed imperative that he erase the evidence as quickly as possible. Only afterward, listening to Betty's even breathing, did he ask himself why. On the other end of the line he'd heard Guido the parrot put in his two cents—"Can't be trusted," the bird said.

"Therapy," Betty advised. "For her, and for you, too. The whole fam-damily." He couldn't feel right about spending money that way. He could not be convinced that a complete stranger would ever fully understand the complications of his life, let alone be entrusted with its details. He was a private person, raised with a firm belief in strong character, taking what was coming. For therapy, he used his friend Betty. She knew that his mentality was still one wherein people snapped out of their problems. They did not solve anything by talking them to death. Talk is cheap, he liked to say, although in the instance of the psychologist, talk was not cheap. It was quite pricey.

Months later, when Mona had been taking medication and attending weekly sessions, when she was out of the woods, alive, still his living daughter, he said to Betty, wryly, "I hope she's happy."

"Oh, bub," said Betty sadly, not recognizing his tone, taking him at his word—was there anything more disconcerting than flip sarcasm construed as true sentiment? "She'll never be as happy as she ought to be," Betty went on to tell him, and he felt thoroughly chagrined, like a shallow tightwad, inadequate in his appreciation of either his daughter or his friend.

Now, in her hospital bed, Betty said, "He likes you." It took a moment for Professor Mabie to understand she meant his son.

"He doesn't like me," he disagreed.

"No, I said, 'He's *like* you.' " She thought his son was like him. "He's like you." Betty then reached her far hand out of sight to fiddle a button. The bed began to hum and rise, the two of them lifted together, as if suddenly exalted.

"Oh, my," said Professor Mabie.

"Shocking," she said, blinking those large dry eyes, inhaling methodically. She loved her W.S.U. faculty ID, the one that promoted the school's wheat-shock mascot and called itself "Shocker Card," featuring her leering face.

Betty had nothing more to offer, in the way of conversation; in her own words, she'd shot her wad. It would have been tidy for her to die, then, him alongside, their thoughts in harmony, but she did not. She died two days later, when no one but her ill-tempered bird was near. Last words would be withheld, Professor Mabie assumed, Guido holding his big little prehensile tongue. Betty's voice and inflection, inside that green creature, keeping her secrets behind his ugly red eyes.

Eventually Professor Mabie had climbed down from Betty's deathbed, leaving her raised nearer the ceiling as she approached sleep, *lulled,* he liked to think, as in *lullaby.* She was murmuring as she lost consciousness. *What's gonna be your last words?* "Not quite," she'd said. Or perhaps, "Knock twice."

HE INHERITED the bird, much the way he'd inherited his mother's dog. Not a fan of pets, he turned this one, like the dog, over to his daughter Mona. Mona hung Guido's cage in her bedroom and studied its contents. She'd not owned a bird before. At the zoo, she passed by the talking birds quickly, as she did the baboons. Animals with human attributes scared her. Mightn't they mimic or mock? Unforgiving as a mirror, blunt as a big-mouth child?

Like her answering machine, Guido was liable to say or not say anything. His feathers sometimes flared, as if he were prepared to fly away. Occasionally in the night he would yell at her, incomprehensible syllables, language from startled dreams. Perhaps not even his own dreams, but those of his owner's, a human nightmare in his mouth, its dreamer dead and gone, her dream left incoherent in the head of a vacuous creature.

Or perhaps not so vacuous, for he seemed to study Mona, too. He liked to move himself from his perch to the wrought-iron bars of the cage, cling and slide three or four inches downward, angled like a snowboarder, skillfully, then bob, peck, preen, shout. He was an old man, arms behind his back, thoughtful, philosophical, grumpy, dressed in a not-natty green suit, bib stained maraschino red.

What could they think, these animals, apes with their fingers and dogs with their eyelashes? Poor Guido with his gullet of Betty Spitz, laughter and hacking and whimsy and criticism? When Winston visited Mona's room, he brought a spray bottle of water. "Shut up," he'd say, and aim, and the bird would raise its wings, shake like a dog, like a drunk, glory in the mess. On each upper wing was a bright blue spot, like an epaulet, hidden till he flexed proud as a general. "Little Dictator," Winston called him. "Little Dic."

Other times the bird paced, as if plotting his escape, think, think, think. "He reminds *me* of Dad," Mona confessed. "Of all professors. Kind of eccentric? Or misunderstood?"

"What's to understand? He's a bird. His brain is the size of a peanut. If you turned him loose, he'd kill himself before he got beyond the city limits. Don't go soft on me, Mona."

But she was afraid she'd already done so, gone soft, sentimental and sad. Having your heart broken did that to you. Occasionally she tried to believe it was a worthy outcome. Look how close to the rest of humanity she'd come, suffering rejection, a wounded ego, what her therapist had named a narcissistic injury. The playing field was even; misery had found its own level, the survivors wandered wearing the same shabby clothes and rejected lethargy, recognizing one another. They hung around at bars. They watched late-night television and called psychics, they read their horoscopes and hoped for five-star days. They sought willing ears into which they would spill their tired story, familiar as all the saddest songs, full of the same clichés and hyperbole.

They left their answering machines alone for long periods of time, as if, unwatched, something might germinate. As if they didn't care, one way or the other, what that heartless red light said.

It had been two weeks since she'd spoken to Nicholas Dempsey, and she wished she'd never met him. She wished she didn't know how much she loved him. She desired to return to a feeling of distance from the rest of the miserable human race.

"Bonbon," she told Guido the parrot. "Strumpet." What word might he like to learn? What might she do to make his life more fun?

KOJAK did not like Guido. The bird scared him. Hanging above his head when he visited his favorite human's room, the bird kept scritching about, mysteriously, ominously. Every now and then he would give the dog a command: "Shut up!" or "Sit down!" Without exception the dog would startle and comply. A being hated its instincts, sometimes.

5

"WHAT IS IT you like about Marilyn Monroe?" Mona asked Marty Song on the telephone. She was drunk, still drinking, and talking on the family phone, downstairs, while everyone else appeared to be in bed. It was 1:30 A.M. and although Marty lived only three blocks away, it was better to converse over the phone. Ever since their night at AA, Mona felt like talking to Marty. He'd proved reliable in the way of family that evening, and she needed another family member, she thought, someone who might grant heartache its particular rightful place in the realm of misery. Someone who didn't have a history with her and her monster breakups. Marty had time. Marty was game. "You weren't sleeping?" she added.

"Please," he responded. "Getting ready to pass out, but not sleeping." Some nights they played "Is It Passing Out or Falling Asleep?" If you woke up in your clothing, it was probably passing out. If you had to ask where you were, it was almost surely passing out. If you couldn't name the party beside you in bed, it was definitely passing out. "What are *you* drinking? he queried."

"Rum and orange juice, she retorted saucily."

"Healthy. Vitamin C. What was the question?"

"Marilyn." His bedroom was full of Marilyn Monroe memorabilia, and she announced it as a topic merely to hear him talk, not because she cared. Who was she to judge a person's obsession, her own room with its massive menagerie of stuffed animals, her heart full of Nicholas Dempsey?

Marty obliged. Marilyn was beautiful, vulnerable, sexy, pure, elusive, completely chameleon-like. "But you can tell," he said emphatically, "she's really suffering. She's really unhappy. It's like behind all the parts she plays is this very scarred girl. That's what I like, the way she's a mess."

"That's what Winston likes about people, too."

"And her walk, very cool walk, a swagger, really."

"She's got a butt the size of Idaho."

"Psshaw. It came with the narrow waist."

"Maybe I like to see people's messiness, too," Mona postulated. "Even though I think it's sick, to like people because they suffer. Maybe that's why I'm talking to you, you big piece of damaged goods. How am *I* a mess?"

"Huh. Well, you're a romantic, and that's a problem. But I only hang with romantics, so you're lucky there."

"Lucky me."

"And I guess I'd say you kind of live in your sister's shadow."

"And?"

"You measure yourself against her?"

Mona nodded, which of course Marty wouldn't have known. "That's smart," she said, surprised. She tilted her glass back, ice dropping on her face as she sucked down the last of her drink.

"I have a high IQ, believe it or not."

The Mabie family telephone was located on a counter before a mirror, so that when you sat on the twirling stool in the pantry you could lean your elbows on the counter, plastic receiver at your ear, and study your big reflection. While talking to Marty, Mona worked on her smile. She had noticed that Marilyn Monroe's top teeth always showed when she smiled. Mona's top teeth, the pretty ones, did not show when she smiled. She created a smile that included them, but it was hard to remember to perform it when genuinely amused, and seemed forced when not. The lighting was soft here in the pantry, in the mirror, always flattering. It made a good place for trying out facial expressions. Many times Mona had rehearsed or recapped conversations. "Oh yeah," she mouthed, head twitching slightly, eyes exasperated, as if tossing off something inconsequential. "I love you," she mouthed. She liked the way the tongue worked on the letter *L*. *L*'s were good; *M*'s were not, because she had thin lips and a tight jaw, and *M* seemed to highlight the absence of sensuality in her mouth. Ideally, the mouth would hinge open and the teeth would glisten, like old Marilyn Monroe. She had the amazing ability to look great when slack-jawed. In fact, as far as Mona could tell, Marilyn Monroe preferred having her photo shot when slack-jawed. Marty Song's room, his shrine to Marilyn, was truly dazzling, dozens of photos, calendars, even refrigerator magnets on his metal file cabinet that made her into a kind of paper doll, several outfits with which to clothe her, negligee and ball gown and army fatigue jacket. Mona had studied them intensely one stoned night, thoughtfully focused. The woman had changeable looks, thin in one photo, fat in another, frowsy, washed, one minute an ad for racy lingerie, the next for pure Ivory soap. Her eyes were vaguely wide-set, often hooded, rimmed perfectly with a steadily drawn smoky eyeliner. Clothing seemed always to be about to fall off of her, slick as oil on her shimmering shoulders. She couldn't keep her straps up or her skirts down. But a smile always lingered near her, as if she were perennially prepared to be happy. That couldn't have been true, given her life and death. Still, it seemed that way, in the archive of her photos.

"Girls will feel inadequate in your room," Mona told Marty now.

"Then we'll be even," he said.

She nodded once more, making her trademark grunt. She liked herself looking dry-witted, not easily amused. Alternately, she liked herself looking alert and quick to laugh, that smile playing around her lips. When was she ever going to be happy with her face? When was she going to recognize it as strictly hers when she saw it in the mirror? It seemed always to possess the expressions and moods of others, borrowed like ill-fitting hats or eyeglasses, wrong in style or prescription.

"Hang on," Marty said. "Lemme unload this other call." He blipped her into electronic limbo while attending to his call waiting. She talked to Marty downstairs because she could not stand being in the presence of her private phone and its answering machine, the empty window that reported her injured heart. Zero. If you pushed the button, the mechanical voice merely confirmed the visual reading: "You have *no* messages." Whom had they hired to say this with such evident pleasure? She wished she'd kept one of Nicholas Dempsey's on the tape, a sweet drunken one in which he confessed his love. For a long time he'd said "I don't know" instead of what he did know, which was that he loved her. Hearing him say "I don't know" a dozen times in a row on her answering machine had used to make Mona's chest vibrate, as if someone had installed a blender there, left on whirl.

"I'm back," Marty said. He was famous for being good on the telephone and was popular; Mona felt pleased to be his priority. He was good maybe because of his laziness, his stonedness, his simple aimlessness, his ease with repartee, and, in her case, his long familiarity with her family. Television, telecommunication, telephones: he had a desk like mission control, rolling chair and headset, imminently tuned in and turned on, big bong ever ready to be put to use. Also, like Mona's mother, Marty Song looked to be someone who would not leave town, who would not feel the rippling discontent that drove road trips or college degrees or doomed romantic quests. Marty relied on the K.I.S.S. motto: He was *keeping it simple, stupid,* blissfully looking at Marilyn Monroe on his walls, greeting his mother daily at the breakfast table to share a meal, doing his mindless delivery job while wearing his white CoCo's Chocolate cap, listening to music, carrying on his nodding acquaintance with a slew of Wichitans, watching twilight reruns of the timeless couples in the seminal sitcoms of the previous decades—Ralph and Alice, Rob and Laura, Bob and Emily, Sam and Diane—Marty anesthetized, ready for a warm dinner, maybe a visit from an old friend, maybe an exchange on the Internet, and, now, chatting with Mona late at night. He had his real life, and he had his fantasy one, in what he named perfect balance. He masturbated every day, he revealed, when she asked about his not having a girlfriend—didn't he have somewhere he should be going, dating, that sort of thing? Didn't it bother him, no sex life?

"I have a sex life. I have a very reliable sex life. I submit to the jury that masturbation is a sex life."

"And that's satisfactory?"

"Whoa ho ho ho there little Mona, let's not cast stones just yet. Let's look at the evidence before we start disparaging with conventional wisdom. First, I have no need to spawn offspring, so the primary brute urge for procreation is basically a moot point with this cowpoke. Second, self-abuse is readily available, right there at your fingertips, twenty-four hours a day, seven days a week. And it's predictable as well as cheap—"

"Like Burger King—"

"Okay, we'll go with that. It's not gourmet, I'll give you that. But you know what you're going to get, you leave with your basic needs met. Afterward, you can go to sleep instead of be sensitive and talk. You know, afterward, some girls cry."

"Right," Mona said, being a cryer herself.

"Okay, masturbation is not always exciting, I'll confess. Sometimes it's like going through the motions, there's A, there's B, here comes C, come on C, let's go C. . . . Sometimes I'd like a little something else, it's true, but let's talk about the relationship thing. Let's weigh some options, do a little analysis, costs, benefits. A girlfriend is trouble. Too much trouble. Someone is *always* getting hurt. Someone's heart is *always* getting busted in a thousand pieces, and if it's not me getting dumped, then I'm responsible for doing it to someone else. Who needs it?"

"Not me," Mona admitted.

"And how long did the good part last?"

"I dunno. A few months?"

"Okay. And how good were they, *really?* Total infatuation is about a three-month, max, experience. Then there's games, which are a drag, and in your case you have the mistress thing to deal with, little miss bimbo, tucked away in your room. You can't have him whenever you want, you have to wait to see him, sneak around, settle for leftovers, get jealous of the wife. You're revved for a few months, going a thousand rpms, night and day it's a mystery, way exciting, and now that it's gone you're spinning your wheels in the blackest, skankiest old pit of a hole. Surely you can see the advantages of self-abuse? The even keel. The self-containment. The all-in-one aspect, like a TV dinner or a really good pocketknife. I rest my case. By the way, you'll notice how the hand falls just there, falls there and knows just what to do. None of that clumsy getting-to-know-all-about-you business."

"True, true, true. But *every* day?"

"Every cotton-pickin' one."

"Wow."

"It's not like you wear out your batteries."

"I guess not. Who broke your heart, Marty? Who made you do this, this TV dinner giving up?"

He was uncharacteristically silent. "Let me get another drink, and then I'll tell you. You come with me, into the kitchen. Here we are in front of the fridge, hear the ice?"

"Yep." Mona stretched her family's phone cord as far as the liquor cabinet, reaching for the nearest bottle, one of brandy.

"And here's the gin, glugh, glugh, and now for some lime, you have your quinine for malaria, your citrus for rickets . . . You know where gin comes from? Juniper berries. Just one more reason to hug a tree." There was rummaging, a drawer opening, another, the reportage on the knife slice and squeezing, the all-important and usual argument for the small rather than large bottle of tonic, Marty's pet peeve of tonic water's premature flatness. "Ahh," he said, taking a long sip in which Mona could hear his throat working. For a second, she summoned Nicholas Dempsey, his scotch going down, and her heart fell. She hated melancholy; melancholy sucked. From the brandy bottle she took a mouthful of fire, let it burn down her throat, shook her head, and grimaced at the mirror in a not very attractive way.

"I'm going to tell you now," Marty said, "I'm going to tell you my problem, my fucked-up love thing, but I want you to say something right back. Do not hang up. Do not sit there in what we call dead air. Speak immediately."

Mona agreed, swore, then prepared to hear her sister's name. Was she strong enough to hear Emily's name, to have Emily win once again? Emily always won. Marty would at least understand her sarcastic reply, her—

"Your brother," said Marty Song. "I fell in love with your brother in seventh grade, and I'll never get over him." Ice rattled over on Devonshire Ave. "Say something, you have to say something, you promised."

"Winston?"

"Winston."

"Winston?"

"Winston."

"Winston?"

"Were you going to say anything besides Winston?"

"I'm working on it."

"Work harder."

"I thought you liked girls."

"I do like girls. And I like one boy, your brother. I don't know why."

Mona sighed, taking another mouthful of brandy. "Nicholas Dempsey used to say 'I don't know' all the time, even when he knew, just because he was embarrassed."

"I adore your brother."

"I love him too. If he wasn't my brother, I'd be *in* love with him. I don't think you're gay, Marty. I really don't."

"Neither do I. Who's worried? I just don't think I'm going to find somebody I like better than Winston to get married to, or whatever. I keep meeting these girls, thinking, well, maybe . . . And then I'll realize how much better a time I have hanging out with Winston—"

"And you can always masturbate."

"Right. So, there you have it."

"Winston is a crush magnet. He collects them like nobody's business. Everyone's got a crush on him, even my grandmother, and look where that went. I'm flabbergasted, Marty. Really. I don't know what to say."

" 'Flabbergasted' is a start. People always say 'I don't know' when they know," he added.

"I've noticed that." The room was now at a tilt; Mona was preparing for a night in which she passed out rather than fell asleep. "You want me to tell you a secret, too?"

"But of course. Nothing would make me feel better than hearing a humdinger of a secret from you."

"Okay. Sometimes, when *I* masturbate, which is not, by the way, every day, but sometimes when I do, I use the electric mixer."

"The mixer? As in cookie dough? Eggs? *That* electric mixer?"

"The very one."

"Yargh, Mona. That seems somehow dangerous. I mean, doesn't the button say *scramble*?"

"Well, I only use one of the beaters. And I put a sock over it. A thick sock. Athletic." Mona felt like an idiot. There was something too pathetic about confessing a masturbation tool. "It's a girl thing," she added lamely. "Like a vibrator, but easier to hide."

"Easier to mail order, too," Marty said, getting into the spirit of the thing. "Sometime I want to inventory your kitchen. I think we've just barely scratched the surface of a very interesting subject."

They sat companionably embarrassed and intimate over the telephone, educated about each other, forgiving. This was friendship,

Mona thought, not getting grossed out, accepting your friend's weirdness. Not thinking less of him for it, not feeling sullied by its fact. This was what had been missing between her and Nicholas Dempsey, friendship. He was not her friend. What they had could not have been love, could it, in the absence of friendship? This was a drunken illumination, but she trusted it, she would cling to it, she would take it to bed with her so that she could pass out.

"Okay, nighty-night," she told Marty Song. It was 2:12 in the morning.

"I'm gonna sleep like a baby," he declared.

"Me too," she said, "kicking and wailing and wetting myself all night long."

6

FUCKING IS A form of fighting, Emily thought as she walked thin and swift as a pair of scissors along the street. Insights hit her sometimes like hailstones, icy ping to the skull. *Fucking is a form of fighting.* She was taking her third walk of the day; she grew so anxious sitting still that she was forced to act, and dog walking led her most simply out the door, Kojak consistently available, grudgingly anchored on his leash. Never in his ratty life had Jackoff justified his existence until now. Outside, in the dry winter air, Emily made herself think of things other than her potential cancer.

She recalled the purely physical urge to hurt her ex-husband, to bite his neck, to bend his penis, to buck her hips against him until the knobs of her pelvic bones impressed. There was anger in that, not tenderness, not particularly love. "Whatsa matter?" he used to mock her, high and slurpy. "Aren't you getting enough attention?"

"No," she said, eyeing the rubbery tendon in his neck as if to sever it. His attention was of the limp heavy variety, the long-term taking-for-granted sort, and she wanted more—rigidity, rage, a run for her money. She wanted a passion competitive enough to clench its fist. Jerking sideways, she sought the angle that better suited her, impatient, a gesture meant to convey her displeasure with his slackness, his uninspired anesthetized soft sexual blasé. Naked and entangled, she was beating him up, but he wasn't even aware they were having a fight. It seemed her job to pummel him into action.

And, Emily thought, sex is like tragedy, turning a corner, turning to another metaphorical mental calisthenic, yanking the dog up short when he couldn't read her mind. "Moron," she called Kojak, because he was available, because he made an excellent punching bag, because hurting him wasn't taxing. Sex was tragic because it declines and ends, rises and falls like fortune and fate and a satisfying story, introduction, flirtation, climax, denouement, disappointment, and then the resolute closed covers of a completed book. And sex was also like returning home after an absence. You embrace, you kiss—or you yell and cry and hate. These emotions reside within the same web called your marriage. "*Fuck you,*" her husband had said to her, more than once. He'd been twenty-two when they met, Emily twenty-seven. "Fuck you" was casual in his mouth, could be spoken as a joke or epithet or salutation, in funny accents and at inappropriate moments, in lieu of "thank you" or "eat me" or "no shit," but it was never so elastic for Emily—as if the five years between them represented a whole generation, its fuddy-duddy shockability.

She'd learned a great deal about fighting, living with Barry, and maybe she felt grateful. It was so unlike living with her own family, where people merely got their feelings hurt, maybe fled a room or slammed a door. No grand outbursts, no boxed ears. It wasn't their style. They did not outright speak their minds, opting instead for the festering mode of heartache and embitterment.

But Barry permitted Emily to glimpse her family with true distance. He did not find them daunting, or entertaining, or quirkily endearing. He thought they talked too much—and about one another, of all dull things. They *did* too little. He himself owned a powerful truck he liked to attach gadgets to and drive through the city listening to pounding reggae and rap music, heel of his palm active on the steering wheel. His money came from a trust fund, an arrangement that required him to go annually to Florida to visit an aunt and uncle who were his only remaining relatives. For these trips he saved an arsenal of drugs, floating armed and immune through the obligatory weekend, giggling as he wandered the retirement community grounds, cheerfully performing the small duties of repair in his aunt and uncle's condominium, knocking golf balls into ponds, cutting a dashing figure among the blue-rinse crowd at the swimming pool. Back in Wichita, he was consummately unfettered, finding his companionship with *friends,* people he often pointedly told Emily that he had selected rather than resorted to, as one did with family, that bunch who had no choice but to hang with you.

Up ahead the dangerous cars rushed by on Douglas Avenue. As usual, Emily could not seem to stop herself from plunging west, into the arctic wind in the direction of her old house, dragging ungrateful Kojak after her on his leash. What form of self-punishment was this, putting her face constantly up to be slapped by the sight of her failure?

She didn't like to slow down too noticeably before the house, its current occupants still tenderly new to the place, their impact upon it not yet evident. They were no doubt prioritizing, making lists of where to begin, lamenting the failure of the former inhabitants, cursing the previous owners who'd let their home go to hell.

Emily concurred, felt the proper guilty shame: she'd made a commitment to the structure, she thought, to the literal house itself. She'd pledged to aid it in its function of protection, shelter, warmth, family, and she'd not lived up to her end of the bargain. The house had tried, she thought. Its floors had sustained the weight of refrigerators and motorcycle engines, raucous dancing and cartwheels, the incessant clatter of falling silverware and toys and tools, the clicking toenails of visiting dogs. Its roof had runneled off rain, snow, sleet, mulberries, BB pellets, bird guano. The house couldn't be held responsible for the damage it had endured, the battered back porch, the broken clay tiles, the patches of plaster everywhere, outside and in, that had fallen as if under mortar fire, the shattered full-length, funhouse-like mirror, the scorched nook over the kitchen stove, the incriminating cigarette burns in the carpet. Its walls had stood, despite the assault of noise and Crayola and simple brute pounding. The frames hadn't split when the doors were slammed. The chandelier had swung without dropping. The bathroom tile had held firm when the sink had been ripped free.

It was either the sink, or her, she understood as Barry muscled it from the wall and flung it. She could drive him to this, inspire finally fury, make him want to hit her, to shake her and shut her up. "Shut up," he would plead, begging because he was never as good at words, because the way she bested him was cumulative and invisible, impossible to explain, those verbal nets, all turned to vapor and blown away when the sink landed on the floor at her feet. From the wall they watched water pulse instead of blood, both stunned and impressed by what they could do together: they fucked, they fought, they'd made a baby, they'd made a mighty mess. The trusty pipes had sent water onto the cool tile, faithful in their blind function, no matter the mayhem, the enraged man and the bitchy woman and the whimpering child. Her marriage inside this house had been a wrecking ball, loose and calamitous, and despite the dumb pendulous heft of her mistake, the house still stood, withstood, rocking on its foundation and yet here.

And no one had ever known, the walls and windows just that impenetrable. Enclosed spaces were the dangerous ones, she thought, locked doors and airtight glass, houses and cars, those soundproof bubbles of domestic secrecy dotting the landscape, on lawn or street, containing within the chaotic and unhinged. Once, she and Barry had begun struggling in their van on the highway, sending the vehicle from one side of the road to the other, half-joking, half-sincere, punching, lurching, they wished to injure each other. They wanted a crash. The intact shell had a desire to fly into pieces. But those structures had not broken. Emily and Barry had crawled out of the car, away from the house, apart from each other and into other lives like those spindly little crabs on the beach, scavenging shell to shell. Now Emily lived only within her own cavity, the body itself, a functional package inside which a cancer might be burning, like a charcoal briquette, radiant and smoldering.

At her ankles Jackoff began turning tight circles, ready to shit on Emily's foot if she didn't move fast enough. "You are an absolute asshole," she murmured, quickly unfurling his leash. She turned her attention to her former next-door neighbors', checking for witnesses. These were the ones who might have heard, known. But they'd given no indication of objecting, no sense of looking askance particularly. Tonight they appeared to be preparing one of their famous winter barbecues. They had long ago tiled the majority of their front yard, fenced it with white wrought iron, hung Chinese lanterns from the catalpa branches, installed outdoor heaters and stereo speakers and patio furniture, decked the place out in blazing tiki lamps and a fancy gas grill. It seemed you could flip a switch and the party would begin, rain or shine, the elements be damned, Las Vegas in the Midwest. The Shindigs, her brother Winston had dubbed them, a jolly middle-aged alcoholic couple, retired Texans whose grown daughters came to visit with their swarms of impervious blond children. "You can just go to Hallelujah!" the

Shindigs exclaimed, so smug to sidestep profanity. Every variety of lawn ornamentation or patio improvement they owned: swimming pool, hot tub, Ping-Pong, hammock, glider, volleyball, croquet, fountain, statue. They were garish and generous, drunk and raucous, dressed in the gaudy colors of tropical birds. When Barry grew bored with Emily's complaints, he would wander over to visit the Shindigs and listen to their Republican ranting, laughing hysterically. Among the three of them they shared a love of the superficial, the festive glow of chemical alteration, never mind the stage set or sound track. The Shindigs had enjoyed her husband but Emily they seemed to pity, or perhaps fear. She had a graduate degree, after all, and no capacity for bawdy jokes. She always asked for dry red wine, and they never had any.

No way would she reveal her current problem. Emily walked by, catching a whiff of cigarettes, of bourbon, of roasting pork. What did this combination remind her of? Not just the Shindigs, but something further away, more elusive and melancholy. She stopped once more, summoned from the other side of her life, the one belonging purely to recalled senses, the one that could, as it had now, literally stop her in her tracks. Her grandmother's house, before it was Billy's house, a Sunday meal long ago, those curtains drifting on the hot western wind, the black oscillating fan, the ham glistening on the table, deep pink pincushion full of clove, the bourbon decanter lifted from the sideboard. "How Dry I Am" its music box tinkled out. Her beguiling grandmother, who loved the fat ease of a Sunday, whiskey and ham, a ride on the front porch glider after, children's tired heads on grown-up laps, train whistle in the distance. Nineteen sixty-five, Emily guessed. Her age then the one of Roy now. What would constitute her little son's nostalgia? What odor, what wind, what sweet sentimental taste?

"Emily Mabie!" She'd been spotted. Lois Shindig minced over her white tiles wearing a muumuu and a hooded sweatshirt, white earmuffs made of rabbit fur, leading with a very long skinny cigarette. "Hon," she said, "are you iyull?"

Ill, Emily deciphered. Was she ill?

"Kinda."

"You look a little under the weather. Come have a toddy. Dad's got a Hot Pot just overflowing of buttered rum. Dad, lookit who's here."

"Dad," she called him. "Mother," Al Shindig addressed his wife. Barry could never get enough of their goofiness. They cheered him up immeasurably, their desire to have fun, to loll and laugh, to share the wealth of their funky inebriants. Still partying, all these years later, nothing would ever step into their lives to disrupt this routine. They were blessed, as if their refusal to dive below the surface had ensured them a smooth ride right over the top. Emily sighed, pulling recalcitrant Jackoff as she followed her former neighbor across the tiled yard through the porch door and into the party, florid sixty-something friends, comfortable in rattan chairs and white loafers, as if it weren't 26 degrees outdoors and due to snow. As if they'd taken a cruise together to the Bahamas. Even the dog was welcome, the two yapping Shindig pugs circling him just the way their owners circled the human guests, ready to play, tails perky with fun.

"Anus face," Emily's brother had called these dogs, their punched flaccid heads.

"What's old Barry up to?" the Shindigs asked.

Old Barry. "He's in Florida," Emily said. His divorce from her had coincided with a drug deal gone wrong; he'd narced on a half dozen of his friends just to keep himself from prison. He was a coward, at heart, without stamina or loyalty. Fortunately, he had an aunt ready to welcome him back, a maternal compulsion prepared to open its arms and claim him. Had Emily ever been more than a surrogate mother to Barry? A younger model, granted, brighter and sexier, but just as willing to take care of him? He had a need to be held, sometimes, hugged tight against his own self-destructiveness, reassured that Emily was not mad at him. He was not unlike little Roy, in this way. Perhaps that had marked the beginning of the end of their workable arrangement, the arrival of a real child, a bona fide baby. Emily had discovered the true object of her own motherly affection, and could no longer be happy shoring up her husband, being his designated driver, his bail bondsman, his support system.

The real end, the one Emily would never tell a single soul, had come about when Barry had permitted little three-year-old Roy to get hold of a hit of LSD. It hadn't been intentional; Barry's friends had been over playing music, getting stoned, and the tiny windowpane had been neglected on the coffee table, only accidentally within reach. He'd put it to his tongue, Emily supposed, the way he put most things there, just sampling, just aping his elders. A thousand times she chastised herself for not having taken Roy with her to the liquor store, which is where she'd been. Her decision had been made in order to spare herself the castigating look of the liquor store lady, who was Chinese and frowned with an awesome moral authority upon patrons who brought in children. Had Roy been alongside her, all the trouble could have been avoided. Or, she often thought, simply put off. Sooner or later, something like an acid trip was bound to have happened, with Barry.

No one had realized Roy was tripping until he began pointing out Christmas lights that weren't there, following with his finger the tracer trails. And then Emily's heart had jangled like an alarm clock in her chest. While she forced Barry to tag after the hallucinating child, she'd called the hospital, pharmacy, and poison control, and to the anonymous nurse, pharmacist, technician gave her hypothetical situation: *What if* a thirty-two-pound child were to ingest just a *small* amount of lysergic acid diethylamide? Just what if? But no one really wanted to speculate, even hypothetically. No one wanted to be held accountable for suggesting wait and see. Roy wandered like anyone in the throes of LSD, fascinated by the mundane, contented to sit and stare and name the new strange world, unafraid because he was a toddler, unimpressed because he hadn't lived straight long enough to find straightness tedious—and therefore necessary to escape. His lucidity never flagged, and Emily waited the full twelve hours for it to do so, prepared to go public, summon an ambulance, risk losing her child to protective services, but she never had to. All of the band members kept reassuring her, as the night passed, that the acid had been disappointingly mild, hardly a trip at all; many of them had tripped at young ages, eleven, thirteen. Barry sat rolling his head in his hands like a melon, tangling his dirty blond hair, chagrined, chastened, sweating and stinking, waiting for Emily to spank him. He was a hopeless adult, Emily saw, unfit for any part. When Roy's pupils finally shrank, when he quit grinning and chatting and grabbing at invisible worms, when he lay on the couch and slept soundly, breathing evenly with his little boy's face back in place, Emily had opened the front door of her house, preparing to walk through it and away. She told her husband she wished never to see him again. Ever.

And no one was to know. Not her pediatrician, not her parents, not her sister or brother or best friends, no one. Winston would have had his judgment of Barry confirmed. The Excrescence, indeed. Moreover, her pregnancy, only a few weeks positive at the time of the acid trip, she refused to divulge. Barry had no rights to his children; he was nothing but a random sperm donor, in her new opinion, someone shooting in the dark. She banished him, from them, from her heart. Not six weeks later he turned evidence for the state against his friends and fled to Florida; every legal document she'd asked him to sign he had returned in the next mail.

Now the Shindigs waited for an update on his life. Emily told them he was making television commercials. "For orange juice," she said. Why not? Oranges and theme parks and alligators and Cubans. Florida. Emily could almost imagine the squirrelly commercial Barry might put together featuring those disparate details. He had a way with non sequiturs. The Shindigs nodded appreciatively. They liked having the story finished, the chapter closed on old Barry.

"He was always a funny boy," Al said in summation, wistful.

Emily nodded. He was funny, all right. It was the Shindigs who'd allowed Barry to tap into their electricity when the power had finally been shut off in Emily's old house. The yellow extension cord had snaked across the tiles and through the fence, atop the drive where it was daily run over by his truck tires, and up through the kitchen window. Barry plugged in the fridge for most of the day, along with a trouble lamp. Sometimes at night he switched to an amp and electric guitar, leaving the food to thaw, the ice cubes to briefly melt. Barry. "What a card," Al Shindig said, as if reading Emily's mind. As if wanting to change her bitter memory into a benign one. "And what about that boy of yours, Nolan?"

"Roy," Emily corrected. Did she look like someone who would name her child for a ballplayer? "He's fine. Potty trained and everything." They weren't going to ask about Petra because they didn't know she existed. It had been a year and a half since Emily had visited the Shindigs, and yet in that short space of time she'd been able to not only have a baby and lose her postpartum look, but finalize a divorce, sell a house, and perhaps contract cancer. She was an amazing girl, she told herself wryly, full of latent talents. The Shindigs queried her on all the topics they could dream up, her folks, her siblings, the weather, local political shenanigans, but Emily wasn't as much fun as her ex-husband. She sipped at her thick hot toddy and watched as the party's good cheer seemed to slip from the room the way the light had from the sky. The Tom Jones CD ended, leaving everyone at a loss. With her last bit of energy she made her good-byes, pulling Kojak away from the pugs and Las Vegas and into the Kansas cold once more.

"Don't be a stranger, hear? And bring little Nolan, next time, we'll let him feed the piranhas."

"Will do," Emily called back. Walking Jackoff through the dusk toward her parents', she felt logy with small talk and sweet greasy alcohol, sticky as melted caramel. Her current drink of choice was scotch, which, like the smoke it tasted of, did not fill you up, which seeped directly into your system like a drip, which held there like a steady painkilling IV.

On her block, wind at her back, her parents' home within view, she came across the boy and girl. They were walking before the Episcopal church in baggy clothes, hand in hand ahead of her, ambling in the manner of teenagers, without destination. They'd been at the park, it seemed, possibly smoking pot, possibly just watching the brave winter tennis players or baby strollers, maybe in the church creating mischief, no doubt making sport of all the people who had missions in this neighborhood, the industrious and old, mortgage holders and taxpayers, dog owners and speed-walkers. These two were the same height, the same build, hair the same boys' cut, outfitted similarly like fraternal twins. There was something appealingly asexual about them, as if they just must be the best of friends, sharing jeans and boxer shorts and earrings and flannel shirts and hair products. They rocked as they walked, leaning on each other, socking each other's arms, pointing at each other and laughing. Teens without wheels, wandering the dreamy limbo of adolescence, aimless this evening, the whole of adulthood ahead of them. You could envy that, abstractly, fondly.

Then they suddenly stopped, hardly fifteen feet in front of Emily, and fell upon each other, mouth hungrily to mouth, body to body, spontaneous combustion, as if they might fuse and flame and disappear right off the face of the earth in the ignition of their ardor. The boy's hands were on the girl's cheeks, which had gone hollow with the airless suction of their kiss. Emily pulled up short, jerked Kojak's leash, put her fist to her rib cage to keep it from collapsing. She swallowed to prevent moaning out loud. They were not the same, under those layered saggy costumes. They had complementary parts, ones that yearned toward each other, and you could feel the heat despite the thick loose innocuous covering. This was what they were about: desire, pure and burning.

The surprise of this kiss made Emily's eyes tear, her nose sting with the prelude to ceaseless weeping. This kiss embodied the unfairness of the carnal world, its thoughtlessness, and these children of course took for granted the number of times they could indulge in such feverish passion, find each other and entwine, ahistorical, symmetrical, synchronized, inarticulate, whimsical, sexual. Once upon a time she had loved Barry this way, physically, ravenously, ignorantly—before the terrible chain reaction of their marriage, the set of events whose cause and effect could never be satisfactorily explained to an outsider, which always ended with the man banished and the woman left holding the spoils.

Yet she did not feel victorious. She felt lonely. She'd felt that then, too, the secret marital paradox nobody told you about in advance, the way you could be desperately, suicidally lonely, and yet have not one shred of privacy.

Still she ached for that brief period of happiness, that season of promise, those months of living in a body that needed nothing more than the body beside it, easy limbs languid in a warm bed, mouths that mutually required nothing but kissing.

Kissing: the secret of life was kissing. Feeling newly tuned to death, Emily could see that. You spoke, you ingested, you complained, you amused, you resuscitated, but the most vital thing you did with your lips, the most useless and necessary, was kiss, and you would miss it most. She did not want to be fucked, or understood, or talked to, or even cared for. More than anything, she wanted to be kissed.

7

For years Professor Mabie had been aware that his wife was in an ever-increasing retreat from the world. The world frightened her, its bustle and busyness, its unseen sources of noise. When she stepped out of her house and into it, she covered herself in hats and long sleeves and sunglasses, insisting that someone else drive. Her skin was pale and moist as mushrooms. Professor Mabie sometimes held her in the dark and marveled at how little the feel of her flesh had changed, despite the passage of time. As always, he was tentative when he approached her. He'd never forgotten that she could be hurt, offended, reduced to tears. She'd always been a modest woman, secretive only because she did not feel the need to tell everything she knew, not because she was keeping secrets. Shy. Fiercely shy, and proud, and vulnerable. She was, in some ways, still a mystery to her husband, and he supposed that accounted for some part of his desire to stay put, as if he might someday figure her out.

Besides, Professor Mabie had always had Betty Spitz for social complication and sarcasm and gossip and trouble. His wife had seen early on that she could not compete with the sharp and bright and gleaming intelligence of this woman. She was the wife, the woman to come home to. Reliable, contented, steady. With her husband she shared the understanding of family: As long as there were family members around her,

Mrs. Mabie knew what to do. She did not need people in the same way as Betty, who needed them as her audience; they could be dull because she was the agent whose arrival would produce chemical reaction. Betty needed people to bounce off of, those padded bumpers that sent the pinball flying. Mrs. Mabie, on the other hand, was often forgotten in a crowded room, lingering on its periphery, observing. One of Professor Mabie's delights, in the aftermath of department parties, was to listen to the two versions he'd hear from his women. His wife would have seen loneliness and gone to meet it, seeking the solitary and the uncomfortable, bringing them drinks, giving them tours, simply asking them polite questions. Her presence was like an antechamber, a place to go when you were tired of verbal antics, a place to relax briefly from the fray, an off-ramp from the frightening social cloverleaf. Betty Spitz would find herself in the knotted center of a group, mostly men, telling jokes in competitive fashion, drinking heavily, laughing hard. Whatever that group emitted had its own energy, spun in the moment, suspended fragile and transient among them, a hard bursting flare of spontaneity and surprise. No one made him laugh the way Betty could. She was queen of the ensemble, the life of the party. He should have been ready to touch her, to take her to bed.

What kept him from it? What had prevented his entry with Betty into the sticky region of adultery? It was a stickiness like blood, tacky with black betrayal, tempting as that famous tar pit to the creatures that perished there.

He loved his wife. He loved having saved her, and having his attempt pay off. She had become a person capable of thriving. Once she had been his student, a shy girl of old bewildered parents who had died before fully launching their only child. A girl who looked at her first professor with a tilted head, a squinted eye, as if he gave off a blinding light. She studied him carefully, as if able to absorb only a part at a time but ready to come back until she'd learned it all. He could still see her in that pose, sitting near the front of the room, where she had installed herself semester after semester, fair shapely legs tucked beneath the desk and heart-shaped, dimpled face turned adoringly his direction, the faithful local girl who would never leave her hometown.

Of the continents, she'd stood only on North America. From Wichita she'd strayed a time or two—a funeral in Seattle, a high school jaunt to L.A., a train trip to Texas, some car rides into the Rocky

Mountains—but she'd never been away from Wichita for longer than a week. Never east of Kansas City. Of the languages, she spoke exclusively English. She'd dated a boy or two but fell in love only once. Fell there and did not climb out. Made herself a bed and lay peacefully in it.

Her life obviously did not span the globe, did not cover a wide variety of experience, did not consist of a long résumé. But it plumbed deeper in the limited region it covered. Though she could no longer drive the streets of her hometown, she knew Wichita like the back of her hand, its history, its inhabitants, its moods. She could predict both the weather and the subtlest needs of the people she lived with, husband, daughters, son, grandchildren, and attended to them like the well-trained servant, quietly, unceremoniously. Her concentrated attention, Professor Mabie believed, meant that she had at her disposal a thick core sample.

His wife claimed a migraine on the day of Betty Spitz's funeral; the sky bore out her story, a new front having moved in overnight. So Mona, who disliked her parents' disappointing each other, showed up in the kitchen in a loose black dress that hid her recent weight gain, caftan-like with a pattern of distracting purple flowers sprinkled through it.

"You want me to drive?" she asked, raising her voice as she now did when addressing her father. She adjusted to her parents' ailments quite naturally; she understood lapses.

"Don't you have to work?" He knew she didn't have to work. Her teacher's aide job permitted her endless flexibility. She could do anything for anybody, anytime, at the drop of a hat. She could come when called.

"Let me drive," she said, taking the keys from their hook.

"Good idea." Professor Mabie had not expected either of his daughters to go with him, certainly not Winston; and it hadn't even really surprised him to have his wife bow out at the last minute, dutiful as she was concerning the appearances of things. More and more, lately, she could not seem to bring herself to care what his former colleagues thought of her. She'd been a faculty spouse; now her husband was emeritus, and Betty Spitz had often teased her, anyway, in a manner that was hard to describe later as cruel, as if Mrs. Mabie were paranoid and Betty merely clever. "She's just joking," Professor Mabie would explain, feebly.

"No," his wife would say, uncertain, holding no master's or doctorate degree herself, perhaps excluded from the tough club of sarcastic taunting they, as a bonus perk, could both take and dish out. Social custom held that teasing meant affection, but Professor Mabie's wife wasn't convinced this was the case. Betty Spitz had not liked her, and had not really been an official friend of the family. She was *his* friend, not illicitly but specially, protectively. She thought better of him than he deserved; she thought he worked too hard and was misunderstood. Unlike a marriage, the daily annoyances did not build up. He was always on his best behavior, she on hers; they wore their street clothes instead of their shabby pj's, they performed their toiletries in private, they greeted each other in halls and passed notes during meetings. They did not have to sit up on Saturday nights fretting over the late state of their daughters' arrival home from dates with dubious delinquent boys; they did not witness each other's soiled laundry, foul morning breath, regressive tantrums. Instead, Betty and Professor Mabie continued to charm rather than grate upon each other. At parties the two of them would gravitate toward each other like the betrothed prince and princess, the hub of a continuous bit of ensemble humor, Mrs. Mabie's role unclear, ancillary, a kind of escort for her husband as he dressed, then drove through the streets of the city, and promenaded up the walk to the party, where, once he was armed with a drink and the attention of Betty Spitz, she was left to her own devices. She would find the other morose spouses, the less amusing, the shy, wallflowers and misfits and lumps, their interest in the history department nonexistent. The props of the spouses had been highballs, the sound track loud foreign music, the vague hope new blood, somebody's recent second or third wife, or a fresh hire. It seemed unlikely that a funeral would provide those diversions, everyone middle-aged, at best, aged and infirm, at worst, the next in line.

Mrs. Mabie claimed a legitimate headache, elevating it to migraine, and took to her bed with an ice pack on her eyelids and a bowl of pharmaceuticals at her side. As soon as the car left the driveway, she crawled from bed to make coffee and read the newspaper. She did not want to listen to her husband eulogize the woman she had feared for forty years. She did not want to imagine the expressions on the faces of his colleagues and students radiating in the wide area that was her blind spot. Most of all, she didn't want to leave her house.

She didn't like to leave her house, but she also didn't like to be there alone. Sometimes she volunteered to baby-sit Petra and Roy just to have company, to think of the children as a kind of collateral, as though otherwise she might be abandoned. Today she sensed Winston's sleeping body upstairs, insurance that allowed her to let her husband go off without her.

Professor Mabie held a rolled typescript in his hand, thumping it gently on the dash while Mona drove, erratically, which was her style. He'd taken an antianxiety pill and didn't feel adequate to the task of driving, his body a few paces behind his mind. The eulogy had been completed before his friend died, inspired by his visits to her hospital room, the review of their enduring odd intimacy her long illness had insisted upon. He had rehearsed reading it aloud in the privacy of his study, and the tears that his own words brought to his eyes had already been shed. His labor on the eulogy was a bit embarrassing, because he was proud of what he'd written, because he'd grown excited at its development as a piece of prose, because her death had inspired him to write something he found beautiful and moving. As if he'd traded her for his own eloquence. The process felt predatory, coldly pragmatic— *academic,* he realized, that dreaded term—and he wondered if he disliked it. Through him raced the old collegiate excitement, a caffeinated buzz of phrases that, once started, metastasized, spawned their own intricate proliferation of like sentences, one tumbling after the other, a lava flow. In the middle of such a bloodletting, it was difficult to remember the long fallow times, the stumbling stupid prose, the brain tourniquet, fingers fumbling on the keyboard like the paws of a monkey.

At the same time, writing about Betty had permitted him to think clearly about her, to say what he wondered, to amend it, to revise, to come to some sort of conclusion. Nothing else would ever allow him the same luxury, not talking with his wife or with Billy, not stewing in his own juices.

"Death is always surprising, isn't it?" Mona observed, in the car on the way to the mortuary. There was to be a service there, then a procession, then the burial.

Professor Mabie glanced at her, but she was asking an innocent question, as if she'd not, just three years ago, tried to ingest enough pills to kill herself. Maybe the *desire* to die had surprised her, then. Her attempt at dying surprised him; the thing itself would have driven him mad.

She went on, "We know it's coming—if there's anything we know, we know that—and it still manages to shock us when it happens, doesn't it? It just seems like you walk around forgetting that the person who died is actually dead."

Professor Mabie swallowed; he could not help thinking about the morning Mona had been found lying outside her bedroom door, sallow and groggy with her cruel overdose. And there Betty had been, ready to answer his desperate phone call. "A human being's business is to deny death," he said now. "You should take Hillside instead of these tiny streets."

"I like tiny streets. They're prettier and with less cars."

"Fewer. But they're slower. And less safe." He checked the car's clock, the blinking digital display that always thwarted him, stunned him briefly with a sense of secret code, the swift mental transmutation he had to perform in shifting its message to the round face of a true clock.

"They won't start without you, Dad. You're delivering the speech. You're the emcee. The last funeral I went to was Bunny's," she added.

"I go to at least one a year, these days," Professor Mabie said. "That's the difference between being sixty-nine and twenty-nine."

Mona smiled grimly. "Thirty," she told him; her birthday had been last month.

He himself had looked forward to the funeral, in a way, because it would be the last of his university obligations, the final closure on his life as an academic, and he could exit glowing. Betty Spitz had been one of the most popular teachers at the university, and his role as her best friend had given him more cachet than any other role he'd inhabited there.

Billy and Sheila met them at the mortuary, Sheila wearing two black garments that did not cover her navel, which was infected looking, tottering on shoes made of wood and fur, as if by Neanderthals.

"Where's your mom?" Mona asked before Professor Mabie could ask the same.

She turned out her lower lip. "How'd you know she was gone?"

Professor Mabie shared a smile with Mona. Then they entered the crowded vestibule, listening to Sheila sob for a moment about Betty Spitz's saving Eddie Shakes from a failed Western civ semester. As if that was as much as a person could hope to accomplish in this life, god bless her. When queried on Eddie's whereabouts, this morning, Sheila revealed that he was buying shoes at the mall, size 18. Professor Mabie hadn't known that shoes came in sizes that big.

"Shaquille O'Neal wears size twenty-two," Sheila said brutally. Who was Shaquille O'Neal? Professor Mabie wondered.

His brother Billy, who smelled of mothballs, leaned close and said, "You know how Hank Williams died?"

"No." Who was Hank Williams? Where were these names coming from?

"It was just plain partying, drinking and smoking and what-all, but the coroner called it 'Death by Misadventure.' " Billy showed his crooked teeth when he grinned. Betty Spitz would have appreciated that epitaph, Professor Mabie thought, Death by Misadventure.

" 'I'm So Lonesome I Could Cry'?" Billy prodded. " 'Five Miles to the Graveyard'?"

Professor Mabie was only confused by these statements put in the form of questions. Billy was always uttering nonsense. He brushed his brother's words aside, recalling the ones he'd written himself. "History," he'd begun his eulogy of Betty, "is the study of heroes. . . ."

BECAUSE he quit wanting her, Nicholas Dempsey became a different sort of obsession for Mona. She pictured a tree of thoughts, every branch a memory of Nicholas, her leaping from limb to limb an exhausting and relentless activity. She replayed their relationship as if to find, finally, the source of trouble, as if some explanation would clear everything up, make her feel sane once more.

At first she had charmed Nicholas Dempsey, but later he began to grow critical of her apparel, her music, her ideas. As he became more critical, she began to change, to believe his opinion the correct one, to lose confidence in who she was.

"I think these guys you like are pretentious," Nicholas had said of her music. "Their lyrics are just too obscure. What's this mean, 'I'm buried to my neck in contradictionary flies I take pride as the king of illiterature I'm very ape'? What kind of bullshit is that?" He'd often borrowed a CD in order to study Mona; apparently this time he found her lacking. Once he would have been intimidated instead of contemptuous, reverent rather than rude. Since her taste in music had been one of their first points of contact—Mona's acknowledged field of expertise—the fact that he now sneered did not bode well.

She flushed; she'd sincerely mourned Kurt Cobain's death.

Next came her thrift-store clothes. "Been in the Dumpsters again?" he asked snidely. "Chasing that AmVets truck?"

"Go to hell," Mona said, trying not to cry. Instantly he'd turned her own clothing against her. And after that, the fact that she didn't shave her legs.

Her response, the wrong one, she came to learn, was to retreat from what she thought she loved, to question *it* rather than *him*. She bought khaki pants and a dull button-down shirt, running shoes, footies, envisioning the ninety-eight-pound wife in tennis whites. She quit wearing black eyeliner and washed her hair every day, brushing it back from her face. She spritzed Chanel. She listened to the Top 40 station instead of the campus alternative shows, turning her attention to the truth of easy rhyme schemes and uncomplicated guitar chords. Maybe everyone really was just that pop simple. She took a razor to her legs.

This was the day that Emily had found her on the bathroom floor, post exfoliation. Stubble floated in the smooth chilled water. Cuts on her calves and knees had left brief streaks of dried blood, as if she'd been attacked by a rosebush. "Mona," Emily cried. "What's wrong?"

"Bluh," said Mona.

" 'Bluh'?"

"How come everybody knows how to act, anyway?" Mona asked, down on the bath mat. "How'd you get so confident?"

Emily stepped around Mona to sit on the toilet. "Do you mind? I have to pee." Ever since her recent gynecology trips, her need to urinate was twice as frequent. Often when she laughed, she leaked, like an old person, the way she had during pregnancy.

"Pee freely," Mona said dispassionately.

"You're getting goose bumps."

"Some of them are flea bites. Hence the blood." She waved a hand as if to show a product for sale.

"Let me cover you with a towel." Emily flushed, then spread a bath towel over her sister. "Remember bottling vodka and orange juice in here?" she asked. They'd taken their father's bottling device upstairs, borrowing the caps and funnels from his beer-making operation in the basement, decanting a lethal screwdriver concoction into Fanta bottles to carry clanking around all evening in backpacks. Mona's first drunk, she'd stumbled along behind Emily and Frog and Toady that night, becoming their entertainment, then their project: how best to spirit her totally inebriated fourteen-year-old body into the house without detection? She'd wet herself before making it to the toilet, then spent the night on this very floor, beneath a similar bath towel, vomiting, sleeping, vomiting, sleeping, drinking water from the tap, accepting bland saltines on her tongue like communion wafers. Half a lifetime later, here she was again, reduced to a fetal position, covered with a towel. And here was Emily, ministering. Were they ever really going to grow up, change roles, or at least take turns?

Emily hadn't been living at home when Mona had tried to overdose, but she still ended up at the hospital, bedside, calmly holding Mona's pale hand, promising the future, one that Mona could have faith in. Her job, always, was to ferry her sister from despairing drifting sea to solid worthy land. Her parents depended on her for that; she had no choice but to maintain the illusion of her own confidence that Mona would make it, that worse crises had been overcome.

But what had put her at sea, now? Last time, it had been Barry's leaving her—Emily shook her head, unwilling to dive into the snaky pit of her sister's affair with her husband. You could get nowhere, trying to assign blame in such a circumstance, trying to pin guilt or innocence, since everybody seemed both victim and perpetrator. But Mona, it could not be disputed, had been the loser. Barry had won, stolen so much from her she was left empty, everything upended and wrong. And poor Mona, who'd had no one in the family to confide in, no one to reveal the reason for her despair. Their parents, Emily was certain, to this day wondered what had brought on such sorrow.

"What happened?" Emily asked, kneeling at Mona's head. "Tell me, Mona, please."

And so came the story of Nicholas Dempsey. Emily listened, unsurprised. Was there any lesson more often reiterated than the one that history repeated itself? That people had a will to live and *not* learn? Her married boyfriend quit calling her; Mona expected the worst. Was there any reason not to?

Mona said, "I just don't get it. I can't get it. He just stopped caring. Where was I when they were handing out that particular gift?"

"Don't feel that way," Emily said. "Please don't feel that way, I can't stand it. He's a jerk." She sat solidly on the floor and tried to recall the piece of literature that told of the best thing a friend could do for the spurned, following her about, bad-mouthing the brute who'd broken her heart.

Nicholas Dempsey did not phone her. Days passed and scenarios flourished; Mona looked for his name in the obituaries. She envisioned his wife—the woman who would have discovered her husband's dalliance—dangling by a rope in the kitchen, that horsey ponytail swinging on a secondary axis, or asphyxiated in the garage, driven by grief to suicide. Nicholas Dempsey couldn't very well phone Mona if he or his wife were dead. Perhaps it was one of his children who'd died, dashing into the street or jamming a fork in an electrical outlet.

Mona finally drove by his house, noting no signs of disaster. The car sat contentedly in the driveway; every light in the smug little home was on. The place radiated coziness, insulation, health. She pulled into a 7-Eleven parking lot and wept on the steering wheel. Later that week, she phoned him, and when his son answered—"Hehwo?" he said, like some child actor on a sappy sitcom—she gruffly asked for his father.

"Hey you," she breathed when she heard the voice she loved more than any other in the world.

"No," Nicholas Dempsey said blandly, "we don't accept phone solicitation," and hung up. This was the last time she had spoken to him; prior, he'd broken a long-standing arrangement to meet for a car ride to Emporia where he had to take a deposition—explicable abandonment, if you wanted it to be.

"Oh Mona," Emily had said, upon hearing her sad tale.

"Oh me," Mona said, beneath her towel.

Still, it seemed to help to have told her sister. Alerted, Emily watched. Mona wandered devastated, pale, unable to summon a smile. The world looked to be shifting in unpleasant familiar ways. Worst-case scenarios were not supposed to come true, Emily thought, certainly not twice. You were supposed to use worst-case scenarios for deterrence, for loin girding, security system, overprotection. But Emily sensed the implosion of Mona's sanity, the unraveling having already begun in her heart. She was going to fall apart. Once more.

"What?" Emily demanded of Mona's mopiness as they loaded the dishwasher one night. Then, "I wish he were dead."

"Me, too," Mona said sincerely.

At Emily's suggestion she wrote a letter, designated a night and time, insisted on the personal appearance. So, cocktail hour of the day of Betty Spitz's funeral he was to meet her at Outlaws.

Nicholas had a window of time between getting off work and arriving at home that he and Mona had inhabited for a few months together, the meeting at the White Glove Motel, the drinks at out-of-the-way bars all over town. This time of day could kill her, if she wasn't careful. She drove deep into the northwest side, into the cloudy winter sunset, and then sat alone at the dim dotty counter of Outlaws, surrounded by rough men wearing all manner of headgear and canvas coveralls, steel-toed boots and flannel shirts. The parking lot held nothing but pickup trucks with gun racks, and although she felt no affinity for her companions at Outlaws, she also felt no fear in their midst. An advantage to having nothing to live for was a kind of fearlessness, she supposed. Was that what courage was, having nothing to live for? She ought to pursue a dangerous occupation, war correspondent, stuntwoman, AIDS volunteer . . .

"Here you go," said the bartender, looking her over critically, as if wondering whether she were ridiculing his bar and patrons, slumming in order to make sport.

"Thanks," she said, leaving a big tip. Her vodka tonic came in a plastic cup; maybe she looked like someone who might take it into her head to break a glass and carve someone's face with it. And maybe that face would be Nicholas Dempsey's.

Pretending to be interested in the pool game in front of her, she tried to be invisible at the bar, the only woman there, the only person drinking a mixed drink, the only drinker without a friend or at least a role. She still wore her funeral outfit, as it seemed fitting for cocktail hour, and looked to conceal her slightly wider hips. Fretting about Nicholas Dempsey had sent her more often to the cookie jar and the liquor cabinet these days.

"You want another?" one of the pool players asked gruffly, of her empty plastic cup. Mona hadn't supposed anyone was paying attention, but she'd just that second finished the drink. The lemon slice lay sodden and orphaned on the bottom.

"Oh no, I'm waiting for someone."

"You want another while you wait?"

Mona sighed, shaking her head, smiling pathetically. She couldn't imagine how he envisioned her, the working girl waiting for her happy hour girlfriend? Or the lonely girl looking for an anonymous forgettable evening? Morose mourner, grieving after the funeral? She had, after all, been to one that day. How lovely to be considered bereft—and perhaps of a husband. The wife of a dead man: not rejected, but abandoned nonetheless, love life interrupted by fate. It was the perfect explanation: widow. She hoped she didn't look like what she really was, which was the opposite of widow, the stood-up date, the jilted lover. She tried not to watch door or clock, hoping she'd feel Nicholas's hands on her shoulders, his lips at her ear, a joke ready to connect them once more, separate them from everyone else in the universe. Mona went over their latest conversations, realizing that she'd instigated them all, leaving him messages at work to phone her, then her recent letter. When, she wondered, had things changed? She tried to pin down the moment when he'd retreated, taken his toys and gone home, and she tried to locate what it was in her that had earned it.

He didn't come. An hour and a half had passed, dinnertime and then full dark. Mona let the pool player buy her a drink and then suffered his annoyance when she could do nothing but watch the door, which never opened to reveal Nicholas Dempsey.

Driving home, Mona looked up at the moon and forgot why it should appear as it appeared, what principle of the universe made it three-quarters visible, the fourth quarter shadowed. Into her mind she heaved the cosmos, the planets spinning hugely around the sun, the sun now shining on the moon, obscured by . . . what? The earth itself? It troubled her to forget how to think about this, how to wrap her mind around the moon and space, in general. What could her forgetfulness foretell? Soon she'd be prying the lid off the milk container with a screwdriver, or sitting before this very automobile instrument panel, clueless as to how to proceed, jabbing the key into the air-conditioning vents.

It was now 7:30 in the evening, and she'd volunteered to look after her niece and nephew in order to avoid playing bridge with her parents and siblings. Betty Spitz had been buried today; everyone was on his or her best behavior. Mona's part would be that of baby-sitter, because, of course, she didn't understand bridge; she'd always been the emergency substitute player, since Emily and Winston had been taught first. She had never quit feeling the onus of being extra, in her family. Her parents had their girl, their boy, and then they'd had Mona, extraneous as a sixth finger or tail, the fifth wheel. Emily had proven bright and sensitive, a caretaker and overachiever, spawner of grandchildren, part owner of a thriving business, and Winston had been beautiful and beguiling, sensitive and mysterious, lately prodigal, but where did that leave Mona? What useful part was she to play? Whatever talents her brother or sister lacked, Mona certainly wasn't going to make up for them. Rather, it was Mona's fate to measure herself against Emily and to perpetually come up short. This comparison was not her own creation; she'd felt her family doing it since she and Emily were children, an expectation established by Emily's precociousness, later and consistently failed by Mona. Emily lost her first tooth at age four, began reading shortly thereafter, sped through school as if using only half her energy, devoting the other half to a burgeoning social life, one that in adolescence included bad boys and wild nights, thievings and drug use, a secret wantonness that their parents never perceived. It was as if Emily led two lives simultaneously, split in an admirable way between her mind and body, sustaining one during the daylight, indulging the other in the night. She had supreme self-control, astonishing drive, graduating from college after only three years, later finishing two master's degrees, supporting her addict of a husband, giving birth to healthy children, all the while maintaining the best of relationships with her parents, running a business, keeping contact with old friends. She was loyal and good-hearted and wry and reserved. The evidence was overwhelming: Mona would never measure up.

Even her love interest wasn't interested in loving her. To think about this evening made Mona's chest constrict. Embarrassment, anger, hurt, hopelessness. She pulled into the driveway of her home aching to find an explanation on her answering machine. She prayed for a family tragedy, his wife in an accident, him the widower. His children were small enough to learn to love her, weren't they?

Inside she found leftovers in the oven. Because her mother had bailed on the funeral, she'd gone overboard on dinner, coq au vin. Mona ate without a plate or fork, simply pulling meat from the bones, popping mushrooms and little onions into her greedy drunk mouth, fingers greasy with the rich Burgundy sauce. The sound of the dishwasher drowned out the other household noise and Mona indulged the comfort of hot water, hot food, inebriation—a succulent amniotic moment in the warm kitchen.

"There you are," her mother said, the bright overhead light blazing on. Mona swallowed guiltily, that small irritation in her windpipe she sometimes noticed, wiping her slick hands on a pot holder.

"Here I am."

"Go tell your sister you're home."

Mona climbed the back stairs slowly, passing her opportunity to check her answering machine for a little while longer. Emily was eager to leave her children in her sister's care; it had been a long day. "Roy's having an allergy attack," she said. "How are you?"

"*Awful.*"

"Oh Mona."

"I don't want to talk about it. They're waiting downstairs."

"Have a drink," Emily advised as she left, pointing at the wine bottle on her kitchen table. "He's a shit," she added, a briefly cheering refrain.

Alone, Mona went to the bedroom and looked at little Roy. He resembled his father, her other lost lover. She could forgive his father because of this resemblance, she thought, that dirty blond hair that always needed cutting, those long eyelashes. For a moment she entertained the fantasy of a phone call to Florida, of seeking out Barry and seeing how he was. But Barry didn't really interest her anymore. And she couldn't forgive Nicholas Dempsey. So she bent over Roy and hugged him tight, soaking in self-pity. Maybe she should have a baby, force her parents to think of her as a grown-up. But she couldn't even find a boyfriend of her own—only other women's husbands; even that indisputable loser Garth Blewski had not phoned her after their AA date—let alone a man willing to impregnate her.

"Stop choking me!" Roy declared, struggling to escape her mushy embrace.

From far below, two stories down, Mona could hear laughter. On the one hand, it cheered her to think that Winston might win his way back into his father's heart. On the other, their laughter certainly excluded Mona herself. She didn't find bridge amusing in any way, didn't understand the little sayings they tossed back and forth and giggled over—*He who hesitates is lost,* or *Get the boys off the streets,* or the one about leading to and through strength and weakness—and mostly suffered through hands hoping not to fuck up in too dramatic a fashion. She was always relieved to be named dummy, to be sent to the kitchen for snacks or drinks, to change the radio station or check on children. Dummy: who else better qualified?

"I'll be right back," she told Roy, deciding she'd been away from her answering machine long enough.

A few months ago it would have shown six messages, which would have thrilled her. Then, she would have pressed the button to hear what Nicholas Dempsey had to say to her tonight, what small moment he'd been allowed away from his wife and children to think of her. "All the time," he claimed, when she'd asked how often she was in his thoughts. Could that have been true? Certainly she thought of him incessantly, then and now, convinced she had loved no one more or better. Her brain and heart were at war, two fierce organs, each with a large winning army and a lengthy argument in its stable, at its disposal. Things were at an impasse but that didn't mean peace. All day long they had once argued the point of Mona's obsession. *He won't leave his wife. But he's smitten with me. He has children, babies. I have a right to happiness. Not at the expense of someone else's misery. But what of my own misery?* Mona had no idea how to settle this battle. At the moment, she mourned the loss of that lovely luxury, happiness, adoration, love. Some nights a dozen phone calls had collected on her machine, Nicholas in his basement or backyard or office or pay phone murmuring into the receiver his desire for her. Only after she'd hung up, heart vibrating like electric currency, would her brain send the image of one or the other of Nicholas's little family, a child's or wife's face at a window, watching him sit on a swing, swaying in the dark, lusting into the telephone out there beyond the circle of a lighted home.

Mona had often heard the swing-set chains squeak over her answering machine.

Nicholas Dempsey drank before he phoned her. Three miles away, Mona drank as well, wondering if they matched each other drink for drink. He had an amazing capacity for alcohol, for one so slender. Some nights he relied on beer; others, he resorted to whiskey. Mona had tried to learn to enjoy whiskey, but with little luck. Its one virtue was its quick uptake in her system. Straight to her head it went, and the wonder of alcohol was the way it drowned the argument of the brain. Those smart soldiers fell silent, then, and the heart's army swelled through her system. As usual, she was tempted to phone his house, hope he answered, tell him she still loved him, hang up. But as usual, she resisted. She could not bear to hear how he no longer loved her.

She wished again that she had saved a few of his messages. "Hey baby, just sitting around with nothing to do, wishing I could do nothing with you. Time for the first beer." The sound of his throat working had made Mona want to hold his neck, the hot stubbled warmth. "You can track the dull course of the night because I'm going to call you every time I get another beer. 'Kay?"

In her room, the machine said o.

"I love you, Roy," she told her nephew, when she returned to him upstairs in his garret. See? She had healthy affections, as well.

8

"PARTY OF one?" the hostess greeted Emily.

She caught her breath. Everything was striking her in the solar plexus, these days. *Party of one* seemed the saddest phrase she could imagine, so oxymoronic. Or like a code name for masturbation. Or for death.

"No," she was glad to be able to say, "I'm meeting somebody."

Had she known them, the hostess might have been amused by the circumstances, or, just as easily, unimpressed. Emily had come to meet her sister's lover, who was breaking her heart. Who had the power to kill her.

The Grapevine had been improved since high school, when Emily and her friends used to come here for lunch. There hadn't been a hostess back then, dressed in black with spike heels, and there hadn't been tablecloths. Back then there'd been a useful absence of bright light or stringent requirement about valid ID. You came to the Grapevine because anything went.

Tonight she was here to meet Nicholas Dempsey, and who knew how that would go?

He was identifiable as the most antsy man at the bar. "You look like Mona," he said, standing up awkwardly around his barstool, which rocked on its four legs. In his suit he looked disguised, a youngster trying to sucker someone into believing him grown up, and there was a faint whiff of adolescent body odor when he stood, boy sweat. He was handsome in the bland unmarked way of youth, someone whose suffering was minimal, someone who took his tall fitness for granted, who in later years would no doubt develop a paunch over his narrow hips, trade the rosy glow of his cheeks for gin blossom, lose some of that wavy brown hair, wear with growing confidence his suits and pressed shirts, necktie loosened in a two-fingered gesture that would become habit. A lawyer. Winston's lawyer, to be exact. He wore a wedding ring, gleaming and unscarred, a ring that had not yet fallen into the garbage disposal or gotten lost for days at a time in the backyard.

He extended the hand without a wedding ring for Emily to shake, and she thought what she always thought when she shook a man's hand: the last thing that hand had gripped, and in just this way, was his own dick before a urinal.

He was drinking a black and tan, which looked rich as chocolate, almost like something healthful, molasses floating a layer of cream. "You could be her twin," he said, sighing, pushing his glasses to the top of the bridge of his nose, his wedding ring catching the bar's subtle light and reflecting it like the teeth of a superhero. He had a faint rim of foam on his thin upper lip.

Emily wiped her palm on her thigh as she climbed on the barstool beside him. "Merlot," she told the bartender.

"Your sister always orders whatever I order," Nicholas Dempsey said.

"She's easy."

He shook his head, lips pursed as if to whistle. "She's not easy. That's just the problem."

Emily had to agree; it was why she was here.

The signature trellises still lined the bar's walls, plastic grapes hung from dusty synthetic leaves. Once she and her friends had celebrated a birthday here—whose?—an extended lunch, pitchers of golden beer in the afternoon sunlight, a blood-colored chocolate cake called Red Velvet, their hands and lips crimson with rosy dye when they returned—as if from a crime scene—stoned and sated, ribs sore from laughter, to honors fifth hour. Emily missed her adolescence with a sharp pang, like a beautiful dream on the verge of dissolving, unraveling before her waking eyes: come back!

Nicholas Dempsey's knee knocked suddenly into hers, forcing their eyes to meet, the present to descend. Emily sighed. He knew that Emily knew about his affair and that she had intimated blackmail. But all Emily wanted to do was instruct him on how to better break up with Mona. Her sister might otherwise try to kill herself again, the way she had on her last breakup from a married man and father. Emily had watched that chain of events with a kind of horror, most horrifying of all her part in setting it off. She had confronted Barry with her ultimatum, and then weeks later found herself shrieking at Mona to take her antidepressants and go to therapy after the suicide attempt. Somehow her own right as injured party had been neglected, pushed aside for the larger issue of her sister's life. And Mona still believed the affair had been secret.

Emily knew Nicholas Dempsey had two children, the ages, more or less, of her own children. He did not seem qualified to be a parent, but who was she to judge, given her own weak husband? Perhaps his wife would be the one to rescue the children.

"How's Mona?" he finally said, his tone weary.

Emily pictured her sister on the bathroom floor. She'd opened the door after knocking and not getting an answer, pushing into the room while unzipping her jeans, the door hung up on what turned out to be Mona's feet. She lay on the bath mat, half-dressed, fists at her eyes, sobbing silently. The tableau bore the appearance of insanity: tub full of water, still surface broken every few seconds by a slow drip, lights off.

Mona's eyes were bruisy with smeared makeup. She pleaded with her sister for an explanation. "What I can't figure out is how he simply turned off his love for me."

That this man, this random breathing organism, could be responsible for such devastation seemed like a cruel hoax, a preposterous premise. He'd asked how her sister was, and Emily did not know how honest she wanted to be with him. Mightn't it be her job to convince him of her sister's worthiness?

"Mona is confused," she said, which seemed safe, something you could say of anyone worth her salt.

"So am I," he said quickly.

"I bet Mona is more confused."

"Well, I don't want to get into one-upping misery."

Emily appraised him, recalling her sister, whose misery hung on her like a shroud, and a heavy one, at that. On the bathroom floor, Emily had wished it were summer, that the windows were open, the sky blue. Like the waiting bathtub, winter stretched out gray and chilling, a stagnant uninterrupted surface of damp.

Her sister had laid her head on the cold tile. "How could he just stop?" she asked once more.

"It's self-protective," Emily said, guessing. Didn't men do that, the preemptive strike?

"Would *you* be able to just stop? Let's say you'd been having a raging romance for about six months, obsessive, every waking minute spent thinking about each other, calling each other, leaving messages, meeting in parking lots and weird motels out in Augusta and Pratt. I mean, I know it was reciprocal. I don't have any doubts about it. So how does he just pull the plug on that? Could you?" Her open wounded face made her look like she was four years old again, appealing to Emily for an explanation of the cruel world, the boy who'd sucker punched her and stolen her candy. Innocence like that was stunningly dangerous.

"I could," she confessed. She had. "Although I sort of wish that I couldn't, if you want to know the truth."

"Why?" Mona cried. "Why would you want to suffer like this?"

Because it was pure, and because it meant that its inspiration had been just as powerful, on the other end of the continuum. This kind of distillate pain could only have come from sublime pleasure; Emily pictured a huge shade tree, under which grew a root system exactly as knotty and veiny and vast, mirrored there beneath the beautiful elm in the dark subterranean, inhabited by slick eyeless centipedes instead of songbirds. Was that not some definition of perversion?

What was difficult was reconciling Mona's response with the figure beside her at the Grapevine. Nicholas Dempsey sipped his creamy drink. Emily wanted to push him off his stool and kick him, repeatedly, in the groin where his reckless penis hid and in the ribs that housed his tiny tiny heart. Instead, she said, "You kind of have the upper hand, right now."

He nodded, sighed mightily. He seemed to enjoy his adult issue, the disposal of his first mistress. Emily had no doubt there would be others. "My favorite thing about Mona is how, when she wakes up, she stretches," Nicholas Dempsey said, trying a new tack. "I love how she makes fists and how her navel gets exposed and her face sort of squeezes into a hedge apple. You know?" He stared into Emily's impassive eyes. So what if he could speak metaphorically; she was trying to figure out if he was a sweet person or not. These days, she had more skepticism than usual concerning sweetness, the aspect of people's affection. She couldn't afford to be fooled. She had no time for games, however complicated they might be, however intricately fashioned they revealed the player to be. Talking about her sister rising from bed seemed unappealingly intimate, some strange come-on line. Or perhaps merely naive. Was he flirting? Or simply eager to talk with someone about his secret life? Moreover, the last time Emily'd seen Mona's fists, they'd been grinding into her weeping eye sockets.

"I just can't manage having an affair anymore," he said abruptly. Emily felt some shift in him, some veil of coolness slip off.

"Because . . . ?"

"She's too intense. She was messing with my home life." He ran his fingertips over his cheek as if to check for five o'clock shadow. *Too intense:* here they went again. Barry couldn't handle that intensity in Mona, either. Wasn't Emily intense? She focused on two separate thoughts: first, the fact that intensity frightened cowards like her ex-husband and this current jerk. Second, she wondered how Mona managed to become *too intense* over this one, as opposed to some other? What about that one over there, a friendly outdoorsy type with laugh lines and hiking boots? Like Barry, there seemed little to attach to in Nicholas Dempsey, his charm utterly elusive, or yet to develop. But of course that was beside the point. Love was all about creating the beloved, concocting whole cloth in a fantasy the object of one's affection. Mona's version of Nicholas Dempsey resided in her mind and body and heart, a character Emily couldn't begin to hope to understand or know. She'd heard all about their long conversations, their secret assignations, heard in Mona's voice the man she had made up. Who bore little resemblance to the man before Emily now.

"I mean, it seems like she changed the rules," Nicholas Dempsey said.

"Her feelings changed," Emily said. "She likes you more than she thought she would."

"But the deal is, I told her right up front that I was married, that I wasn't going to get unmarried. I have been in no way leading her on."

He was a "letter of the law" sort, she thought. "Sometimes people fall in love," she told him. Emily knew Mona fell hard. Fell hard, and hurt herself, and then felt in every important way the full correctness of being rejected. Sure enough: she was unworthy. Every one of Mona's relationships ended without her permission. That she would let herself fall in love over and over—open herself like a flayed animal—seemed to Emily both beautiful and insane.

The way Nicholas Dempsey stared into Emily's face let her know that this wasn't his first drink, that he'd been here for a while, fortifying himself. She had the sudden wild impression that, if she wanted to, she could go with him to wherever it was he went for these sorts of things, and make love. Why would he meet her here for a lesson in how to break up with her sister, and still be capable of sending out a message of availability, willingness, downright readiness? Or was this just the effect of alcohol, a seducer's sleepy smile on his face? But Emily would have bet a thousand bucks that he had a fresh condom in his wallet, waiting in its little puff of sterile air.

"You look so much like Mona it's scary," he said, blinking deliberately behind his lenses.

"I'm five years older, and an inch taller, and my head is smaller while she's got this great heart-shaped face. I always wanted to have her dimple." She prattled on some more about the differences between her and her sister, but Nicholas Dempsey was peering into her in a familiar and unsettling manner. If she resembled her sister, and if he had undressed her sister, then he was capable of seeing inside her clothing. All the exercises Emily had been taught in high school forensics did not apply; her audience had a complete understanding of not only her underwear but what it covered. His frank expression of longing was flattering, there was no denying it. A body wanted to be loved, wanted to recognize and respond to desire. She sighed, feeling she was getting far ahead of herself. Sleeping with Nicholas Dempsey would make her and Mona even in some way, since Mona had slept with Barry, yet Emily didn't sense that revenge was necessary. Barry and Mona both had been kind of helplessly beholden to Emily in ways that required outlets. They each had a need to hurt her, and it was oddly elegant—economical—that they'd done so together, one fell swoop. Emily had forgiven them long ago, she realized, and so sleeping with Nicholas Dempsey would not be revenge but something else, a fresh joust, a new wounding of her sister. She could afford it because she was ill; her sister would have to forgive just about everything.

Nicholas Dempsey had ordered another black and tan before he'd finished the one on the bar. He was the kind of drinker who doesn't like to be left empty-handed, waiting. This made him more interesting to Emily, put a dent in his generic demeanor. He was becoming distinct to her now, someone with personality, and though it was one she disliked, it at least had edges and angles. "Wine?" he asked, raising his eyebrows at her half-full glass.

"Sure."

"Here's the thing that clinched it," he said. "My daughter—she's eleven months old—she crawled over to me a few weeks ago, after I got home, the last time I was out with Mona—'working late.' " He used both hands to make quotation marks, bunny ears around his euphemism. "Anyway, so I get home, all glowing and smug, and there's little Ella, doing her thing with the furniture. Almost walking, she pulls up and goes around from one piece of furniture to another, then kind of sits down and scoots to the next chair leg. Very cute. So she crawls into my lap and starts patting my face, like she'd forgotten what I looked like, like I had been gone for a while. I can't tell you how"—he searched for the word, the future crow's-feet at his eyes appearing briefly— "*despicable* I felt. How low and repulsive, how I'd been looking into Mona's face when I should have been at home with my daughter."

"Uh-huh," Emily said blandly. He'd patted his own face when he imitated his daughter, and she couldn't help thinking about Petra, *her* toddler, who might have to get along without her mother. This made Nicholas Dempsey's problem seem so mild to Emily, so self-indulgent and ridiculous, she wanted to punch him. Fuck you, you little punk, getting all angsted out by a love affair. Moreover, she was glad he wouldn't be around in Mona's life. She sure didn't want to have to imagine her own daughter someday sitting on his lap, patting his facial features.

Emily drained her first wine, setting the glass down so sharply that the stem snapped. Nicholas Dempsey looked alarmed. "What's the matter?"

"Oh nothing." The bartender swept away the two pieces of the glass without expression. All in a day's work. "I don't know why wineglasses have to be so delicate, do you?" Emily asked brightly into his face. A more complicated man, a mature human being, would have known to take her in his arms, literally or figuratively, but Nicholas Dempsey, hopelessly young and self-absorbed, grew afraid, and addressed the issue of stemware instead of the forceful hand that had brought it down.

"Hush," Emily said to him finally. He bristled, but he closed his mouth. "My sister is fragile, even though you think she's tough." Emily did not want to disclose Mona's suicide attempt; if Mona hadn't told him, then he oughtn't to know. "Do you think you could possibly work this out so that she thinks she broke up with you?" She had to restrain herself from going into a rant about his ability to pull off such a trick, because she knew he wasn't good at such orchestration. You could see it in his haircut, in his manicured hands. He did not want to be the one who got dumped. Period. He was not someone who got his heart broken. And it was Emily's job to persuade him how truly manly it was to commit such a thing, his fabricated broken heart. It was true that he had the most to lose—his wife, his son, and baby—but Mona had no one to cushion her fall, no one. Parents and siblings and even a cute niece and nephew were not the same, not nearly. And so far, Petra wasn't really that cute.

Emily drank her second glass of wine quickly, felt it take up glowing residence in her head and arms and throat. "Okay," she said. "The deal is, you can do this really easily, really slowly. Just go make yourself miserable in front of Mona, suffer some guilt, tell her the story about the baby patting your face. That's a really good story about your guilt. And you have a son, right? He probably talks, and could say some things about missing you? Maybe your wife could get sick?"

Nicholas Dempsey stared at her, probably thinking, *Although this woman looks a lot like Mona, she is totally not Mona.* Emily waited.

"What kind of sick?" he asked.

"I don't know. Ovarian cancer?"

He made a face. Emily swallowed something bitter, trying not to squint unkindly at his youth, that arrogance that had revealed itself. His wife would never have ovarian cancer.

"Mono? Anemia? Give one of the kids strep, that'll keep you home for a few days, then you can get it yourself. Let your immune system run down, get some bags under your eyes." He would be vastly improved with bags under his eyes, Emily realized. He might turn into something, with bags. "Start looking bedraggled and hopeless, and let Mona take the initiative. Let Mona rescue you by ending the deception." When he didn't respond, Emily said, "The deception that is eating away at you."

"Right."

"Are you patronizing me?"

"No," he said, throwing his head back, swallowing the last of his black and tan, Adam's apple working in an ugly fashion. "No, you're patronizing me, is what's going on here."

"Another?" said the bartender, eyebrows raised, unhurried, familiar with scenes. Would it be interesting to tend bar? Would it make you wise? Or just jaded? Were the two the same?

"Mona's sister," she'd told his snotty secretary that morning, when a name had been demanded. He came instantly then to the phone, agreed readily to their meeting. Now, Emily leveled the same threat. "If you don't at least try to do what I've suggested, I'm going to call your wife and tell her all about Mona. And I might give you a few other girl-friends." She stood up and nearly fainted, so quickly did the blood leave her head. She bent over, took a deep breath. "You seem like someone who needs to have a whole stable of girlfriends."

"Fuck you."

For some reason, this made Emily laugh. The last person to say *fuck you* to her had been Barry. He could inflect in a hundred different ways, a whole continuum of shadings, like Nicholas Dempsey, in anger, and wholly unlike, as in the middle of sex, *fuck . . . you,* with longing and release and pure animal pleasure. Emily missed Barry just now—young and useless as he was, he was still preferable to Nicholas Dempsey. How had she ended up with Nicholas Dempsey saying *fuck you* to her in his cold, mean manner?

"She's way too good for you," Emily couldn't help telling him, and feeling the truth of what she'd said swell in her made her want to slap him for not being what her sister deserved. Her love for Mona was big-ger than him, better than him, and it couldn't help matters in the least, a fat impotent fact, a gun loaded with blanks.

"Yeah?" he said, like a bully, "well, you're nothing like her, not one thing."

9

THREE DAYS BEFORE Christmas Emily left her children with Winston and Mona, the boy with the boy, the girl with the girl, and returned to Dr. Love's office to hear her biopsy results. Mona knew now what they were waiting for, although she had been sworn to secrecy. "I don't want to get Mom involved unless I have to," Emily had said grimly. Their mother worried medical matters in the way of the honor student, consulting sources, reading up, her tunnel-visioned attention focused like a spyglass on her mission, its new expert and convert. Mona could remember her college herpes scare, just how thoroughly researched the subject had gotten in her mother's hands, the frightening pictures and the nauseating testimonials, the dinnertime discussion during which everyone was supposed to be so high-minded and mature, Mona burning in shame while shoveling mashed potatoes to her mouth. Apparently Emily had learned the same lesson, and now wanted to practice discretion.

On the third floor, Mona contemplated her sleeping niece, who, at fourteen months, still did not yet walk. She had all the makings of a perfectionist, not a risk-taker. Until she could do it just so, she wasn't going to let go of chair legs or the big people's hands. She would evaluate your attempts at entertaining her, your face behind your hands, your exaggerated expressions, your phony smile: at all she frowned, unimpressed. Roy could make her laugh, and Winston, and of course she loved Emily. Toward Emily she had a very sad response, Mona thought, Petra's face always fell into a nearly tearful aspect, as if she'd been holding back everything until her mother was there to take it from her. If Mona felt impatient with her niece, she had only to remember how pathetic the baby looked when Emily opened her arms and reclaimed her, the way relief filled the child like a good drug.

In her crib, Petra snored, mouth ajar, strand of spittle connecting her to her bedsheet, where a puddle had formed. Mona lifted the child and carried her downstairs, sleeping, so she wouldn't have to be alone in Emily's apartment. It was a nice apartment, but lonely. Too clean. Its cleanliness bespoke anxiety. The person who lived there had been busying herself—alphabetized spice rack, toys in Tupperware, immaculate grout—for the sake of distraction.

Besides, Mona's cousin Sheila was due soon. For Christmas she had made a private request of Mona: birth control pills. Today was the Planned Parenthood visit. Mona teetered as usual, poised on the typical double-edged sword of family, rocking in the breeze: if she told Wenda and Billy about Sheila's request for birth control, she was not only betraying Sheila but perhaps contributing to lethal unprotected sex. If she didn't tell Wenda and Billy, then she was going behind their backs with the underage daughter. Similarly, she was flattered Sheila had come to her, but also miffed. "Why not Emily?" she'd asked.

"Emily is so perfect," Sheila'd said, shocked at the suggestion that her perfect cousin be implicated. Mona had wanted to spill the beans on Emily, the party girl whose reputation had somehow never been tarnished. Now, of course, she was feeling sorry for Emily, scared that her sister had cancer.

"Ma ma ma ma," said Petra insistently, right off the bat. Her peanut-shaped head was covered with a pale fuzz and her eyes, which were hooded like her father's, looked accusingly up at Mona. *Imposter!* her expression said. *What have you done with my mother?*

"She'll be right back," Mona promised. "Right back." But the baby didn't believe her. Mona had enjoyed Roy's babyhood. He'd been cute, but Petra felt like a rerun. This again. Poor Emily.

Mona carried Petra on a tour of the dark house, allowing her to press the light switches, which were the old-fashioned variety, two resistant metal buttons atop each other on the switch plate, one black, one white. Petra's ability to work the buttons distinguished her from all the other babies who'd tried over the years. She was a strong dexterous child, and she stuck out her tongue like an extra finger when she exerted herself. The tongue also came out when she managed to lay hands on Kojak; getting what she wanted took terrific concentration and sometimes included crossing her eyes. When Roy was her size he would be seized by the need to hug his aunt Mona, just wrap his simian arms and legs around her and lay his large head against her chest, as if replenishing a reservoir. Roy had been a terribly affectionate baby, a hugger and a kisser and a cryer, and Petra was none of these. When she fell down, she pulled herself up dry-eyed. Today she was more interested in the weighty pool balls in the basement than in her aunt's affection. She turned the black eight ball in her palms, brought it to her mouth, and sucked its cool hard surface, her four tiny teeth clicking.

Mona's mother had decorated for Christmas, which meant that she'd harvested the customary cuttings of cypress and that the house smelled both woodsy and clean, like a forest, like Pine-Sol. The tree in the living room was undisturbed, this year, because Inkspot wasn't there to knock off ornaments and claw at the light strands. Mona missed her kitty, the soft noisy indiscriminate affection. No one else loved her the way that cat did. On the piano sat the mechanical Santa with his demonic flashing eyes and swinging hand bell, although it looked more like he was after you with the intention of bludgeoning you than ringing in the season. All children, Petra included, were scared of him. Her method was not to cower and cry, but to strike back. "Ba!" she said to him, banging a few notes on the piano to punctuate, to drown out his sputtering fiery rage.

"Ma ma ma ma," said Petra, when the piano lid was closed, the notes silent, Santa fizzled out. They had to keep moving.

At her father's study, Mona knocked.

"Come in," he called, after clearing his throat. He'd been asleep in his chair, Mona saw when they entered. Her father seemed possessed by a new kind of slackness these days—it was in his face, loose and dull, dented red this afternoon from his snooze against the leather headrest. Betty's death had brought this on. Mona experienced a cold brief wave of nausea: what exactly was his relationship with Betty Spitz? Oh, she hated thinking of her parents with sex lives. Why did that nasty inevitability have to rear its head the way it did, only now and then, always surprising? She was now forced to wonder if her father and Betty had once—or even recently—been in love. Veteran of two affairs with married men herself, Mona possessed sympathy for the practice. But not if her father were one of the parties, and not if she had to put herself in the shoes of Betty Spitz. Betty seemed too wise and sarcastic to be a mistress, more like Emily than Mona. Betty seemed like someone you would want to aspire toward, like a disciple on a higher rung in some spiritual ladder.

"Where's Emily off to?" her father asked. On her hip, Petra kicked; she liked her grandfather's eyeglasses, which he could move with his eyebrows.

"Did I wake you? I'm sorry. Petra's bored and we're looking for diversion."

He nodded. He wouldn't ask again about Emily, which was one of the very best things about their father: he understood discretion, understatement, subtlety. His deafness was starting to interfere with that subtlety, Mona thought; it was hard to be nuanced at high decibels. Their mother would assume that *you* hadn't heard the question and ask again, and again, and again, relentless with her right to know everything—as if having produced her children entitled her to their secretest secrets. Professor Mabie handed the baby the snow dome on his desk. It had been Roy's Christmas gift of last year. From him everybody had received a snow dome enclosing a nun or a moose or some other forlorn figure in a flurry of cheap dizzying white. This year, with Winston's aid, Roy had discovered gag gifts such as cans that advertised peanuts but in fact contained green snakes, or the ever-successful plastic pile of dog shit. Roy's grandmother was particularly susceptible to such practical jokes, which, since Winston had been away in jail, had not been perpetrated upon her for a few years. Roy was really looking forward to Christmas morning, when she would be bamboozled and shriek gratifyingly.

"Ma ma ma ma," Petra said, snow dome at her lips, the nun inside upside down, stoic and stuck. Mona raised her voice and quizzed her father on his Christmas purchases. He generally selected one day, one store, and accomplished all of his shopping therein, typically in the company of Uncle Billy, whose wife insisted on purchasing only edible or potable gifts. This year he would not reveal his store of choice, which meant it was a specialty venue, such as The Cutting Edge, or The Luggage Rack, although the family had already received from him Swiss Army knives and suitcases.

"Loose lips," he said.

Petra threw the snow dome down and demanded her mama once more, straight-arming Mona in outrage.

"There's Sheila," Mona told her father as her niece roared into the driveway in Eddie Shakes's Camaro. Their alibi was Christmas shopping. "Petra's going to have her first ride in a Camaro," Mona told her father loudly.

"Hmm," he said skeptically.

PROFESSOR Mabie had been only lightly sleeping, and was grateful for Mona's interruption. He'd been unintentionally reviewing the moments of his life when things had taken a turn, always in the direction of seriousness, always a matter of mortality. The first was his brother Billy's strange accident when he was a little boy. In Uncle Lyman's garage in Oklahoma, he blew himself up with a rocket and almost died. It happened in the quiet dust of a Sunday afternoon, the hour of the nap, the postprandial torpor, sunshine on the tar-paper roofs and shrinking clapboard houses, behind the corrugated tin garage door that had been pulled shut, an enclosure lit with one lamp, porcelain-based and featuring a decorous well-dressed lady, pilfered from the parlor while the family lay exhausted and each solitary in a bed, arms flung out, eyes heavily shut as if with coins, as if of the dead, desperate for the end of the day, the fall of the merciless sun from the white summer sky.

The small hissing flare—it never ceased to amaze Professor Mabie how little ignition was required, one wooden match, red head a flickering piece of insubstantial light—spark, and then instantaneous catastrophe. *Pow!*—and the neighborhood came alive: the eyes flew open, the limbs swung wildly into action, houses virtually shaking in a sort of aftermath. The garage door lay on the ground, little Billy twitching at a workbench, inexplicable fragments of what appeared to be bone in his neck and arms (the lamp, its splintered white china base now embedded shrapnel). To the hospital in Oklahoma City the ambulance had rushed, eldest brother Daniel Mabie riding on his knees beside his youngest brother, making bargains with God. *On your knees, boy,* the Baptist minister had recently chastised him, and this sudden explosion—the literal one, and the familial one that had immediately followed—felt to seventeen-year-old Daniel Mabie like his punishment. If he thought it was his own life that would knock him from his feet and land him on his ass, he was sorely mistaken. It was precisely this: his brother, bleeding and unconscious, so clearly at the cusp of life and death, teetering as the vehicle veered, Daniel helpless at his side. You could not hold life, he saw, it could lift like a current of rare air and simply float away, that capriciously. It came to him that were there a god, he was not one worth loving, that a soul as tender as little Billy's could not be ripe for plucking. Others abounded: the minister himself, foul-breathed, unkind, hair whipped into a vain meringue-like formation on his head each Sunday, stiff there while he pounded his fist, swore the vengeful nature of their unhappy lord.

What then to make of Billy's survival? Recovery against odds that left his surgeons puffed with silly pride. They'd approached him like some challenge from medical school, a life-form found floundering in the surf, or a cadaver and a set of curious tools, a hopeless case wherein their wits and improvisation would prevail. On a gurney in the same room lay Daniel, arm splayed, a steady supply of the same blood type. He'd have let them have that arm, let it be taken at the shoulder, patch together two incomplete boys rather than let only one leave the room alive. He half-listened, half-swooned, God still large on his mind, his anger subsumed by his fear, heart and brain in battle, as usual.

And now these other men, a banter among them he could not reconcile, would not understand until adulthood, until he'd been to war, the necessary humor of a unit at the hardest labor—to understand the joke was to be unified in the task at hand.

Billy's scalp they replaced with less important patches of skin, snipped quickly from elsewhere, thigh and buttock, the almost-fleshy underside of a seven-year-old upper arm—more whimsy, Daniel thought, random selection. "He's coming around," one of this team exclaimed.

"Then knock him down," said another. And for hours the Mabie boys lay in that clanging room, room like a restaurant kitchen, an open drain in its tiled floor, utensils in drawers, splattered blood casual as tomato sauce on walls and aprons. Cooks, constructing something palatable out of leftovers. One boy sedated and dreaming of flight, bursts of rocket and stars, flare of morphine and hallucination of heaven. The other fully conscious, more than awake: rattled yet utterly rigid, heart waiting as if at the end of a long and tangled, serpentine and endlessly knotted, particular sizzling fuse.

Billy's forehead, according to family lore, had originally been his armpit.

"That would explain why his head sweats so much."

"And why his brain is under his arm."

"Speak into the pit. Hello? Hands in the air, please."

Yes, his brothers believed his brain was damaged, although they also knew that he had moments of uncanny brilliance. As if sparks were still going off in there, the rocket he'd intercepted still discharging spottily inside his funny covered noggin.

It kept him from gym class, it kept him from the military. It kept him forever in Professor Mabie's vision, that boy who'd brought him to his knees, who'd brought him to the crucified position on a hard table, arm open and blood siphoning. You didn't get over a debt such as this.

He'd lost his parents, which was to be expected, and he'd almost lost his daughter, his Mona whom he hadn't, in all honesty, been in favor of conceiving, way back when. And he'd lost Betty Spitz, last month. These deaths, and near deaths, depleted him. Christmas seemed ominous this year, as if dressed in black, as if closing not only the year but a big coffin-like box inside of which Professor Mabie was living, tired and worn out, insufficient to the task of fending off the lowering lid.

WHEN Mona returned from Planned Parenthood the boys were in the yard, Winston holding a shovel, Roy standing on a stump pointing. Sheila, eager to go pop her first pill, screeched out of the driveway; Mona could just imagine her father's annoyance.

"Thanks, Cuzzy Mona!" she'd exuded, over and over, so delighted with her dial of contraceptives, the little calendar, the pamphlets and serious chat about side effects. Mona had resisted the strong impulse to remind Sheila to hide all of this stuff. "Wouldn't your mom want you to practice safe sex?" she'd asked futilely on the ride to the little cottage that housed the east side Planned Parenthood.

"My mom doesn't want me to practice any kind of sex," Sheila said definitively.

"Ah," sighed Mona, accomplice and loser in this scenario. She reflected that her own sex life was so sporadic that she'd not used birth control pills in about eight years. What was the point of taking those things, day in, day out, getting fat, when you only fucked every three weeks? Her cousin's joy irked Mona. Sheila was so happy she'd given her full attention to Petra, playing a loud game of peekaboo from the front seat until Mona snapped. "Do you think you could act your age?"

Sheila stuck her tongue out. Petra did, too.

Through the kitchen window, Mona watched Winston begin digging a hole. His shoulders braced as the blade met the ground. He stopped and asked Roy something. Roy held out his hands to indicate a size. Winston returned to digging, taking bites out of the earth. They had interrupted their usual feeding to dig this hole, a gardening project, Mona guessed, Winston ready to bury some object that wouldn't grow, Roy's hope for a fire-truck tree or a pop-gun vine. They'd taken out a sack of dried corncobs to nail to the trees, a bag of seed to dump into the bird feeders, and scraps from last night's dinner for the other creatures. Soon the hole was deemed large enough and Winston plunged the shovel into a pile of leaves; instead of something silly he came up with a bright red cardinal—like a magic trick, a spectacular crimson scarf yanked from a dull sleeve—the bird plump and perfect as one of Mona's stuffed toys, fake-looking with its absence of motion. Winston brought it to the hole, nudging it down the shovel blade until it tumbled in. Roy stood by, frowning. Winston leaned the shovel against a tree and sat down on the stump beside it to smoke. Roy began dropping one handful after another of dirt onto the dead bird in its grave.

"Ma ma ma ma," Petra said behind Mona. She spoke the word monotonously, as if understanding her demand was not to be met, yet duty-bound to make it nonetheless.

"There's Roy," Mona told the baby, who looked up briefly, then went back to insisting on her mother. She was a stolid, dedicated baby, intent on her rights, clear on her desires, undistractable. In her high chair she surveyed the offerings: Cheerios, shredded cheese, frozen lima beans, chunk of banana. Methodically, she ate, stopping every few minutes to suck lustily at her cup of water, inquire after her mother, sigh, resume eating. And then, while Mona forgot to pay attention, Petra fell asleep in her high chair, face in her food. Mona was thinking of Nicholas Dempsey, once again stunned dumb by his betrayal. She stared out at Winston and Roy and their nice grave but what she saw was the rumpled sheets of a motel bed, the last piece of happiness she'd known, waking in his arms with the television the room's only source of light, muted music videos. She'd wakened that night and marveled at the rare span of hours they had together, sunset to sunrise. The simplest most useful lie, his occasional business trips with the window at one end or the other left open for Mona, just Mona. The ache seemed to her unbearable. How did people bear it? She leaned over the sink and cried, sobbed and sobbed like an extra faucet.

Outside Roy knelt on his haunches to pile rocks on top of the cardinal's grave. The activity finally drew Mona out of her self-pity. From his stump, Winston bent down now and then to heft a stone in Roy's direction. Roy would add it to his pile, each time squatting in his small-child's squat, one hand holding up his pants.

And then she heard Emily's car in the drive. As usual when left with her sister's children, Mona had a moment's panic wondering whether she'd somehow neglected to be a trustworthy baby-sitter. The slumped form of Petra, head in her Cheerios, didn't look good. On the other hand, if she released the tray and pulled the baby out, there'd be tears, and that wouldn't look good either. Plus those many indentations, all those rings of O's . . .

Besides, surely Winston was a worse influence, smoking in front of Roy, handling dead animals, throwing rocks at the child, Roy out there with a runny nose and no coat, just barely keeping his pants on. Mona looked again, squinting, which is where Emily found her, at the kitchen window, peering out in disbelief at the little boy.

It was Emily who started laughing. At first Mona couldn't make out what she was seeing, as if a pale half-dressed mythical creature had entered the yard and stopped before the window, flesh and garment somehow wrong. And then the creature came clear, Roy with his butt aimed their direction, pants and underwear around his ankles, defecating. So unexpected was her angle that Mona had not recognized what she saw, Roy's scrawny bottom centered there before them as if on television, plugs of excrement appearing as if from a cookie press to fall soundlessly to the ground. Both women laughed so hard the baby woke up. Who else could laugh this way, Mona wondered, at such a sickeningly hilarious image, her nephew's pale cold-pimpled bottom and its widening aperture, her brother calmly looking on, daydreaming over a cigarette, legs crossed at the knees in his careless feminine way?

"I hate when I laugh so hard that I cry," Emily said, sputtering, weeping.

"If only it worked the other way around," Mona said when she was able, "that you cried so hard you started laughing."

"If only."

Mona knew the results had to be negative. Negative is good, she'd trained herself long ago, when her Bunny had had similar testing done with barium and X rays. In the field of medicine, positive is bad. It ran counterintuitive, against what she'd been told in junior high assembly, when a *positive* attitude was encouraged, a *negative* one frowned upon . . .

"It's positive," Emily said, wiping her eyes, watching as Roy hefted his drawers.

PART THREE

PART THREE

I

HEN IT WAS spring again, and clouds sat on Kansas like a big wet sponge. Weather was the state's news—weather and season and prevailing wind, which tipped all the trees sideways. From corner to corner the little communities were regularly polled, and without exception, from Liberal to Goodland, from El Dorado to Manhattan, be it Pittsburg or Delphos, Rome, Yoder, Harveyville, or Otis, Arnold, Bird City, Fowler, Friend, Amy, Tennis, Paradise, or WaKeeney—ask any Kansan anywhere—the most stressful pressures were barometric, matters of meteorology, your heat wave and your cold front, frost line, dew point, jet stream, flash flood, hailstone, rainfall, winterkill, wind chill.

Mrs. Mabie did not like spring; it was spirited, unruly, the halting coltish gawkiness of rudimentary life. Outside, the wind tried to knock all the new little leaves off the trees, but they hung on, tenacious and brave and pale. Inside, shutters and doors were banging like firecrackers. Mrs. Mabie went around lowering the raised windows, sealing away the tomboyish blast as if battening down a ship in a tossing sea.

"Don't you dare open that," she warned Winston.

"Air," he pleaded.

Something was amiss in the universe. Mrs. Mabie felt worse than flustered, she felt threatened, held hostage by her own lack of control.

Her neighbor, the shaggy little man who had moved last year into the Vaughn house next door, appeared at her back door one morning to demand if she'd seen anyone in his yard the night before.

"No," Mrs. Mabie said, keeping the screen door between herself and him as if it were bulletproof. He had his hands on his hips, which stance, taken with his long frizzy hair, his scorching expression, made him resemble a clown or a gnome, Rumpelstiltskin stamping his foot.

"*Some*body cut our wires," he said menacingly.

"Goodness!" she responded. He pointed and she looked. Black cords dangling from his home, snipped as if to unmoor him.

"Who would do such a thing?" she asked, somewhat rhetorically.

"I don't know who would *do such a thing*," he responded, intimating, she thought, that her family was capable of exactly this outlandish behavior.

The spring wind. The sinister wire cutters. The unsummoned witchery of the universe.

Mortal illness had the same explosive effect. Catastrophe, disaster. Of course she would never have wished cancer upon her daughter. No. But when she consulted her truest thought, she could not deny her sense of sureness in dealing with it. Here was something to bite off and chew; here was a way to matter. She felt her emotional repertoire wholly engaged, fully activated. There had been a few significant instances in her children's lives, after they were adults, that this had happened. One had been Winston's car accident—the mild wound at the base of his neck that had required stitches, his fearsome remorse and shame as he continued to live in his bedroom, shunned by his father, waiting for his sentencing, hulking about like the accused, those cruel black stitches in his neck as if overtaken by some alien implant. Another had been Mona's suicide attempt, the ensuing weeks and weeks of numb druggedness, her lumpy unlovable persona as she crawled around the house hating herself, behaving with utter unpredictability. And now there was Emily's cancer. These matters concerned death, her children pushed to extreme edges, their mother alongside doing the best she could to prevent their suffering. Was that what it took, she wondered, to make the world seem full of color once more? Her son had killed someone, her youngest daughter wished to kill herself, and the eldest was being killed. If that was what it took, how could Mrs. Mabie face herself in the mirror?

But she was good in emergencies, at the point of extremity. It was something she and her husband did together well because it was selfless activity. Their generation honored selflessness, sacrifice to the greater good. Concerns fell into place like money in the change sorter: big coins here, little ones there, order and priority and the end of superfluity. She felt tears now ever ready to flow, a certain charged reservoir. Her role, in these mortal times, was *Mother:* the unconditional state of acceptance, pure love, she supposed it could be called. She felt called upon, in the past with Mona and Winston, and as she did now, to forsake particular bodily form. Essence mattered, the invisible force like its own season that moved through the house in the manner of dust motes, of odors, of religious persuasion, a confident helpful ghost on whom you could rely. In the face of bad luck, there she would be, on your side, at your service. *Mother.* If you called, she would come. If you needed bathing, she would cleanse you. And if you disappeared, she would be there to take care of your children.

And so she envisioned, as her grandchildren sat in her lap one stormy night, that they would be bestowed upon her. In many ways, this seemed like a second chance. Roy and Petra leaned their hot heads against her breastbone when the thunder rumbled and it seemed to Mrs. Mabie that, were she their only mother, her heart would open fully beneath that bone. They could enter as they had not yet entirely entered. A second chance, she thought, suggested she'd somehow failed the first time out. Was that the way she felt? Her relations with her three grown children were complicated, their childish selves obscured by time and injury, layers of scar tissue—hers, theirs—thickening between them. Wasn't that the apt metaphor? Scar tissue—a protective covering acquired to hide a wound, to keep you from suffering. It included the passage of time, the accumulation of experience, the pres-ence of more than the immediate maternal influence, all of it necessary to mute an otherwise overwhelming pain. Her children had left her embrace; she'd lost them to the world. But these children in her lap trusted her; she could trust them, too. Emily would leave them in the care of her parents. Mrs. Mabie was sixty-one years old, could see her-self at Roy's high school graduation thirteen short years from now, it wasn't so unthinkable. Roy's graduation, and Petra's puberty. Their lives could turn out differently. Their grandmother could do for them what she seemed to have neglected to do for her first set of charges.

"I like when it rains," Roy said, his voice vibrating at Mrs. Mabie's sternum, "when it rains and we're inside," he amended.

"I like that, too," his grandmother agreed, clasping him and his sister against her. Love was physical, she thought. If you were an orphan, if you had been busy armoring yourself, if somehow your vision had become a narrow ray of clarity burning through a shadowy world and you were afraid, you could forget such a thing. A touch could hardly resonate through a tough skin; you might forget to look for or welcome it. But Roy and Petra reminded Mrs. Mabie: You needed always somebody to hold.

"I don't love thunder," Roy said. "Lightning," he added. "Lightning, however, is 'lectricity."

EMILY'S illness insinuated itself. It was everywhere at once; it was terror, embodied. Like parenthood, it could not be forgotten. It seemed suddenly to define Emily, to have eaten like a drop of corrosion straight through all the other elements, worldly as well as ethereal, unifying them as it nullified them.

From her doctors there came nothing but bad news, one positive test result after another, which news gave Emily the feeling of falling: she kept expecting to land, to go thunk at last. But instead the bottom continued to open beneath her, affirmation of all worst-case scenarios, a swift decline from dull ache to malign tumor to widespread lymphatic distress. Her disease had sneaked up on her while she was busy not worrying it away, like weeds, like rust, like corruption. She'd been vigilant about pregnancy, these last few years, pregnancy and then her babies' health. In her absorption in the lives of others, she'd forgotten to concern herself with her own status as mortal being. She'd let down her fretting guard. And look what had come in to hijack her, to cut her cables and send her plunging in this black shaft.

"It's not fair," her sister wept. Her sister could not bear it, and so Emily had to bear it for her. Found herself patting Mona's back as if it were Mona who was suddenly faced with demise.

"Statistically, this is so unlikely," said Toady.

And Frog reminded her that their friend Emily had never figured into statistics. Her whole life had been one preposterous distinction after another: accelerated, precocious, brightest, earliest, first, best, most. Here she went again, outstanding in her field.

Oddly, Emily and her brother were getting along. He was the only person who didn't treat her any differently, he and her two children. The children didn't count, however, because they were in the dark concerning her cancer. Her brother impressed her with his genuine respect for the differences they'd harbored between them for so long. He did not forgive her her trespasses, nor did he do any rehabbing on his own. Things were the same, and for this Emily was profoundly grateful. With him, for brief periods of time, it was possible to ignore the fact that she was dying. With him, she could still reach heights of absurd annoyance over trivialities, a trait of hers he'd been working since they were eight and ten years old.

"I hate how the syrup collects in his ears," Winston said of his Mickey Mouse waffle, sincerely vexed.

"Don't eat," Emily advised, having consumed 1,000 milligrams of ibuprofen, six vitamins of various sizes and textures, one mood elevator, and two very fine bright red painkillers for her own breakfast, washed down with terribly strong coffee. It was an agreeable buzz.

"Why aren't *you* eating?" he asked.

"I'm not hungry."

"I haven't seen you eat anything in days."

"I eat. I just don't need witnesses."

For her thirty-sixth birthday, in February, he had not bought her a gift. "I don't *get* gifts," he told Mona, meaning both that he didn't buy them and he didn't understand them. She was appalled. Usually her brother could not make her angry but slighting their dying sister on what could very likely be her last birthday seemed somehow beyond the pale, something even Winston wouldn't do.

"She doesn't need anything," he argued. "I don't have any money, anyway. It would just be a hollow gesture."

"What do you know about hollow gestures?" Mona cried. "I brought you presents in prison all the time, *all the time,* just because a present cheers a person up." She hated resorting to such bald manipulation and guilt inducement, but her brother was threatening to become insensitive, so far gone no one could reach him. Mona felt it her duty, an imperative, to retrieve him.

"That's right," he said, "you did, and I accepted them because you needed to give them to me. Those gifts were about you, not me. Don't even be fooling yourself otherwise."

"Oh, I can't believe we're talking this way, arguing about presents when Emily is dying." Now Mona sobbed in earnest, and she thought she could tell that her brother's sigh, when it came, was sincerely pained, damp from his throat. He hurt, she hoped. She made a wish that he did not want his sister to die.

Over waffles on that cloudless day, Emily felt weak, a little light-headed and drifty, as if some piece of her were sliding loose inside, like a drop of water in a taut balloon. She asked Winston to drive her to her radiation treatment. It was the first time they'd been in a car together since last summer when she'd picked him up from the airport, and, as far as Emily knew, it was the first time Winston had driven since 1991, since George Bush was in office; he probably possessed no license, although neither broached that technicality. She let her thoughts linger on his last passenger, her grandma Bunny whom she had loved. Like Emily, Bunny had had a brush with cancer and was very frail; it seemed to Emily, who had helped decide how to accessorize her grandmother in her coffin, that the auto accident injury that killed her was, in fact, minor, ancillary. Her grandmother had been a fragile parcel, one jostled just slightly too hard by her unlucky chauffeur. "Good-bye, Bunny," Emily had whispered, clipping turquoise earrings on her grandmother's soft, cool earlobes.

It was her mother, Emily recalled, who'd said something inspiring about Bunny's death. "I like to think parts of her are still with us," she'd said of her mother-in-law. Emily had taken up her grandmother's elegance as her desired legacy. Wry elegance.

"Do me a favor," Emily said to Winston. "Mom's going to want to put something insipid on my gravestone, like, 'Here Lies Emily Mabie, A Chipper Sort.' "

"You underestimate her."

"I was kidding." And she was glad he thought she underestimated their mother; it made him bigger than Emily in some way.

"I won't let her call you chipper," he added, later.

"Thanks." He was easy to be with, now that Emily was unwilling to do the harder work of initiating, asking, orchestrating their exchanges, making things ordinary and pleasant. She now had the right to expect others to pick up the slack.

And if anyone had asked her how she had managed to glide so quickly from terror to pragmatism, she would have said, "What choice do I have?" There wasn't any other way to be.

"Not here," she told Winston as he found a parking place near the front door of Saint Francis Outpatient. "Over there, in the corner." To his credit, he did not question the decision. Would there ever be people in the world who accommodated more willingly, with fewer interruptions, than siblings? They parked far from the front door, and then walked slowly across the lot. "I like to make the cars mad," she said, tapping the driver's keyhole of a white Cutlass. Sure enough, it whooped: a dowager, goosed. "Remember when the alarms talked? 'Step *away* from the car.' I miss that." She tapped her heel gently on the bumper of a black Jeep, which responded by saying its own name: EEP, EEP.

The cars squawked and bleated as they passed along. "I can make the whole place come alive. I've been counting but I forget what . . ." Winston took her arm when she suddenly sagged. ". . . my record is."

The front door was still yards away, across the shining lot. All this glass and metal, reflecting the cold plains sun: the automobile. Its presence in the world seemed so heartlessly permanent. It would be fashioned into other useful products, wouldn't it? Smashed flat and square, melted and soldered, crushed and ground, spread thin and polished, heated and transformed into a new tool, another toy.

The human body, she thought, just so much compost.

"I gotta rest," she told her brother. She eased her shoulder against his and leaned into him, more than she needed to, enough to make him brace his feet. She simply forced him to hold her up. She would insist that he touch her. She breathed in his odor, which was cigarette smoke, old clothes, unwashed skin. When she could, she took in his expression. On his face was not the customary guardedness, the scathing judgment Emily often believed he felt toward her. He met her gaze without looking away and what she saw there in his vivid blue eyes was apprehension, and sadness, a question the answer to which they both understood.

Inside, in the bright hallway decorated with fake philodendrons,

Emily's least favorite technician made her usual greeting—"Hello beautiful!"—beaming like an ad for fluoride. The woman treated the patients like children—and they took it, by and large, all of them pleased to be complimented, grateful to be greeted with a smile. Emily looked away, angry beyond words.

"Now now," said her brother. "Maybe she meant me."

"She's an asshole," Emily told him. How she hated false cheer. How she wanted to kneecap it.

"She's just a fool," Winston said. They'd reached the waiting area outside the radiation lab. "She doesn't mean any harm."

"But she's not harmless."

"No, I guess not."

"You wanna see the machine?"

He shrugged, agreeable. Another technician was arranging the bolsters on the gliding table. The machine itself looked like a giant KitchenAid mixer, antiquated round edges, colors those of a Ford Falcon the family had owned in the seventies, bay leaf green and Pet Milk ivory. "They line you up with lasers," Emily said, "like that weird blue chalk on construction sites. Then they blast me with two hundred rads."

"Rad," Winston said.

"It's dark and quiet, and I just lie here kind of meditating, or praying."

"Praying to what?" Winston was taking in the room slowly, gazing up and around. He'd been to some odd places in his life, Emily thought. Why should this one amaze him?

"I don't know what I pray to. To my gyno onco? To beating the odds? Maybe to those funky rads."

They returned to the waiting room. Winston dropped down on a chair and riffled through the magazines and brochures. You could pick up a lot of information about cancer while waiting in such a place.

"I should have told you to bring something to read," Emily said, standing in the warm square of sunlight coming through the window. She was cold all of the time these days. Out in the parking lot, the last car they'd passed on their way in was still making its objections, a faint persistent noise through the glass. The red Corvette in the handicap space had been simply begging to be thumped. Winston had done it, with his fist, leaving a momentary dent in the fiberglass hood. Its wounded howl continued looping through the air, sweeping through

Emily in the way she imagined radiation did, a wave of incendiary power, blinding, deafening, annihilating.

"You could nap, I guess," she told Winston vaguely.

"Doubtful."

"Well, I'll be back in fifteen," she said when the cheerful technician came clipping back down the hall with her file folders and motioned Emily through the door.

"I'll be here," her brother said, "boning up on the old prostate."

TEN YEARS earlier Professor Mabie had not been in favor of Emily's decision to become a part-owner of Kick, the shop she and her twin best friends ran. But it was precisely Emily's stubbornness in investing in the business that now impressed him. She was a smart girl and she'd made a lucky gamble.

During what was known as a bitter divorce, the twins' father had bought a seedy comic book shop in a strip mall, providing a destination for his daughters besides the ballet studio, which is where his ex-wife wanted them. Funny, Professor Mabie thought, that no one had suggested college to the Lee girls. It was their father who had pumped money into the business, floating it for years out of a kind of obstinate refusal to be wrong. First one and then the other of the girls lost her anorexic grace and pallor, hanging around there behind the glass case full of the accoutrements of drug consumption: pipes and rolling papers and tiny spoons and delicate clips. Was this what their father had had in mind? Prior, the girls had been famous for fainting, living on lettuce and Fresca, for being absolutely identical, starved and fair, red-headed, heavily freckled, pale as illness, with their blistered and bleeding toes, their serious laughable ambitions in the world of art. Professor Mabie remembered them from his own dinner table, pushing their food around the plate as if to make it ugly, adamantly not eating. He couldn't recall which had let herself go slack first, Roberta or Tonya, just that whichever it had been, she'd acquired a sense of humor along with her heft, some color in her face, so that when the other followed suit nobody but their mother minded. Their juvenile-delinquent customers certainly didn't care what they weighed—running a head shop was guaranteed to make you more popular than dancing *The Nutcracker* every Christmas.

Professor Mabie could still picture the yellow brick fire station that had once stood on the corner, torn down to accommodate a strip mall in the early seventies. Lucky for Kick and its owners, the neighborhood surrounding it had gone steadily upscale. These days the little cement block mall had been resurfaced with pebbles and thatching, trying to look British, sporting a few planters full of heather, and a couple of houses next door had been turned into other trendy shops: kitchen and bath supply, coffee shop, bike repair, baby boutique. The twins—when had they lost their real names and become Frog and Toady?—had slowly changed out their merchandise, from comics and vinyl albums and bumper stickers promoting the legalization of marijuana to cheap imported silver and flimsy patterned fabric and folk art totems from Central America to, these days, one-of-a-kind jewelry, shoes, lingerie, dresses. Emily, of course, had changed the store's direction slightly, when she came on board, aiming them toward the conservative and salable. But they'd moved so slowly through and into these phases that the alterations were nearly imperceptible, like the aging face of a relative, and always they'd retained a few pieces of the store's last incarnation, nostalgically, a poster here, a Guatemalan sweater there, vintage lamps and bolts of imported lace and bric-a-brac, the store thick with atmosphere, old chairs to sit down upon, toys to play with, a few cats wandering around or resting in the windows, a loud sound system, oilcloth-covered tables, and dim light. Eclectics, Emily was quick to say, when someone asked her what she sold. The store reminded Professor Mabie of the home of an old woman, layered with the business of moving through time, vaguely cat stench–scented, and hosting a loyal clientele, family-like, people who had also proceeded through stages: stoned adolescence, impoverished college hip, trendy young parenthood, and impending comfortable reluctant middle age. Amid the slick bright homogeneity of most retail stood Kick, prepared to make you feel distinct yet not alone.

And they carried plus sizes, Emily always reminded her family. "Fat Chicks," Winston had long ago suggested calling the store.

Ballet would never have worked out as well for either twin as Kick had. Professor Mabie didn't understand why the business had thrived, only that it had, and that his daughter, contrary to his warnings, had finished two master's degrees while also making a solid profit. Rebellion pleased him, when it worked out as this one had; he didn't mind being proven wrong. In fact, his relationship with Emily seemed built of just such episodes: her sage defiance.

Professor Mabie and Winston both happened to be awake when the police called the Mabie household at four in the morning to report the robbery. They'd arrived at the telephone at the same moment from their separate nocturnal activities of TV watching and guitar playing, Professor Mabie's heart beating rapidly: one of his brothers, dead—and him, sleeping soundly before a television.

"I'm not waking Emily," Professor Mabie declared when he hung up. His daughter napped all of the time, usually upright in the living room recliner, as if lying down meant giving in. Her health was now a presence in the house, like a rare orchid or exotic pet, like an expensive piece of art, to be attended meticulously, formidable with its fragility. "She had radiation today," he added, and Winston did not mention that he'd been the one who took her there.

By mutual silent agreement, Winston and Professor Mabie climbed into the Toyota and drove the mile to Kick, Winston wearing not just flip-flops but *weathered* flip-flops—as if to spend $2.98 on a new pair every season or so would be too much to ask. Professor Mabie breathed deeply, determined not to fly into a rage.

Retired, possessed of insomnia, Professor Mabie often found himself out and about in the wee hours of the morning, visiting the twenty-four-hour grocery store or gas station. He conducted his business against the flow of ordinary commerce, visiting the video or liquor store at the moment they opened, for example, thereby avoiding the late afternoon rush. He banked also in the morning. Emptiness comforted him, on streets or in offices. He came to see that businesses counted on tradition, much as others might lead you to believe tradition was faltering. Based on his observations of traffic flow, for example, he gathered that it was still traditional to work from eight in the morning until five in the evening. Lunch hour ran at the customary time. It was traditional to work, period; rarely did he find reputable company in the odd hours. Instead, he found ragamuffins and retirees. Pregnant women, occasionally, teenagers who should have been in school or bed. People like Winston, consummate unemployed deadbeats. Wearing flip-flops. In March.

Tonight the street was all theirs, all the way to Kick, a trip father and son made in complete silence. The radio muttered at an indecipherable volume but neither adjusted it one way or the other. At the store parking lot they found the Lee twins with their arms crossed, glowering as the red and blue lights spun crazily against the houses and shops and the faces of the neighbors, who stood wearing bathrobes and scuffs. The scene of the crime. It was funny how people didn't mind being caught in their pajamas, Professor Mabie thought. He liked to think that he would have gotten dressed before stepping outside his home.

"Whassup," Winston asked the twins, his first utterance of the evening. Professor Mabie marveled at the casual palm slapping the three exchanged, this generation's version of the handshake.

"The real cops are arguing with the rentacops," Toady explained.

"Turf battle. Cock of the walk," said Frog.

"We decided that rentacops are cuter, but the police are better armed."

"So," Winston said. "You *date* the rentacop but *marry* the real deal?"

"Basically," Frog agreed.

Professor Mabie asked about the damage.

"We're just robbed, thank god, no damage exactly except a busted lock and some mud on the rugs. The kitties are fine," she added, as if Professor Mabie had even remembered there were animals involved. An attachment to pets, like slapping hands in greeting, eluded him.

"Kilim rugs," emphasized Toady. "The rentacops tracked in the mud, so insurance probably won't cover dry-cleaning. I knew we should have upgraded our security. Those buff bastards from Rest Assured . . . Where's Em?"

"Sleeping." The four of them stared off in different directions, each, Professor Mabie assumed, fighting despair over Emily's illness. The wave passed and he was able to take some mild comfort in the night, despite the occasion, its gentle temperature a reprieve from the long close winter. For days and days, spring had been coming, backing off, coming, backing off.

"Well, *I'm* going for doughnuts," the twin called Frog said, as if someone had threatened her right to eat food as well as finish the night's sleep.

"Chocolate-covered cake," her sister requested.

"Bear claw," said Winston. "And coffee, white."

"Nothing for me," Professor Mabie said, placing a tiny TicTac on his tongue. "Thanks," he added. The Lee twins had always scared him. They worked as a pair, like magpies, speaking alternately so that you had to keep shifting your gaze nervously back and forth, as if one might peck at you while you were distracted by the other. Their voices were similar, their appearance identical, their sensibilities indistinguishable. Double irony, double sarcasm, double silent scornful observation when you entered the room. But tonight he had a new appreciation for the women. When one handed the other her wallet and then tucked the label of her sweatshirt in, he suddenly was able to see them the way he saw himself with his brothers: protective sibling affection. They were less scary, in that light. And, of course, they had been nothing but loyal to his daughter Emily for years and years. Bad influences, probably, but abiding.

The thick-necked men in uniforms settled their differences and finally allowed the owners inside to fill out forms.

"Intruders took their time," one of the cops noted, looking around.

"Meaning?" Winston asked. The cop evaluated Winston head to toe, gaze settling on the flip-flops for a second. Though they might be the same age, there was little else to indicate similarity. Would Professor Mabie have preferred his son to be the cop? Tough? Clean-shaven? Hard? Employed, yet unforgiving? This officer called the twins "Ma'am"; he had a toothpick twitching between his lips as if he wished it were a needle, as if he could spit it with deadly accuracy into somebody's eyeball.

"No frenzied bits," the cop said, summing up the composure of their intruders.

The place looked fairly normal, a little empty, picked over not by nervous boys but calm ones. The cats slept in their accustomed bed, blinking lazily up at the people, useless witnesses who wished somebody would turn the lights off. The velvet was gone, all of the expensive jewelry, all of the silver cigarette cases and hip flasks. The cash register itself was missing, as was the deposit bag stored habitually in the office file cabinet. The mannequins had lost not only their accessories but a couple of their hands. "Why would you steal mannequin parts?" Professor Mabie asked.

Toady glanced at the figures. "Those were already missing."

He didn't ask why you'd want to display clothing on broken mannequins. There was a sloppy aesthetic at work that he didn't quite apprehend; it was related to his daughter Mona's fashion sense, too, the desirability of used and tatty things, junk from times Professor Mabie was happy to have passed through and forgotten.

"Two guys," the cop speculated, "to get the register out the door."

"It took two of us to get it in," Toady acknowledged.

"But no broken glass. Just the busted lock."

"Well, you'll excuse me if I'm not exactly grateful." The cop shrugged; he was only trying to show her her good luck; she wasn't attractive enough to spend much time impressing.

"Spare," her sister said upon return, of the store's new look. "I like it. So few options, so much room to move around." She held out a big yellow box. "Doughnut? When I told them we'd been robbed Winchells gave me two dozen free. Who knew?" Everyone trudged around the store chewing, noticing the specifics of their break-in. Professor Mabie felt oddly vulnerable—as if the thieves might come back and turn into killers or arsonists—and kept peering out the plate-glass windows to the parking lot, which still flashed blue and red. He felt like he was onstage, being watched. When the cuckoo clock sounded, he jumped. Jesus God, *cuckoo clocks.*

Winston touched the remaining clothing and shoe boxes. He had been offered a job by Frog and Toady, last summer, but he hadn't taken it. He wouldn't put himself in a beholden position with Emily, Professor Mabie guessed, even if it were the last job in town. Now Professor Mabie had an unkind thought: what if Winston had robbed the store? Winston had been awake, knew the habits of the owners, needed money. . . . He watched his son move among the racks, make jokes with the twins, and hated him, briefly, imagining him here just a few hours previous, stashing earrings in a bag, hauling off the stereo system. He did not trust Winston, and the lack of trust was precisely the crux of his problem with his son. Not trusting him made Professor Mabie angry, cautious, afraid, ashamed.

But clearly he was alone with this suspicion. Toady and Frog trusted Winston. It had never occurred to them to suspect him of robbing them. On some reel of super-8 film, somewhere in the Mabie archives, the Lee sisters chased Winston around a kiddie pool with a garden hose, shrieking, grinning, naked torsos, stringy children's hair, the flickering faded colors of 1970, Winston untarnished, identical redheaded girls two years his senior focusing all their attention upon the task of ambushing him, soaking him, Emily standing in her floral two-piece with her customary smirk on her face while her friends preferred her brother. In another of those films the girls dressed Winston in his mother's cocktail clothes, black silk dress with cut-out midsection, and he looked lovely, a better girl than his sisters or their friends. Professor Mabie could still recall the uneasy reaction he'd had to seeing his son in a dress, the moment just before recognition when he'd thought: *Sexy girl*. After Winston's voice changed, he did other favors for Emily and her friends, screening phone calls from bad dates and jerks, sometimes ushering ballet performances. By virtue of his position—little brother—these two women had never been intimidated by Winston, never interested in flirting with him, sleeping with him, adoring him. They liked him; they grew irritated with him; they were tolerant and familiar. They trusted him.

"I miss the herb paraphernalia," Winston said, after the cops and the bumbling security patrol had left. "Ah, patchouli." He had nudged his rear end onto the stool behind the counter, propping his hideous sandaled feet on the rungs, comfortable here, as he was most everywhere. Professor Mabie resented the ease. Winston yawned emphatically, setting off a chain reaction. Outside, the sun was rising and traffic had picked up.

"Those Rest Assured guys pump iron," Toady noted.

"You think they're hiring?" Winston asked. The twins laughed. "What?" Winston made a muscle inside his secondhand shirt and flexed it a few times for their amusement.

"Do we open today, or what?" Frog asked.

"Dunno. Clearance sale? Everything twenty percent off?"

"Because we've only got twenty percent of our stock? Open because we've got no way to close, no lock?"

"We don't even have a cash register. It's charge plates or nothing, today. Hey, they took the fucking telephone. Unbelievable. Sorry," she added, realizing she'd sworn in front of Professor Mabie.

He waved: don't mind me. With them, that was what he'd always wanted.

The sisters looked tiredly at each other. "Do you feel *violated*?" one asked the other, quoting some conventional wisdom or other.

"*Ter*ribly."

When he asked if there were any last jobs he could perform, Professor Mabie was finally handed a broom. His daughter's friends were awkward with him, which made Winston, for once, an asset. The four of them moved through the store rehanging what had been deemed unworthy of theft—"We can't *give* this stuff away," Winston said, suggesting a sales tack—sweeping the doughnut crumbs and dirt from the floor, switching on the remaining lamps, plugging in a radio to fill the role of the stereo. Winston went on foot to the hardware store three blocks away, returning with a new deadbolt, chisel, and Phillips head screwdriver to replace the lock. His ability surprised his father; Professor Mabie could not recall having seen Winston work with tools before.

"There," his son declared, demonstrating the lock's smooth action. He knelt and deftly swept up the sawdust, containing it in his pants pockets the way soldiers did cigarette butts. His hands were pretty hands, inherited from his mother, nothing like the Mabie brothers' large rough Okie models. Were those fingerprints rampant in this building? Had he been here earlier, filling Marty Song's delivery van full of Kick merchandise? Professor Mabie stared at his son's back, hating the fact that he could not know.

The Lee sisters thanked them both, standing there identical and newly middle-aged, Toady's shirt unbuttoned on a freckled bit of cleavage. Professor Mabie couldn't help wondering if they were absolutely identical, if they'd played tricks with that odd power, left behind a trail of fools. Furthermore, what about the husband of Frog? Wouldn't it be useless for the unmarried twin to subscribe to a certain kind of modesty before the husband of the married one? What would be the point of covering up what he already had supreme intimacy with, her naked body? His familiarity with Frog would completely obliterate Toady's privacy. If a man knew either twin, he knew them both.

"Doesn't Roberta have a husband?" Professor Mabie asked Winston on the way home, just to speak.

"*Had*," Winston replied. "Past tense. Seems like he went off with some other girl recently."

"Oh."

In the driveway they found two pigeons copulating. Professor Mabie halted the car short of the garage and jumped out, swinging his arms. Their guano on his concrete was an affront. He waved his arms and swore. "Goddamn birds," he said, to no one. Winston was slow to ease out of the car, standing with his head tipped thoughtfully toward the eaves where the birds had retreated while his father ranted. "I hate them," Professor Mabie said, smoothing his own ruffled hair. In the kitchen, he realized his tiredness. It was a feeling left over from former late nights, the sore eyes, the dusty raw throat, the desire to plunge his head into a pile of pillows and disappear. "Milk," he said to himself before the refrigerator.

"Yeah," Winston agreed, getting the glasses down and checking them for dishwasher sand, while his father opened a new gallon of skim. And that was the extent of their conversation. Five hours together, and that was it.

WHEN KICK was a head shop, back in high school, Mona and her friends shoplifted there because Frog and Toady owned it, and not only did the consequences seem minimal, but those two deserved to be ripped off. Back then, Mona thought so.

When her sister became a part owner, Mona wouldn't steal from Kick anymore.

The morning after the robbery, Mona called in sick at Starkey.

"Just 'cause you were killed," said Percy the gay secretary. He plagued Mona by being the perfect stereotype.

"What?"

"You were killed yesterday, Raymond said." He meant in the ongoing game of Killer that Starkey personnel played. It was a bizarre game; a little like serious hunting, a little like tag, it probably accounted for Mona's long tenure at the school, the fact that she would play. "Good sport," her letter of rec would someday read. "Esprit de corps."

"I was not killed yesterday," she said now. "I was nicked in the thigh."

"I heard direct hit."

"Raymond lies. Plus, I thought there was no using a magic bullet. This one ricocheted off the wall into my leg. Anyhow, I'm sick. Not killed, not even wounded, just plain old sick."

Mona liked her teacher's aide job for a number of reasons, prime among them that she could be sick often; the real teacher would be there—frazzled, pissy, but there. She also felt kinship, or something like it, with the emotionally frail, the physically disabled, the mentally retarded. She really did. But this morning she was sick in order to work at Kick. The twins were going to be tied up with insurance claims; they'd already decided to have a Rip Off Sale and hung signs announcing the fact.

"Pussy," Percy said. He got away with the meanest teasing because he was gay. "Crybaby."

"Whatever."

Mona had been awake at four in the morning, too, listening to her headphones and crying. She owned old-fashioned headphones, the kind that sat on her ears like two plastic baseball gloves, their enclosure total, leatherette material suctioned to her face by her tears, which ran down her cheeks. The songs she liked best now were the ones about hopeless unrequited love. Before, when Nicholas Dempsey had been hers, she preferred the songs concerning secret lives. There would always be a sound track, she thought. That was the beauty of music: it never failed to accompany you, to fuel whatever fire you found yourself in. She could have made a compilation tape of her last year of emotional upheaval, an operatic roller coaster of highs and lows.

Things were worse now than they had been over Christmas. At least back then she'd believed that Nicholas Dempsey had quit loving her, his thorough silence signal enough. But in recent weeks he'd been calling her every now and then, chatting, being friendly, although noncommittal about meeting. This was his version of "let's be friends," a relationship Mona couldn't envision. "I don't want a friend," she told Marty Song. "I want a lover."

"There must be a pill for this," Marty advised.

"I've already tried all those. One made me dizzy, another made me yawn so often my jaw ached. A few turn you inorgasmic. Not that I'm having orgasms, anyway."

"Talk to your therapist." But Mona didn't dare. In therapy, she discussed her sister. Emily's health was leaking away; she had cancer in an ovary and her lymph nodes; she had been through surgery and chemo and was now on radiation therapy, processes that had left her weak and bald and a little dumbfounded, sleepy. It seemed to Mona crass and immature and downright evil to dwell on her obsession with Nicholas Dempsey when her sister was dying.

Dr. Lydia had sighed mightily when the recent affair was exposed. Not because she was disappointed but because the two of them could have discussed Mona's emotional state when it was something besides depressed and rejected. "Your fantasy life is more powerful than your real life," she pointed out. "You've invested very heavily in it."

"I know."

"And now it's kind of gauzy."

"I know."

"And you're alone."

"Right." Mona cried, sorry for herself, sorry for her hopefulness, that open face waiting at a window for him to return. And then it was right back to Emily, whose stoic bravery seemed something Mona might learn from. She actually did have complicated feelings about Emily's illness, her own guilt about the affair with Barry, her envy of years past. . . . But yesterday, Dr. Lydia had interrupted Mona, finally having had enough. "Stop talking about your sister." Startled, Mona blinked, gathering her loose words and lazy phrases back around her to take a look at them. Had she been talking only about Emily? Sometimes in therapy she forgot to pay attention to what she was saying, just rambled and digressed down the paths of her thoughts, brought up short only by Lydia's sudden scribbling on her pad. Lydia looked angry. Mona resisted the urge to apologize, having been scolded in the past for that habit. She noted that her therapist had three new piercings in her ear, twinkling diamond studs lined up along the firm rim where it was supposed to be painful. "You're using your sister's problems to avoid your own."

"Hers are bigger."

"Bullshit."

Mona sighed. Lydia had dyed her hair a different color, last week, and this week she was hostile. It heartened Mona to recognize that these things were not about herself; previously, she would have felt responsible for the way the session was headed. Instead, she evaluated Lydia candidly, from her big brown eyes to her clunky black boots, coming to the conclusion that Lydia had been recently betrayed. Having been betrayed herself, she thought she recognized the symptoms in others.

"There's just not much going on in my life except Emily's illness," Mona said, which was true. When tempted to think of Nicholas Dempsey, she inserted her sister's problem like a slide over the image of her own. This felt clarifying to Mona, calibrating, but Lydia seemed to think of it as distortion, instead.

"Comparison is not going to get you anywhere," she declared. "You could find a hundred people with worse lives than your sister's within a three-block radius of this building."

"That just seems so cold," Mona said, her eyes tearing. "Why are you being so cold?"

"I'm not being cold. You're avoiding the subject of your obsession. Don't adopt your sister's cancer. That's no more useful an obsession than the old one. Have you had contact with Nicholas?"

His name on Lydia's lips made Mona feel like she'd been hit, so unexpected was the sound. For days and days she could fortify herself against succumbing, against memory and desire and longing and melancholy, but his name, in an unguarded moment, could still undo her. His phone calls—erratic in timing as well as tone—were driving her crazy. She wished she had the strength to simply not answer them. She knew that was what Lydia would recommend.

"Occasionally," she offered weakly.

"Cut him off," Lydia said, suddenly forceful, leaning forward and clasping her blunt-nailed fingers, trapping them with each other, *Here's the church, here's the steeple, open the doors . . .* "Take action."

"Like?"

"Revenge," Lydia said intently. "Go ahead. Do something to hurt him. Why should you be the only one hurt? He wants to pretend nothing happened, phoning you up just to chat. Well, don't let him pretend that. Don't let him get away with it."

"That seems like awfully unconventional advice," Mona observed, frowning.

"So?" Lydia leaned back and crossed her heavy feet contentedly.

Maybe Lydia was suffering her own breakup. Her hair color had changed from nutmeg to eggplant, and those new studs winking in her ear, painful as they obviously were, signaled something. Mona had assumed that Lydia was a lesbian and therefore outside the dictates of the usual mating game problems. But of course those problems would find you, no matter your sexual orientation.

"Call his wife?"

Lydia shrugged, as if this were the most minor of potential avenging activities, small potatoes. As if Mona ought to be able to come up with something more inspired.

"I'd like him to disappear," Mona admitted. "I'd like him to die," she confessed. Sometimes she wondered which would be better, his death or her own? Given a gun, where would she aim it?

"Your anger is more interesting than your woundedness," Lydia told her. "Work from strength."

"Kill him?"

"Don't *kill* him. But do something to give yourself some power. You can't go around so undefended any longer." She squinted dazzlingly, daring Mona to disagree. Mona's other confidants, Emily and Marty, sympathized with her broken heart, patted her head and gave her hugs, but not Lydia.

"Is this some kind of tough-love strategy?"

Lydia smiled at last, dismissing her gruffly. "We just need to make progress," she said, standing, shaking a foot. She was tall, fit, knees knobby like a boy's. "I can feel you getting bored here, repeating yourself, slipping into Emily's problems in order to avoid your own."

Mona took Lydia's advice home and mulled it. Revenge, huh? She enlisted the aid of Marty Song, whose first idea was a personal ad. "Hefty gals wanted," he said. "And then Nicholas's number."

"I like it."

"It's good," he agreed. "The wife will go nuts, fat girls calling all day."

"The wife," Mona said, speculatively. "Maybe I'll befriend his wife. Maybe I'll get to know her really well."

"What does she do?"

"I don't know. Wash her hair? Lactate? She works out. Every day she works out at this club. She has a personal trainer, Nicholas used to make fun of him, Alphonse or something."

"You could get some calf definition out of the deal."

"I'm liking this plan. Don't you think it's odd that my therapist recommended revenge?"

"What's her number, that therapist of yours? She sounds right up my alley."

AND THEN Nicholas Dempsey's wife came to the Kick Rip Off Sale, pushing a stroller holding the two children, the whitest white children with their fervently black names, Ella and Miles. The wife did not look large enough to have given birth to them, as if she were of another species, or as if the children would soon overwhelm her, parasites destined to consume their host. The boy looked like Nicholas, like Beck Hansen Jr., his eyes, his teeth, which teeth Mona could still feel beneath her tongue. "Hey, Miles," she said to him, squatting, knowing how to act with him because she had a nephew at home just like him. The wife eyed her appraisingly.

They had never met. How did Mona know her son's name? "Your husband is my brother's lawyer," Mona said, rising smoothly, easy with the information, not waiting for the connections to make sense to Nicholas Dempsey's wife. "I saw you guys in his office once." Now that they weren't sleeping together, she wasn't having an affair with Nicholas. She could talk about him all she wanted. Let the wife worry, she thought. Christine, her name was. Mona was pleased to see crow's-feet at her eyes, dark roots, a harried embarrassment as she maneuvered the cumbersome double stroller in the narrow confines of Kick. Mona adopted the confidence of the saleslady, dressed up, entitled to go behind the counter, in charge of the merchandise, limited as it was. In others she hated this stance, as if selling nice stuff made you nice stuff yourself, as if you owned or could even afford the goods in your care. But she was grateful for the disguise, today. Clearly Christine Dempsey believed in saleslady poshness. Clearly Mona's fingernails on the calculator and then charge receipt, separating the copy from the original, meant something.

It was Emily who had pointed out fingernails to Mona. There were jobs, she explained, that were all about fingernails. Bank tellers, restaurant hostesses, salesclerks, those women whose elaborate handwriting is loopily convoluted because they're busy protecting their manicures, protecting and showcasing, simultaneously, gripping the pen just so, always sweeping their gorgeous fingernails before your eyes, as if to distract you with magic tricks from the fact that they were just selling makeup or underwear, spending their days giving pedicures or waxing bikini lines, plunging their great beautiful hands into someone else's permanent wave, and always obliged to smile at and fawn over the customer.

A whole fleet of the working force donned their best clothes in order to go serve. Some of those salesclerks even put on lab coats, as if cosmetics were a science, and they were the doctors.

"That color is wonderful on you," Mona said of an ocher turtleneck.
"Do you have it in *petite*?" asked tiny Christine Dempsey, twisting
her torso in front of a three-way mirror while her children gazed on.
Mona smiled to think of how she would tell Emily about this later, her
lover's wife asking for an ugly-colored sale shirt in size *petite*. Not since
she was four years old had Mona worn something labeled petite. If only
the turtleneck were tight enough to squeeze her throat. . . .

"Just what's out," Mona said, looking so sorry for the inconve-
nience, motioning with her fingernails toward the merchandise. Christine Dempsey was flattered into buying a pair of large dangly earrings
that were absolutely not her style. They weren't Nicholas's style, either,
big interlocked distressed-copper disks, and Mona enjoyed imagining
his reaction. "Looking pretty ethnic," he would say sarcastically, flip-
ping them with his casual cruel fingertips. And the wife would say,
"This very nice woman helped me choose them, the sister of one of
your clients, she was so sweet to the kids. . . ." And maybe Nicholas
would blanch. Flinch. *Blinch*, Mona remembered: something Winnie
the Pooh did. She liked very much envisioning his blinching.

2

EMILY'S CHILDHOOD bedroom was now the guest room. But in the old days, when the children were in their teens, Emily's room was the place to go when stoned. Her bed was always made, for starters, and the wallpaper, an innocuous pattern of swirled white and pink and gray, vibrated beautifully under the influence. You seemed to be enclosed within a snowstorm, swirling flashes of white pulsing around you, yet warm. Plus, it was down the hall, sort of isolated from the other bedrooms, near a bathroom, just in case, and it had three big windows that, when fully opened, allowed a refreshing cross-breeze.

Emily was good at creating atmosphere. Her apartment on the third floor, up there where once, when the house was new and the customs different, the servants had lived, she had made wholly her own, walls adorned with paintings and masks and photographs of her children and the family, rooms comfortable and functional, furniture eclectic and arranged to suit a variety of pursuits: reading, sleeping, eating, talking, playing. There were only four rooms: a large bathroom with claw-footed tub; the kitchen, which had housed Winston's photography lab when he thought he might become a photographer; the living room with its bookshelves and array of pretty lamps; and the bedroom, which, like the bedroom of the notorious bears, held three beds, big, medium, and small all in a line. Through the dormer window was the roof where once the three Mabie children had crawled out to look at their neighborhood and city, over the trees and power lines and church steeples, to listen to the cicadas and the soothing hum of a passing car. Now the window was cleverly latched, preventing little Roy from doing the same. At night, when her children slept, Emily unlatched the window and slid out, smoked a cigarette in the dark there while the city glimmered and the trains made their noise of longing.

In the hallway linking these four rooms Roy's toys were arranged, shelves with clear bins, his plastic and wooden sets organized in the way of day care. He pulled a drawer and placed it on the floor, removing the blocks or dolls or trucks or balls or trains, sitting in the timeless M that only the loose-limbed, the child or yogi, could perform so effortlessly, and would stay for a long while, making his way through his game. He was a large-headed boy, blond like his father, big-eyed like his mother, and his fingers, spatulate masculine ones, resembled neither parent. They came from his grandfather, Professor Mabie, working hands, destined to become sturdy and guiding. Emily loved to see him move his fingers, which had never been pudgy and tapered, the way Petra's were, the way most babies' were, but had always been simply small versions of her father's hands. She liked to sandwich them between her own. She liked to nuzzle her boy, to have his head on her chest. She had been fond of sitting on the hallway floor with him, leaning against the wall, merely watching, drinking a glass of wine while Petra nursed. Petra had nursed all the time; she was a girl who would eat and eat and eat, nothing like Roy, who'd had to be convinced he was hungry, who had not recognized his own hunger pains and still did not. His tummy hurt, he would complain, doubled over, and only after he'd been fed did he feel better. Yet he never connected the pain with emptiness. He would not, next time, say that his tummy ached and therefore he was hungry.

On a late April evening, Emily swallowed a sleeping pill to stop her worrying insomnia. The pill seemed to have given her someone else's dream. She dreamt that it was not her sister who'd once taken an overdose of pills, but she herself, right this moment, and that she was pregnant, besides. Horrified, her dream self put herself before the toilet, finger in her throat as it had used to be all those years ago when staying thin meant throwing up most of what she swallowed down. Now she wanted the pills gone, those pills that were even now dissolving, on their way into her bloodstream to harm her baby. Never mind that she hadn't had sex with anyone for over a year. Never mind that the thing growing in her was cancer, not infant. Never mind that she was facing her own demise. It was the baby she thought about, the baby whose life she felt most concerned to protect.

And in this way, Emily saw the truth of her situation: better she should die, leaving her children, than one of them should die and leave her. From this she took the only shred of solace available: at least she was not losing one of them.

Her illness felt like many things simultaneously—for instance, it seemed that gravity had some sort of extra power, these days, that she was heavier although she understood that in fact she weighed less than she had, as if her body had grown denser, like mercury—and now it felt like wisdom.

Emily slid out of bed and crossed the floor, resentful of the creaking boards beneath her feet, the fact that she was walking on the ceilings of her mother and sister, who no doubt lay awake below her, wishing they could do something to help her out. So many feelings, loose in the house, so many misconceptions, missed cues, hopeless misunderstandings never to be set right. All she wanted in the whole world was to put Petra beside her in bed, sleep with her baby nestled beneath her armpit. It was not difficult to understand the parent who, facing crisis, turned inward toward annihilation, destroying the entire group, and, last, turning the gun on himself. Everyone would go; it was too awful to consider one without the rest. Or the rest without the one.

But Petra fussed, did not want to leave her crib, tossed her heavy head under Emily's arm like a bowling ball and made sleep impossible. The child apparently did not like to touch anything as she slept, wanted nothing but vacancy to greet her as she rolled over and back. Finding Emily there, warm and engulfing, irritated her, made her swat and grunt.

In fact, Emily thought, Petra might not quite notice her absence. After a certain blank curiosity over what had happened to that old maternal odor, Petra might very easily attach herself to Mona, to some other blend of pheromones. She would cling to Mona's chest, pull Mona's hair, fall asleep in Mona's arms.

It was Mona whom Emily imagined, not her own mother.

Petra had had to stop nursing in January when the chemotherapy began. For weeks she scowled at Emily, reached for her buttoned blouse and muttered her intention to get inside it, where Emily's breasts were bound with a wide Ace bandage, so painfully truncated was the weaning. Neither party had wanted weaning; each mourned, in her way. Once or twice Petra had found the plastic MediPort, ran her finger around the mesh center the way Emily sometimes traced the perimeter of the baby's fontanel.

Solid Petra, confident baby with cheery stubborn habits, would make her way through the world in the way of the bully, but Roy would suffer. Returning the baby to her crib, Emily next visited Roy's bed. He lay breathing through his nose, snoring mightily, covers kicked off as usual. Where he'd scratched his dry skin were long red streaks; as she watched, he brought his hand to his neck and clawed furiously, furrowing his young brow. His fingernails were not only long but dirty. Emily hated herself, then, for neglecting those nails, for permitting him to fall asleep without rubbing lotion onto him, for all of the negligence he would suffer as a result of her abandoning him. Her attention was wandering from the small things he needed, she was indulging some sort of strange self-pity that made her feel sanctioned in forgetting how to lead her son through a normal day. "What's the matter, Mama?" he had asked, more than once, when he caught her staring mutely at the vast future she could not hope to occupy. "You happy, Mama?" he used to say, when she was pregnant with Petra, divorcing her husband, little Roy desperate to have her deny her tears.

"Mama's sick," she told him this year, beginning the more troublesome weaning, his.

Her children. No one was ever going to love them as much as she did. She sometimes wished they simply didn't exist, that she'd not made them and thus not have created the tragedy they were about to endure. Poor Roy, he who would miss her most. He would not change as he grew older, sensitive and obtuse, at once. He would never understand how to make the simplest pain go away. And to whom could she explain this adequately? Who would attend and know, when she was gone? It overwhelmed her, the fact that she had so many loose ends to tie up, that she could not simply let go and die, the way her sister had tried. It made her furious, and panicked, and resigned, and she longed more than ever for an arm around her, a man's arm, somebody she could envision leaving the children with who would take good care of them. Certainly this was not Barry's arm. Her ex-husband had never been able to convince her of his maturity; in fact, the point of their marriage might have been to convince herself of her own, having him as her first project, and his children as her next. Now she wished someone would hold her, assure her that she needn't fret.

She retrieved another sleeping pill, and, in the thirty minutes before it took effect, having crossed the creaking floor once more and alerted her sister and mother downstairs to her insomnia and grief, Emily again desired those masculine arms, those arms into which the burdens of the world were to be placed. *Here,* she imagined herself saying. *Hold this.*

She slept, finally, and this time dreamt of walking on a high stone wall. It was a deceptive wall, springing up innocently enough, a flat band of rocks to navigate, a lark. But then it suddenly grew higher, and she balanced precariously. As she felt herself about to fall, she noticed that her father stood below. He was calmly watching her as she teetered on the wall, his hands at the ready. "Catch me, Daddy. Daddy, catch me," she called, knowing he was frail, aware also that she didn't call him Daddy, hadn't for years and years. She did not want to hurt him, and yet she saw she had no choice but to fall, and that was what she did, fell into his arms, where he caught her.

ROY COULD barely remember his father, only the flimsiest of details. But his nightmare seemed somehow about him, nonetheless. An invisible man, who was his father, stood in his third-floor bedroom and opened the window, repeatedly, exposing a pacing sinister monster just outside it. The monster was hazy, yet terribly present, and though Roy's mother closed the window time and again, his invisible father continued to open it when she wasn't looking. For inexplicable reasons Roy himself could not speak, could only observe, knowing that his mother could not see his father nor the monster, that she was just concerned about ordinary things like rain getting in, or cold air, or Petra falling out. It must have been a flying monster, Roy considered later in the day, unless it was even larger than he'd previously thought, tall enough to walk on the ground and still look in Roy's window three floors up with his ferocious eyes, snarl with his dreadsome teeth.

"Monster," he said to Petra, not unkindly, just getting rid of the word.

"Ma ma," she said. It was all she knew, poor little thing. Roy petted her pityingly. His uncle Winston liked to tease the baby. "You cayan't talk," he'd taunt, head pendulum-like on his neck. "You haven't got any tee-eeth." Roy thought this was awfully amusing. For just a few days, when Winston had first come to live with them, Roy had hoped that someone would tell him that he wasn't his uncle but his father— surprise! *This* was the invisible man, back at last, visible. But nope. When they went out, Winston always introduced Roy thus, with his hand on Roy's head: "This is Roy, my evil companion." Roy loved that.

MONA WATCHED Winston and Roy playing with Legos, sipping at a beer and feeling tender. "He's barely beyond five years old himself," her father had said of Winston, sour as usual about her brother. And it was true that part of Winston's charm for children was his immaturity, his genuine investment in childish activity. Tonight, following a Sunday family dinner, Roy was building Sherwood Forest with Winston's assistance. Mona had entered the living room just as Roy asked if they could make a jail, to which proposition Winston replied doggedly: "I told you, Roy, no jail." As if the boy were teasing him, provoking him. As if Roy could possibly want to upset his uncle Winston. It was on the tip of Mona's tongue to correct Winston's thinking, but then Sheila appeared, motioning frantically.

"Play pool, Cuzzy Mona?" she implored, eyes big as two spiders with mascara. Sheila had been sulky during dinner, nothing new in that, but she had also insisted on helping with the dishes and now sought out Mona, pulling her toward the basement stairs, guilty as sin with something.

"Don't call me 'Cuzzy,' " Mona said. "It's insipid."

Downstairs in the poolroom, Sheila began to cry, her black makeup of the variety unaffected by tears. "I'm pregnant," she sobbed quietly.

"What?"

Sheila nodded emphatically, reaching her arms around Mona, who did not want to touch the girl. This outburst seemed remarkably like a performance, and not a convincing one. Foolish histrionics. Mona patted her back while Sheila hiccuped. She was a big soft girl, smelling of strawberry shampoo and pot smoke. Her hair, curled and teased and sprayed, bunched stiff as doll's hair against Mona's chin, and she fell heavily, like a bag of sun-warmed sand, into her cousin's arms.

"Does Eddie know?"

Here Sheila convulsed again. "No oh oh!"

Mona, supporting her cousin, felt some vertebrae in her back shift uncomfortably, pinching near her tailbone. "Let's sit, Sheila." They shuffled awkwardly to the love seat before the drafty fireplace. Sheila nestled in next to Mona, laying her head on Mona's shoulder, one thick leg crossed over Mona's knee, as if she would next pop her thumb in her mouth, curl right up into the little girl she'd been not so long ago. Mona wanted to ask what had been the point of that Christmas trip to Planned Parenthood. Sheila hadn't felt like telling her mother about birth control, so of course she wasn't going to tell her about its failure. And poor Billy—Mona could very easily picture his deflated, disappointed face as he received the news that his only daughter not only had sex but got knocked up.

So Sheila had come once again to Mona, her last resort, and now Mona had to decide once again whose wrath would be least tolerable, Sheila's or Wenda's. The quandary was not unfamiliar, especially in the Mabie family: damned if you did, damned if you didn't. Now she was damned, anyway.

"I forgot to take my pill a few times," Sheila was saying. "I have to get up so early in the morning for school, nobody else in the family has to get up as early as me. That bus comes at seven twenty-five A.M. and they won't wait even if you're a tiny bit late. If Daddy would just have bought me a car . . ." She sat back petulantly. "The curling iron—" she began.

"What are you thinking about doing?"

"I don't know!" She broke into fresh tears, threw herself against Mona's shoulder and sobbed and sobbed. "I don't want to tell Eddie, or Daddy, or anybody." On the one hand, Mona felt flattered to be Sheila's confidante. On the other, it troubled her that Sheila would think of her as the person to come to, as if she were the family black sheep, repository of all ugly secrets. More than anything, Mona wanted to consult with her sister.

"Pregnancy isn't the worst thing that could happen," Mona told Sheila. "You could have gotten AIDS. That would be worse."

Sheila pulled away to give Mona a horrified look. "Maybe I have AIDS, too!"

Perhaps it was a sign of being thirty years old, but Mona felt only like giving maternal advice. She did not identify with Sheila so much as have the desire to shake her. Any idiot could remember to take a pill every morning. A great majority of the world rose each morning uncertain of having food to eat. How hard could it be?

"Have you ever had an *abortion*?" Sheila asked her, whispering the last word.

"No." It was on the tip of Mona's tongue to reveal Emily's two abortions. She could start one by one in the family, erode this image of perfection Emily had constructed around herself, this image that was now making her cancer seem the suffering of a saint instead of the suffering of a secret cigarette smoker, of a closeted bad girl who'd lost count of her sexual partners. Mona would begin by setting Sheila straight. It had been Mona who'd gone with Emily fifteen years ago for her first abortion, Mona the student driver. They'd stopped for discount doughnuts afterward, the way they did when they went to the dentist. Emily sat drugged in the car, then popped doughnut holes into her mouth the whole ride home, white powder on her chin and black shirt. Her sister's life had struck Mona then as the most exotic thing she could envision. Its thorough hiddenness had also impressed her, the way Emily could have it both ways. On the surface, successful, straight, smart, self-possessed, bossy, and underneath, reckless, promiscuous, unreeled and wild as a wind-tossed ribbon. That white powder lasted from the car to Emily's bedroom laundry hamper, good-bye mess, good-bye baby, end of story. Mona's mistake, for many years, was assuming she could replicate this life, that she ought to. This goal was a difficult taskmaster, and now she felt its total collapse, her competitiveness false and meaningless and shallow. Besides, her nature was not to hide herself, as Emily's was. She might lock her bedroom door, but on her face she wore the expression of who she was. If it had been Mona sick with cancer, the whole house would be suffering her theatrics, wouldn't it? Yet Emily exhibited an unnerving calm, not martyred, not pathetic, just matter-of-fact. She was so competent as to be ready to take anything.

Sheila sniffled wetly and said, "And I'm going to get fat."

"That's the least of your worries, you dope. First, we have to make sure you're pregnant. Then we'll deal with the rest."

"Eddie already has one son," Sheila said, wiping her nose on her sleeve. "In Oklahoma."

"Unbelievable."

"Antoine. His mom's in the army. Eddie left her after she got pregnant, so that's why I don't want to tell him, okay?"

"Eddie is immature." And so was Sheila. Unfortunately, their bodies thought otherwise. Their bodies believed, and rightly so, that they could do anything a fully qualified adult could, and better, no doubt. The human body wanted to mate, wanted to procreate, wanted to have biological fun. Mona knew that.

Therefore it was Mona who drove to Safeway later that evening and bought a pregnancy kit. And Mona who, at six the next morning, parked her sister's car at her uncle's curb. Billy's house had once been Bunny's house, but its old lady looks no longer prevailed. Wenda had painted the clapboard bungalow turquoise and pink, and Sheila had hung a wind sock from the flagpole. It whipped in the icy April wind, a yellow rip in the pewter sky. Bunny's house seemed, to Mona, desecrated, garish, and wild, rather than revivified. Wenda didn't like the neighborhood, which had fallen on hard times since Ruth Mabie had lived there, but Billy wouldn't move. His mother had left the house to him because she had wanted Billy to own something solid, to be able to make a contribution to the marriage. Bunny had long ago understood how powerful Wenda was, and how necessary it would be to provide for Billy. Mona wondered what her grandmother would make of her old home, the two cars sitting in the drive, the two others in the yard, vehicles Billy would be repairing. Next door needed paint; on the corner a house had burned down and never been cleaned up.

Mona rapped gently at the front door, the pregnancy kit in its brown paper bag, eager to hand it off to her sullen lumpy cousin and return to Pearson Avenue, the house that had not yet fallen to ruin, as this one had. "Wait," Sheila whined, stepping up and down on the cold threshold, feet bare, her sleepwear a giant shirt with a coy cartoon rabbit on its front: *I Am Loved.* "You are fucked," Mona muttered, following Sheila inside. And so it was that she found herself in the funky downstairs bathroom of her grandmother's old home, listening to a tinny radio screaming "Slow Ride," sitting on the edge of the tub with her feet resting among the soiled towels and discarded outfits, waiting while Sheila held her nightshirt up with her chin, reading an instruction booklet, trying to urinate into a plastic cup. "What does this mean, mid-flow?" the girl asked petulantly.

"Pee in the cup," Mona said, yawning. "How hard can it be?"

"Be nice to me."

"I *am* being nice to you."

Mona watched the dipstick while Sheila went to get ready for high school. Her music was stuff from twenty years ago; just think, Mona was old enough to see the second coming of elephant bells and Steve Miller, Aerosmith, ZZ Top.

"Which shoes?" the girl asked, five minutes later, red platform sandal on one foot, brown clog on the other. Mona pointed at the clog.

"You're pregnant," she told her cousin.

"Dang!"

"Red shoes," Mona added, as an afterthought. Why not?

IT WAS ON that same stormy morning that the dog disappeared. For a few hours, no one noticed. He was not a very nice dog, with his wiry gray fur that resembled nothing so much as pubic hair when shed around the house. He was not a dog the Mabies would have chosen. They thought of themselves as a large dog family, golden retrievers, chocolate Labs, but what choice had they had when Bunny died? How rare it must be for the dog to survive its owner; things usually worked out another way. Professor Mabie, who knew better than anyone else how dearly his mother had loved her pet, took a moment to be grateful she'd not had to suffer the animal's death.

He was at least ten years old. Only Mona loved him; she'd been there when he was chosen at the pound, she might have actually made the choice herself, with Bunny's permission. She felt a kind of willed loyalty because he was hard to love, it couldn't be denied. She loved him because no one else would. So it was she who missed him when he turned up absent.

"Where's Jackoff?" she asked her mother. She could not bear the loss of animals, and this particular pet had required more than the usual amount of peddling in her family. He was not a good specimen. He failed to charm in even the most rudimentary ways. Mona's own strategy for loving him was to remember the way he used to ride alongside Bunny in the Cadillac, feet scrabbling on the plastic-protected front seat as she swung around corners, sharp varmint face scanning the landscape as it flew by, Bunny's instinctive hand thrust against him as they came up short at a red light. His black eyes were often frightening, and it was true he could not be trusted either with children (he bit them) or small objects you loved (he hid them) but still Mona had been his protector. And after Inkspot's departure last year, he was the last of the family pets. He'd been the full recipient of Mona's maternal affection these past twelve months.

It might have been coincidence, but Kojak hadn't seemed himself since the arrival of Betty's bird Guido in her room. Guido and Nicholas Dempsey were to blame, also Sheila's pregnancy. Distracted, Mona had forgotten and left the dog out in his pen overnight while an April shower whipped up. When she returned from Billy's, he was nowhere to be found. Had he interpreted her negligence as a sign of things to come? Further forgetfulness, forsaking?

His pen gate was still latched with its bungee cord, his food bowl inside untouched, the chow bloated and pale with rainwater. His leash hung on its customary hook in the mudroom, and no one remembered having seen him since last night, after dinner. In his youth, he'd climbed the fence, scrabbling up in what Mona had assumed was his vain sad attempt to find his owner, his Bunny who had without explanation simply vaporized from his world. At the top of the fence, he would free-fall dangerously, and then run as if with direction as fast as his scrappy legs would take him. The family would be forced to comb the neighborhood, scan the streets for his run-over body, post silly notices on phone poles with his Xeroxed photo and vital stats.

She moved methodically through the house in search of him, basement to attic, whistling feverishly. Roy, still in his pajamas, followed her, as she was the most animated in the search. Like Roy, she did not entertain the gruesome hope that Kojak had truly vanished. Both Emily and Mrs. Mabie would not have been very sorry to see him go. They cared more for the safety and reciprocal affection of the children; they'd invested their maternal love elsewhere.

"Jackoff," Roy called, dumping his long blond hair upside down as he checked beneath beds and ottomans and end tables. He could not whistle so he made do with a "Whoo whoo" meant to resemble whistling. The dog had never been known to respond to Roy's calling, but Mona wasn't going to hurt the boy's feelings. At Winston's closed bedroom door, Mona did not hesitate to knock brusquely and inquire if Kojak had spent the night with him.

"No," Winston said sleepily. "You can't find him?"

"Come help us look, Winston," Mona called as she and Roy thumped down the stairs. Winston had no doubt seen the dog last, as he stayed up the latest.

When it became clear that Kojak wasn't inside, Mona stood on the front porch and waited for her mother to return from her search of the neighborhood, afraid herself to look in the streets. The worst thing about a missing pet was the scouring of the roads, the way every crumpled grocery bag or pile of leaves looked exactly like your animal, dead and cast off, victim of hit-and-run.

But Mrs. Mabie returned with no evidence of his having been killed by a car.

"Could he have gone with Dad?" Mona asked. But of course Professor Mabie would not have taken Kojak with him on his errands.

Winston joined them, groggy, smelly, unshaven, shirt unbuttoned, first morning's cigarette dangling between his lips. Some might have been able to find him charming in some rumpled, postcoital way, but Mona wanted to kick him. "Did you see Kojak last night?" she demanded.

Winston merely stared at her, blinking like a lizard.

"Did you see him last night?"

He turned his back on her, and headed for his bedroom once more. He'd never enjoyed being accused, first thing in the morning.

Mona phoned Percy at Starkey and told him she was sick.

"Were you killed again?"

"Negatory. Just sick."

Every day when she came home from work, she knelt on the floor and rubbed Kojak's oily belly, offering the refrain she always offered him: "I don't like my job, I like my dog, I don't like my job, I like my dog." Kojak enjoyed this affirmation. No one else was likely to sing his praises in so religious a fashion. Some days before she left for work, when she still had some minor excitement in actually having a reason to wake up and put on lipstick, Mona would tell him insincerely that she wished she could stay home with him and eat kibble. But it was utterly heartfelt when she returned to tell him of her love after a long day in the special ed trenches.

Alone she searched the dog pen, looking for Jackoff's escape route, slugging through slimy leaves and disintegrating dog shit, clutching her coat around her. Kojak had spurting desires, although in recent years he had seemed to accept his fate, pen-bound in his stinking kennel, in fact had seemed to enjoy it—stuck out there, his own place.

On the other side of the fence, beyond the crusty honeysuckle, the Nakeds were outside, screeching. Their voices particularly annoyed Mona today, as if, inside the dog pen she'd acquired that mystical method of hearing the humanly inaudible, dog ears. There was a Pixies song she liked to put on the stereo for Kojak. Three minutes into the music some synthesizer activity tuned into a nerve solely in the dog's ear. Suddenly he would twitch, his eyes would dart wildly, as if someone were speaking to him, seducing or tormenting, hard to say which, and he would dart to the window, trembling. Excited.

Suffering or enticed? Mona applied this to herself, there in the stinking mulch of her family's neglected dog run. A phone call from, a sighting of, Nicholas Dempsey would excite her in the same way. She'd be riveted, poised, alive, heart throbbing. It was a physical sensation like fear, love was. It flipped all the same switches. It distracted and overwhelmed in precisely the same manner. It had the power to ignite and consume your life.

"Ay ay ay," the Nakeds shrieked, and Mona winced, the shrill sound piercing a little-used nerve, as if a hot needle pricked the pit of her brain.

Maybe she was in heat, she thought. She could hear like a dog, she could suffer desire like a dog, animal need, native urgency.

"A THOUSAND dollars is a good figure," Emily noted of the ransom letter. "Serious, yet modest."

"Modest?" Mona protested, she who made only a fraction of her sister's income.

"Well, it's hard to say no to a thousand dollars," Emily said. "Isn't it?"

Emily would have agreed because it wouldn't set her back. Mona would have agreed because she loved Kojak, despite his serious shortcomings as a pet. The note had arrived in the afternoon mail, plain envelope, plain American flag stamp, a typed request folded within, nothing distinctive, addressed, also in typeface, to "Mabies" without a zip code or even the name "Wichita," but "City," which seemed old-fashioned. Also, it had been typed on a typewriter, and the typist had a weak pinkie, witness the faint *a*'s. The note posed a question: "Is your dog worth a thousand dollars?" Emily found it amusing, as she did not like the dog and also had a thousand dollars to throw away on such things, should she choose to. At least, that was how her father perceived her response. He also knew that she would gladly give her family a thousand dollars, all the while disliking the dog, and that she would never mention it again. She had a generous, vaguely cold heart, one he appreciated for its candor. Money had never meant to her what it meant to her parents. She made it easily, dispensed with it cavalierly, also behaved with some shrewdness, investing as her financial adviser recommended, deposits here and there for the impending rainy days.

"A thousand dollars," Emily went on. "You'd have to ask for at least that much to make dognapping profitable. Yet, it's not over the top. You probably wouldn't end up holding the bag."

"Keeping the dog," Mona interpreted.

"I wonder if there's a lot of this going on," Emily said. "I'm going to call the police and find out."

Professor Mabie watched his son as the family pored over the innocuous yet incriminating piece of mail. Winston held himself in the background, aloof, playing that irritating guitar. He knew only a few chords, apparently, and strummed them incessantly, as if punctuating conversation, as if the tone of his music set the tone of the room, as if Winston had designated himself some sort of Greek chorus, announcing to the audience how to take the drama being played before them. The basic blues intro, his favorite ditty, four notes, the second one squealing upward. On a recent late night, under the influence of bourbon, Professor Mabie had been tempted to destroy that guitar, throttle its throat and bang it on a handy rock. . . .

"This is so ridiculous," Mona cried, "a ransom note for Jackoff! How can that be? Who would do such a ridiculous thing?" In the corner, Winston strummed a kind of reiterating question.

Someone desperate for money, Professor Mabie thought. Someone so stubborn as to turn down job offers from friends and well-wishers, someone who had yet to make amends with his family. Someone who had been incarcerated, who'd fallen so far from grace he might never clamber back into the land of the reputable and upstanding. That's who would steal the family dog and demand a thousand dollars. That's who would rob his sister's business while she languished at home under the reign of cancer and radiation therapy. Professor Mabie found himself nearly choking, so outraged was he at his son's bad character. What would be next? Arson? The abduction of one of Emily's babies?

"What's wrong?" Mona asked him, laying her hand on her father's arm, she who attended worriedly to his expression. She who actually loved Kojak, where the rest of them merely endured the dog. It was Mona who would insist on paying the ransom. It was Mona's heart that was in the balance here, not the life of the miserable dog. The question really came down to how much Professor Mabie was willing to pay for Mona's peace of mind. He'd already paid plenty for it, and he wasn't ready to stop doing so. But the fact that Winston was the recipient of this windfall galled him. And to make such an accusation, to lay it before them all, to believe in it, would be to further injure Mona. Mona most of all. Professor Mabie sighed. And Winston played that same irksome four notes, *dow dow de dow.*

3

KOJAK HAD BEEN gone three days when a new dog suddenly appeared in the little pen. Emily found him, early in the morning when she took out a bag of trash, and his presence made her lift up on her bare toes, shriek.

"Who the fuck are you?" she asked. In response, he paced behind the closed gate of the old pen, humming. Who had put him there, slammed the latch, attached the bungee? He was a large dog, proportioned like a jackal, fur variegated, tongue a mottled purple, eyes two different colors so that he seemed wild and unpredictable—as if he'd stolen those eyes from two different animals—and emitting a noise like a high-pitched engine. "Did you eat our dog?" Emily asked him, squinting into his funny eyes, nearly serious.

"This is what I like about life," she told Mona later as she loaded her children in the car. "All of a sudden an ugly dog shows up in your yard, just when *your* ugly dog was missing."

The animal paced, showing his large clean teeth as if laughing. He growled at men but seemed to like the women. Unless they wore hats, then all bets were off. "Get used to it, bub," Emily told him, shaking her bald, capped head at him.

Even if Kojak had been Emily's beloved grandmother's beloved pet, she hadn't liked him. She hadn't trusted him with her children, and she liked thinking of him in the past tense. Jackoff always looked to her as if he were plotting how to get away with something. He was so blatantly self-interested. She preferred the lunky gregarious breeds. She preferred dogs who could clean themselves; what did it say about a dog that could not clean himself? She did not mind that he'd disappeared. For three days she'd had a thousand dollars ready in an envelope, prepared to drive to some designated drop site, prepared to retrieve Kojak from his abductor, allow his squirming stink into her car, but there'd been no further word. Besides, she was drawn to this new dog, who was good-natured, despite his nefarious looks. He had chosen them, as opposed to having ended up with them as a last resort. Emily was ready to let the new dog stay, spend her thousand dollars on chew toys and collar and shots and chow, consider Kojak killed and gone, done and done. Emily had firm feelings about nostalgia, these days, and she wasn't going to waste it on that hateful dog.

"Whattaya think?" she asked Roy, as if she'd summoned and then delivered the animal to him.

He clapped; replacement seemed as good as restoration to her little boy. Should Emily have been relieved, she wondered? He named the new dog Curly after the Stooge he and Winston liked best.

"I HAD A dream," Mona was saying in Dr. Lydia's office, recalling the dream for no good reason, swamp and fog and fence posts like knife blades. "I dreamed I found Kojak." The poor dog had been starving to a skeleton in the basement, right under the family's noses, rotting away like rubbish, eyes luminous with betrayal. And what else? "My brother kidnapped Kojak," she said, light dawning, the hair on her arms lifting. That information hadn't been part of the dream, but she knew suddenly that she was right. Winston had taken their dog! Just being in Lydia's office, sitting in her chair, staring at her reassuring sardonic face across the surface of her messy desk, made the truth pour forth. "How could he do that?" she asked, horrified and stunned. Where had he put him? In what small space did Kojak now sit, shivering misery, little canine heart aflutter?

— — —

AT HOME, Professor Mabie walked outside to make the acquaintance of the new dog, who growled as he approached. His wife was thinning her plants, wearing peculiar yellow shoes designed for gardening. She had whole ensembles for this hobby of hers, tools and aprons and little flags with Latin names on them. Catalogs arrived nonstop, roses, bulbs, pots, poison. Her ankles were swollen, he noted, pale and shot through with tiny blue veins. Against the cool green of the ground her skin had an unhealthy pallor, bloodless, the same shade as the worms she'd unearthed, which squirmed in her wake.

"I'm going to get to the bottom of the Kojak affair," he announced.

"Good," she said without looking up. "Hand me that spade, will you?"

He knelt to lift the shovel and the dog showed his teeth.

"Enough of that," Mrs. Mabie said placatingly.

"At least Kojak liked me."

"Tolerated," his wife corrected. "Kojak tolerated us. He liked your mother, and he liked Mona, and the rest of us he merely endured."

"Where do you think he is?"

"I haven't the faintest idea." She looked up squarely into his face then, the blue of her eyes faded, vaguely damp, a soft wet pocket beneath each eye, bloodshot as gravity tugged her features downward. What could she see? How did he appear to her? She would go blind, he would go deaf, they would huddle together as their days came to an end. . . . The breeze blew then, which coolness did not faze Mrs. Mabie, but Professor Mabie returned to the house chilled.

His wife had begun taking leave of the world perhaps ten years earlier. She'd gone simple in interesting ways, letting loose of her desire to compete, not minding what many women seemed to as she aged. First was the clothing, a general untrussing that left her in fleece garments and flat shoes. With dinner she drank only one glass of wine so that she could still attend to her book reading later. The wild yard, historically under the purview of Professor Mabie's indulgent anarchy, she entered and tamed, in the form of cultivating a little garden, back near the dog run, a series of lines like parted hair, surrounded by a delicate fence of string, inverted seed packets on Popsicle sticks designating carrots, basil, tomatoes, lettuce, parsley, things with which to create a salad, a piece of tender organization in the yard's tangled wilderness. Simple

258 — ANTONYA NELSON

pleasures, Professor Mabie would have named his wife's new philosophy. She took long slow walks around the park, stately, her feet moving steadily, her straw hat seeming to float on her gray head in the summer, replaced in the winter by her furry Russian-esque one. She kept busy, she kept abreast of world events. She kept a calendar of her family's activities, she kept to herself.

From the window of the mudroom he watched her patiently uncover the earthworms, gently pull up the nascent weeds, rub her nose with the back of her naked hand and leave mud on her face. This image troubled him, as if she were out there on her knees digging her own grave, as if her self-sufficiency and self-containment would come to that, reduce her to clawing at the dirt and rocks with her fingernails.

His attention was suddenly drawn to noise behind him, inside the house. Winston, just now coming downstairs. Everybody had a pattern in their descent down these stairs. Mona trilled, three steps at a time, like someone accompanying music, *la*-la-la, *la*-la-la, and Emily struck all of them lightly and swiftly, someone in a perpetual graceful hurry. Little Roy still brought his feet together on each stair as he proceeded, as if he were dragging a lame limb after himself. Mrs. Mabie came down both carefully—as if afraid she'd fall—and silently—as if afraid she'd annoy, but Winston thumped over the treads as if ready to put his foot through every single board, as if he were the giant and this was his home, look out below.

Everyone else was up and about, Mona at her therapist, Emily delivering her children to day care before going to the shop, Mrs. Mabie in the garden. From the porch Professor Mabie heard his son making a phone call, the beep of numbers, then Winston's muttering, his brief spurts of weak words. The boy had never learned to articulate, to stand up for himself, to assert an opinion. It wasn't a long conversation, nor a congenial one; soon Winston left the house, out the side door so that he wouldn't encounter either parent, on foot, and, as Professor Mabie hurried up half the set of stairs to observe from the landing window, wearing a brand-new blue jacket.

Had that jacket been purchased with the spoils of the Kick robbery?

Professor Mabie trod back down the steps in the style that was his— steady, cautious—and picked up the telephone. He studied the buttons on the keypad, weighing the heavy moral quandary within which he found himself. His children's rights to privacy had never seemed to him a simple issue. He wouldn't read diaries, he wouldn't search purses or pockets. He supposed he might have discovered useful information, had he indulged the temptation to suspect his children. Perhaps he could have prevented a portion of their trouble; quite possibly they *wanted* him to meddle, leaving their doors and their underwear drawers open, beer caps and condom wrappers on the car floorboards. Equally possible was that not meddling permitted his not knowing, a form of cowardice or laziness. He consulted today his memory of Betty Spitz, who reminded him in her smoky voice that he suspected Winston regardless, that not pushing redial wouldn't aid that fact. "*Do* something," she was known to say, inflection on the verb.

He poked the button tentatively, as if resistance would dissuade him, listening fearfully to the little seven-note tune it produced.

"Blewski," the voice on the other end answered.

Professor Mabie hesitated. He knew a Garth Blewski. The math professor, one of Betty Spitz's prized targets, a fervent committee joiner and rabble-rouser—she claimed he had no sense of humor, the kiss of death, in her book. Before Professor Mabie could speak, the voice continued. It was a machine, mercifully, and its message announced that Blewski was screening his calls so the caller would have to prove his worthiness before Garth would pick up.

Professor Mabie set the receiver down, grateful not to have to speak, telling himself the coy message had prevented it. When his own phone then instantly rang, he knew better than to answer. This would be Blewski, returning the hang-up. Not only did the elaborate abilities of telephone technology mystify Professor Mabie, but he had no notion what havoc such technology had wreaked on the rules of etiquette; he felt suddenly caught in a game, eager to disengage, throw up his hands, unplug the cord. And how—and why—had his son entangled himself with Garth Blewski? Did it concern the dog? Despite disliking the man, it was hard for Professor Mabie to imagine Blewski involved in dognapping. He seemed someone who might worry over fleas or be allergic to animal dander. Betty's words concerning their colleague in the math department returned to him now: "Garth Blewski is like a bad smell, wafting around the campus." The man did seem to waft as he walked, springing on his heels, nose in the air as if convinced he could drift.

Professor Mabie's fingertips played Betty Spitz's old phone number longingly. His wife's nearness seemed then an affront, Betty so thoroughly gone, his wife nearby but insufficient. It was a flash of unfaith-fulness that made him wretched. To offset it, he quickly called his brother Billy and told him what had just occurred. Betty would have laughed hilariously, defusing Professor Mabie's paranoia, but Billy just grunted. On the line he heard the *weep* that meant another call was coming in. Maybe Garth Blewski would plague him forever like this, dialing and dialing and dialing.

Receiver tucked under his chin, Professor Mabie looked up Blewski's name in the faculty section of WSU's phone book. It was dated from three years ago, the last year the Mabies had been on a mailing list from the campus. Professor Mabie had no idea whether Blewski still resided at the address, an apartment near the dorms. "You go there," he told his brother. "Blewski doesn't know you."

"Yeah, but Winston does."

"True."

"I could send Big O. He's right here." A mumble resonated on the other end of the line.

"Big O," Professor Mabie mused. Billy's friends typically troubled Professor Mabie, rough-hewn and tattooed, felons and drunks and louts and thugs, crazy and usually under restraining orders. "Losers," his daughters named them, one and all. "Is it Big O who meows all the time?" he asked now.

"Aw, just when there's women around," Billy said. "Big O's girlfriend dumped him last night, so he's got a lot of free time on his hands. She told him she didn't want to play second fiddle to his motorcycle. What?" There was an exchange at Billy's house. "He says, '*Third* fiddle. There's the dog, of course.' "

Professor Mabie laughed with them, across town. This was the best way to know Billy's friends, at a distance and through anecdote.

"So Big O's got his panties in a bunch," Billy went on, "so maybe that would help. Put him in the right mood to meet up with a faggot."

Professor Mabie sighed. Billy's friends rubbed off on him, there was no denying it. He had one—Mickey, Dickey?—who spent his days in Billy's broken Nova, with a bottle, just sitting in Billy's driveway. In exchange for this dubious privilege, he cared for Billy's yard. Often in the evenings he could be found at their kitchen table, especially when Wenda was out of town. When Wenda was out of town, these friends grouped at Billy's—for the beer, for the television, for the domestic comforts.

They occasionally said disturbing things to Sheila, who defended herself admirably. Big O would yowl, and Sheila would flip him off. All of Billy's friends tended to walk around with no shirts on, ready to scratch themselves constantly, yet also ready to complain about Sheila's appearance. "Thunder thighs," one might say, out of nowhere. "Asshole," Sheila would reply, calmly curling her lip. They'd toughened her, Professor Mabie supposed. His own daughters, especially Mona, could have used some toughening. Most disturbing about these blockheads was Billy's belief that he was among them, of them. Professor Mabie knew better, and more than hating his brother's friends, he hated knowing that Billy felt no different from them.

"I could round up a posse," Billy was saying. "Everybody's out of work and looking for something to do."

"I'm afraid of what they'd do. They're not a subtle bunch, Billy."

"He says we're not subtle," Billy repeated for Big O's benefit. There was much racket over this accusation. "SUB-tle? Who says I'm not subtle? I'm subtle as hell."

"You just want to know Winston's business with him, right?" Billy said.

"Right. Never mind. I don't know what I was thinking."

"We'll go there."

"No, I've changed my mind. Forget it. Forget everything."

"Dog come back yet?"

"No. And no more notes, either."

"On TV, you'd be getting a lock of hair or a video proving the victim was still alive." He turned from his phone to explain the situation to Big O, who laughed heartily—as one might, Professor Mabie thought, as one very well might. It was absurd, stupidly tragic. At least it was amusing. Emily had found it so, as well, and seeing her amused had briefly pleased her father.

Someone else joined Billy and Big O; the rattle of doors and chip bags and the hissing pop of beer bottles came over the phone, amazing electronic fidelity, and Professor Mabie made his good-byes. "Tell him sayonara from your subtle friends," Big O shouted. "So long from subtle us."

By this time Mona had returned from her weekly shrink appointment. Her eyes were red, her face mottled. She shared her mother's fair skin, on which all emotional business showed instantly, unappealingly.

Typically her father made a point of disappearing when she came home from Dr. Lydia's, allowing her to scurry safely to her room, if need be. Today he was caught in the pantry, phone warm under his palm. It rang and they both ignored it. "Hi, Dad," she said, passing without looking at him. Why was she crying?

"Honey," he said, following down the hall to the stairs, leaving the jangling phone behind. She waited at the bottom of the steps with her back to him, willing to talk though not wanting to. "You all right?"

"I'm fine," she said. "Therapy makes me sad, sometimes."

"Okay." When she lifted her feet, one step to the next, he remembered her as a toddler, taking the stairs on all fours, fat diaper on her rear, proud gleam in her eyes when she made the landing, gleeful tiny-toothed grin. His heart tore; his daughters' sadnesses, from completely different sources, pained him. He used to be able to make them happy, to refute whatever had convinced them they hurt. Once, he'd known how. He'd lost the knack during their adolescences, when their pain was covered by a veil of ugly anger and assumed identities, when he had been repulsed by them and their problems, their crude contorting sexual evolutions. Later, as young women, they'd slowly lost the rebellion and rage, discarded the fashionable teenage passion, discovered once again grace, femininity, leaving then only injury in their expressions, pure and transient, some part of their scarred surface a kind of pity toward him, for he'd lost his own passionate aspect, too, turned impotent in the face of their piteousness. Both sides, he thought, had disarmed themselves.

He would have done anything to make Mona happy today. She was as defeated as he'd seen her since her suicide attempt, and he felt the same frightened ineptness, his weak capacity to shield her. Halfway up the stairs, with the light from the landing window flaring around her head like a halo, his daughter appeared ethereal, powerful, far beyond his hope of rescuing her. "What is your brother doing with Garth Blewski?" he asked desperately.

Mona shrugged. "That guy is weird," she said, sniffling. "I don't like him."

"Betty didn't like him, either."

"Really? Betty seemed to like most everyone."

"Not Garth Blewski."

"Well, that makes me feel better about hating him." She sighed, wiping her nose. "I like having permission to hate someone."

They both turned as they heard the mailman open the front door box. It clanked once, twice, three times as he deposited envelopes, flyers, magazines, catalogs. The Mabie household took in a great deal of mail. Professor Mabie retrieved today's lot, scanning for the envelope that would announce the fate of Kojak.

"Anything?" Mona asked.

"Nothing," he said, handing her a real estate office postcard; the Nakeds were putting the old Vaughn house on the market. "Maybe they didn't like us," he added, meaning the Nakeds.

"Maybe they found out about Mr. Vaughn dying in the basement. I dreamed Kojak was in *our* basement," Mona said. "He was down there starving to death, trapped in some pipes or boards."

"Kojak isn't starving," her father assured her. Was that what made her weep today? "Kojak is fine." Since the arrival of the ransom note, Professor Mabie had quit thinking of the dog as in jeopardy. Something else was in jeopardy, something less obvious than a pet. Its ruin was quiescent, rising through the house like a slow leak of noxious fumes.

MONA HAD also noticed Winston's new jacket. Where had it come from, expensive lightweight weatherproofing, designed for alpine sports and the like? Its vividness set off Winston's eyes, contrasted beautifully with his hair, and resembled nothing else he had ever owned. It was a shade of blue invented in the '80s, Mona thought, a color of the new Jell-O or Sweetart or Skittle, a kind of child's candy that had no natural flavor correlative, a hue without background, uncredentialed, mimicking neither sky nor sea, nothing organic except perhaps the plumage of some exotic bird or fish. Winston's new jacket was this color, this Jell-O blue, this un-Kansas article. It was as unlike him as it was anything else in nature.

"Where'd you get that?" Mona asked him when he came through the back door later in the evening, rustling in it.

"At the gettin' place," he said.

"Gettin' place!" Roy laughed.

Mona found herself feeling the way her sister had used to claim to feel around Winston: like he was holding out just to enrage her. He wouldn't answer a question put in such a defensive tone; she ought to know that. Still, she had no patience for his style. She thought he'd stolen her dog and was preparing to take a thousand dollars from their sick sister.

"Where have you been?" she asked as he aimed himself out of the kitchen, hands full of food his parents had paid for, Roy at his heels like a truant in training. She hadn't seen him all day.

"To quote Betty Spitz, 'None of your beeswax,' " he said.

"Beeswax!" Roy crowed. "Beeswax comes from bees' *bottoms!*"

Mona took her suspicions to her sister, on the third floor. Sunset burned through the west windows, dust motes floated over the stained pine floors, and Emily's apartment smelled of comfort food, macaroni, applesauce. Emily was changing Petra's diaper on the bed. Petra had a rash on the plump folds of her vagina, and Emily was waving a diaper over the area, glass of wine in the other hand. "I'm a shitty mom," she said.

"You're not a shitty mom," Mona replied. "You're a great mom." Compliments, now that Emily was ill, fell off her tongue. If only Mona could feel this way toward all of humanity, beneficent with the praise, eager to give aid, ever ready to eulogize.

"Where did she get this rash? Where was I when this rash came up? It's like blackouts, or something, I just wake up and she's got diaper rash to beat the band. Don't tell Mom," Emily added.

"She wouldn't blame you."

"She'd just get that look."

"Emily," Mona said, sitting beside her niece's fat waving legs and raw privates, "what if Winston stole Kojak?"

"What if he did?"

"What would you think, if he did?"

"I'd think he was getting back at us for whatever it is he has to get back at us for."

"Ma ma ma ma," said Petra, shaking her fists, annoyed with Mona's arrival, the slight tip of the bed.

"She still misses nursing," Emily said, sipping at her wine, waving the diaper.

Mona speculated on their brother. "He did have a huge inheritance taken away from him."

"That's not the half of it." Emily emptied her hands and lifted her big baby. She gently slapped her bare bottom. The sound was pleasing, and Petra didn't seem bothered. Mona wanted to spank her niece, too—she wondered why.

"What's the other half?" she asked her sister.

"I don't mind giving Winston a thousand dollars," Emily said. "I'd give him five thousand, if he asked."

"Really?"

"Truly. I bonded him out for five grand, once upon a time. Hand me my wine, will you?"

Mona took a mouthful before giving Emily the glass. She lay back on the same bed Petra had just lain on, and looked up at the moon and star mobiles, the posters of babies and kittens. "I forgot about the bail money. Didn't you have to do that for Barry, too?"

Mona knew she had; she just wanted to say Barry's name.

"Sure enough," Emily said. "I know the drill."

Mona swung at a twirling Styrofoam Saturn. "I wish you had been *my* mom," she said, disloyalty and loyalty flaring simultaneously. She'd betray her mother, she'd take a bullet for her sister.

"I *was* your mom," Emily said, smiling grimly down at her. "You want a diaper change, Mona? Want me to wipe you up?"

"Wah."

"Listen you big baby, don't worry about Winston and the money. Kojak is old, the money is a drop in the bucket, and you're going to get over whatshisname."

"Oh whatshisname. I forgot about whatshisname for a minute." But only for a minute. Then he was back, monstrous, eating the universe like Pac-Man.

"You know what I keep thinking of?" Emily asked, jiggling Petra.

"What?"

"How much Roy loves Winston. I worry all the time about Roy, and he adores Winston. If Winston weren't here, I ask myself, where would Roy get his fun? Who would play with him and make him laugh? That's what Winston is doing for me. So if he feels the need to make me pay for some past sin, well, that's his problem. I'm going to pay. I can afford it. Whatever's going on between him and Roy is more important. He's what Roy has to look forward to, you know?"

Emily's figure had reduced in the same way as her character, to essential elements. Holding fat fleshy Petra she looked skeletal yet beautiful. And she sounded so wise. The friction of their past relationship had virtually disappeared in the last few months. Mona realized she ought to be pleased with that fact. For a second, her worldly worries fell away, and Mona felt pure, too. Whole.

"Will you take her for a minute?" Emily asked, turning her daughter over to Mona's care. Mona blinked as the bare baby landed in her lap.

"I don't think it's Winston, anyway," Emily said. "I think it's more likely Billy. Some dumb prank he and his friends pulled."

"Billy," Mona said. But she knew her uncle wouldn't do such a thing to them. "The Nakeds are selling their house," she told Emily.

"Maybe they're tired of us and our barking dog. Hear that?" her sister asked, crossing to the dormer window. "That's our new dog, barking his fool head off."

DOWNSTAIRS, directly under her two daughters, Mrs. Mabie also listened to the dog. His barking was methodical, unhurried, as if he were pacing himself, ready for the long haul of unanswered cries. This was unlike Kojak's barking, which had been yelpy and desperate, which sounded as if someone were throttling him.

"In dog years," Roy had sincerely informed his grandmother, "I'm not even one years old."

The barking sounded over the mute throbbing of Mrs. Mabie's headache. She hoped her neighbor was listening. It was Mrs. Mabie's opinion that he, the gnomy man who'd come accusatorily to inquire about the wire cutting a few weeks previous, the one her children had named Mr. Naked, had stolen Kojak. This would be his idea of setting things right. "Revenge," Winston had written his mother from prison, "is the simple man's justice." Mr. Naked was a bitter, limited man, Mrs. Mabie believed. He would steal his neighbor's dog for ransom enough to repair his wires.

Mrs. Mabie feared her neighbor; she hoped the house would sell quickly. And, she confessed to herself, she hoped they lost money on it. That would be his due.

It was interesting to consider the terms of revenge, how one act equaled another, how the human race had a need for equity, or its impression. Betty Spitz's death, for example, had seemed to close some kind of unbalanced account with Mrs. Mabie. She would not have wished death upon Betty—would not have hastened it, certainly—but was not unhappy to have it happen. That was a kind of revenge, wasn't it? Surviving her? There was in Mrs. Mabie that slim slice of what felt like malfeasance.

"If I was a dog," philosophical Roy had claimed, "I would *not* lick my bottom. No way."

She would not take her suspicions of Mr. Naked's deed to her family. This was because they were braver than she, every one of them, even Roy. Even Roy would carry his outrage recklessly through the yards dividing the houses, storming up the steps and into the faces of the Nakeds, righteous and ready to demand the return of his dog. Mrs. Mabie wasn't of their ilk. She could wait for things to happen of their own accord rather than initiating them. Her gift, she thought, was patience. Patience was the ability to wait, and it had been Winston who'd pointed that out, too. It was another of his insights from prison, lifted from his letter, engraved and preserved now in his mother's mind. She missed their correspondence. She missed their long-distance kinship. If he were still in prison, it was him she would write and tell of her suspicions regarding Kojak and the man next door, Winston who would not be able to act on such information, merely absorb it. Were they still in the midst of their letter-writing, she would not have hesitated to let him know that it was their neighbor who'd taken their dog. It was an instinct she would have bet her life on.

4

EMILY'S HAIR had always been thin, and now she could not find a wig that looked like her. "I used to make jokes about having chemotherapy hair," she told Frog and Toady, "and now I really do."

Her friends had brought a wig consultant to the shop after hours. In her van she had a dozen Styrofoam heads, each sporting a hairdo, not one of them remotely close to Emily's former modest cap of hair. "That," she finally said, choosing a relatively innocuous brown model, which sat on her head like a rodent pelt. The consultant exclaimed over it, but Emily could see the truth in Frog and Toady's faces: awful.

She ended up wearing the wig only with a scarf or hat over it, so that it acted mostly as fringe, the equivalent of a dust ruffle. She found herself scratching beneath it with pencils, chopsticks, paper clips. She couldn't help trimming it every time she put it on, reducing it, cropping it in ways that a natural hairdo might forgive but that a wig didn't particularly. She had to wash it with shampoo, dry it on her fist, style it on its Styrofoam holder. Emily's Styrofoam head had a nose and chin, yet totally empty eye sockets. She and Mona, one drunk evening, applied makeup to the white surface, Red She Said lips, VeryBerry eyes, Cappuccino eyebrows over the soulless sockets. Still, the head looked much better under the pelt than Emily did, possessing a more shapely skull. Obviously the Styrofoam bust could not reside in Emily's apartment. It was all too easy to envision Roy's nightmares as inspired by a hairy faceless form on the bedroom dresser. So the whole unit was tucked away in the linen closet, a cupboard in the main hallway opened only by the women of the house, where it never failed to startle Mrs. Mabie. She would clutch her heart, breathe deeply, retrieve the sheets and pillowcases she needed, and slam that awful head away once more.

At first Emily hadn't wanted to consult her mother about her cancer because she knew what her mother would do. With her sister she shared a rolled eye, an ironic anger, a sad terror, but it was the certainty of her mother's fear, the killing horror of illness in children, that prevented her from wanting to tell her what was wrong. Not the fact that her mother would research the illness and report back; not the fact that she would take action, but the fact of what that action masked, kept at bay: fear. Nothing scared a mother like the risk of losing her child. Mona couldn't know this, yet. So with Mona their mother's worry was a kind of joke, a fond joke, an inside joke, a sisterly intimacy, but the real intimacy Emily shared was with her mother. She, too, was a mother. And she knew.

So when her mother threw herself into scarf shopping, Emily permitted it, wearing without complaint the flamboyant silk. Emily was vain, they all knew that about her, and she would be, she swore, until the day she died. Vanity seemed to her something to seize, something to retain as a piece of volition and life, a lively trait that once would have plagued her, reminded her of her self-absorption and superficiality. But now it would be an illustration of her ongoingness, the trite concern, the shallow silliness. She would have to manufacture vanity. She would have to summon it the way she did good humor with her children, patience, other qualities that one might label *virtuous*. Vanity would be another among those, she decided, because it was not a typical feature of the saintly or good. It was a bratty trait, and Emily wanted to hang on to a few of those so as not to become tiresome.

Emily realized that knowing your days were numbered was just a speeded-up version of aging. She'd been stumped by aging before. She hadn't liked the way her body was betraying her, the forces of gravity, the scary lines in her face. Even then, in her innocent thirty-fifth year, she'd resented the fact that nobody carded her. Once, in the liquor store run by the Chinese lady, her sister Mona had been asked for ID. "What about me?" Emily demanded. "Why not card me?"

"Card her," Mona pleaded with the humorless proprietress. The woman glared, crossed her skinny arms, and refused.

In the car Emily swung the rearview mirror toward her face and stared at the crow's-feet and laugh lines. "How old do I look, anyway? That much older than you?"

"You *are* older than me," Mona reminded her.

She resented that in CD stores she was not required to surrender her backpack like the younger patrons, just waved through. Why was she no longer considered a shoplifting threat? The suburban matronly message of that knowledge annoyed her.

So one Saturday at the mall, Emily went shoplifting. This was an antidote to invisibility. She'd not been quite so aware how many mirrored surfaces the mall contained, and not only the ones made of glass. There were, of course, the mirrors other people made. In their faces her appearance revealed itself. Her looks, once at least drawing occasional sexual curiosity, now drew almost nothing. Eyes swept over her and nothing registered. It was as if she'd been neutralized, overnight gone from flesh and blood to cardboard.

"There's Patty Abbott," Mona whispered to her outside The Wild Pair. And Patty, with whom Emily had had a brief confusing love affair in college, passed by her without noticing, not ignoring her but simply unable to see her, chewing a pretzel, daydreaming. Once she'd shared a futon with Patty, beer bottles, secrets, awkward gropings and laughter; once, Emily had been the subject of that dreamy look in Patty's eyes. Emily turned to check the inevitable mirrored front of the store: wasn't she here? It seemed she was; but the red bag dangling from her wrist was more colorful than any other aspect of herself.

"She's put on some weight," Mona observed. They watched Patty as she swayed in her distinctive style, her back pants pockets riding the curves of her rump as she walked away. "You guys got along afterward, didn't you?"

"She didn't see me." Patty's inability to see Emily was not an isolated instance. Emily tested her theory at Dillards.

Mona couldn't believe it when a few minutes later they walked out of Dillards and Emily pulled a child's silver tea service from the caverns of her purse.

"I cushioned it in Petra's diaper," she explained. The tiny sugar bowl sparkled in the subdued lighting of Towne East. Two dazzling sterling spoons that reminded Emily of cocaine tools, of the tiny earring Barry had hung from his earlobe. He liked to make jokes about earwax.

"Unbelievable," Mona said, fingering the booty. Then they began laughing hysterically, leaning on a statue of a horse. Hysteria, Emily remembered from college, had to do with wombs, historically speaking. It was the craziness particular to women. Oh irony, Emily thought, her with her tainted private parts, here at the mall suffering another kind of female trouble, shoplifting. Hysteria was why a woman would never be elected president.

They had planned to get pedicures and facials, enjoy high tea at Lemongrass Restaurant, act like society ladies. But the prospect of having other women attend to her suddenly oppressed Emily. She couldn't help thinking about her grandmother's dead body being cared for similarly, made up and dressed. The most she could summon the energy for was a stop at The Replay on the way home. Nobody at The Replay would have had a pedicure or facial or taken high tea lately. Nobody at The Replay was planning on dying anytime soon.

Emily's prognosis was a year, maybe eighteen months. The cancer had spread, and although the chemo and radiation could argue with it, possibly stall it, they could not stop it. For herself, she wanted less than she might have previously imagined. It was why shoplifting now drew no consequences. In high school, she had *needed* that underwear and makeup and music, but now she didn't need much, and certainly not what you could steal at the mall. She was tempted to further test this theory, heft a television onto her shoulder and stroll away.

"Let's sit down," she said, suddenly exhausted. She wanted to be home, in the cavernous dark of her family's big abiding home, where mirrors and strangers and former lovers wouldn't leap up to surprise you. When she felt herself panicking like this, when she needed to focus, she ran through her plans for her children's future. Her friends Frog and Toady would invest her share of the business profits into an account for them, college funds. Her parents would let them live in their home until grown. Her father would investigate universities, when the time came; her mother, meanwhile, would visit their schoolteachers, pack their lunches, take them to Girl Scouts and soccer practice. And her siblings? What were Mona and Winston's roles? Emily let the four figures— Winston, Mona, Roy, Petra—cluster in a family-like configuration to give herself comfort, Man, Woman, Boy, Girl. Her own allegiance to the memory of childhood asserted itself. Her children would like to think of their aunt and uncle in the place of parents. They would need it.

Without a lot of alternatives, she turned to the ones at hand. And they did not seem so terrible to her, anymore. She had a newfound belief in the ability of people to rise to an occasion; probably because she felt she was rising to her own. This involved a leap of faith, on the part of her unreliable siblings, melancholy Mona and mercurial Winston. But in the nine months since Winston had been home, he'd never hurt little Roy. He loved her son, she thought. Mona could learn how to care for Petra. Mona had a whole menagerie she loved, and her affection for her pets could translate to that for a baby. Wasn't that what pets were for, practice? With enough involved adults, her children might move with a minimum of suffering into their waiting adulthoods.

Ultimately, it would be out of her hands. Like this ongoing fracas at the local mall, life would proceed without her, continue in its clatter and flow as if she'd never been there to interrupt. All her life Emily had worked against that premise, that she was distinct rather than ordinary, that she could stand out instead of merely blend. But the mall told her otherwise. Her cancer confirmed the message. She would have to succumb, turn the keys over to others to continue the trip, to her family, who loved her children, if at a slight distance and with a distracted attention, but loved them nonetheless. It pained her that Roy's father had so easily left his son. Barry was young and self-absorbed, and her belief had always been that she could reform him, turn him into the man he seemed to have inside him, that she was just that powerful. He was weak, it was true, a virtual embodiment of impotence, constantly making a promise that he couldn't keep, wanting to follow through, but always at the crucial moment limp. Yet his weakness was only part of their undoing. It was her fault, too, she with her conviction. She'd thought she was strong enough for the two of them. That had been her arrogance, once upon a time, assuming she could do the work of two.

"Facials give you acne, anyway," Mona said, when Emily admitted she just wasn't up to it. "Well, not you, but me. Everything gives *me* acne."

AT PLANNED Parenthood, Mona had to pose as Sheila's mother in order for the girl to get an abortion. Was this the same woman who'd bought their last mother-daughter act, back in December? The receptionist looked skeptical, as well she might. Mona found it hard to picture herself as Sheila's mother. She would have had to have been a fourteen-year-old pregnant girl. At fourteen, she'd not even been kissed yet.

"I don't want my daughter to have the same life I had," Mona claimed, an inspired lie, she thought. It helped that their driver's licenses showed the same last name and that, in some obvious picky bickering familial way, they were related.

The receptionist wore a wig, a thick stiff head of brown hair like a big inverted tulip so clearly fake that Mona wondered if it was a joke. The woman was terribly thin; maybe chemotherapy accounted for it all, her whites hanging from her shoulders and hipbones as if from two hangers. To her credit, Emily had managed the ravages of chemo and radiation more successfully. She wore exotic scarves wrapped around her baldness. She slept all of the time, making it a priority, handing over the children to her family with an unworriedness that was not her former nature. She adapted, Emily, refiguring herself so as to be best prepared for what came next. This clinic nurse had bigger personal problems than Sheila Mabie's reckless pregnancy; she didn't care who was the responsible party, who signed what. Sheila sulked on a leatherette couch, paging through last year's January *Redbook* as if Mona had dreamed up the whole appointment and was forcing Sheila to accompany her.

"Doctor will be right with you," the woman claimed. Her eye makeup was as phony as her coif, blue shadow, thick mascara, heavy pancake cover-up. Yet she smiled, finally, sealing the deal, taking away the clipboard and consent forms.

Mona's MasterCard was rejected, so she wrote a check. Sheila gave her two wadded-up twenties, promising to pay the rest.

"I thought there'd be a protest out front," Mona told her, deflecting the money issue. Mona didn't pay rent; she owed her family various debts, and Sheila was as fine a project as they came. "There used to always be protests," Mona went on, although she didn't recall one during Emily's abortion of 1981, either.

"Hmm," said her cousin, possibly not even aware of the controversy of abortion. Maybe she'd missed all of that. Abortion, for her, seemed to be merely a cumbersome form of birth control, to be endured the way one did any penalty, the makeup exam, detention, being grounded.

So Sheila was engrossed in an article about the male perineum. Apparently it was an extremely erogenous zone. Mona wanted to ask if Sheila thought Eddie went around reading advice about improving Sheila's sexual pleasure. She was going to turn into a bitter spinster, she thought, nagging the generation behind her of their obligations to their predecessors, all those women who'd suffered so that girls like Sheila could take for granted their freedom. Girls like Sheila went around forgetting their birth control pills in favor of their curling irons. Girls like Sheila thought about their boyfriends' erogenous zones. No matter; Sheila and Eddie obviously had fantastic sex. Mona wished she'd had sex at sixteen. She didn't make love until she was nearly twenty-one, and by then it meant too much. Sex equaled love. And love equaled a broken heart. Her second lover had been her sister's husband. Her third Nicholas Dempsey. She was dying to meet her fourth. When did she plan on learning, she asked herself. Planned Parenthood, indeed.

Afterward, she drove to Winchells, for doughnuts, as if this were now a family tradition. "I'm nauseous," Sheila complained, lying on the backseat.

"Nauseated," Mona corrected.

"Whatever." But she accepted a doughnut anyway, and ate it slowly, in her Valium-induced languor, as her cousin took her home. She would tell her parents she had the flu. Or perhaps PMS. They would believe her because it was Friday, and what was the point of faking illness on the weekend? Mona would phone her in the morning and hear that Sheila felt nearly normal, her biggest complaint the fact that she had to wear a pad instead of a tampon, and what was she going to tell Eddie Shakes now that they couldn't have sex for six weeks? She would be panicking about that, tomorrow morning. But Mona would be speaking to her after a restless night, one filled with nightmares of her cousin's death by hemorrhage.

THE SECOND ransom note instructed the family to leave the thousand dollars in a milk carton in a sack near the swing set at College Hill Park at six that evening. It was Emily who'd received the mail the day the note came, and she pulled Mona aside as Mona returned from work. "I don't want to tell Mom and Dad about this," Emily said.

"Why?"

"Because they're weird about money. Because I think Dad'll get angry with Winston. Because I don't know why. Just because."

"Okay." Like the first note, this one was typed on plain paper, straightforward, addressed City.

"We're walking Curly," Roy shouted to his grandfather through the closed study door. "He said 'Umph,' " Roy reported to Emily and Mona.

Mona pushed Petra's stroller, the sack with the milk carton swinging from the handle. They'd had to empty the milk into jars, then stuff the bills inside the damp plastic gallon container, which still smelled. Too bad; if you asked for money in a milk carton, you were going to get a rank ransom.

To the park they went, Curly tugging mightily on Emily's left hand, Roy pulling on the right. They left the sack by the swings, weighted with a rock, appearing for all the world like trash. Roy wanted to swing, but his mother and aunt didn't think it wise, and convinced him to cross the street into the area with the tennis courts and basketball hoops. Mona kept looking back at the thousand dollars, waiting to see someone pick it up. It was 6:07; anyone could take the bag, throw it away, investigate it, ruin the drop-off. She expected to see her brother, that blazing blue jacket he'd been wearing the last few weeks.

But near the shuffleboard courts they came upon a boy without arms, he and his friends, who were galloping along pulling a plastic tractor on a jump rope. The tractor was designed for smaller children, a riding toy now converted to a cart. One boy pulled it, jump rope yoke-like across his chest, while another rode with his gangly legs thrown over the plastic handlebars. The others charged along beside, laughing, jostling, now and then falling. Their hair was cut in the ragged manner of the poor, in the way of simple neglect; it had never been sculpted by a hairdresser and had now been permitted to grow long. They shook their heads to get it out of their eyes, habitual, patient. One of them, who smiled reflexively, was missing a tooth, a boy too old to be waiting for a permanent tooth to emerge. They looked like ruffians from some bygone era, boys of the Mabie sisters' father's generation, wearing out-moded clothing, the sort you found at the Salvation Army. In a movie, they would be misunderstood impoverished boys with hearts of gold,

teetering always between the path of virtue and the seductive temptation of going bad.

The sisters stopped to watch the ruckus. Petra clapped when the
trailer went flying by, and Roy tugged on his mother's sleeve. "Where's
that boy's arms?" he asked.

"He hasn't got any."

"Why?"

"I don't know."

Mona glanced back at the swing set across the street and saw that
the white sack was gone. "It's gone," she told Emily.

"Amazing," Emily said. "That was fast."

But Emily had gotten caught up in the chaos of the ruffians. She
liked them because they seemed to be surviving despite some desperate
situation. They treated one another well, leaving no boy on the outside
of the game, including the boy with no arms, naturally. They disre-
garded their bad luck. It would have been simpleminded to claim that
attitude was everything, a kind of sentiment one attached to posters in
counselors' offices, the sort of notion one scoffed at in high school and
then later began assessing for its truth. Faced with death, Emily
thought of all adages as bearing central truths. If you didn't have your
health, you didn't have anything. And the truth was, her children would
survive, and would know happiness, and would mourn her but not
inordinately. It was as much as she could ask, she told herself. It was all
she was entitled to. Fear sometimes leaped up in her mouth like a monkey, gripping her with its clawing fingers, and she was practicing
squelching it. Down, monkey. She was alive today, able to walk with her
children, capable of appreciating the joy of racing through the park on
the back of a pull toy.

Mona, however, had another response. The children reminded her of
the downward turn her old neighborhood was taking. She didn't like to
be reminded of this, as it seemed to implicate her in its plunge. No one
would be surprised to find a fat girl in a secondhand skirt wandering the
park. Parks were well-known havens of the lost and unseemly, the
drunken and disenfranchised, the schizophrenic preacher and the doz-
ing junkie. Mona never passed easily through this territory, recognizing
at her core some kinship with its nomadic natives. Her sister, fortunately, added an element of the respectable, the upstanding. Emily was

fashionable, as usual, dressed in the expensive subdued contemporary style that was her trademark, and she pushed her stroller with impunity. The boy with no arms ran after his friends halfheartedly: he could not join in their game except to track his friends' progress from one end of the length of sidewalk to another, running behind them, hollering. This reminded Mona of a bird she once saw at an aviary, a dove separated from the other birds, on the outside while they were on the inside. This dove had been pacing up and down, tracking his beloved as she paced up and down inside. The bird on the outside had no interest in his freedom, the wide world he could soar off into, leaving the other birds in their cage. No, he wanted *inside* the cage with them. Mona thought Dr. Lydia would like this image, the bird who desired to be trapped, who could not recognize the larger beauty of being free. Lydia would apply it to Mona and her obsession.

Lydia would have liked it, but the metaphor didn't do anything for Mona.

The boy with no arms in fact reminded her a bit of a bird as he hopped alongside his friends, the long stretch of chest without defining interruption of appendage. He did not mount the tractor, nor did he shoulder the jump rope harness. He spotted Mona and Emily and Roy and Petra, and brightened visibly. But it was Curly, the new dog, he moved toward; Curly whose head came to the boy's blank chest.

"Does he bite?" asked the boy, his eyes immediately on Mona, who told him not usually. They'd had the dog for a week; his personality was still emerging. The boy's short green sleeves flapped; beneath his shirt pockets Mona could almost believe his arms were tucked except that there wasn't enough bulk. It could almost have been a prank, but she knew it wasn't. He bent at the waist to greet Curly, making contact with his nose like another dog. He lifted a leg gently to rub the sole of his shoe along Curly's flank. There was nothing to suggest he had ever had arms, ever known what it was to use them. His torso seemed painfully long to Mona, wrong in some way that he didn't seem the least bit bothered by.

The human body ought to be shaped like a starfish, Mona thought, not a clothespin. Nothing in nature had this odd absence; even birds, armless as they often appeared when pecking at the ground, took on their own beautiful integrity when launched into the sky. She tried to picture the armless boy in a swimming pool, asleep, at a desk or table, riding in a car. No setting accommodated him. He made neither sense nor grace in any position. And this was perhaps what made him fascinating.

"What's your name?" he asked Roy, finally looking up from Curly's lapping purple and black tongue.

Roy told him but the boy didn't hear, tilting forward to put his ear closer, the same gesture usually accompanied by a hand at the ear: Eh? The boy turned his large brown eyes to the Mabie sisters.

"Roy," they said in unison.

"I'm Marco. What's his name?" He nudged his chin toward the dog.

"Curly," Roy announced.

When asked where he lived, the boy tossed his head to indicate the block behind them, one falling more quickly into disrepair, houses weathered gray in need of paint, plastic-covered broken windows, bald lawns. Emily's old house was within view, now teetering between ruin and restoration.

The boy nudged his head down once more to receive the dog's furious licking. The sisters had not seen the animal quite so animated before. "This dog looks just like our old dog," the boy said amiably. "But his name was Brutus, and he got lost a while ago."

"How long ago?" Emily asked. Roy threw his arm around Curly, already guessing where the conversation was leading. He could not bear to lose his new dog. Mona watched tears spring to his eyes.

"Oh a long time ago. Last year, or something. Are you Brutus's brother?" he asked the dog. "Do you have a brother named Brutus?"

Curly waved his tail enthusiastically, humming his odd noise.

"Did your dog do that?" Emily asked. "Whine like that?"

"No. Our dog just ran away a lot." Now his friends called to him, and he nodded at the Mabies. "'Bye."

It would have been convenient for Curly to have been Brutus, to have gone away with the armless boy and his friends, case closed, because when the foursome returned home from their walk, they found Kojak waiting in his pen for them.

AFTER THAT, Emily always thought of the armless boy when she was feeling sorry for herself. Him, or of the fact that she preferred her own death to those of her children. She had only to be faced with the pretend choice, her or them?

While watching *Suddenly, Last Summer* with her family one night, Emily nearly broke into tears when Katharine Hepburn descended from the ceiling and began talking about her dead son. There would be no way to live with a dead son. She would have to have killed herself.

There were jokes about armless, legless boys. What did you call him at the baseball game? Third base. What did you call the limbless boy hanging from the wall? Art. And what if he were lost at sea? Bob.

And so on.

She also took solace in drinking. Drinking made her relax. Drinking made her calm. Drinking made death a metaphysical inquiry, fuzzy and ephemeral. Her fear was physical, that crazy monkey, and alcohol made it sleep, soften its prehensile grip on her.

THE DOG was none the worse for wear, his strange lost week. In fact, he had beefed up during his dognapping. No matter how hard you looked at him, he could not reveal his whereabouts, nor the name of his abductor. Professor Mabie surveyed the two dogs in the pen as his wife, once more, gardened. "Why was he returned?" he asked.

"Why do you care?" she replied blandly.

"What sort of question is that?"

To this she had no answer. Maybe she would become sanguine and enigmatic. Maybe he would grow to appreciate that about her.

The dogs liked each other, oddly enough. Kojak had taken to standing beneath Curly's legs, as if inside a doghouse, staring out at the world from a safe space. When they ate, Curly allowed Kojak to go first, waiting patiently until the little dog was done, then stepping up to the bowl and emptying it. This respect from the bigger younger dog toward the older curmudgeon nobody could have predicted. Curly adopted the role of bodyguard, as if Kojak were some frail dictator or mob boss. They slept together at night in the pen, no complaints. Separated, each of them made noise, one humming, one growling.

"I don't like not knowing how this happened," Professor Mabie said.

"It's a mystery," his wife said, unperturbed.

"Winston did it," he said to her; he said it perhaps to encourage the response he received.

"How can you think such a thing?" she cried, vehemently. She blinked up at him from the ground, brandishing her tool as if to dig into his chest. "I forbid you from thinking that!" He nearly laughed he was so surprised. "How can you live, thinking the worst of your son?"

"How can you think otherwise?"

"Easily," she said. "I think so quite easily." She turned back to her worms and dirt as if dismissing him. As if he'd disappointed her.

Professor Mabie stormed into the house and phoned Garth Blewski's number. Once more he reached the machine: "Blewski here. I'm screening my calls, so let me know why I should take yours."

Professor Mabie stated his name, when the time came, and then was at a loss. Had he believed he could phone a fifty-something-year-old man, a university professor, and accuse him of stealing a dog? Was that something he wanted Garth Blewski to have on tape? He slammed the phone down, embarrassed and angry, his usual emotions in matters related to his son.

"Do you need money?" Emily asked Winston.

"No," he replied, "and I don't want you to give me any." They were watching a movie about famous drug addicts. Emily preferred tragic plots, oddly enough. She liked to have the shape of life—which is to say death—ratified. These particular rock singers had been riding a fast-rising star for the last hour, and now were due to come crashing down for the next hour.

"Where are you getting money?" she asked him, pursuing the topic during commercials, unconcerned with tact.

Winston faced her. "You really want to know?"

She considered the question. "I do," she decided, prepared to be told that he'd robbed her store and held the family dog for ransom. She'd forgiven him in advance, if those were his infractions.

"I am what we call A Paid Companion," he said, instead.

"Really?" Emily took a moment to absorb this, then, to be sure, asked, "As in sexual favors?"

He didn't answer, which seemed answer enough. His profile was beautiful, as always. It was not hard to imagine that someone would pay him for sex. Emily envisioned the old women of her grandmother's bridge clubs, which image made her attend to the television once more. The commercials for this movie suggested that the only people watching were ones who were bad credit risks, who were tempted to consult psychic healers, who enjoyed beds that could fold them into a number of positions with just the touch of a button, who were likely to make collect phone calls. It was not a favorable demographic, Emily thought, but it appeared to be hers and her brother's. When the movie came back on, the girl in the famous couple was shooting up backstage, then smearing lipstick around her eyes and mouth, holding the bullet-like tube in a salacious manner.

"Paid companion," Emily repeated in the echoing method of the psychiatrist, prompting gently. It equaled humiliation, paid companionship, although she thought she'd rather be a prostitute than the person who had to go to one. She wondered if the word that popped suddenly into her mind—*privation*—was related to *deprivation*? Or maybe it had its origins in *private,* or perhaps both. Which would make its opposite, its antidote, *un-private, un-alone.*

"You ever try heroin?" Emily asked.

"I haven't. Been tempted, but. You?"

"Nope. I wish this movie was in black and white instead of color. Color tends to date film. Wouldn't it seem artier in black and white, noir-y and all?"

Winston eased his long legs out and crossed his ankles. Emily had the impression that he was glad he'd told her how he was making money, acquitted somewhat, relieving him of his private privation. Terminal illness had the effect of truth serum sometimes. In its face, what was the point of deception or modesty or evasiveness? She had the liberty to speak her mind these days, and the right to expect others to answer in kind. It pleased her.

"I wonder who'll bomb out first?" Emily asked of the movie. "Him or her? Who'll embarrass themself first?"

"There's gonna be tears," Winston warned, the way their father always had.

"And vomiting. We haven't seen anyone toss their cookies yet.

"Will you do something for me?" Emily asked him at the next commercial, which promised a brand-spanking-new car for absolutely no money down.

"I might," Winston said, "if you ask nice."

"Will you stop being a paid companion, whatever that means? Will you quit that euphemism, and take over my part at the store, instead?"

"It's not like I stand out on a corner soliciting," Winston said, smiling now. "It's just one pathetic guy, and he's clean, and it's fine. You don't have to rescue me, Emily. I only go for the victimless crimes, these days."

"Still," she said, then decided to forgo the admonition about being careful. People in their family were forever advising you to be careful. It was practically a family motto—she could envision the insignia, an alarmed open mouth, frightened splayed hands. She nodded at the movie. "I wish my drugs were as fun as those drugs look. But my drugs are all of the nonaddictive, no-fun variety. My painkillers are all cut with some wet-blanket agent, like the narc at a party. I could never get addicted to the stuff I have."

"I'll work at your store," Winston said abruptly. "Let me get you some fun drugs, and I'll take the job."

"Yeah?" Emily said. "I'm good with that." They sat in the movie's 1972 psychedelic glow, waiting companionably through the blaring rock and roll and the long swinging hair of the dancing orgy members and the undulating navels of the hip-huggered girls and the overdramatic twitching fingers of the Afro-haired band members on guitar strings and drumsticks, the music swelling ominously, Emily and Winston content to stick it out to the bitter end, the inevitable overdose that always closed shows like this.

5

Roy's grandmother had a key to his aunt Mona's
bedroom. One day the two of them went in. He knew they were not
allowed, even though his grandmother had brought her dust sock and
spray bottle. She bent her face close to the keyhole, close to all objects,
because she was going blind; Roy knew this. Still, she looked like she
was smelling things, the way dogs did.

"This is a surprise, Roy," his grandmother told him. "Don't tell
Mona that I dusted her room."

"Why do you have a key?"

"Mona gave it to me."

Nuh-uh, Roy thought but did not say. "Why is it a secret?" he asked,
instead.

"Not a *secret*, a *surprise*." His grandmother wore her sock on one
hand like a puppet, which she used to wipe with while opening drawers
with the other hand. Roy did not pursue his inquiry because his uncle
Winston had forbidden him from asking more than once any question
beginning with the word "why." Besides, Roy had his eye on the nest of
cats, the spotted ones and the striped ones, the tiny kittens nestled in
among the wild leopards and cheetahs, the old friendly faces of the
standing lion and the sleeping tiger, the father and mother of all the animals. He bounced onto her bed and settled among them. In the old

days, Mona would tell him stories about the creatures. She would make them talk, fall over, have fistfights, dance. The flamingo and the frog and the walrus and the lemur had a rock and roll band, instruments made of cardboard and tinfoil and buttons and tacks; the fox was always in jail, rattling his bars; one of the rabbits thought he knew everything, so he got to host a talk show.

"Can't be trusted," squawked Guido the living parrot all of a sudden. "Good morning. Good morning. Be quiet, Betty." His grandmother jumped; everything startled his grandmother.

"Can I take off his sheet?" asked Roy. He'd forgotten about Guido. The covered cage quivered like a ghost.

"No, honey, we'll let him sleep until Mona comes home."

It was on the tip of his tongue to ask her why, but he didn't. His grandmother was sniffing behind books in the bookcase, then behind the bookcase itself, then in the closet and under the bed. She got onto her hands and knees and reached behind the radiator, frowning. Even Roy knew you didn't dust behind books or radiators. If she'd asked, Roy would have advised looking inside the zippered animals. Mona had a few stuffed toys with zippers, a bear and an alligator and a kangaroo and a Dalmatian with hidden interiors, places to put your toothbrush if you were going on an overnight, places to store money if you had a brother and sister, places to keep secrets. But his grandmother didn't ask Roy. From Winston, Roy was learning that it was best not to volunteer everything you knew.

"Shut up Guido," said Guido. "Chin up bub."

"I could not live with that bird in my room," Roy's grandmother declared, blinking furiously. "Let's go, Roy. Everything's clean." Roy patted the heads of his favorites among the animals and they left Aunt Mona's room, locking her door again.

"It's a secret," he assured his grandmother when she asked him why they weren't going to tell anyone what they'd done.

He located his uncle in the garage, where he was sleeping on a tarp, curled against the wall. Winston often took naps; he could do it anywhere. All around him were boards and wood chips, tools and a saw, a sack of nails. Cigarettes were slipping from his shirt pocket, and when Roy reached delicately for one, Winston woke.

"My man," said his uncle.

"What are you doing?"

Winston rose, stretching and shaking his head. The tarp had left a crease in his cheek.

"What are you doing?" Roy repeated. "Can I help?"

"These are torture devices for pigeons," Winston told him, yawning as he sat up, patting for his smokes. On the far side of the garage floor lay stacks of boards, all with a lot of nails sticking up in them. "I'm going to climb a very tall ladder up to the roof, and underneath, all along the eaves, I'm going to attach these boards so the pigeons won't sit there. This is a bed of tarp," he said, rising from his napping spot. "But those are beds of nails."

"Beds of nails," Roy repeated.

"For suffering. Even idiotic pigeons will find the beds of nails extremely, excruciatingly, uncomfortable."

"Me, too."

"You can keep your old bed, porky. Your grandfather hates pigeons."

"He's your dad," Roy pointed out.

"True, my man, so true."

"Grandpa tried to shoot them, but Mona wouldn't let him."

"Mona doesn't like to kill animals."

Roy shook his head. Aunt Mona loved animals. He'd found her crying one day about Kojak, when Kojak was missing. If there were bugs in the house, she caught them in her cupped hands and led them outside, telling them to fly free, rather than squashing them. Roy liked that about Mona.

"Once," Roy said, "once Grandpa put some rubber snakes up there to frighten the pigeons, but that didn't work, either." Roy recalled how placidly the birds accepted the snakes, sitting beside them, building their nests behind them, acting as if they were simply decoration, while Roy himself had hated the snakes. On the third floor, where he and his mother and sister lived, the pigeons sat just outside their windows, sighing, muttering like ladies talking at a party. They had red feet, they had red eyes. Sometimes they sat on top of each other and flapped their wings, shook their fannies. Roy did not like them, they reminded him of his mother's friends Frog and Toady, so he aided Winston in the construction of the beds of nails meant to discourage the birds, hammering enthusiastically. Later, he stood on the ground and watched Winston climb the shaky ladder up the three tall stories of the house, holding the first board under his arm, hammer tucked in a back pocket, nails in his mouth.

"You need a tool belt," Roy told him when he climbed down a few minutes later. "And you have a hole in your shoe."

"Keep it coming," Winston said. "I love advice from the peanut gallery."

WHAT happened first on May Day was that Mrs. Mabie caught Mona in front of the pantry mirror making faces at herself. It didn't look good, Mona grimacing and contorting, looking at herself with venom in her eyes. Her mother gave a frightened exclamation, then wondered if she could cook Mona some scrambled eggs before work, perhaps squeeze a glass of juice? As if eggs and oranges might solve anything.

Next, on the way to work at Starkey Elementary, Mona saw a one-armed man on the street. He was an example of the kind of event that was making Mona scare herself. In all ways he seemed a perfectly acceptable man except for the missing arm. She began making a case for this, that she could love a one-armed man, that she would tend his stump lovingly, bathe it, caress it in the fashion of a sexual partner. . . . Then the man lowered what she'd thought was his missing arm—he'd been vigorously scratching his back as he walked—and smiled at her, lifting the hand that she'd thought absent to wave at her. Maybe he approved of her speed—slow, since she was gawking—or maybe he liked her looks.

"Pathetic," Mona whispered, of herself: she'd want him more if he were damaged goods, which meant, she supposed, that he'd be less likely to leave her, grateful for her attention, as if he were the one who should wonder about worthiness. It was sad, the way her mind worked. Nicholas Dempsey's rejection made her feel universally rejected, rejected in advance.

Tears came, warm and salty down her cheeks, and she enjoyed the bitter ripeness of her emotions. *Overwrought,* she whispered. She was overwrought. *Poppycock, hogwash, utter rot,* she thought. This was the one thing she might have shared with her grandmother Bunny, the love of words, the comic nature of their coupling. The lyrics to a song her brother had made up came to her.

Oh granny, how the world has gone wrong,
I'll tell you all about it, in this little song.
We used to court our women, using all the fancy phrases,
Now you say you'll phone her, there pass by many days-es.

At Starkey she lied to Percy, who found her in the hall, unarmed, alone. He leveled the Nerf gun at her temple. "I'm already dead," she told him flatly.

"It's not posted!"

"It just happened in the parking lot."

"Who's the shooter?"

"Poison."

"Poison?"

Mona slipped down the hall, into the girls' room. "Self-inflicted," she called to him. Killer seemed dangerous to her, now, unfunny. She needed to focus on one task at a time, not be looking over her shoulder for some fool with a paint balloon or a water pistol. Killer was for people with self-confidence and love lives and goodwill. She aided in three different classrooms during the day. Art was first. Art was easy. Art was going to give her a lot of time to gather her wits.

"You can't kill yourself!" Percy yelled through the bathroom door. "That's a rule, no suicides! No Human Shields, No Public Hits, No Suicides!"

"Fuck you, fag," Mona muttered.

Then, when she came home from work, she drove over some board in the driveway and ruined her mother's front right tire. "What are you doing?" she asked Winston, who emerged from the garage with a circular saw in his hand and a cigarette in his mouth.

Instead of answering, he revved the saw, as if to slice her in two.

"Now Mom's car is trashed. And guess who'll get blamed?"

"You shouldn't have driven over my board."

"Fuck you," she said, slamming the door and raging into the house, where her mother had made brownies, as if to turn Mona into a blimp. Entrapment, she thought. Her family was trying to lead her into her worst tendencies.

Then, upstairs, Nicholas Dempsey called from his office "just to chat." It was that turbulent hour that had lately turned malicious, the hour when they'd used to meet in bars, the chamber between work and home, what was often referred to by the uninitiated as Happy Hour.

"Chat?" Mona said, stupidly, chewing a brownie. She'd heard from him ten days earlier, another sober afternoon phone conversation, adamantly unflirtatious, truncated when Mona asked why he was calling her. For, while she was dying to hear from him, she was also always uncertain where things stood. What was he doing? Did he want to start their affair up again? For what reason on earth would he want to "just be friends"? It was impossible to move on, Mona thought, with Nicholas Dempsey standing in the path of progress this way. And it was also impossible for her to shove him aside.

"Chat," he said now. "Give-and-take, tit for tat, how are you, what's new. Like that. Oh, just a sec." He took another call, leaving her with music, a peppy marching tune. After these calls, Mona always wished she had thrown a little tantrum and told him off. *Fuck you,* she wanted to say to him, plus a lot of other business. Because nothing came of Nicholas Dempsey's phone calls. They were perhaps designed just to assure him that he still held her heart, to restore a sensation of daring, to boost his confidence, to make him strong by taking the small bit that remained of Mona's strength.

"Sorry," he said unapologetically. "So tell me what you're doing, Mona Mabie."

"Nothing. I just got home from work." Mona swore to herself to be cold today, to take the first chance available to tell him he was messing her life around with these phone calls, misleading her, holding his affection in front of her like a baited hook, and she was tired of being caught and released, ensnared and thrown back, so would he please just stop. She wanted to tell him she didn't trust him, not one little bit, that he'd had her love, that he'd hurt her terribly, that he didn't deserve her friendship. . . .

"How was Starkey?" he asked.

"Starkey was fine."

"And how's Crazy Mary?"

"Also fine."

"She didn't strip?"

"Nope."

"And Nancy-pants?"

"He kept on his clothes as well."

"*Any*body strip?"

"Nope."

"Hmm. Anybody kill you?"

"Nope."

"You kill anybody?"

Mona paused. *Myself,* she was tempted to confess. *And it's all your fault.* "Nope," she said, instead.

"Okay. Good. Clean living. Stars in the heavenly—"

"I met your wife." Mona interrupted, a flat accusation.

"And you talked her into some butt-ugly earrings," he replied.

Mona couldn't help laughing, melting into their former back-and-forth, intimate banter. As usual, she would succumb to his knowledge-able persistence and warm up, tell him about her day, forming the anecdotes she was accustomed to forming, laughing, and sort of losing track of her firm decisions concerning his calls. She asked about his day, his secretary, his cases, and then, when she said, earnestly, passionately, forgetfully, "It's so nice to hear your voice," she could not even be surprised when he sabotaged her by suddenly having to go.

"I've got to hang up," he said abruptly and then did so, leaving her with a dial tone that made her want to strike somebody with the receiver, bludgeon first him, then herself senseless. She was sorely tempted to phone his wife and not just drop a hint but a bomb. As usual, this call unhinged her, made Nicholas Dempsey fresh once more, right in front of her and totally out of reach. For the next few days she would play the call again and again in her mind, attending to the inane comments he'd made, looking for something in the inflection or phrasing to tell her he still loved her.

The repetitious flavor of his interference oppressed her; she knew it would be weeks until she felt anywhere near normal once more. Every time he threatened to inhabit the back burner of her obsessive mind, he managed to insert himself front and center, its hottest topic, its bright-est flame.

Moreover, it seemed someone had been in her room. The animals seemed rearranged, just vaguely so, their eyes looking askance as if ashamed on her behalf. But this could have been her imagination. Her dreadful overdriven imagination.

Worst of all was the open house going on next door at the Vaughns' old place, a parade of visitors and real estate agents, a few nervous glances cast in the direction of the Mabie property with their trees and wildlife. The Nakeds, it was rumored, could not afford their mortgage; until she saw the sign, Mona thought they were throwing a party, the bright lights, the many cars on the street. She had gone to retrieve the barking dogs, crossing the driveway holding a stiff drink, hushing Kojak and Curly, avoiding the beds of nails Winston had left strewn about, when she saw Christine Dempsey, pushing her double stroller with Nicholas's children up the Vaughn driveway. Mona stopped, stared stupidly, swore to herself. "Goddamn." What if Nicholas Dempsey moved in *next door*? What if she had to see him every morning, whistling as he left for work, kissing that wife and those children? What if his son became best friends with Roy? The two sons of her lovers, little bitty Miles and Roy, plaguing her for the rest of her years, growing up together and getting in trouble. "Unbe*liev*able," she said aloud, following the dogs as they tripped over each other on their way into the house. "Unfuckingbelievable."

That evening after dinner, Mona took herself away from home, the scene of the crime. Roy seemed to be wearing on everyone's nerves, so she invited him along and they went to DQ to make themselves sick on hot fudge and peanuts, then to drop in on Billy and Sheila, who were at loose ends since Wenda was in Dallas again.

"Huh," said Sheila without interest when she found her cousins on her doorstep. Ever since her abortion she'd been a little cold toward Mona, the way people were after you'd witnessed their low moments, as if Mona were blackmailing Sheila. You couldn't win, doing favors such as those.

"You want a drink?" Billy asked, opening his refrigerator. The only thing he had was a bottle of expensive Champagne left over from the holidays. "Champagne!" he declared happily, popping the cork before Mona had a chance to decline. Not that she would have. In their family, with the exception of Winston, no one ever declined the offer of a drink.

But then Big O came over and he wouldn't drink Champagne, so Billy only drank one small glass, shifting to cheap beer served in naked lady glasses, and that left Mona to finish the bottle, remembering too late what a lightweight she was in the face of Champagne. Roy had fallen asleep watching something thoroughly inappropriate on television, Sheila stroking his back while she talked to Eddie Shakes on the telephone. Mona hated the tenor of her cousin's end of the conversation, the way Sheila teased, argued, flirted, made pillow talk the way people in love did. This accounted, in part, for the fast intake of alcohol, as well as the volume. Her cousin, the seventeen-year-old nitwit who'd managed to carry on a relationship for over a year now, a public relationship, a sexual relationship, one that had survived an abortion, one that was clearly thriving . . .

Billy was fixing tomorrow's welcome-home dinner for Wenda, marinating an enormous piece of bloody beef in a concoction of lemonade and beer and soy sauce, and was too absorbed in Big O's mumbled anecdote to pay particular attention to the conversation he had been having with Mona. This allowed Mona to wander, both mentally and physically. It was comforting, Billy's home, warm and untended, noisy and benign, unrecognizable as her grandmother's former tidy home. And it was also discouraging and depressing. How had brainless Billy and slutty Sheila managed to find true love—even Big O had had a girlfriend, one he'd had the luxury of breaking up with—while Mona, tender and good-hearted and smart, had found only assholes like Nicholas Dempsey and The Excrescence? At ten-thirty, when Sheila hung up and the last of the cooking utensils were in the dishwasher, when the meat in its plastic marinade bag had been fitted in the crowded refrigerator, Mona finally rose and realized the extent of her inebriation.

She pretended that the hand she extended for balance was intended for Big O to shake. He shook. On his knuckles he had individual letters tattooed, but Mona couldn't arrange them into a word—like random Scrabble letters—and didn't want to ask.

She would drive home very drunk, yet safely, she told herself, carefully charting her course as she strapped Roy into the Volvo backseat still asleep. The Volvo was safe, she told herself as she waved to Billy and Big O. The white road marks made good guidelines, and the yellow ones were ridged so as to rumble your car should you transgress. Over the train tracks she bumped gently, past the slaughterhouse and the oil refinery, glad for the evening's balminess, for the impending promise of summer. She was narrating to herself, trying to cheer herself up, telling herself that she fell in love, some summers, and maybe this would be one of them. She wanted nothing more than to fall in love again. She wanted to think of some other head of hair, some other neck, some other pair of hands and voice. She wanted to cringe when she thought of Nicholas Dempsey, to feel vaguely incredulous that he'd ever attracted her. Thank god for so little traffic, she told herself. In the back Roy snored, face slumped against the middle headrest when Mona checked as she entered the freeway.

She had just returned her gaze to the road ahead of her when she saw the lights, two rows of them facing her, approaching with alarming speed, blossoming furiously as if unleashed from a starting gate. She was traveling south on a northbound lane, the divider on her right raised so that claiming the proper lane was a matter of briefly high-centering her sister's Volvo. Sobriety washed through her as she swerved, a flush of adrenaline and fear, simultaneous with the image of a crash, the impact of Roy's death on her dying sister, the brief prayer that she not overcompensate, the spinning car on I-35 wrapping itself round a pole or stump . . . Stunning how much she could imagine in such a split second. But after the initial horror and heart-stopping thrill of bumping over the median, realizing the happy fact that she had landed in a clear lane, that the car still operated, that her nephew still slept, that there appeared to be no witnesses, that as far as she could tell there were to be no repercussions, no police, no other southbound traffic to interfere with her correction, Mona drove the remainder of the freeway clenching the steering wheel, sweating fiercely, doing a dutiful 45, and then pulled into a 7-Eleven to phone Marty Song.

"Help," she said piteously, watching Roy through the car window as he continued his innocent uninterrupted slumber. Mona held the phone receiver the way she'd held one earlier, as if to knock some sense into her head, hating herself, afraid of her own destructive inclinations. She could not incline this way with Roy on board.

"Sit tight," Marty said. "Buy yourself a soda and then go turn on the radio. Find Dr. Laura and listen to that bitch. I'll be right there."

John Denver played on the radio, and Mona was so upset that she didn't switch the station, as if this was what she deserved, John Denver and his jet plane. John Denver, she realized, was rumored to have died drunk in an airplane. Irony on him, irony on her. Her hands shook so much she had to use them both to bring the Crush to her lips. And she didn't even like Crush, she had no idea why she'd chosen it, and had she taken her change from the attendant?

Marty brought Winston, who went inside to buy his own can of soda and then plopped down behind the wheel of the Volvo. Mona, beside him, passenger, breathed heavily. Cans of soda reminded her of visiting him in Larned, the heavy pocket of quarters she was allowed to bring to the visitors' room, the thick black line taped to the floor that neither she nor he was allowed to cross, as if they were meeting on a basketball court. Mona and Winston staring at each other, no props other than their cans of Pepsi.

"Orange Crush gives you baby aspirin breath," Mona said and Winston shifted the car from park.

"Bunny's the one who taught me how to drive drunk," Winston said, steering them onto empty First Street. He went no further with what had sounded like the beginning of a story. Mona wasn't going to ask; obviously it hadn't been a foolproof method. The three of them—man, woman, boy—drove home to the oozing noise of The Captain and Tennille, Marty following in his mother's Riviera. Mona was fully aware of the complicated ongoing conversation beneath the hum of the car's engine and innocuous rock radio, Winston's thoughts, her own, and Roy's innocence, Emily's entrusting him in Mona's care, all of it. "I'll carry him," Winston said when he turned off the car engine in their driveway. "You go ahead." The Volvo's doors *ponk*ed shut behind her; some insect or frog ceased its racket and everything was still.

Her parents were in bed and Emily, Mona noted thankfully, slept in the living room, Petra limp and angelic on her lap. Winston laid Roy on an adjacent couch, covered him with an afghan, and turned to Mona. "Everything's fine," he said, his blue eyes boring into hers. "Everything is absolutely fine. Mona," he added, her name a piece of forgiveness. He took the Crush can from her hand.

"Okay," Mona agreed. In her bed, she slipped into sleep immediately, her drunkenness returning to ease her into oblivion.

But four hours later she woke, rigid, horrified, unforgiven: indubitably unforgiven. It was three-thirty, the most devilish of the evil hours. In nightmarish proportions came her drunken drive home, the awful image of those rows of oncoming headlights, her nephew sleeping in the backseat, her phone call from Nicholas Dempsey, his persistent abandoning of her, his wife in her neighbors' home, Winston's prison term for doing precisely what she'd done tonight, Emily's unfair illness and her affair with Barry, Kojak's kidnapping and her suspicion of Winston—everything flew toward her, tickertape flurry of her flaws and failures, and she was in a cold sweat, wave upon wave of chilly emission. Mona was weeping, afraid beyond the catalog of disaster, leery of her own self-hatred. The urge to simply dump herself, take herself to the edge of the city and leave herself there, toss herself off a bridge in a weighted gunnysack, anything to put a stop to the insistent nagging raging pitiful hatred. She crawled out of bed and drank a full glass of stale water she found on her nightstand, gulping so desperately she soaked her shirt. She turned on the light by the dresser and observed herself in her mirror. The face that was getting old, that had been kissed by Nicholas Dempsey and then deserted—and rightly so, she thought, playing out the evening once more, the car she'd driven drunk, the arrogance of sitting behind that wheel while the other cars came at her with her little nephew asleep . . . She was ready to call Lydia, to tell her good-bye, this was the notification of her suicide. Not an attempt, but a success. She would never again merely make an attempt.

And then she recalled her mother's keening voice after her overdose of nearly four years ago, and her pets circling her warily in that other early unhappy morning. Her father stunned into silence. Her sister at the hospital a few hours later, Emily who'd then been breast-feeding Roy, the two wet patches on her dress when she visited, Emily who'd not had time to put on a bra or insert nursing pads before rushing to the hospital to see her sister, Emily whose husband Mona had been fucking . . . Mona could turn to no image that would act as a firm place for her to stand with herself. Everywhere were land mines, ready to blow her into a thousand tiny pieces. Her old ally Winston she could not talk to, the way she'd somehow spit in his face, driving drunk and poorly, and then getting away with it. She had gotten away with something, and now she could not move, could not visit her sister, scare her mother, disappoint her father, or burden her brother. On her stereo were lyrics that only confirmed her worst fears: *you're not safe in this house; poor thing, don't you have someone you'd die for?*

She told herself she dialed Marty's number to keep herself from killing herself, but to be honest, she knew her helplessness was beyond suicide, she was tangled in a net, a caught animal, no better than the toy creatures sitting blank-eyed around her. They weren't benign; they were dispassionate, full of dusty stuffing inside stitched limbs. The larger suffering was to continue to live, struggling nightly in the sticky trap of herself. That was how she would punish herself, by *not* dying. And even to think this way was to wind so tight as to turn inside out, the way a rope contorts as it's twisted, tightening and spastic.

"I'm sorry," she said, her tears overtaking her and washing away all the other words, the effect of discharging the full weight of her guilt and trouble, the twirling untangling rope. "I'm so sorry."

"You know what, Mona?" he said, sleepily, patiently. "You start every conversation with an apology."

"I'm s—"

"It's okay," he said. "Just hang on. Don't move one muscle."

Mona switched off the light so as to avoid her reflection in the window and lay down the aching burden of her head and face. Once more a kind of drunkenness seemed to wash over her, a swell of horror and obliterating emotion. So that, who-knew-how-much-later, when she saw the shape of a man standing beside her bed, she thought it was Nicholas Dempsey, that he'd returned to her, her desire sufficient to summon his form. She lifted the blankets in welcome and only when he sat on her bed did she understand that Marty had joined her. Marty had come to rescue her for the second time in one evening.

"I thought you were Nicholas Dempsey," she whispered hoarsely, not yet disappointed in the mistake, still taken with its glittering afterglow. "I thought you came back to me."

"Just me," Marty whispered. He eased into a half recline, elbow near Mona's ear, shoes politely off the bed's edge.

"Lie down," Mona said, her arms around his warm shoulders, suddenly so grateful for company, for *his* company. "Who let you in?"

"I broke in the basement. Just like high school." He seemed to have known she could not leave her room, and so he broke into the house, using the methods they'd all used, once upon a time, through the old coal chute into the wood room, up the back steps, then up the main ones, clearing the three noisy treads, right through her door.

"Wasn't my door locked?"

"You opened it," he said. "When I tapped, you unlocked it."

"Wow." She heard his shoes thump to the floor, then felt his socked feet beside her own bare ones. It was so wonderfully comforting to feel with her toes the warm socked feet of someone else. "I thought I was asleep."

"You *were* asleep. You opened the door in your sleep. I watched you get back under the blankets. It was cute."

Mona laughed, burrowing into Marty's shoulder. She had a fond-ness for placing her forehead against a solid object when she lay down, ideally a shoulder. Stuffed animals made adequate substitutes, but it was certainly nice to have a warm living form beside her, beneath her forehead.

"How're we doing now?" Marty asked softly.

"Much better. Much much much better." She started to cry then, let-ting Marty put his arms around her. She made a mess of his T-shirt, a big slick mess, while he held her, murmuring in her ear. "I'm sorry," she threw in now and then, a refrain, a liturgy. It felt good to apologize, a catchall confession: she was sorry, sorry, sorry.

"Stop apologizing, Mona, you just have to let time pass. Time will pass, everything will change, you'll feel better."

"Hold me," she said. "I'm sorry," she said. "Hold me." He lay there for what was left of the night, right through the snotty phone call from Percy—"You ain't dead, girl, no matter what you say! Get your bull's-eye butt to school!"—just holding her. It turned out that that's what she needed. He simply held her. He was simply there, providing the easiest, most obvious gift.

6

THERE WERE A lot of things it seemed Roy ought to know how to do and didn't, things either a father should provide, or that a mother would if she had her wits fully about her. Emily spent yet another horrifying night considering all of the many things she had failed at, turning in her bed like a rabbit on a rotisserie, around and around, stretched out and skinny, hot and doomed, and rose in the early morning intent on setting Roy on a path of accomplishment.

He must learn to tie his shoes, for example, and how and when to use toilet paper. He must start to flush, too. He needed to recognize the pain in his stomach as hunger. He was forever failing to understand that he had simply to eat something in order for his crippling cramps to go away. He had to get desensitized, although Emily couldn't believe taking away a child's sensitivity would benefit anyone, in the long run. But what she did understand was that his crying over every little thing was going to be a bad idea, as life progressed. Nobody would tolerate his tears the way she did, and she would not always be around to help out. This would be true if she weren't dying, but given that she was, it seemed especially imperative to train him to toughen up. Once she might have optimistically, stubbornly believed that the world ought to conform to him rather than the reverse, that it ought to treat him with kid gloves, respect his tremulous feelings, that to toughen up was to lose his essential self. But now she thought in much more practical terms. He needed protection, head gear and gloves for his time in the ring.

To her list of Roy's deficiencies she added swimming, placing a few exclamation marks after. The boy had a terrible fear of water, and Emily vowed she would not let another day pass without doing something to make him water-safe. It was the least she could do, equip him if only in this small way for the rest of his life.

At the pool Roy was careful to disguise his fear of water. He didn't fetch the coins the instructor tossed but instead cleverly circumnavigated, parting the water as he walked as if preparing to dive down any second, waiting for some ambitious other child to hand him an extra penny. One day the boy named Brent, whom Emily did not trust, clung fiercely to Roy's shoulders at the side while waiting for the teacher to ferry them across the pool, arms flailing. Emily, in the observation deck a floor above, could sense her son's unease, the way Brent's hands on his shoulders made him fretful of dunking. Emily herself was anticipating having to jump over the rail, into the pool in her clothes—shoes, wig, wallet, wristwatch—and go save her boy. She held her breath while her son seemed in trouble, the brat Brent toying with him in the manner of the bully. She was on the verge of calling out to the instructor when the boy moved on, found another victim, the girl Destiny, whom Emily also did not particularly like.

Roy's swim class was full of the unfit, a one-legged girl whose prosthesis was two shades too dark for her skin, as if her parents had purchased a black child's fake leg. On its fake toes were a pink water shoe and white sock. In the locker room Emily couldn't help marveling, the child maneuvered her fake leg so deftly. She had pretty blond hair that fell to her waist, still the downy hair of a child, ringleted, soft. She was a sweet child. Like the armless boy at College Hill Park, the girl seemed evidence that the partial and unfit were gravitating in her direction to teach her something.

Brent was not only a bully but his face was made strange by his right eye, the pupil of which was wholly dilated all of the time, big black circle like the pitiless eye of a camera. Could he see with this unnerving eyeball? Naturally, he seemed to train that lens exclusively on Roy. Was he waiting for the moment when he could dunk him like a float toy, drown Emily's beautiful and only boy? Brent seemed to want to injure Roy simply for the pleasure of inflicting pain. Roy's own hobbling was invisible, possibly chromosonal from his early acid trip, and soon he would be orphaned. His swim classmates were named Destiny and Mesa and Hayu, which was pronounced I Ii You. Roy was in favor of Hayu. Emily, on the other hand, liked to tell her family that Roy was playing with Destiny.

"For godsakes be careful," said her father.

"Destiny!" shrieked the swim teacher, glancing up to the gallery balcony to see Emily smile. This was Dwight, head of the Guppies. Guppies was the name given the group of children afraid of water, of which her son Roy was king, crying every June morning as Emily forced him to pool's edge. He would swim, she promised herself. Her staunch belief in swimming lessons precluded all else; Roy could not talk her out of them, no matter his tears, no matter the betrayal. She would not leave her boy until he was seaworthy.

The instructor Dwight had not made much of an impression on Emily at first. He seemed dim and defused in the way of middle age, jolly enough, game, a bit laconic, yet kind. But when, on the eighth day, as Roy did not cry and snuffle at water's edge and Emily could finally look upon the rest of the tableau rather than merely at her son's part in it, she found Dwight appraising her. He nodded, unconcerned with his absence of anything but swim trunks, eyes the same tawny brown as his buzz-cut hair. She began studying him, and he did nothing but improve in her estimation. This was unlike her last adventures in flirtation, where the object of her affection only kept falling.

Many times during class he had his Guppies poke their thumbs on their foreheads and waggle their fingers like the combs of roosters. When class was over, they clustered together to utter a little cheery phrase or two, like a prayer, then lifted their hands in victory: survivors of swim class, once again!

And if, for example, Dwight came upon a wad of chewing gum in a drain or on a life vest, he simply stuck it on his trunks after offering it to one of his charges for a chew. He was forty-something, casual with the fraidy cats he taught, coaxing them into the element they feared by pretending he couldn't care less if they joined him, he'd be out here tossing pennies and toy boats about, handling these gaudy Hula Hoops and gadgety eye goggles . . . totally unself-conscious as he frolicked by himself in the shallow water while his class sat on the deck with nothing but their feet wet, sober as a jury. He'd been in the military and not yet abandoned the look. He had his own inner tube of soft flesh around his middle, above his bright Red Cross bathing suit. When he came up from the water, hair plastered on his forehead, sputtering, he resembled one of his students, childish, adorable.

"He's a champ," he said of her son when she wrapped a towel around Roy's shoulders. Her hat slid off then; she could feel the wig slip, beneath. Dwight retrieved the hat and handed it back, staring deep into her eyes under her bad crooked hair.

"Thank you," she said, coldly, face flushing. But he did not turn away. And when she returned, a day later, he was still ready to gaze upon her, interested, fearless, sincere.

Thus Emily found love—late, and in the unlikely locale of the YMCA swimming pool, in the even unlikelier person of Dwight. He was divorced, yet retained a huge confident heart over which he wore a silver monogrammed whistle. He was the kind of man meant to be married; he would ask her, Emily knew.

He was like no other man she had ever loved, but she thought perhaps the body knew its needs better than the brain. She had to do almost nothing, concentrate nearly no effort, make no excuses, tell not one lie. Forget the labor and conjecture and fantasy and squinted appraisal; she did not have to contort who he was in order to like him. It was like stepping into warm water, this relationship, being surrounded by an element the precise temperature of her own body, one that permitted her to float, to forget the ache of gravity and pressure and friction.

They had odd dates, grocery shopping or line dancing, one evening repairing a dimmer switch in Dwight's divorced-man's kitchen. He was very interested in the nightly news, so they did that. It was as if they'd known each other for a long while, as if they'd been married not to each other, but to people just like each other—even though that wasn't true. He was familiar, yet entirely strange.

"I hate the Y toilets," Emily told Dwight one morning after class.

"Why for?"

"The seats are always wet."

"Little girls' little wet butts."

"Plus, the logo on the stall door annoys me. Hiney-Hider. What kind of self-respecting company calls itself Hiney-Hider?"

"Wankers," Dwight said mildly. "Let's kill the bast[a]
their fucking factory. Watch the toilet seats rain down on
"You think I'm bitchy."

He grabbed her suddenly, squashing the breath out of her, a r[.]
lich hug right there in the Y lobby. He put his scratchy face at her ear
and growled something intimate that reverberated down to her toes.
She went limp in the clutch of his rough readiness. She had no choice.
She was caught. She could wish that he had entered her life earlier, but
of course she wouldn't have been ready for him any earlier than the
moment he had arrived. Such was the way of love, of lifesaving.

In his last class, Roy himself was learning to save lives. Emily
watched as he threw the big white lifesaver ring with exuberance, far
into the pool. There was applause among the other students. Then
Dwight made a dramatic O with his mouth, hands flexed at his chin:
Uh-oh, SpaghettiO! Roy was clapping, too, using both free hands
because he'd forgotten a key element to pulling in the drowned: hanging
on to the rope.

"SHE'S NEVER going to really know me," Emily said of their
mother.

Mona's first impulse was to disagree, but after considering for a
moment, she told the truth. "No, she isn't."

"I don't like that, not one little bit."

"Well—" But there was no use in going on about it. They were sitting at the demolition derby, anyway, and the noise was terrific. This
was the first thing the three Mabie children had done together in quite a
while. Roy, in Winston's lap, pressed his palms to his ears as if to keep
them pinned to his head. It was a beautiful summer evening in Kansas,
the temperature balmy, the fields surrounding the derby track loamy
and dark, the derby as alien as a UFO landing, as gaudy as a circus, as
loud as a rock concert, as beguiling as a revival tent—all things the
Kansas plains and its farmers had endured and entertained before; a
whole school of art celebrated such carnivals, Thomas Hart Benton and
John Steuart Curry with their massive murals of simple folk at a spectacle. Everyone drank beer and shook fists. People surrounding them
seemed pleased to indulge this odd childish sport, grown-ups who'd

.ade toys out of life-size automobiles, brought them together in the mud and dirt, then rammed them with utter conviction into one another. It had been Winston's idea to come, and it was a good idea. Mona thought her family's timing was impeccable: they'd arrived just as what was named the Consolation Heat began. All the battered wrecks, the maimed ugly losers, gathered on the track to bash into one another one more time, insult to injury, last hurrah, swan song.

It was true that their mother didn't know Emily in the way that others did, but it was also true that she was home baby-sitting Petra, that she knew where they were, that their destination did not surprise or disturb her. Their mother knew a version of their lives, didn't she? She'd been an accomplice, even if they didn't want to give her credit. It wasn't often that any of them called upon her to tell it, but she certainly must have her side of the story. For an instant, Mona could envision the day she would ask her mother to talk to her. Long after Emily was gone they would mourn together—*that* day. It wasn't going to be anytime soon, but it would come.

The demo derby was not the place to argue the finer points.

"Of course," Emily shouted in Mona's ear, "of course, I don't really know Roy or Petra, either, do I? So why am I giving Mom so much grief for not knowing me?"

"*Some*body's got to take the grief."

Beyond them the cars smashed mercilessly, a huge pileup punctuating the moment. *Everyone,* in the consolation heat, was taking the grief.

"WHY AM I three-D?"

"Pardon?" said Roy's grandfather, stalling automatically, although he'd heard the boy perfectly clearly. Already Roy knew to speak loudly to his grandfather, to face him and shout. The kitchen smelled of Sunday morning, syrup and coffee and wet newspaper, which was in the oven, crisping. Roy repeated his question, intent on getting to the bottom of it. An Animaniac had sung a confusing lyric; Roy wanted answers.

"Why am I three-D?"

His grandfather was growing accustomed to Roy's style. The child had become more human, less protoplasmic in his fifth year. He did not now mean *why* was he three-dimensional, but what defined three-dimensionality. Professor Mabie enjoyed responding in part because he didn't have a full answer at the ready. It was a philosophical issue, to some degree, although Roy's initial interest was in what distinguished him from what he saw in books and on screens.

"Three dimensions," began his grandfather.

"Dimension is for D," Roy understood, tucking this first fact away.

"Three dimensions," Professor Mabie began again, launching into lecture mode. How rarely outside a classroom did anyone require it of him.

His grandfather described length, width, height, depth by use of fruit and newspaper insert illustrations and a syrup bottle in the shape of a woman, Mrs. Butterworth, Roy remembered, but also suddenly read. The letters on her chest came clear to him abruptly, not recalled, not random alphabet members sitting out of order, just asking for trouble, but as two distinct words, sounds, one meaning. Mrs. But-ter-worth, the syrup.

"I read her name!" he proclaimed to his grandfather, who was still talking.

This, too, Professor Mabie was growing accustomed to, the switch of subject, the non-sequitous next thing. With his own children, he'd believed such flitting concentration illustrated rudeness, a short attention span, a bad attitude, all blamable on television. But with his grandson he was willing to take what came his way. He observed Roy more than influenced him. It was interesting, slightly objective, pleasing precisely because he could so easily step away. Grandparenting was to parenting as retirement was to work. Professor Mabie approved.

"I can read!" Roy said, his face abloom.

DWIGHT was very good at kissing. His lips were large and faintly chapped. He liked to hold Emily's lower lip between his and flex or chew. His kissing had a wonderful sense of humor, a patient of-the-moment Zen quality, a serious thoughtfulness. Some instinct told him to start at her mouth and then to move around her neck, concentrating on the diamond-shaped area at the base of her skull, shoulder blade to shoulder blade, nape to hairline. Was this because she could not touch that place herself? No matter; he touched it for her, with his lips, and then the onus of Time fled.

"After a while a person gets ugly," Dwight had warned her. "Ugly in looks but that's not the least of it. Ugly in personality. Picky. Grumpy. Paranoid." He apologized in advance for his calcified qualities, the parts of himself that no longer went with the flow. Who was Emily to complain? She fell into his life without one regret, no reservations.

Dwight had keys to all of the Y doors, including the pool and sauna.

"I saw a girl masturbating here today," Emily said, when they met at the lobby door in the dark. Dwight grunted, undoing the door while glancing behind him.

"Security," he muttered savagely. "Always lurking around when you don't need them."

"This girl was standing in front of the water jets," Emily continued. "That one that spews warm water? At the shallow end?"

"We have to take the stairs," Dwight said, inside the black lobby. "The elevator has its own power system, shut off after ten."

Emily checked her glowing watch, which read 11:05. Her children were asleep; her mother attended to the monitor. Emily herself was free for hours and hours, here in the dark, damp, seedy downtown YMCA. The steps were concrete, lit only by a glowing light two flights down. She stumbled on the unforgiving strips of sandpaper designed to aid wet-footed swimmers. Dwight caught her, stopped, and gave her a squeeze. "I like you in compromising situations." Emily felt cool and lost, here in the bowels of a closed building, held by a man she didn't know all that well. Anything could happen. And what if anything did happen? Her children were safe; she was dying anyway, so a hastened end would only represent that: preemptive strike. In this mood, she made a grab for Dwight's pants zipper. He bit her earlobe. She felt his zipper harden beneath her hand, quickly, a reflex she approved of. Behind him was a concrete wall and a metal rail, on which she placed her hands and his back. He unzipped himself and freed his erection.

"No underwear," she noted.

"I don't like underwear."

He lifted her dress, which was a simple black dress, and lowered her underpants to her knees. She started to raise a foot, to free herself, but he objected. "Let's have some obstacles here. The wall, the standing up, the panties around the knees."

"The blackness," Emily added. He was merely shadow and then substance, but nothing wholly seen. His eyes reflected the dim light from a flight down, two glassy spots in the near dark. She leaned in and nibbled at his ears, which were small and vaguely furry. He liked this, she could tell by the way he ducked and giggled. Her hands were tired from pressing against the wall. "Could we find somewhere to be prone?" she asked.

He did not zip up his pants, led with his erection like a dowsing rod down the stairs, while Emily deftly removed her panties, stuffed them in her bag. It felt good to step downstairs without underwear, the cool pool air rising between her legs, chilling the wetness that had begun.

In the women's locker room they paused, adjusting their eyes to further dark, listening as the door wheezed shut. "The weight room has mats," Dwight whispered. "Or we could get in the pool and play with that jet."

"Pool," Emily said decidedly. She had enjoyed watching the girl masturbate. She could well imagine the thrill of a jet of water between her legs, bubbling, warm. She'd tried to imagine Petra, all those years down the road, finding some clever way to make herself feel good. They stripped at pool's edge, the water lit by three bright red EXIT signs, its lapping slurp at occasional intervals like a lake. Emily plopped down her hat and wig as if they were equal to purse and shoes. She used the steps but Dwight cannonballed off the board. When he found her, his erection was gone. His penis floated at her thighs as they kissed. She squeezed him until he was hard once more. He took her nipples between his fingers and rubbed them tenderly. Nobody but a chemo technician had been anywhere near her nipples since she'd weaned Petra, five months ago. The sensation was fully sexual once more, not one shred maternal or therapeutic. Emily welcomed this. She lifted a leg to his furry thigh. He was furry everywhere, head to toe, his back included, all of it a tawny copper, all of it bristly. Only the skin of his penis was smooth, and she made a fist around it happily.

"I've never fucked in a pool," Emily said.

"Chlorine does something weird to semen," he replied. "Makes it solidify."

"Hmm."

"Also, lubrication is an issue." By now they were attempting the insertion, him into her, hard object into waiting warm entrance, length into width, breadth into breadth. It was a good fit, and he didn't require a lot of thrusting, so there wasn't much chlorine to interfere. Instead, he

pulsed and she flexed. It was awkward standing thus, so they moved to
the tiled edge of the shallow end, where Emily rested her backside. Now
Dwight leaned into her, fingers still active on her nipples, erection growing inside her, pushing faintly, faintly, faintly. Emily spread her legs and
lifted them to his hips, encircling him as if to pull him fully inside herself, every part of him. "I'm going to come inside you, Emily Mabie,"
he said in her ear. "I'm going to just fill you right up."

"Now?"

"Whenever you say."

Beneath her naked head he twiddled the lobes of her ears and was
patient while she bit him on the shoulder, tilting right and left, wobbling
his hard-on inside of her, playful, teasing, while she shifted her hips,
seeking the right place, and when the sensation suddenly hit her she
sank her teeth deeply into his flesh, locked her ankles together at the top
of his ass, and pulled him into her until she could feel him at her con-
demned cervix, which led to her tainted uterus, the tip of his penis
painful and yet just what she required. He filled her up; before her burst
a blinding series of purple rings, lightning, salty tears, splashing water.
She said, "Aha." The rippling effect of his ejaculation made her come
again, immediately. It had been too long between fucks, she thought,
she had stored up all of her sexual energy for just such an event. He
came without the high drama of her ex-husband. He came slowly, without pulling out more than an inch or two, he came with a beautiful
unself-conscious grateful grown-up moan. His hands arrived at her
breasts, his voice at her ear. "I love to fuck you," he said worshipfully. "I
love it so much." He dived under the surface of the water then and
found her newly denuded pubis, where he burbled something inaudible,
then kissed her. Emily, above the surface, laughed, put her hands to his
swaying breezy buzz cut and held on.

PROFESSOR Mabie watched his skeletal daughter move about the
house. Her face was aging but her body had grown even lankier, like the
body of a dancer or of a teenage boy, and therefore seemed younger.
Her movements in this angular frame then became like those of a praying mantis, hyperattenuated and prettily gawky. She wore her pajamas
more, a transparent set of wrinkled white linen things, top, bottom,

robe, through which you could see her underwear—black—on her skinny backside. It troubled Professor Mabie that she would seem somehow sexy in this new body, but perhaps that was because she had a boyfriend. Dwight, the swim instructor. Dwight, the lifeguard. Professor Mabie wished with all his heart he had the sage counsel of Betty Spitz to consult on the subject of Dwight. He wished he hadn't taken such an instant dislike to the man. Probably Betty would tell him it had to do with Dwight's being so much older than Emily, somebody between the generations separating Professor Mabie and his daughter, somebody who could take his place, veteran of a more recent war.

Betty would make a case for Emily's preferring to be cared for rather than supplying the care. Betty would remind Professor Mabie of The Excrescence, how unhappy that man had made him, how Dwight was a vast improvement over Barry. She might even suggest jealousy, Professor Mabie's never approving of his daughter's boyfriends, personalities be damned. Professor Mabie sighed, burdened with the endless intelligence that was Betty Spitz. He assumed that this was how he would commemorate his friend, by summoning her wisdom to influence his action, by imagining her and thereby enlivening her. The dead had only that gift to impart to the living.

Like history itself, Professor Mabie thought, its solid presence, its permanence in the face of human perishability. This big-minded philosophy was a comfort, globally, but offered nothing when he considered his daughter's mortality. Her swift decline scared him, made him abruptly aware of his own negligence of death. He was letting death insinuate itself while Emily, in the manner he most admired about her, took it by the horns. It seemed to Professor Mabie that she had figured out a kind of clarity and pointedness. It was no longer mysterious to her what ought to occupy her time. This trait, he thought, she had learned from her mother. She spent what was left tending to her family, the old one and her little nascent one. In his opinion she was trying always to present to her children a face confident with purpose, a face that knew how it wanted to be remembered later, when it was no longer around. In his mind, this was the ambition of heroes and the study of history. If somebody had asked, he would have named his daughter another one of his heroes. If somebody had asked, she would have topped the list.

—   —   —

"MORPHEUS," Emily informed Mona. "The god of dreams, according to Ovid. That's where *morphine* comes from."

"I don't care how it got here," Mona said, turning the canister languidly in her hand. "As long as it's here." They lay together on Emily's old canopy bed, heads on the pillows, feet under the spread. Once the party room, now the guest room, soon the sickroom. A summer breeze blew through the windows, lifting the gauze and dropping it, as if the walls were breathing. Mona looked at the wallpaper, the windows, the spring trees. The morphine came in a nasal spray; Emily was sharing with her. She could feel it as it worked its way up the passages in her head, flooded along the surface of her face and skull. It made her giddy, there could be no denying it. The effect was quick, and a very vague odor of illness she'd suspected in the air had disappeared.

"I like this drug," she told her sister. "Right on, Morpheus."

"Me, too. Maybe I can get a scrip."

"Where'd Winston find it?"

"Marty Song."

"That was nice of Winston."

"Also maybe dangerous."

"Maybe." Mona was touched, given what Winston had to lose in getting caught with illegal pharmies. She assumed Emily had already gone through the gratitude emotion. Emily was always a few steps ahead of Mona. Now her limbs tingled, her chest opened, her mouth fell into a smile. And there was that lovely blizzard to contemplate on Emily's wallpaper.

"The pigeons are gone," Mona noted, the first time she'd realized what was missing, their burbling noise.

"Winston got rid of them," Emily said. "I don't even know if Dad's noticed yet."

"We should tell him."

"I don't think so. I think it will be better if he just one day realizes they're gone. I dreamed they came back, inside the house."

"I hate birds in a house."

"Everyone does. But then I realized it was only a dream, so I just let them fly at my face and grabbed at them. I don't seem to be having anything but lucid dreams anymore. What would your Dr. Lydia make of that?"

Mona thought hard. "That you needed control over some part of your life?"

"She's one smart cookie, that Dr. Lydia."

"Emily," Mona said, in a spurt of bravery, putting her hand on Emily's arm, feeling suddenly forthcoming and confessional. "I wanted to tell you something."

"Something what?"

"Something bad from a while ago, something I did, a while ago."

"You mean having an affair with Barry?"

Mona, despite narcotic calm, was taken aback. She removed her hand and considered confessing to some lesser bad deed, whipping through a scrolling list of them. But it was too much to bother with. "You knew?" she said.

"I knew."

"You knew then?"

"I knew then."

"Wow." Mona had the conscious need to consider this information, make it fit with the rest of what had happened since. Morphine was making her slow on the uptake, insulated from outright shock like a bed of feathers all around. Ought she to feel somehow betrayed, that Emily had known and not said anything? Or merely bested, once again, by her sister's superior skill in matters personal, psychological, and, it appeared, judicial? Her sister had apparently forgiven this trespass. Or considered it unworthy, insignificant. For a second, Mona envisioned Emily and Barry laughing about her, teamed together against her, when all along she'd believed the alliances more fluid, equal. "This is some painkiller," she finally said, since it was her turn to talk. She could not trust her feelings; she never could, but at least now she understood to withhold immediate judgment.

"It's okay, Mona." Emily rolled her head to stare into Mona's eyes. They lay on the pillows in the bed as if preparing to spend the night there, as if ready for any pajama-party intimacy. Emily's eyes were huge, given the loss of weight in her face. "You know what your problem is?"

"What?"

"Your problem is that you don't know any marriages except Mom and Dad's. That's your whole experience. Marriage is weird. An affair can mean hardly anything."

"Oh."

"I mean, Barry and I had problems. If it hadn't been you, it would have been someone else. It probably was someone else, too. Barry wasn't made to be married. Barry was the biggest bachelor on the planet. Anyway, being married is kind of boring, after a while. You want to be all passionate and overwhelmed, and you just can't keep having that. I think everyone wants to be swept away."

Mona watched her sister talk, aware suddenly that she was listening as if her life depended on it. From whose lips would this wisdom come, when Emily was gone? There was Winston, thankfully, and Dr. Lydia, and there was Marty Song, and there was the whole glorious stockpile of song lyrics and music, past, present, and future, but it was specifically *Emily* to whom Mona had always come for the final word. It was Emily she would eventually be weaned of. Not her rock idols or her parents or her brother or therapist or bad boyfriends, but her sister.

Emily was still talking about Barry, saying, "I mean, look at his habits. He couldn't say no to passion of any sort. He was always looking for the next party, the next high. He really liked to be happy—"

"Emily," Mona interrupted.

"What?"

What? "Nothing," Mona said, her insight rolling away under the wave of morphine, jewelry washed to sea in the tide. "You are the best person to do drugs with."

"Think how horrified Mom would be, if she knew." Emily laughed, pleased with her brattiness.

"I wonder what Dwight would think." Mona said his name shyly. She didn't know what to think of him. "Wasn't *Dwight* the most common name for serial killers?"

"That was *Duane,* not Dwight. Dwight," Emily repeated. "Dwight, Dwight. If you say his name too many times, he metamorphoses."

"Metamorphoses," Mona said, dreamily looping the word in and out of *morphine.* "What about guilt?" she asked later, when her thinking returned to Barry, to the subject of her betrayal of Emily. She wanted to make sure she had followed up on all the angles. It was important to leave nothing unsaid or undone, as they might never come back to this subject again, never find themselves side by side beneath a blanket, altered in chemically compatible ways, talking in bed.

"Guilt!" proclaimed Emily. "Get over it. Are you guilty about what-shisname and whatshiswife? You have no idea what's going on in a marriage. Nobody knows but the people in it. If you want to feel guilty, go ahead, but personally, I think it's a waste of time."

"Do you think Dad slept with Betty Spitz?"

Emily pulled the bedspread to her chin, fists balled at her throat. "Not a literal affair," she said. "But I think Dad had a *kind* of affair with Betty, even if they weren't sleeping together. There's all kinds of intimacy. He's obviously grieving. Isn't that an affair, having intimacies with other people? So what if it's not physical? So what if there's no fucking involved? I submit that Dad had an affair with Betty. And furthermore, I don't think there's anything the matter with it."

Mona found herself crying; it was like finding flies suddenly on her cheeks, a tingling. Her sister's big-mindedness was daunting. Doors were opening, freedom resounded, but it seemed that the last door might swing wide to reveal the blank nothing of a borderless sky. That unbreathable space between you and the stars that rendered everything inconsequential, valueless, adrift: marriage meant nothing, affairs meant nothing. What distinguished this kind of meaninglessness from the kind that made Mona convinced she might as well die as do anything else?

"Why are you crying?" Emily demanded. "This is a *happy* drug, not a drag. It said specifically so on the label."

"It did not! I don't know. I feel like you're forgiving me. It makes me happy." That it scared her as well seemed beside the point.

"Don't let Roy see you. He'll get confused. I just got him all straight on the crying thing. Poor Roy. He's got a lot of stuff to sort out. Jesus. Someday he's going to be lying on a bed under the influence of morphine."

"I hope he likes it as much as I do. I'm totally in favor of this."

"Tell . . . me . . . about . . . it." Emily extracted her arms from the spread and stretched them over her head as if reaching for the faded pink canopy. Mona did the same. As usual, Mona's arms were plumper, less elegant. "Look at those veins," Emily said dreamily, twisting her wrists.

"Whenever we do drugs, we end up looking at our veins."

"Just think: these are the same veins from when we were fifteen."

"Yep."

"And on acid."

"I remember."

"And from when we were five, and four, and just born. I remember when you were born. 'Can I hold her? Can I hold her? Lemme hold her, lemme hold her!' "

"Isn't that weird?" Mona said. "You probably remember a time when I wasn't born, but I can't remember any time when you weren't there. You were always there."

"That's me, all right, always there." Her sister laughed but Mona couldn't. "Hey," Emily said, turning her face to Mona's, putting her fingers to Mona's cheeks in order to line her up like a mirror image, like someone steadying a round rolling object on a flat surface. When they were face-to-face, eye-to-eye, Emily said, "Listen up, party girl. I want to give you and Winston custody of the kids. Is that all right with you?"

Mona furrowed her eyebrows. "Oh my." Outside the dogs barked, first one, then the other, as if they, too, were conversing. A siren sounded, far enough away to seem pleasant rather than disarming. Under the old canopy, Mona rolled into Emily's arms, nodding emphatically into her sister's knobby shoulder. "Sure," she said. "That's great with me." Mona felt full. Of everything. She made a note to remember this feeling, she upon whom this ultimate compliment had been bestowed, this unsurpassable bit of flattery, to let the sensation claim her like gravity, to hold her upright like one of those wobbling dolls from her past, the weighted Weeble.

"The thing is, you have to make me a promise," Emily added, rubbing with her knuckles her sister's scalp. "There's a few things a parent just can't do, but the main one is—"

"I know." Mona swallowed hard, past the irksome catch in her throat. With that swallow she took down into her body and through her coursing veins what her sister was requesting of her: the promise that she would continue choosing to live.

FOUR IN the Morning, the family affliction, its source worry, its symptom sleeplessness, its solution—pacing, painkillers, vodka, letter writing, list making, music, mystery novels, hot baths, car rides, crying, telephone calls, television, the aimless application of a fearful forehead to a cool pane of window glass. Even Roy woke sometimes to tell his mother he was worried. About what? He did not know.

At four in the morning this morning, Professor Mabie turned to a cigar and a car chase movie. Unlike Roy, he had reasons, and they hung like ornaments on the branches of the worry tree. His movie distracted him. Its action was such that he did not require volume, which would have perhaps wakened others, and he could read the captions, if dialogue came up. Like the rest of his adult family, he wanted solitude for his bout of Four in the Morning. He wanted no witnesses to his method of escape, his bad cinema and foul cigar.

But without a sound track, the movie could not keep him from slipping into sleep, and the cigar, radiant in the blue room like a punk in the night, soon fell from his fingers to the floor, where it burned stolidly for a good half hour, then finally lit the rug. The rug, which was wool, smoldered rather than flared, and its fumes seemed to act as a kind of intoxicant, an accompaniment to the exploding vehicles on TV, the extraordinary repeated image of ignition, the car intact and then dissembling, again and again, the flaming mushroom and the flying debris, by far the most artful element of the film. The acting was stiff, the cinematography amateurish, the sets phony, but, in slow motion and with an apparently abundant budget, the explosion of the car was a work of beauty. In its luminescence Professor Mabie dreamt of doing battle, a war that seemed both personal and indiscriminate, as if Death had come calling in the place where it appeared most likely to succeed. Lazy, Professor Mabie wanted to name Death, lazy cunt, to arrive here where there was no challenge, an old man in a daze before the tame flaring rays of television. In his car chase movie, justice was served by indirect means: the bomb, set by an evil character and intended for an innocent one, claimed, instead, the life of the villain. The residue of this uncomplicated Hollywood logic rollicked and detonated in Professor Mabie's head, and in its wake he was ready to strike bargains, trade his life for his daughter Emily's. Simple enough: an old man's life for a young woman's. Woozy as he was, he nevertheless understood that Death would not follow formulae dreamed up in Hollywood. Death would in fact make certain that justice would be obscure, poetic, and skewed, at best, blind. Professor Mabie would not die alone, autonomous and deserving. No, Death would allow the house to fill with smoke and then with fire, to ensure maximum suffering, to let it first drift up the stairs and insinuate itself, then consume the place with its greedy licking laughter, the great joke and irony of Professor Mabie's long-standing vigilant protection, every room ablaze, the world blown apart once more, top to bottom, two tiny children, three worthy women . . .

Cold air rushed over his feet like the tide, and a shape passed before him, there and gone, taking with it the burning carpet like a boat washed abruptly to distant sea. "Dad?" said someone, and Professor Mabie struggled not quite out of his smoky dream to respond. "Dad?" The two of them made an exchange he could not later recall, although he retained the memory of saying *some*thing to *some*one, that someone who was not Death, who had whisked away the danger and then disappeared himself. Words, he believed he had uttered, or the idea of words, gratitude, explanation, apology, a muddled monologue to a tolerant audience. It was Winston to whom he'd said these words, and it wasn't Winston. It was not the Winston who had come home to inhabit a sullen existence this last year in his parents' house. Rather, it was Winston in a dream, Winston playing cleanup at the tail end of a nightmare, Winston as he should have been.

Professor Mabie slept, he had to have slept, for the next thing he knew it was indisputable benign daylight and his grandson was situated on the sofa beside his chair, viewing some piece of animation without sound on the television, hand rummaging in a noisy box of Apple Jacks.

"Grandpa," said the boy when he saw his grandfather was awake, "now will you unmute?"

For a moment Professor Mabie reviewed the scene, Roy's innocent request, the gruesome night he had apparently passed through. For a moment it seemed to him that either reality—his bout of Four in the Morning or his grandson's present daylight appearance—might be illusion. Either he had burned the house up in the night and this continuing normality was a sick and vengeful hallucination, or he'd dreamed the disaster in the night and this was just another Saturday morning. Either scenario would have convinced him. Winston, he realized. Winston was the one who knew.

"Unmute?" Roy pleaded. Stuck on his lip was a pink circle of cereal; he wore boxer shorts and Band-Aids; now there were commercials for

Pop-Tarts and Play-Doh and Hot Wheels and Super Soakers pouring forth from the television, material so alien that Professor Mabie could never have dreamt it up. A strong case was being made for current reality over last night's horrific version. Had he in fact smoked a cigar? It was not like him to smoke anywhere but in his study, and then only in the late afternoon with a tumbler of bourbon. There was no evidence of a cigar, no ashtray or stick match or odor. He sniffed his own fingertips, on which he could detect nothing incriminating.

"Where's the 'mote control?" Roy asked.

"Mote control," Professor Mabie pondered. It was only when he rose unsteadily to his feet that he realized *both* time sequences were true. For the Turkish carpet that should have been beneath him was gone, having left a mere smudge of charred wood in its place like a signature—no larger or more obvious than a pointing index finger.

Everything else was fine. From the morning cartoons he proceeded through the remainder of his daily Saturday routine. His wife and daughters and grandchildren looked upon him as they looked upon him every day, fondly, vaguely impatient, faintly sympathetic. Winston sat on the side porch, plucking his guitar, filling a coffee can with butts.

"How'd you sleep?" he asked each of them, as the hours burned on, one into the next and further from Four in the Morning.

"Fine," they responded wryly. As well as could be expected, they meant, given their common ailment. Nothing unusual.

It was only a rug, he told himself, and just a cigar. He hardly ever smoked, once a week, tops. Armed with her vacuum, his wife would inquire into the carpet's whereabouts and he would claim that the dogs had peed upon it, that it stank, that it was stained. He himself could not locate it. Not on the front porch, not in the basement, not in the outside trash cans. The evidence was missing. Professor Mabie would be left with nothing but his crucial moment of sleepiness, his house full of smoke, his negligent second, his fractional forgetfulness. Yet of course he felt continually haunted, knowing he had been saved in the night from nothing more nor less than himself. Also, knowing he would never be reminded of this fact by the person who had done the deed.

AND SO HE was paying particular attention a few days later on the sixth anniversary of Bunny's death, curious as to how any of his family now commemorated her. Professor Mabie sat in his leather chair that June day studying the view, holding a fresh unlighted cigar between the blunt fingers of his left hand, stick match in his right. His brother Billy had once lit a stick match to ignite a homemade rocket and instead blown his life open, begun a process of bloodletting that for his older brother had never ended. From Professor Mabie's window he watched the comings and goings of his family, who sought the driveway because it was warm, unshaded by trees, because it was cheery as compared with the dark gloom inside the house. Later in the summer, they would be grateful for shade and coolness, but for now everyone was eager to see the sun, to stand in it, to squint at it. Billy came by to show off his new braces, having decided to finally fix those snaggled teeth of his, aiming his grin in such a way that he went off like a flashbulb, over and over. This was his idea of humor. Sheila and Eddie Shakes washed his Camaro using the Mabie hose, making a soapy stream that drained down the driveway, slapping each other with rags, leaving the hose stretched across the pavement to get run over and ruined. Professor Mabie's wife appeared with a mask over her nose and mouth and began tentatively applying bug poison on her modest garden of salad greens. The dogs barked and were told to shut up, barked and were told to shut up, were sprayed by the hose and stood shaking, waving their tails, then barked and were told to shut up. Mona pulled out an ancient aluminum lawn chaise with its tattered nylon seat and situated herself in the sunshine, once more working on a tan, once more ignoring all warnings her family had annually supplied since she was thirteen years old. Her music, as usual, was a frightening discordant presence, terribly at odds with the flowers and birds and blue sky, as if someone were throwing razor blades into the air.

No one appeared to recall the date. But should this have surprised Professor Mabie? He was, after all, the only historian among them. His wife would give him a hug tonight in bed, put her soft skin against his; she would let him know that she, too, remembered, even though for her the anniversary was about Winston, not Bunny.

Winston himself seemed undaunted—merely unaware?—hair wet, shirt untucked, pack of cigarettes in one palm, car keys in the other. After lunch, Emily was sending him and Roy to the zoo. Petra sat on Emily's hip like a bear cub on a sapling, clinging as if to topple it. Meanwhile, Roy strapped himself happily into the backseat of the

Volvo, babbling gleefully, and Winston situated himself behind the wheel of the car. Easily, as if he'd made peace with the process.

Did he have a license, this mysterious son of his, this bane and savior, this miscreant and beneficiary? Professor Mabie sighed, found himself believing the question, suddenly, wholly irrelevant. The relevant question was coming to him, he thought.

"Good-bye, good-bye!" Professor Mabie heard them yelling, beyond the thick glass of his study. He hadn't cracked the window yet, hadn't lit his weekly cigar. He was waiting. Out there the air smelled of June: cut grass and gasoline. Emily and Petra waved, a big hand and a little one. Roy bounced—radiant with expectation—while Winston craned his head around so as not to hit Mona in her lawn chair or the trees along the drive or the house itself, taillights, brake lights, backing patiently out. A year ago, Professor Mabie would have been outraged, alarmed, his son driving his grandson to the zoo, Winston driving *anyone* Professor Mabie loved *anywhere*. He could imagine the gearshift in his own palm, ratcheting down from reverse to drive; he measured his acceptance against the paralyzing pang he felt in striking the stick match— before his eyes its quick snap, its pop of sulfur and whisper of flame. Betty Spitz would have been proud of him, he thought, pulling smoke into his mouth, this old dog who had learned a new trick: forgiveness. "He's like you," she'd said of his boy, and not so long ago. "Not quite," she'd added, and meant "but close enough." Beyond the window, the car eased out into the traffic of the summer street, his son behind the wheel, his son who could be entrusted with the care of a child.

LIVING TO TELL

DISCUSSION POINTS

1. Antonya Nelson has said that she set *Living to Tell* in Kansas because she grew up there and was familiar with the kind of house the Mabies might live in. In what other ways do you feel that this book is reflective of its midwestern setting? How might the Mabies and their story differ if Nelson had set her novel in, say, New England or California?

2. The first chapter of *Living to Tell* and the beginning of the second reveal two nearly diametrically opposed sides of Winston: one, the obsessively anxious flyer, and two, the cool, playful uncle. What does Nelson accomplish by revealing, so very quickly, these two poles of Winston's character? How does this move influence our feelings about Winston as the novel progresses? Do you believe that Winston is responsible for the robbery and the dognapping?

3. Over and over, Winston's beauty, and its hold on the people around him, is affirmed. Do you think Winston takes advantage of his magnetism, or is he casually unaffected by it? Can you think of characters in other works of literature whose good looks have exerted a dramatic influence on the story?

4. Does *Living to Tell* have a "main character"? If yes, who? Which of these many characters appeal to you the most? Do you feel that it's important for a significant character, in any work of fiction, to be likable, or admirable, in order for readers to be moved by him or her?

5. Discuss the book's title. What is it that each of the Mabies has "lived to tell?" Ironically, given its title, for a book this size, there is relatively little dialogue, relatively little "telling." What does Ms. Nelson achieve by allowing so much of her characters' stories to remain inside their heads? In light of the dead grandmother's idea, "Funny how talk defused the explosive while also substantiating it," consider the relationship between what these people feel and think and what they speak aloud.

6. Discuss the incidence of sexual love in this book. Basically, nobody gets a whole lot! Why do you suppose Nelson separates her characters from the thing they all might need the most, pro-

viding Emily with an affectionate, passionate attachment only so fleetingly and so late? Do you feel that the image of so many people doing without sexual love is peculiar to the Mabies, or representative of a lot of us?

7. Inasmuch as the story may be influenced by its midwestern setting, the real sense of place in this novel emanates from the house itself. Remembering that "parts of 133 McPhearson went without hosting its inhabitants for years, then suddenly became popular," discuss the significance of the parts of the house, its rooms and passageways, its stairways, zones, and hideaways. What role does the house play in the family dynamic? Discuss some of the houses you've lived in and how they might have affected your life.

8. Emily asks what might someday constitute her son's nostalgia. See if you can answer her.

9. One of the ways in which authors of fiction develop characters and make them important to readers, is to expose their fears. Each of the characters in *Living to Tell* is afraid of something, whether they know it or not. Mrs. Mabie is afraid of something terrible happening to her children, while Mona is afraid of not being special in some man's eyes, a fear for which she comforts herself by surrounding herself with the adoring eyes of stuffed animals. Of what are the other characters in the novel afraid? And how do they, in turn, shield themselves from the objects of their fear?

10. Recalling her assault in the Ladies' Room, Grandmother Mabie reflects that it is "up to total strangers to let you know your common, brutal heritage, your dark desires." Contemplate the way in which the rest of the book either supports or refutes this notion.

11. Thematically, all of *Living to Tell* appears to emerge from a single event, that is, the car accident in which, with Winston at the wheel, Grandmother Mabie is killed. Having created an ongoing family history so filled with tragic, complex moments, why do you suppose that Antonya Nelson chose to anchor her story in that particular one? Did that accident alter the family dynamic, or did it only bring an already existing dynamic to a head, forcing it to reach some kind of resolution?

12. Some schools of fiction writing insist that for a book's ending to work it needs to feel "inevitable," as if the story, all along, has been laying the groundwork for its conclusion, creating, unbeknownst to the characters and to the readers, a narrative whose ending feels as unexpected as it does inescapable. In this context, discuss Emily's illness.

13. Discuss the "pure and transient . . . injury" that Professor Mabie sees in his daughters. Do you suppose he would see the same thing in other women if only he looked? Would he see it in his wife?

Would he have seen it in Betty Spitz? Perhaps the "pure and transient . . . injury" is a universal side effect of female coming-of-age. Do you think so? What might be, according to *Living to Tell*, an analogous side effect of male coming-of-age?

14. Antonya Nelson has said that she imagined all of the Mabies still living together in the family house in order to exemplify the enduring nature of all family bonds. Do you think that family members who live apart experience ties as powerful as those binding the Mabies? Would the Mabies be better off under more than one roof? Artistically, what kind of power does the book achieve by virtue of their living together?

15. Do you think the Mabies fall into the category popularly known as the "dysfunctional family"?

WHY I WROTE THIS BOOK BY ANTONYA NELSON

I was raised in a large family (five children and many extended relations) and have always felt conflicted about the intense closeness—and appalling heartache—family has represented to me. One of my books is called *Family Terrorists*—and I still believe that the pairing of love and war is what makes families the special terrain of American writers. We are a nation whose central political affiliation is familial; the home is where our bloodiest battles and most heartwarming successes take place.

Living to Tell is a story written in an attempt to understand the curious role family plays as it evolves away from simple relationships between parent and child. In a house of five grown-ups, the position of leader, of follower, of seer, of protector, shift, depending on situation. In this way, conventional roles are required to adjust, and new relationships develop. My fictional family, the Mabies, live in a large home together, forcing them into dramatic interaction. They are also all involved in mortal crises: one sibling has accidentally killed his grandmother; another has attempted suicide; and the third has a terminal disease. The book became a contemplation of mortality and permitted me to understand the true benefit of having faith in the institution of our family that will sustain us.